FINGAL O'REILLY, IRISH DOCTOR

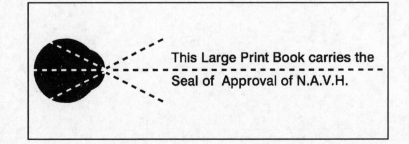

This Large Print Book carries the Seal of Approval of N.A.V.H.

FINGAL O'REILLY, IRISH DOCTOR

PATRICK TAYLOR

THORNDIKE PRESS
A part of Gale, Cengage Learning

Detroit • New York • San Francisco • New Haven, Conn • Waterville, Maine • London

GALE
CENGAGE Learning®

LIBRARY OF CONGRESS CATALOGING-IN-PUBLICATION DATA

Taylor, Patrick, 1941–
   Fingal O'reilly, Irish doctor / by Patrick Taylor. — Large print edition.
      pages ; cm. — (An Irish Country novel series) (Thorndike Press large print core)
   ISBN 978-1-4104-6350-0 (hardcover) — ISBN 1-4104-6350-8 (hardcover)
   1. O'Reilly, Fingal Flahertie (Fictitious character)—Fiction.
   2. Physicians—Fiction. 3. Country life—Northern Ireland—Fiction.
   4. Northern Ireland—Fiction. 5. Medical fiction. 6. Large type books. I. Title.
   PR9199.3.T36F56 2013b
   813'.54—dc23   2013026621

Published in 2013 by arrangement with Tom Doherty Associates, LLC

Printed in the United States of America
1 2 3 4 5 6 7 17 16 15 14 13

To Dorothy

ACKNOWLEDGMENTS

In the acknowledgments section of *An Irish Country Wedding,* I wrote, "A friend recently remarked, 'You always put acknowledgments at the start of your book. Why? Nobody ever reads them.' " Four days after publication, a reader e-mailed me, and her letter was not a happy one. She took pains to inform me that she invariably read acknowledgments, felt cheated if people who had contributed to a book were not recognised, and was certain she was not alone in this.

I stand corrected.

Fingal O'Reilly, Irish Doctor would not have been written and published without the unstinting assistance of a large number of people. They are:

IN NORTH AMERICA

Simon Hally, Carolyn Bateman, Tom Doherty, Paul Stevens, Irene Gallo, Gregory Manchess, Patty Garcia, Alexis Saarela, and Christina Macdonald, all of whom have

7

contributed enormously to the literary and technical aspects of bringing the work from rough draft to bookshelf.

Don Klancha, Joe Meir, and Mike Tadman, who keep me right in contractual matters. Without the help of the University of British Columbia Medical Library staff, much of the technical details of medicine in the thirties would have been inaccurate.

IN THE REPUBLIC OF IRELAND AND THE UNITED KINGDOM
Rosie and Jessica Buckman, my foreign rights agents.

The librarians of The Royal College of Physicians of Ireland, The Royal College of Surgeons in Ireland, and The Rotunds Hospital Dublin, and their staffs.

To you all, Doctor O'Reilly and I tender our most heartfelt thanks.

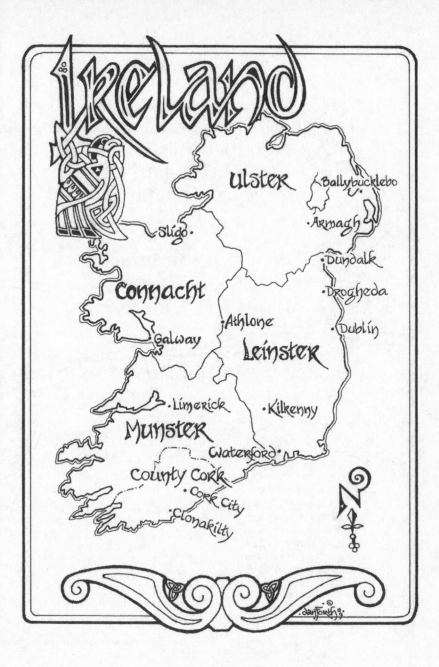

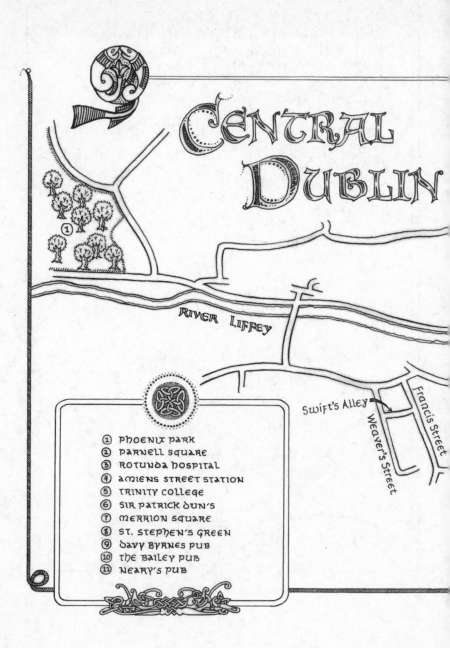

CENTRAL DUBLIN

River Liffey

Swift's Alley

Weaver's Street

Francis Street

1. PHOENIX PARK
2. PARNELL SQUARE
3. ROTUNDA HOSPITAL
4. AMIENS STREET STATION
5. TRINITY COLLEGE
6. SIR PATRICK DUN'S
7. MERRION SQUARE
8. ST. STEPHEN'S GREEN
9. DAVY BYRNES PUB
10. THE BAILEY PUB
11. NEARY'S PUB

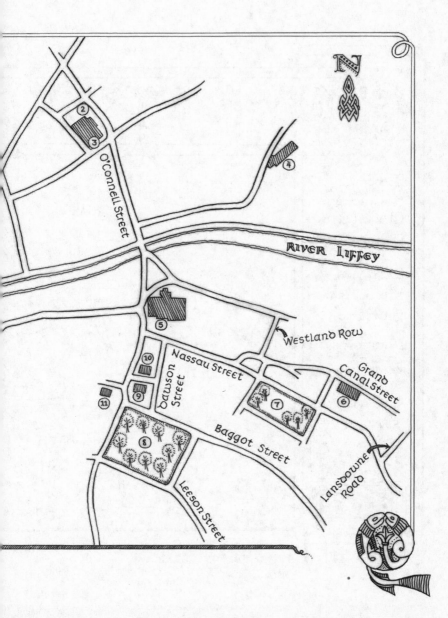

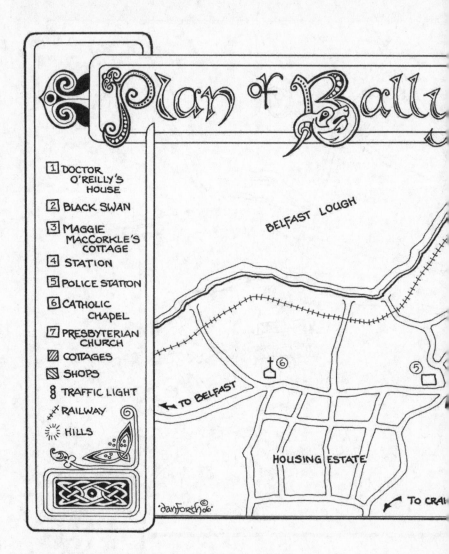

Plan of Balli...

1 DOCTOR O'REILLY'S HOUSE
2 BLACK SWAN
3 MAGGIE MacCORKLE'S COTTAGE
4 STATION
5 POLICE STATION
6 CATHOLIC CHAPEL
7 PRESBYTERIAN CHURCH
   COTTAGES
   SHOPS
8 TRAFFIC LIGHT
   RAILWAY
   HILLS

BELFAST LOUGH

← TO BELFAST

HOUSING ESTATE

TO CRAI...

danforth ©

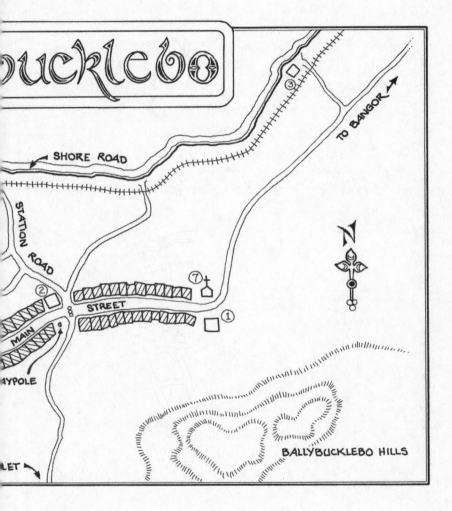

ucklebo

SHORE ROAD

STATION ROAD

TO BANGOR

N

② ⑦ †
STREET
①
MAIN
YPOLE
LET

③

BALLYBUCKLEBO HILLS

1
I'll Give You Leave to Call Me Anything

"Our first breakfast together as man and wife in our own home," said Doctor Fingal Flahertie O'Reilly, beaming at the suntanned woman across the table. "And how does it feel to be back in Number One Main Street, Mrs. O'Reilly?" Three honeymoon weeks in Rhodes had given them both healthy glows and brightened the silver streaks in the raven hair of Caitlin "Kitty" O'Reilly née O'Hallorhan.

"It feels very good to be home, Fingal, and in what's now my home, too," she said, stretching out a hand and covering his.

"And it does be good to have you both back, so." Mrs. Maureen "Kinky" Kincaid came in bringing a tray with two plates, each bearing a full Irish breakfast. She set one in front of Kitty. "Now eat up however little much is in it, Miss —" She frowned.

Oh-oh, Fingal thought, Kinky's having difficulty working out the proper form of address between the housekeeper and the mistress of the house. "Miss Kitty" had been fine before the wedding. "Mrs. O'Reilly" would be too formal. "Mrs. Kitty" sounded odd. He waited, a tiny smile playing on his lips.

"Kinky," Kitty said, "plain Kitty's fine. Aren't we friends?"

"We are, so." Kinky's two chins wobbled as she chuckled and said, "Indeed we are so, Kitty, bye. And there's your breakfast, sir. I've done the rashers crisp, the way you like them."

The telephone in the hall began its double-ringing clamour. "I'll see who that is," she said.

"That was gracious, Kitty," O'Reilly said, feeling his mouth water, "and it's a great relief to me that you and Kinky are getting on so well now." He stabbed a ring of black pudding, sliced it, and shoved half into his mouth. Greek grub had been all right, but it was great to get back to Kinky's proper Irish cooking. He was, as she often remarked, "a grand man for the pan."

"We'd better," Kitty said, and smiled. "It'll be a whole new experience for you, having three women in the house and no fun at all if two of them are at loggerheads."

"True enough." Young Barry Laverty, who had been O'Reilly's assistant until recently, had gone to Ballymena for training in obstetrics and gynaecology. His place as temporary

16

assistant had been taken by one Doctor Jennifer Bradley, who was out on a maternity case this Saturday morning. "At least," he said, "having Jenny living and working here lets me have some weekends off. After breakfast, let's pop in and see Donal and Julie Donnelly and the new chissler. Kinky tells me the wee lass arrived three days after we left, so her birthday's July 6."

"I'll put that in my diary when we've finished breakfast —"

"Sir." Kinky stood in the doorway. The colour had left her cheeks. "It's the marquis. His sister, Lady MacNeill, has had a riding accident."

Fingal ran to the phone, bolting the black pudding as he did. Young ones being born, middle-aged ones falling off their bloody horses. The daily round of the country G.P., a job he'd loved for more than twenty years. And he was duty bound to answer this call even if it was his weekend off. He grabbed the receiver. "John? What's up?"

He listened as John MacNeill, marquis of Ballybucklebo, explained how his sister had been thrown when her gelding, Bramble, balked at a jump. "You reckon her leg's bust? I see. Is she conscious? Good. No trouble breathing? Good. John, don't try to move her. Keep her warm, don't give her anything to eat or drink, and I'll be right out." He slammed the receiver into its cradle. "Kinky, get an ambulance out to Ballybucklebo House." He stuck his head into the dining room. "Kitty, the marquis's sister has been hurt. I'm heading straight out there. Shouldn't be too long."

"I'm coming —" Kitty started to rise.

"Finish your breakfast." There was no time to waste on politeness or explanations. He had to get out there now, and even if she was a nurse, there was nothing Kitty could do. As he crossed the hall, O'Reilly's stomach grumbled. Couldn't be helped, but Lord, that soupçon of black pudding had been delicious. He grabbed his bag from the surgery and charged down the hall. Lady Macbeth, his white cat, leapt for the stairs, scrabbled between the bars of the banister, arched her back, fluffed her tail, and spat.

He raced through the back garden yelling, "Stay, Arthur," when the big black Labrador stuck his muzzle out of his kennel.

In moments O'Reilly was in the long-nosed Rover, roaring along the main Belfast to Bangor Road. He barely noticed a cyclist taking refuge in the ditch. Up the gravelled drive, past the oddly shaped topiary in front of Ballybucklebo House, round its Virginia-creeper-covered gable end. The gate was open to an adjoining paddock, where he saw a saddled bay horse, reins dangling, cropping the grass. Two men squatted beside a figure lying near a two-bar jump.

The old Rover jounced across the field, shuddered to a halt, and O'Reilly, bag in hand, dismounted close to the marquis and his butler/valet Thompson. Both were coatless, their jackets covering the prone Myrna even though the sun was splitting the heavens. Fingal felt its early-morning heat and heard the burbling of wood pigeons from a nearby coppice and the *Kek-kek-kek* of a cock pheasant.

"Fingal," John O'Neill said. "Thank you so much for coming so quickly. Thompson and I have done as you told us."

"Good." He knelt. "Myrna, please don't turn your head, but can you hear me?"

Until he was satisfied that she hadn't hurt her spine it was critical that Myrna not move.

"I can hear you perfectly clearly, Fingal, thank you."

"Where are you sore?"

"I'm sure I'll have a bruise like a soup plate on my backside, but it's my right thigh. I distinctly heard the bone snap. It's aching now to beat Bannagher and I can feel the muscles all knotted up." He was impressed by how calm she sounded describing what was, almost certainly, the muscle spasms associated with fractures of the femoral shaft. "And no, I didn't land on my head." He noticed that her John Bull top hat was still firmly in place. "I was getting ready for next week's gymkhana. Bloody horse has never

19

refused before and I should be putting him at the jump again, but clearly I'm not fit to do that."

"Lie still, Myrna," O'Reilly said.

"I wonder, Thompson, if you'd be good enough to catch Bramble?" said the marquis. "Take him back to the stables." He spoke to his sister. "I don't want you fretting about your horse. Don't worry, Myrna. I'll get him over that damned jump once I know you're settled."

"Thank you, John."

O'Reilly ran through the routine assessment of a patient who had fallen. When he examined her lower limbs, he had already satisfied himself that she had suffered no head or spinal cord injury at least as far down as the first lumbar vertebra, and if she was feeling pain in her thigh and could sense the spasms, it was probable that the second and third were unaffected too. The fuller neurological assessment could wait until she was in the hands of the orthopaedic specialists at the Musgrave and Clark Clinic, the private hospital associated with the Royal Victoria Hospital. Right now, he had no concerns about moving Myrna once her leg had been splinted.

O'Reilly glanced at his watch. "I've sent for an ambulance," he said. "Should be at the hall soon. Could you meet them, John? Bring them round here."

"Of course." The marquis left.

"I need to have a look at the leg, Myrna," O'Reilly said, not relishing what he had to do.

"Go ahead, Doctor." She smiled, then winced.

O'Reilly looked at her right riding boot. The toes were pointing to the side at an unnatural angle and the whole leg seemed to be about an inch shorter than the left. He took a deep breath and gently laid both hands on her jodhpurs at the top of her right thigh. When he approached mid-thigh he heard Myrna sucking in her breath. "Sorry," he said.

"That bloody well hurt." He saw how pale she was and a drop of blood where she had bitten her lip.

O'Reilly was certain Myrna had fractured the shaft of her right femur. "Your diagnosis is correct, I'm afraid," he said. "It is broken. We'll have to get you to the Clinic and have it set. In fact, I think I hear the ambulance arriving now. I'll give you something for the pain."

The ambulance driver and attendant were efficient, waited patiently until the quarter grain of morphine he had given her took effect before they applied a Thomas traction splint to immobilise the break, realign the ends of the broken bone, and reduce muscle spasm and further soft tissue injury. Introduced by the Welsh surgeon Hugh Owen

21

Thomas in 1916, this type of splint had reduced the mortality rate for femoral shaft fractures from 80 to 8 percent.

The ambulance driver tied a label to her hacking jacket collar. The red "M" indicated she'd been given morphine.

She said drowsily, "Thank you, Doctor O'Reilly," as they loaded her into the primrose yellow Northern Ireland Hospitals Authority ambulance. It drove off, slowly at first, across the irregular ground in the field. The injury, now the splint had been applied, was hardly life-threatening, so there were no accompanying flashing lights or screaming sirens.

"She'll be grand, John," O'Reilly said to the marquis. "As good as new. Broken bones are pretty routine stuff today." Not, he thought, like in my student and junior doctor days. Fingal decided not to worry the marquis by talking about potential complications like nonunion of the bones or deep venous thrombosis in an immobilised limb.

"I appreciate your coming out, Fingal, and your reassurance," the marquis said, "and I'm sure she will be fine. Myrna's a tough old bird." He nodded toward the house. "I suppose it's a bit early for a Jameson, but if you'd like a cuppa?"

"Much too early for whiskey," said Fingal, "and as I hadn't even finished my breakfast. I'll be trotting on, thank you, John." He opened the car's door and chucked his bag inside.

"Understood," said the marquis, stooping to retrieve his and Thompson's coats, "but now you're home from abroad you and Mrs. O'Reilly must come round soon. Have a bite."

"We'd like that," O'Reilly said, thinking how much he liked the "we," "but it's home James, and don't spare the horses for me now."

On the drive back to Number One, O'Reilly let his thoughts roam. He'd phone and arrange for Myrna MacNeill to be looked after by Sir Donald Cromie, one of O'Reilly's classmates and close friends from their student days in Dublin. Cromie'd studied under Mister Jimmy Withers, the first orthopaedic surgeon in Northern Ireland. Fingal's other great friend, Charlie Greer, was now a consultant neurosurgeon at the Royal Victoria.

It had been an interesting road Fingal O'Reilly had travelled to get here; G.P. in Dublin, junior doctor in the Rotunda Maternity Hospital there, then assistant to Doctor Flanagan here in Ballybucklebo before the war. He'd been briefly married when he was a naval surgeon on a British battleship, and then after the war the widowed principal in his present practice. He frowned. The first years here had been lonely ones without her, but Fingal was single no more and he knew his first wife Deirdre would fully approve of Kitty, and that thought drove away his frown and brought a smile to the dark eyes he'd inherited from his father.

He could recall in detail his interview for that very first job, and his first-ever case as a newly qualified doctor. That had been a patient with a fracture too, but unlike today, in 1936 the outlook was not as good.

It took no effort to see himself twenty-seven, one week qualified, standing in Aungier Place in Dublin's Liberties slums ready to go into the building that housed the dispensary practice presided over by one Doctor Phelim Corrigan.

2
GOD AND THE DOCTOR
WE ALIKE ADORE

Fingal Flahertie O'Reilly, *Doctor* Fingal Flahertie O'Reilly, looked up past the two-storey whitewashed building on Aungier Place. The sky, what little of it was visible above the tenement buildings on the narrow street, was the eggshell blue of midsummer. He inhaled. The air was noisome with the smells of the city — exhaust fumes, draught horse dung, the oily tang of the River Liffey mud at low tide, and the stink of slaughter from the butchers' shops in the Liberties. Dirty Dublin hadn't got that nickname without good reason.

He straightened his new Trinity College medical graduate's tie. It was only seven days since July 1, 1936, when he'd graduated, finally qualifying for the career he'd had his heart set on since age thirteen. Now it was time to put his skills to use earning his living. He swallowed, fiddled with the tie, and strode through the open front door into an unfurnished hall, its walls distempered and unadorned, the floor covered in worn linoleum.

On his right, a door lay open and a hum of conversation spilled from what must be a waiting room. A woman in nurse's uniform approached from down the hall. "Excuse me," he said.

"Yes?"

"I'm Doctor O'Reilly. I've an appointment with Doctor Corrigan at eleven." He noticed blue eyes behind rimless glasses. Her hair was hidden under the nurse's headdress that encircled her forehead and fell to her shoulders. She looked about thirty.

"Pleased to meet you. Edith O'Donaghugh. I'm one of the midwives attached to the dispensary." She pointed to a closed door. "He's in there with a patient. You go into the waiting room. I'll let him know you're here."

"Thank you." The room was filled with a series of narrow backless benches arranged in rows, the front four occupied. Fingal decided to stand at the front of the room.

"It's me feckin' back, sir," a man sitting in front of him said.

Fingal eyed the man, who was looking at him expectantly.

"You're a doctor, aren't you? You're dressed like one."

"No, I'm — Well, yes, I am a doctor." I am a doctor, thought Fingal, and couldn't help grinning.

"Meself? I'm a tugger. Pull round a two-wheel cart all day like a feckin' oul' horse,"

26

the man said without rancour. "I ricked me back lifting heavy shite out of the cart two days ago. I seen Mister O'Leary, him w'at's got the chemist's shop on Thomas Street, and he made me up a lotion, charged me tuppence. He's a good skin, O'Leary, but this lotion? Stung like a feckin' wasp but done me bugger all good." He curled his lip. "So I come to see Doc Corrigan. But you'll do fine. I'm in a rush."

Fingal smiled. "I don't actually work here. I've come to see Doctor Corrigan too."

The heavily pregnant woman beside the tugger laughed up at Fingal. "Big healt'y young fellah like yourself? You look well filled enough to me, but if you're sick take yer place at the end of the queue."

Rank apparently has no privileges here, Fingal thought.

"My granny from County Clare swears there's nothing like a poultice made of bog onions for sprains."

"Sure," said the tugger, "and w'at would a oul' culchie know about sprains?"

She sniffed, pulling her shawl round her. "Just because you Dublin Jackeens t'ink the place's the centre of the feckin' universe, dere's no need to believe all country folks is stupid. My granny had a County Leitrim prayer too, for sprains."

"Go on den, I'm all ears."

Fingal heard the reverence in her voice as

she crossed herself, bowed her head, closed her eyes, and intoned, "Our Lord was going over the mountains and his foal's foot he sprained. Down he got and touched the sprain and said he, 'Bone to bone, blood to blood, nerve to nerve, and every sinew in its proper place.' " She straightened and opened her eyes. "If it does you any good, and I hope it does, you're welcome to it."

"T'ank you, missus," said the man, "and I'm sorry I called yer granny a culchie. It's the oul' back makes me grumpy."

Fingal smiled. Dubliners. It would be good to be working with them in their own neighbourhoods.

"Doctor O'Reilly?"

He turned. "Doctor Corrigan is just finishing," said Edith O'Donaghugh. "He says to go straight in as soon as his patients come out."

"Thank you." As he headed for the hallway, he heard her say to the pregnant woman, "Come on now, Mary, down to my room and we'll have a look at you. And you just bide, Lorcan O'Lunney. You and your back'll get their turn after Doctor Corrigan has finished with Doctor O'Reilly."

The door to the surgery opened and a woman came out carrying a squalling infant in her shawl and holding the hand of a little girl of about eight. Fingal would have known her cornflower blue eyes anywhere. He bent and said to her, "Hello, Finnoula Curran, Finnoula of the fair shoulders. Nice to see you again."

She smiled shyly at him. "I remember you comin' to Francis Street. You're the Big Fellah, Paddy's doctor when he was in hospital."

"The very one," Fingal said with a smile. Not long ago, a feisty, one-armed ex-army sergeant named Paddy Keogh from here in the Liberties had called Fingal the "Big Fellah" — the same name given to Michael Collins, a hero of the war of independence fifteen years ago. The nickname had stuck and by it Fingal had become known around Francis Street. Fingal straightened and said to the woman, "It's all right, Mrs. Curran. Finnoula and I are old friends. I hope she's keeping well."

"Finnoula's grand, but Aidan's teethin'. His bawlin' has the whole family up at night. Doctor Corrigan's given me a scrip'."

Fingal guessed it would be for chloral hydrate, one grain to be taken by the noisy Aidan at the adults' bedtime.

"I'm sure it'll work," he said, and leaving them, went through the door.

In a sparsely furnished room Doctor Phelim Corrigan sat on a tall stool behind a desk that could have come from a Dickensian counting house. He was a short, rotund man in, Fingal guessed, his middle fifties. His pinstripe-trousered legs dangled well above the floor, and the man wore a badly fitting brown toupee with its parting exactly centred on his head. Wire-rimmed spectacles blurring a pair of pale, watery eyes sat on a bulbous nose. "O'Reilly?" He didn't get down or offer to shake hands.

"Yes, sir." Fingal's naval training had him standing at attention. Today he'd worn the new suit he'd bought for graduation, a good choice because Doctor Corrigan obviously believed the dignity of his profession should be reflected in the practitioner's attire. He wore a wing collar and dark tie under the jacket of his suit.

"Ye sounded like an Ulsterman on the phone?"

"I am. Originally from Holywood, County Down."

Fingal could hear neither distaste nor approval of his northern roots when Doctor Corrigan said, "I'm a Connaught man meself. Mainistair na Búille, County Roscommon."

Fingal knew the town of Boyle and its ancient monastery and he'd already placed Doctor Corrigan for a Roscommoner. They always said "ye."

"Ye've already told me all I need to know professionally, Doctor O'Reilly. As long as I take a shine to ye, ye can have the job. I'm desperate for help." He yawned. "Delivery at three this morning then back here in the trenches at nine."

Fingal hid a smile. Babies didn't keep bankers' hours.

"Now ye're fresh out of Trinity and want to be a dispensary doctor?" He yawned again and made no attempt to cover his mouth. There were dark circles under his eyes. "Ye need yer bloody head examined. I'm going to tell ye what ye're in for — every second day ye'll be on call twenty-four hours, and every other weekend. I hope ye'll be one of two assistants if I can attract someone else. Then it'll be one weekend in three and less night work."

"I'd prefer that," said Fingal, "but I'd be happy to work one in two."

"Ah, youth," Doctor Corrigan said. His grin was sardonic. "Being on call's not all," he said. "By way of an encore, ye get to be registrar of births, marriages, and deaths, and district medical officer of health for a princely ten to fifteen pounds a year, and vaccinator and TB prevention officer. How's that sound to ye?"

"Pretty hectic," Fingal said. He'd had no inkling the work was anything but clinical medicine. Even in the five years of medical school, he'd come to loathe paperwork.

"It is. Still, ye get a generous two whole weeks' holiday annually, so ye can spend yer riches in some exotic seaside spot like Grey-

31

stones or Malahide." Doctor Corrigan slipped down off the stool and stood on the uncarpeted plank floor. "Now," he said, "the old dispensary committee —"

"Dispensary committee?" Fingal asked.

Doctor Corrigan twitched his head. "Lord, did they teach ye nothing at Trinity?"

"Not about how the dispensary system works, sir."

"New graduates? Mewling infants." Doctor Corrigan shook his head. "Babes in arms. Lambs to the slaughter. See those seats?" He pointed at two plain, cane-backed chairs that stood beside a leather examining couch. Horsehair stuffing was jutting through where the leather was torn. "Plant yer benighted arse on one."

Fingal obeyed.

Doctor Corrigan said, "There are three types of customers. The payers are the private patients, and if ye're in practice up on Merrion Square — like Oscar Wilde's dad Sir William, the ear, nose, and throat surgeon was — ye're in the money."

"I don't imagine there are too many payers in the Liberties and the Coombe, or the Quays and the Northside for that matter," Fingal said.

"True on ye, but funnily enough the madams in Monto, the old red light district up by Amiens Street Station, had the dough and some of them like May Oblong and Becky

Cooper would pay for their girls too." He must have registered Fingal's look because he pushed his specs up to the bridge of his nose and said gruffly, "Ye can take that look off yer face, young man. My information is strictly through my professional relationship with the ladies. Now," he said, shooting his jaw and patting the toupee in place, "where was I? Right, three types of customers. If ye do get a payer, ye can charge a fee. It helps bolster the so-called salary we get for looking after the other two classes. The first is those who have jobs and belong to approved societies that workers and their employers pay into weekly for medical care. Those societies pay our salaries for when we see the insured patients. Then there's the poor — and the great gross from the Liberties and the Coombe are in that third category. The poorest divils can apply to a member of the dispensary committee I mentioned earlier and get issued with a ticket for free medical advice and medicine at dispensaries like these or get visited at home. That's the way it has been since 1851, but everything's changed politically with an act of Parliament in 1933 that's finally being implemented this year."

Fingal heard something beside him and turned to the doorway where a youth of about sixteen in ragged pants to his shins and a collarless shirt covered in blood stood panting, one hand cupped over his nose.

"So, Doctor O'Reilly, I seem to have lost yer attention. Ye've the look of a man who cares little for the administrative details of our profession. Bring on the sick and the dying, ye say. Well, I'll tell ye, Doctor —"

"Doctor Corrigan, we, ah, we seem to have a patient at the door."

"Jasus Murphy." He stood in front of the youth and shot his jaw. "Not more bloody fighting, Eamon?"

"No, Doctor, sir. Dere's been an accident on Aungier Street. A tram hit a man on a bike. I was on the tram and the driver braked so hard I banged me feckin' nose."

"Is the cyclist still down?"

"I t'ink so."

"Right. Eamon, take yerself along the hall. Sister O'Donaghugh will fix up that nose. It's a bloody good thing midwives train as general nurses first. Doctor O'Reilly, we are going to run there straightaway and see what we can do. Carry my bag. It's there," he pointed, "beside the door."

3
I'm Not Even a Bus; I'm a Tram

Fingal trotted, holding the battered leather bag. "Carry my bag"? Was he being offered the job of doctor or bloody medical orderly? He'd been used to giving orders as an officer in the Royal Naval Reserve. Next time he'd tell Corrigan to carry his own damn bag.

They ran out of Aungier Place and onto Aungier Street, halted, and looked right to a stopped tram. The pole that connected the tram to overhead wires drooped over one side. A small crowd had gathered and as Fingal passed it he noticed the mangled remains of a bike crushed under a front bogey.

The tram driver was bent over a man lying on the cobblestones. Doctor Corrigan tried to push his way through the press of bodies with Fingal hot on his heels.

A man in a duncher and patched jacket muttered, "Quit your barging, you bollix," but a woman beside him said, "Houl' yer wheest. Dat's Doctor Corrigan."

"I'm a doctor, too," Fingal said, trying to

get past.

The man in the duncher squinted at Fingal, then smiled and said, "Hello dere, Big Fellah." He put his hands on his hips and yelled, "All right, you bunch of bowsies, quit your rubbernecking. Dere's two doctors here, so move back and let the dogs see the rabbit."

As the crowd started to move aside Fingal thought, This man must have seen me out on my rounds as a medical student only months ago. Being recognised by folks like Finnoula Curran and now this fellow was something he'd enjoyed while working among the tenement dwellers. He knew it was one of his reasons for wanting to practice here. His own upbringing had been privileged, yet he felt a sense of belonging whenever he was in the tenement slums of Dublin. Perhaps it was akin to the feeling of community he'd always known from his earliest days growing up in a small village in Ulster and later in the enclosed world of his boys' boarding school, the camaraderie of his medical class.

Finally Doctor Corrigan and Fingal stood beside the tram driver, who stared at the new arrivals. "I couldn't have missed him. Honest to God, sirs." He was pale and trembling.

"I'm sure ye couldn't," Doctor Corrigan said. "It was an accident, and I know about bikes and tram tracks. Anyone who lives in Dublin does."

"T'ank you, sir." Fingal heard the relief in the man's voice. "The conductor's sent for the Peelers and the ambulance."

"Good. Now, Doctor O'Reilly, if ye'll take a look at the patient?" Doctor Corrigan stood aside.

"Me?" Fingal frowned.

"No. The other Doctor O'Reilly," Doctor Corrigan said, and shook his head. "Yes, of course — ye. Get on with it, young man."

Sarky bugger, Fingal thought, and wondered if this was going to be some kind of on-the-spot practical examination of his clinical skills. He cocked his head, darted a glance at the senior man, then knelt by the patient, setting Doctor Corrigan's bag on the ground. By God, Corrigan could carry the bag back when they'd finished here. If Fingal was going to work with the man it would have to be established at the start that while he might be Corrigan's junior, Fingal Flahertie O'Reilly was nobody's skivvie.

He turned his attention to the patient, whose head was pillowed on the driver's jacket. "I'm Doctor O'Reilly," Fingal said. "Where does it hurt?" Even as he waited for a reply he'd taken the man's wrist. The pulse was regular, didn't seem unduly rapid. By his ragged full shock of black hair and clear complexion, Fingal guessed the man to be in his middle twenties. His face was creased and he gritted his teeth, but he was having no difficulty breathing.

"Me feckin' left ankle," the man said. "Don't touch it. For God's sake, don't."

"I won't." Fingal looked the man in the eyes. Young man's eyes. Both pupils were equal in size and neither constricted nor dilated. "Your head feel all right?"

"Me nut's grand," the man said, and grimaced.

"Where are you?" O'Reilly asked.

"Dat's a feckin' stupid question. Do you t'ink I t'ink I'm up in the Phoenix Park lying on the grass wit' me arm round a pretty wee mot?" His face screwed up, he groaned and reached down toward his left leg.

"I know it sounds daft," Fingal said, "but I am trying to help. Just tell me where you are." He glanced up to see Doctor Corrigan nodding in what Fingal took as approval. So he was being tested.

"All right. I'm lyin' on Aungier Street and I've a banjaxed ankle. A horse reared up. A bloody great barrel of Guinness fell off a dray and near poleaxed me. I swerved and the wheels of me bike got stuck in the feckin' tram lines. The poor oul' driver couldn't stop and he knocked me arse over teakettle, but it was an accident."

No disorientation there and no intent to blame the tram driver. Fingal said, "Thank you. That does help. Now I'm going to take a quick gander." His general examination would be rapid because he was already sure that the man had suffered no potentially lethal injuries. Fingal was aware of another presence and looked up. "Officer," he said to a large Garda sergeant who turned from questioning the driver.

"You carry on, Doc," the policeman said. "I'm getting the facts from the tram driver. I'll have a word wit' yourself when you're done wit' that poor divil on the floor."

"Right." Fingal ran his hands over each of the patient's arms. Nothing broken there. An abdominal injury was pretty unlikely. "Are your guts all right?"

"Never better, sir."

Fingal decided he'd leave the belly alone. Nor was there any sign of bleeding. "Mister . . . ?" Fingal asked.

"Finnegan. John-Joe Finnegan. From the Coombe."

"Mister Finnegan," Fingal said, "how's your right leg?"

"Feels grand to me," he said. "Look." Even lying on the cobbles he was able with no difficulty to flex it at the knee. "It's the udder one. At me ankle." He swallowed. "It's not so bad now, if I don't try to move it, but, och, Mother of Jasus, if I do." He sucked air between his teeth.

Either the ligaments of the joint had been badly torn or the ankle was broken. Likely a Pott's fracture. Fingal turned to report his findings to Doctor Corrigan as he might have to a senior doctor when he was examining a patient in his student days, but there was no sign of the man. He must have slipped off back to the surgery. There had been a lot more patients in the waiting room. He might have said "Cheerio," Fingal thought, or "Carry on, Doctor O'Reilly. You're doing fine," but he'd simply vanished. Never mind, there was a more pressing matter to attend to. "I'm going to take a look at the bad ankle," he said.

"Go easy, sir. Please?"

"I will." Fingal gently removed a bicycle clip and eased the leg of the man's moleskin trousers up his calf. Mister Finnegan's left foot lay twisted to the side, an angle of nearly ninety degrees to the shin, and as he wore no socks, the increasing swelling and bruising were obvious. This was no sprain. "I'm afraid it's broken," Fingal said. At least there was no evidence of bone penetrating the skin, unless there was damage he couldn't see without moving the leg. If there was, it would be classified as a compound fracture with a risk of infection, and that could lead to amputation. "They've sent for an ambulance," he said. "You'll need an X-ray and it'll have to be set." And, he thought, the surgeon can examine the break properly once John-Joe is under anaesthesia. Right up Donald Cromie's street, Fingal thought. His friend had taken a distinction in orthopaedic surgery in their final examinations.

"Just my feckin' luck," John-Joe Finnegan said. "I landed a job at Guinness's at Saint James's Gate. I'm a cooper by trade and they make about one t'ousand five hundred barrels a day — barrels just like the big bugger that has me destroyed. I got the bike today from a fellah on City Quay and I was takin' it for a spin because I was goin' to use it to get to my work next week. Fat bloody chance now. Dey'll not keep the position until I'm back on me feet and dere's no shortage of coopers lookin' for places. I've been out of work for eighteen months, I finally get a feckin' job, and now this? Jesus, Mary, and Joseph, it'd make a grown man weep. And me new bike's fecked too."

Fingal already understood how high the rate of unemployment was among the men of the tenements, particularly after the stock market crash of 1929, and how precious a job could be, particularly to a man like John-Joe Finnegan. By doing an apprenticeship for several years and learning a trade, he had made every endeavour to give himself and his family a chance. "I hear you, Mister Finnegan," Fingal said, feeling bloody useless. He tried to remind himself that he was only a doctor, not someone who could solve all of the world's injustice — but it was bloody unfair.

41

John-Joe propped himself up on one elbow. "Would youse do me a favour, Doc?"

"If I can." Fingal wondered what it might be.

"In me jacket pocket." He inclined his head. "There's a packet of Woodbine."

He found the ten-for-fourpence cigarettes, put one between John-Joe's lips, and used the Ronson Fingal's parents had given him as a twenty-sixth birthday present to light the fag.

"Lord Jasus," John-Joe said as he inhaled deeply, then blew out a cloud of smoke, "but there's a great comfort in the oul' weeds." He took another puff. "Where'll they take me to, Doc?"

"I'm not sure. Maybe Baggot Street Hospital," Fingal said, and thought with pleasure about a certain Nurse Kitty O'Hallorhan who worked there. "Or Sir Patrick Dun's. It's pretty close, on Grand Canal Street." Fingal and his friends had spent most of the last two years walking its wards learning their trade. Great years.

He saw the crowd part and two ambulance men approaching.

Fingal stood. "I'm Doctor O'Reilly," he said. "I've examined the patient. He has no injuries except for what is probably a Pott's fracture of his left ankle. He'll need it splinted and you'll have to take him to . . . ?"

"Dun's, sir," the taller of the two said, turning away. "We'll see about splints and getting him on a stretcher."

Fingal was pleased. He bent to John-Joe. "You will be going to Dun's."

"And who'll let my missus know? She'll be going spare when I don't come home."

"I'll ask." For a moment, Fingal thought of volunteering, but on foot the Coombe was a fair stretch and he still hadn't finished his interview for a job with the . . . "different" was the word that came to mind, the different Doctor Corrigan. Nor did Fingal relish having to break the news to Mrs. Finnegan that John-Joe's prospects for a job were now nil.

The big policeman bent over John-Joe. "Where do you live?"

"Ten, High Street. The front parlour."

So, Fingal thought, John-Joe lived in a tenement, but in one of the better sets of rooms, if it could be called that.

"Scuse us." The ambulance men had come back. They set a canvas stretcher on the cobbles. "We have to splint your ankle," the tall one said.

John-Joe took a drag, then stubbed out his cigarette. "All right, but go easy, for feck's sake."

Fingal stood back. The attendants would be far more skilled than a physician at splinting broken bones, and indeed it wasn't long before the break was swaddled in a pillow and bandages and immobilised so the jagged ends of broken bone wouldn't grate together and cause pain when the patient was moved.

"Now, Doctor, could yiz steady the ankle while me and me mate get yer man here on the stretcher? Alfie, take you yer man's shoulders, I'll take the right leg, and Doc, lift the pillow."

Fingal bent and grasped the pillow and in moments John-Joe had been hoisted and lowered onto a stretcher.

"That's her now," said the tall one. "T'anks, Doc."

Fingal straightened. "You'll be grand now, John-Joe," he said. As a medical student he'd got into trouble for getting to know his patients by name, as people not as cases, but damn it all, he liked people.

"T'anks, Doc, you're a grand skin."

"You'll be fine." Those thanks meant a great deal to Fingal. He wasn't a hair-shirt-wearing do-gooder and he'd be lying to himself if he didn't admit that being respected, looked up to, wasn't soul-warming too.

"And never worry about the missus," the big Garda said. "I'll have a constable round on his bike to let her know."

Although his face was pale and beads of sweat stood on his forehead and upper lip, John-Joe managed to smile. "Tell him to keep his wheels out of the feckin' tram lines," he said.

Fingal laughed. Dubliners. Smashed ankle, job prospects up in smoke, and John-Joe could still manage a joke.

"Can I ask a question, Doctor?" John-Joe said.

"Fire away."

"What kind of a doctor are yiz, anyroad? Some kind of specialist?"

"That," said Fingal, "in the immortal words Sean O'Casey wrote in *Juno and the Paycock,* is 'a darlin' question, Captain. A daaarlin' question.' " He laughed. "I'm just finished medical school so I'm no particular kind at all — yet. But I enjoy working in Dublin. I was in the middle of an interview for a job in Aungier Street Dispensary when we heard about the accident."

"Wit' Doctor Corrigan w'at was here? He's a sound man. Sound."

That a local thought so was more promising.

"Fair play to you, sir. I hope you gets it," John-Joe said.

"So do I. And after meeting you, Mister Finnegan, I know this is what I want to do. Thank you."

"Happy to help, Doc." He stuck out his hand.

Fingal grasped it without hesitation. He had never forgotten Ma's teaching, straight from Rudyard Kipling, If you can walk with kings and princes nor lose the common touch.

Even as an apprentice in the merchant marine and later a sub-lieutenant in the Royal Navy Reserve, he'd never felt distant from the crew.

"If I get a chance, I'll try to drop in and see you in Sir Patrick's, John-Joe." The hospital was no distance from Fingal's home, and he was always curious about all his patients' progress.

The attendants hoisted the stretcher and started to load John-Joe into the ambulance. "Good luck to you," Fingal called. He turned to the Garda. "Will you need me, officer?"

"Couple of quick routine questions, sir." He licked the end of a pencil and started in. It wasn't long before he said, "That's it, sir. I don't t'ink we'll be needing you in court."

"I hope not," Fingal said. He bent, picked up Doctor Corrigan's bag, and turned to go.

The sergeant said, "I heard you tellin' John-Joe about lookin' for a job in Aungier Place. It's part of my beat and it's a pretty tough district." The sergeant made a huuuhing noise, compressed his lips, and shook his head. "I hear bein' a G.P. there, drawin' a wage, and treating the poor folks for free can be a hard row to hoe. Good luck to you, sir, if you do get it."

And as he started on his walk back to the dispensary the Garda's parting words echoed in Fingal's mind.

Yes, it had had its rough patches, starting

with my first impressions of Doctor Phelim Corrigan, O'Reilly thought as he ran the Rover into the garage back home at Number One. He let himself into the garden to be greeted by a joyous Arthur Guinness. "All right," he said, patting the Labrador's head. "All right. Soon."

Arthur gazed at Fingal, the big dog's brown eyes full of adoration.

"Kitty and I are going to take a run race down to see Donal and the new baby. You can come too and we'll give you a walk." Fingal's stomach made a noise akin to that accompanying the release of geothermal energy from one of New Zealand's mud pits. "But not until I've seen if Kinky's kept my breakfast warm."

4
WHEN THE FIRST BABY LAUGHED

O'Reilly turned left off the inside curve of the hairpin bend on the Belfast to Bangor Road, the Rover rumbling along a rutted lane so narrow, brambles scraped the car's sides. Despite the warmth, Kitty cranked up her window. "Nearly got scratched," she said.

Now that the car had left the surfaced road for a country lane, Arthur Guinness made excited noises and wagged his tail. "He always does that. Thinks we're going shooting," O'Reilly said as he parked the car in front of a thatched cottage. "Here we are," he said, "Dun Bwee, the Yellow Fort. Home of the Donnellys, and if I'm not mistaken that's Donal himself putting on a lick of paint."

Donal, with most of his carroty hair hidden under a paint-smeared duncher, was putting a coat of fire-engine-red paint on one window sash. He hadn't heard the car coming because his portable transistor radio was blaring the Byrds' recent number-one recording of a Bob Dylan song.

Hey, Mister Tambourine Man, play a song
  for me
In the jingle-jangle morning . . .

"Turn off that bloody awful racket, Donal,"
O'Reilly yelled in his best quarterdeck voice.
" 'Jingle-jangle morning' indeed," he muttered. He liked the song well enough, but not
the volume at which it was being played.

Donal flinched and his brushstroke jerked
over a strip of masking tape and put a red
smear on the pane. He spun and his wide-
eyed look turned into a buck-toothed grin.
"It's yourself, Doctor," he said, bending to
turn off the radio, "and Mrs. O'Reilly. When
you yelled there now I near took the rickets,
but I'm main glad to see youse both, so I am.
Welcome back."

"Thank you, Donal. It's good to be back. Is
it all right to let Arthur out? Where's Bluebird?" O'Reilly asked. The two dogs had been
known to disappear when together, and
O'Reilly wasn't taking any chances close to
the main road.

"In her dog run round the back." Something in the way Donal lowered his voice
seemed furtive to O'Reilly. Donal came closer
to the car and peered in. "So if you want to
let Arthur out it'll be fine."

"Grand," said O'Reilly. "Hop out, Kitty."
He let Arthur out of the back. The big dog,
tail going like a threshing machine with

slipped gears, headed for the fuchsia hedge, cocked a leg, gave a happy "Yip," then headed straight for Donal and licked his hand.

Now the radio was off, O'Reilly stood for a moment listening to the silence of the country. The air was heavy with the scent of clover spiced by the odour of drying paint. He moved round the car and Arthur came and sat at his feet.

"Sound day," said Donal, "for the time of year it's in." He stooped and set the paint-brush on the upturned lid of the paint tin. "I'll not need to let the half of that new coat get too dry before I finish it," he said as if to himself, then turning to O'Reilly, "and what brings you out here, for didn't you only get home last night, sir?"

"Six o'clock Heathrow plane into Aldergrove," Kitty said. "Kinky told us you and Julie had had your baby. We're taking Arthur for a walk, and Doctor O'Reilly wanted to see the new arrival, so we popped in."

"Julie's in the back garden with the wean in her pram."

O'Reilly knew Donal had for the entire pregnancy been convinced the baby would be a boy, but he seemed to puff up when he said, "She's one hell of a — Sorry, Mrs. O'Reilly, she's a right wee cracker, so she is." His grin was vast. "Hang about." He stuck the brush into a jam jar of clear fluid, wiped

his hands on what by the stink of it must have
been a turpentine-soaked rag, then along the
sides of his dungarees. "Come on in and we'll
go round and see the pair of them."

O'Reilly took Kitty's hand and together
they followed Donal to the big back garden
shaded by a row of towering lime trees. Julie,
her long cornsilk hair shining, had parked a
high-sprung four-wheel pram that would not
have looked out of place in an Edwardian
nursery. She was carrying her new daughter
wrapped in a white, open-weave wool blanket.

"Doctor and Mrs. O'Reilly." Julie smiled.
She lowered her bundle and O'Reilly could
see a little face, wrinkled brow, and tiny
pursed lips. "Meet Victoria Margaret Donnelly," Julie said.

Kitty moved closer and bent over. "She's
lovely."

"Victoria for Julie's ma, Margaret for
mine," Donal said. "Prettiest baby in the
whole six counties, but she takes after her
mother so that's no surprise." He puckered a
kiss at Julie.

"Och, sure, and doesn't a baby bring her
own welcome?" said O'Reilly, thinking that if
you lined ten newborns up you'd think they
were identical decatuplets who all bore strik-
ing resemblances to squashed oranges. But
he was too much of a gentleman to say so.

"And before you say it, Doctor O'Reilly,
sir, for I can guess what you're thinking, so I

51

can, she does take after her ma. None of your 'Oh, doesn't she look like her daddy? Never mind. At least she's got her health' *craic*."

O'Reilly laughed. "You know me too well, Donal Donnelly."

Arthur, who had walked at O'Reilly's heel, lifted his head, sniffed at the baby, gave a wag of his tail, and wandered off down the lawn. He passed a mound that bore a sign, on which the words NATIONAL TRUST HERITAGE SITE were accompanied by an embossed sprig of oak leaves, and continued on to a chain-link dog run. Donal's racing greyhound Bluebird greeted Arthur by sticking her narrow muzzle through a link to exchange sniffs with the Labrador.

Victoria Margaret screwed up her face and amazed O'Reilly by how such a tiny creature could manage to sound like an air-raid siren crossed with a banshee. He recognised the niff that assailed his nostrils.

Julie frowned. "I think someone has a full nappy."

Donal took a step back. Maybe times were a-changing, but by the way he folded his arms and inclined his head, it was clear that in his opinion changing nappies was not men's work.

Victoria Margaret's face grew redder and she let go another shriek. Julie shrugged and said, "I'll go and see to her. I'm not very good at it. Miss Hegarty the midwife gave me a few lessons, but seems to me you need five hands, not two."

"Come on," Kitty said. "I'm not a nurse for nothing, and I'm sure, Fingal, you and Donal will have lots to talk about." She took Julie gently by the arm and headed for the cottage's back door. "The trick is to get the wee one by the ankles . . ."

"It's going to take a power of getting used to, this being a new daddy, so it is," Donal said. "Being a carpenter's a lot easier."

"I'm sure you'll manage. You and Julie'll make great parents."

"We're certainly trying, but it's a brave sight harder than training dogs." He cocked his head at O'Reilly. "I do try to give Julie a rest by doing the late bottle feeds, but the pair of us is both a bit sleepy these days, so we are." He grinned his lopsided grin. "At least you can put an ould bow-wow in her kennel at night. Victoria Margaret had us both so knackered with her gurning in the wee hours this morning that . . ." He inclined his head in the direction of the dog run.

"You don't mean that, Donal."

"Not at all. Just pulling your leg, sir. We're both daft about the wee crayture. No man ever wore a cravat as nice as his own child's arm around his neck. We would never let nothing hurt her, so we'd not."

"Good man," O'Reilly said. He noticed that Arthur had wandered back again. He glanced

53

to the dog run. "And how's Bluebird doing, Donal? Dogs can get jealous of new babies."

"Not her. She's as gentle as a lamb. But then I haven't raced her for a brave while. All the local bookies know her and her form. You can't get decent odds at any of the registered tracks, so you can't."

O'Reilly knew that, legally, dog tracks had to meet standards set by the Greyhound Racing Board of Great Britain and their Ulster branch, the Irish Coursing Club.

"I'm going to go in for a bit of flapping," Donal said.

"Flapping?"

"Just between you and me and the wall, Doctor, there's a few unregistered tracks and I've a wee notion how to make a few bob running her at one or two. That's called flapping."

"But surely the bookies would still recognise you and her?"

"I've another wee notion about that, too. Change her looks a bit, like, tell folks I've got another dog, and get some wee lad to take her to the stewards after the race. Dog owners' kids handle dogs all the time, so nobody'll mind." Donal let one eyelid droop in a slow wink.

O'Reilly guffawed. "Jasus Murphy, Donal, I'll pretend I didn't hear that." The man was incorrigible. "But you'll let me know what happens?"

"Och, aye. Sure it'll only be for a bit of *craic,* anyway." Donal grinned. "Now, sir," he said, "I don't mean to be impolite nor nothing, but would you excuse me for a wee minute? The paint's going to be half dry on that sash and I'd like for to get her completely finished the day."

"Off you trot. I'm content to sit in the sun in your back garden, Donal. Kitty and I just popped in and we'll be running along once she's finished with Julie and the chissler."

"Thank you, sir. Come round anytime. Anytime you like." Donal left.

Kitty appeared carrying a now presumably dry and clean Victoria Margaret.

"All is now sweetness and light," Kitty said. "Julie's on the phone to her mum and this wee dote's half asleep."

Kitty looks so natural with that youngster, O'Reilly thought.

She laid the wee one into her pram, turned it so the sleeping compartment was in the shade, grabbed the handle, and rocked the pram on its springs the while singing,

I see the moon, the moon sees me
down through the leaves of the old oak
    tree.
Please let the light that shines on me
shine on the one I love.

Kitty smiled at O'Reilly and put a finger to

55

her lips. She stopped rocking and whispered, "She's asleep." Kitty moved away from the pram and sat, legs folded under her skirt. She patted the grass beside her.

O'Reilly joined her, and not to be left out, Arthur flopped down, head on outstretched paws, and yawned mightily. "I must say you looked very much at home with the babby, Kitty."

"I should do," she said. "I've told you that I took some midwifery training, after we —" She sighed. "Well, after we went our separate ways before the war."

"I'm sorry," he said, not so much as an apology as an expression of his own regret.

She took his hand. "It's all right. It took a while, but we've fixed it, haven't we?"

"Thank you for that, Kitty."

A tiny whimper came from the pram.

Kitty shook her head. "Leave her. She'll nod off."

"I wonder," he said. "I wonder if we had got married back then . . ." He looked right into her eyes. "Do you mind not having children?"

"Your children?"

"Ours," he said.

She lowered her gaze, clearly lost in thought, smoothed her hair with one hand, then looked at O'Reilly. "Truth?"

"Truth."

"Yes. I think I did for a while. All my friends

56

had families. Back then it was what women were supposed to do. I was never one for standing out from the crowd, but as the years went by and I'd been to Tenerife, then specialised in neurosurgical nursing, I began to realise that I was having a fulfilling life and that children weren't the be all and end all. But yes, if we had stayed together I'd like to have had ours, but I'm so happy to have you back now, and we both know we aren't going to be parents so there's no use fretting about it." She glanced over at the pram. "And we can always enjoy other peoples'."

"And that's about how I feel too, Kitty. I'm happy to be with you, my love, and content." And that, he thought, just about says it all.

They smiled at each other and it seemed to O'Reilly that neither he nor Kitty felt any need to talk anymore as they sat, close together, in the sun.

The day was warm and he removed his tweed jacket to sit in his shirtsleeves and thick red braces. Arthur snored gently and bees murmured in the drowsy late morning. Overhead, from somewhere in the heavens, the notes of a skylark spilled in a silvery cascade onto a field of ripening barley, and the hoarse voice of a corncrake rasped from where the bird was hiding in an unmown hayfield.

A far cry, he thought, from the sounds of the Dublin tenements.

5

Not All of These . . . Can Sleep So Soundly

The waiting room of the Aungier Place Dispensary was much emptier than it had been an hour ago. Doctor Corrigan must have been seeing patients at a rate of knots, Fingal thought, as he knocked on the surgery door.

A curt "Come in."

Doctor Corrigan ignored Fingal and stood legs apart, arms akimbo, fists on his hips in front of a woman of about twenty sitting on a hard chair. The parting in his toupee had moved to an east-northeast, west-southwest axis.

She cradled a baby. Unusually for a sick child, except those who were desperately ill, the little one was lying perfectly still and quiet. Probably, Fingal thought, it's fine and she's the patient. The baby's face was bright pink.

Phelim Corrigan's was puce. "Ye stupid, stupid, bloody woman," he said. "I'd forgive ye if it was the first time and put it down to pure, unadulterated, bog Irish buck ignorance, but it's not bloody well the first time, and ye knew exactly what ye were up to. Didn't ye? Didn't ye?"

Fingal couldn't hear her whispered reply, but he flinched, partly for her because he hated to see anyone being bullied, but also for himself. This interview was turning into a roller coaster. Now it seemed the senior man had a God complex and was unashamedly insulting a patient. Rudeness to a colleague was one thing, this ranting another entirely. Did Fingal want to work with this tyrant? He glanced at the door. No reason why he shouldn't simply leave now, but — but his curiosity was getting the better of him, and what about his plan to beard Doctor Corrigan about his earlier behaviour? Would it be possible to have a reasonable discussion with this man? And yet, John-Joe Finnegan had described Doctor Corrigan as a sound man.

"How in God's name could ye do such a horribly stupid thing again? Ye nearly killed wee Manus the last time." The patients in the waiting room probably heard that, but the little one didn't stir.

"I'm sorry," she said, and hung her head. Her unwashed hair fell forward and Fingal couldn't see her face.

"Sorry, Mary Bernadette Foster? Sorry? Sorry be buggered." He moved closer. "Give me the flaming child." Fingal watched as the little doctor accepted the sleeping infant and held it as might a loving mother. He bent his head to it. "Come to me, wee dote, open your eyes for yer uncle Corrigan," and his voice was soft, soothing. He carried Manus over to the couch and laid him gently on the sheet, smoothed his brow, and said, as if noticing Fingal for the first time, "Come here, Doctor O'Reilly. I'd like to show ye this poor wee mite."

Fingal, as he passed the mother, said, "Good day, Mrs. Foster." But she refused to meet his eyes. He noticed a smell of damp underclothes and fresh stout.

As he stood beside Doctor Corrigan, fresh smells assailed his nostrils. The wee one certainly had a dirty nappy, and yet he was still asleep?

"All right," said Doctor Corrigan, "I'll give ye the history as it was told to me — with one critical omission. That stupid bowsie over there said she put little Manus, who's three months and eight days old, and I know because I delivered the wee divil at four in the morning on a pissing wet April Fool's Day, she put him down asleep into his cot, if ye can call an orange box lined with straw a cot, at ten this morning. Says he was fine then." He spat the next words. "Fine? Fine my arse." Doctor Corrigan fished out his stethoscope, slowly peeled back the baby's grubby vest, listened all over the front of the chest, which was as pink as his face, sniffed and said, "At least he's still breathing. The heartbeat's about 120, but that's not too bad for one this age." He pulled the stethoscope from his ears. "Now, I'm not making up what I'm going to tell you next," Doctor Corrigan said. "Once she'd got Manus down, she took her oul' one's wooden leg and pawned it for twelve shillings."

Fingal was not shocked. He knew enough about tenement life to understand that the pawnbrokers — "Uncle" in the parlance of the streets — were often all that kept many families going from one week to the next. The brokers would advance money on the most unlikely items, but pawning a man's wooden leg was a new one to him.

"Then, she took herself to the nearest boozer for a couple of hours," said Doctor Corrigan, "and it wasn't until half an hour ago what passes for her maternal instinct took over. She went home, and to her great surprise" — He scowled at the woman, but picked up the infant and cuddled it. — "found the wee one still asleep. And she couldn't wake him up. Could ye, ye useless trollop? It was just like the last bloody time ye did it."

Fingal was baffled. He started to make a differential diagnosis of causes of what must be coma, and recurrent coma at that, in recently born children. But he had only got

61

as far as meningitis and brain tumours, neither of which caused such pinkness of the skin, when Doctor Corrigan said, "Have ye ever seen such a bonny pink babby, Doctor?"

"No," said Fingal, "I have not." He scrutinised the colour. "The child's certainly not cyanosed, so it can't be from oxygen lack."

"Huh," said Doctor Corrigan. "Can it not? He's been poisoned and he is oxygen-starved."

Fingal tried to remember his toxicology course, but for the life of him couldn't remember any poison that caused pink skin.

"You see, Mammy here wanted to go out for a jar and she wanted Manus to sleep, and he wouldn't because she didn't really know how to change a nappy nor had she the wit to ask a neighbour woman to show her, which is daft because the tenements are huge mutual aid societies."

"I do know," said Fingal.

"But ye don't know what she did to get him to sleep before she put him in his cot, and it's common practice in the Liberties."

Fingal shook his head. "I've no idea."

"She has a coal gas cooker so she turned on a ring and held the mite over the gas until he nodded off. And it's the second time in a month she's done it. That's why I'm so bloody furious."

"Good God," said Fingal. "Carbon monoxide poisoning." The gas dissolved in the blood, displaced oxygen from the haemoglobin, and combined with it to form the pink compound carboxyhaemoglobin, which accounted for the baby's colour. No wonder the child had passed out. It was lucky he hadn't died. Fingal looked at the mother and shook his head. How could anyone treat a child that way? Perhaps Doctor Corrigan had some justification for his anger.

"All right," he said. "We'll ask Miss Jackson to run the wee one over to Baggot Street Hospital in my car. They can put him in an oxygen tent. Little Manus hasn't died yet, so the carbon monoxide hasn't displaced all the oxygen, some is still getting to the tissues, indeed the minute she stopped waving him over the gas he'd have been starting to recover. He's certainly not getting any worse now. If I'd seen him a couple of hours ago I'd have had him straight into the hospital and given him oxygen. There's not the same urgency now, but even so an hour in a tent will bring him round quicker, reduce the chances of permanent organ damage." He glared at the mother. "Then they'll wipe his arse, put some Vaseline on his nappy rash, give poor wee Manus a clean diaper, and probably a good feed when he wakes up." He held the child gently and said, "Doctor O'Reilly, would ye please go and get Miss Jackson, third door on the right, and ask her to come here while I have a short discussion with the sainted Madonna here about my responsibilities to babies with respect to making reports to the Society for Prevention of Cruelty to Children, the Sisters of Charity, and the Garda Siochána."

Fingal headed for the door. That last remark at least brought a response. "Och, you'd not, Doctor, sir. You'd not tell the Peelers, would you?"

Fingal didn't hear the reply. He strode down the hall. The mention of Baggot Street Hospital had distracted him into thinking again of Kitty. He'd be seeing her tomorrow evening. He relished the thought, but before that he had to make up his mind about taking up the position here. The recent outburst, even if there had been real provocation, was not much of an argument for taking the job.

On his left he passed a hatch where a patient was collecting a bottle of a dark fluid that looked like either a tincture or a decoction of some medicinal plant. Behind the hatch must be a room where commercially prepared medicines from the pharmaceutical companies like Bayer or May & Baker were stored, and in-house preparations — the powders, papers, pills, capsules, infusions, wines, and oleoresins — were made up and handed out, or "dispensed." It was from this function that dispensary practices got their name.

Miss Jackson, a motherly looking woman in

her fifties, looked up from where she was weighing a baby. "Can I help you?"

"I'm Doctor O'Reilly. Doctor Corrigan needs you in his surgery, Miss Jackson."

"Fine." She handed the infant back to a beshawled woman who had a three-year-old boy by the hand and what looked like a two-year-old girl in a rickety pram. "Young Mickey's doing well, Moira. Can you bring him back in a month?"

"I will." She put the baby into the pram beside his sister. "T'anks very much."

"I'll just be a minute." The midwife washed her hands. "Come on," she said, "and I'm sorry I missed your name, Doctor — ?"

"O'Reilly. Fingal O'Reilly." He followed her into the hall.

"The new graduate who's thinking of working here?"

More accurately "was," Fingal thought, after having experienced Doctor Corrigan's current display, but he nodded and said, "That's me."

"You could do a lot worse." Her voice softened. "Phelim Corrigan's a remarkable man."

6

ONE LAW FOR THE RICH . . .
ANOTHER FOR THE POOR

When Fingal returned to the surgery, the
"remarkable" Doctor Corrigan was still cud-
dling young Manus and handing a hanky to a
tearful Mary Foster. "All right, Mary," he said
gently, "all right, lass, dry yer eyes. Manus is
going to be all right." He rummaged in his
pocket and handed Miss Jackson a set of
keys. "Here, Irene, run Mary and Manus over
to Baggot Street. Tell the houseman to admit
the chissler and pop him in an oxygen tent.
Accidental coal gas poisoning." He stressed
the word "accidental." So, no reports would
be made to the Gardai or the nuns.

Doctor Corrigan turned back to Mary
Foster and handed her the child. "Now," he
said, "I've given ye an earful, Mary, and I
meant every word. I know he's yer first —
but Miss Jackson and Miss O'Donaghugh are
here to help. Bring the babby here when he
gets out of hospital. They'll show ye how to
change a nappy, won't ye, Irene?"

"Of course. And I'll arrange for a nursing

sister to call every day for a while until Mary gets more comfortable with Manus."

"If I'd had any wit I'd have done that myself the last time." He shook his head. "Och well, we all make mistakes."

The change in the man from hectoring ogre to a seemingly calm and caring physician, and one willing to admit his failures, had false-footed Fingal, who had been steeling himself for a confrontation.

"T'ank you, Doctor, sir, and I'm awful sorry. I'll never do it again, honest til God."

"Ye won't," said Doctor Corrigan, scowling, "because, by Jasus, if ye do, so help me God, it'll be Manus for the Sisters of Charity Orphanage taken away from ye for child neglect, and yerself for Mountjoy Gaol for the same crime. Do ye understand, Mary Bernadette Foster? Do ye?"

The edge was still in Doctor Corrigan's voice. He must stand up to this man.

"Yes, Doctor, sir."

"Run along now with Miss Jackson."

As the two women left, he turned to Fingal. "Just be a tick. I'll go and explain to the other customers that I'll be in consultation with a colleague for a while. Have a pew."

Fingal was still clutching the offending bag, so he set it back in its place beside the door. That aspect of his potential relationship with Doctor Corrigan needed to be sorted out as much as, if not even more than, Corrigan's bedside manner.

Fingal gritted his teeth. He had his own reasons for wanting this job, and most of them were, at least on the surface, altruistic. Ma had taught him her brand of caring since he'd been old enough to understand that not everybody lived as comfortably as the O'Reillys. He did want to help what his classically educated father would call the hoi polloi, the common people. Yet he also recognised that the obverse of altruism was the selfish inner glow that came from the doing of "good deeds." A reasonable question to ask himself: Was the feeling of satisfaction making correct diagnoses and giving proper treatments, those "good deeds," any less if performed for patients with money who could pay a damn sight more than a dispensary doctor's salary?

Probably a lot less. The truly affluent had no difficulty getting medical help. What physician wouldn't prefer to take sherry in a drawing room after a consultation as opposed to searching for the fleas that often attacked anyone who went into a tenement? The money was with the upper class and the newly emerging "middle class" of accountants, managers, teachers, doctors, nurses, and civil servants. Like the cream of society, most of them would patronise the more fashionable physicians. The crying need for good medical help was here in the Liberties.

And to be ruthlessly practical, even if he'd wanted the carriage trade, those jobs were not the easiest to come by for recently qualified doctors, and usually were had by purchasing part or all of the principal's practice. Fingal was in no position to buy in. He needed a job like this, at least as a start to his career in general practice. But with this Doctor Corrigan? Perhaps.

Corrigan returned and climbed up on his high stool. "I'm sorry about that scene. Silly wee girl." He shook his head. "How did ye get on with the tram accident?"

The whole thing dismissed just like that? Fingal clutched the seat of the chair and stiffly leant forward. "Doctor Corrigan, I'm very new at this, and there's probably something I don't understand." Fingal hesitated, realising that being placatory might well be the road to defeat before he even got started. He straightened and looked the senior man in the eye. "I think you were cruel to that patient. Very cruel."

Corrigan inclined his head. "Do ye now?"

"Yes, I do. And I didn't like being ordered around, being told to 'Carry my bag.' "

"Did ye not?" Something akin to a smile flickered on the little man's lips. "Well, well." He folded his arms and leant back.

Fingal felt as if he'd delivered his best punch and Doctor Corrigan had let it whistle by into thin air. Nor had he mounted a defence or a counterattack. Fingal would have to forge ahead again. "I just don't think seniors should treat the juniors like personal servants."

"Go on."

Fingal took a deep breath, folding his arms in front of his chest. "I came here expecting to be treated as a colleague. I don't think being ordered to carry your bag as if I were a footman is very collegial."

"Do ye not?" Doctor Corrigan tilted his head to one side and regarded Fingal. There it was again, the hint of a smile behind the thick lenses. "There's a thing now."

"I do not." Fingal frowned but ploughed on. "And I didn't appreciate your simply vanishing when I was examining the victim. I don't think that was very professional either." He ran a finger under a collar that now seemed too tight.

Doctor Corrigan pursed his lips, nodded, his smile widened. "And just so I'll know where I stand with ye, young fellah, ye've been gathering up yer courage all the way back here from Aungier Street to have it out, haven't ye? Then ye got your fires more stoked up because I was rude to Mary Foster." His voice was calm, if anything amused. "I don't believe ye're a man that would bottle up something that annoys him, are ye?"

"Well . . . no. I'm not." Fingal's collar was definitely too tight.

"More power to yer wheel." Doctor Corrigan was making a sound like dry autumn leaves being blown along a gutter. It wasn't until Fingal noticed that the little doctor's shoulders were shaking that he realised the man was laughing.

Fingal felt his fists clench, knew that the tip of his nose must be blanching. It would have been all right if Doctor Corrigan had reared up, but he was laughing and clearly at, not with, Fingal.

Before Fingal could speak, Doctor Corrigan continued, and his voice was quiet, serious. "That took real courage for a fellah wet behind the ears to risk losing a job before he got it by tackling a senior man head on, and, boy, ye went at it like a bull at a gate."

Fingal started to blush. He had expected an argument, even anger, but not understanding.

"I told ye the job was yers if I took a shine to ye," Doctor Corrigan said.

Fingal hung his head.

"So for once I'll explain. I told ye to carry my bag because ye're young and strong and I wanted to get to the accident as quick as my old legs would carry me. For all we knew the poor bugger could've been bleeding to death. Maybe I should have said 'please,' but there seemed to be more pressing matters than manners."

Fingal saw the truth of it. "I didn't —"

71

"Then, as soon as I saw you knew what you were about, I legged it back here because the waiting room was stiff with customers."

Absolutely rational. "I think —" Fingal swallowed and said, "I think I was a bit hasty about that."

"Ye were," said Doctor Corrigan, "but sure isn't being impetuous the prerogative of the young? And didn't ye have the courage of yer convictions to act? If ye do come to work here, I'll expect ye always to do what ye think is right. Will ye promise me that?" He gazed directly into Fingal's eyes.

Fingal did not glance away. "I will." He took a deep breath. "In that case, will you explain to me why you were so hard on that young woman?"

"By Jasus, O'Reilly, ye are a terrier. All right." He leant forward, elbows on the desktop. "Poor stupid girl. It's not her fault. They leave school at ten, because as any kid in the tenements will tell ye, learning still doesn't get ye a decent job. Some lasses are lucky, end up as one of the 'Jacob's Mice,' the girls taken on by the Jacob's biscuit factory when they turn fourteen. A whole lot of kids start courtin' in the stairwells of the tenements, often get put up the spout or just get married too early. Half of them don't even know where babies come from, and when they end up as mothers it's usually their own grannies who teach them motherhood skills, because their mas are out at work."

"I've seen it," Fingal said, "but what can we do?"

Doctor Corrigan shook his head. "Pick up the wreckage, use whatever treatments we have. Some of them are useful. Try to comfort, and try to prevent what we can." He pursed his lips. "Mary Foster's not going to be persuaded by the Socratic method of reasoned argument."

That brought a smile to Fingal's lips.

"That's twice she's nearly gassed the wee mite. The only way I could think of to try to stop her doing it again was to throw the fear of God into her. I can't give her what she needs, a husband with a decent job, family support — her granny died of TB last year, her own ma sells used clothes in the Iveagh Market on Francis Street. She's the eldest of nine. She lives in a single end on Peter Street with her husband 'Boxty' Foster, he's one of eleven and he's in and out of builder's labourers jobs." He blew out his cheeks. "Do I need to go on?"

Fingal shook his head. "I hear you. My own ma's working hard for slum clearance, decent rehousing, but it's not going to happen overnight."

"No, it's not. Nothing changes fast in this benighted city, and us dispensary doctors keep carrying on pretty much the same as when the first Act of the English Parliament

73

set the dispensaries up in 1851." He shifted on his stool. "That was after An Gorta Mór, the great hunger, as part of the poorhouse system. But things are changing now."

"Before we went to the accident, you'd mentioned a 1933 Act of Parliament," Fingal said, glad the subject of their conversation was being changed. "It was a Pott's fracture, by the way. John-Joe Finnegan's off to Sir Patrick Dun's to have it set."

"They'll do a good job there." Doctor Corrigan nodded to himself. "They'll have him doing toe exercises in ten days, but he'll not be walking on crutches for at least a couple of months."

And after that? No job waiting for him as a cooper, that was for sure, Fingal thought.

Doctor Corrigan grunted and shook his head. "Aye, the 1933 Act of Parliament. Bah. Ye might as well know that I've no time for politics. It's best ye understand that about me, for my sins, right now. Bunch of bollixes, the whole tribe of them, Sinn Féin, de Valera's Fianna Fáil, this new Fine Gael lot, the Labour Party James Connolly founded? Well, maybe I'd give Labour houseroom, but only just. I'd not give ye tuppence for the rest. Never know when to leave well enough alone. A plague on all their houses."

Fingal wondered if his senior colleague might have a fondness for the works of Shakespeare.

"They've decided to amalgamate all the eighty old independent Approved Medical Insurance Societies that administered the dispensaries and paid our wages under one governing body, the Unified Health Insurance Society, for the whole twenty-six counties of the Irish Free State. The chairman is the Very Reverend John Dignan, Bishop of Clonfert."

"Trust the Catholic Church to have its finger in the pie," Fingal said. The church forbade contraception; the government made it illegal in 1935. Was it any wonder Mary and Boxty Foster had eighteen brothers and sisters between them?

"Och, sure, the priests are everywhere. Our concern is how the system's being run now, and I don't think the new setup'll make bugger all difference to us. There'll be no raise in salaries. We might get the occasional paying patient, but the insured pay our salaries. Being situated where we are, the poor, to misquote Saint Mark, will always be with us. They'll still get their tickets for free care." He inhaled and blew out his breath past nearly closed lips. "And many of the toffs from places like Ranelagh and Ballsbridge, rather than going to a posh local doctor, will come here because even though the gurriers can afford to pay, they can get tickets from their upper-class cronies on the overseeing committee for free care, diddling us out of our

pittances. Despite all the political manoeu-
vrings, for us poor buggers in the trenches
it'll be *plus ça change, plus c'est la même
chose.* My two partners here had had
enough. One's gone to Canada, the other to
Liverpool." His smile was lopsided. "So if ye
do take the job, don't say ye weren't warned."

"Thank you for being honest, but — but if
it's so terrible, why do you stay? I mean, I
keep wondering myself exactly why I'm so attracted to this kind of practice. I think I
know, but may I ask you why you like it here?"

Doctor Corrigan frowned, said, "Huh," and
shook his head. "I sometimes wonder myself,
but I will tell ye a couple of things. When I
was a youngster, a country boy from County
Roscommon, I came to Dublin to train at the
College of Surgeons. The bishops won't let
Catholics attend a Protestant university like
Trinity. Like a lot of kids back then I was full
of ideals. I always thought the poor people
weren't treated fairly. I saw the lot of the
tenement folks firsthand. Somebody had to
do something. I've no time for politics, as I
told ye, and I'm not a bloody evangelist
either. I just thought I could make a difference."

"I see," Fingal said. "I think you and my
mother would hit it off. She and her friends
are trying to get the council to move on slum
clearance."

"Fair play to her, boy. Most of Dublin's

76

toffs pretend poverty simply doesn't exist. Or they blame it on inborn character defects of the poor that make them unable to benefit from help. When I was training, I liked looking after poor people. They were grateful for my efforts and needed medical help a damn sight more because of their poverty, their lousy — and I mean that literally — housing, and appalling diets. The crowding in those neighbourhoods is so atrocious, infections go through the tenements like a gorse fire in summer. I thought the system of free care for them, partly provided by workers' and employers' contributions and from city taxes levied on the rich, was a good way to help."

"It is," Fingal said, "and from what I saw as a student, we need more of it."

Doctor Corrigan shifted from one buttock to the other. "True, and how much have ye seen of the other side of medicine? The one for the rich?"

"Not a lot. My folks' friend Mister Oliver St. John Gogarty, the ENT surgeon, has a private plane and a primrose Rolls-Royce. He charges three hundred pounds for one operation done privately. He taught me at Sir Patrick Dun's," Fingal said, "and to be fair, he was absolutely meticulous when he operated on the charity cases."

"I'd expect that of the man. I know him too, and I know about how private practice works in Blackrock and Ballsbridge."

"My folks live in Ballsbridge," Fingal said.

"I'll forgive ye," Doctor Corrigan said, "and I know about practising among the rich because, apostate that I am, I let my principles slide. I was an assistant in Merrion Square for a year after I qualified. Money was good, but I got fed up being treated like a minor tradesman at the beck and call of the idle rich. Half of them had nothing better to do than sit around all day dreaming up new imaginary illnesses to suffer from. There was a wonderful vogue for colitis — whatever the hell that is — among the ladies. You could make a fortune giving high colonic enemas."

Fingal whistled and said, "Really? I never knew."

"And you never saw the highheejins at a hospital like Dun's, did you? They'd not want to be in a bed beside someone like Mary Foster. They get treated in nursing homes or at home." Doctor Corrigan wheezed his dry laugh. "I came here in '07 and I've been here since, and I think the locals are used to me by now. I fit in and it's comforting to be respected, have them value my work, and so I stay, hoping I'm doing some good."

Fingal thought of John-Joe. "Doctor Corrigan's a sound man," he'd said.

"But," and Corrigan laughed, "the real truth is that I am a real Irishman, too stupid to come in out of the rain." The man's smile faded and his voice was level. "I hope ye'll take the job." He shook his head. "I can't promise ye'll have it forever, mind. There's always rumours of the new administration changing the boundaries of the districts of each dispensary or reducing staff. We'll have to see how things pan out."

Fingal hesitated. That didn't concern him greatly. There'd be other jobs. A doctor would always find work, not like labourers or even skilled tradesman like John-Joe Finnegan. But would the satisfaction of being a respected, recognised local figure, of getting a diagnosis right, be compensation enough for what he'd just heard about the long hours, the poor pay, the possible future insecurity? The paperwork? He already had experience of the squalor in the patients' homes. That didn't bother him. And after a certain initial discomfort with Doctor Corrigan, Fingal reckoned he could do much worse in a senior. He had said he'd not mind working alternate nights, but remembering one of his father's adages about "fools rushing in" said, "Can I have a day or two to think about it?"

"Ye can."

"Doctor Corrigan, I'll be honest as well. I love medicine, but there are other things in my life," like Nurse Kitty O'Hallorhan and rugby football, he thought. "You said if you could hire me and another doctor, the call schedule would be much lighter? One of my classmates is still making up his mind. His name's Charles Greer."

"The big red-haired ox that played in the second row for Ireland last season?"

So Doctor Corrigan followed the rugby? "The very fellah. He's one of my best friends. I'm seeing him tomorrow for a jar. I'll phone him tonight, tell him what you told me, follow up tomorrow and see if he's interested, and if he is —"

Doctor Corrigan beamed and said, "If he is, we'd each work one weekend in three. Ye see yer friend tomorrow, and if he wants to find out more, bring him round on Friday at noon." He slipped off the stool, crossed to Fingal, and offered his hand. The grip was solid. No nonsense.

"Think hard about it, O'Reilly." The handshake was broken. "And for now I'll bid ye fair adieu and go back into the trenches with the great unwashed — the poor divils."

7
Ruinous and Old but Painted Cunningly

Fingal let himself into the high-ceilinged hall to find Bridgit vigorously taking a feather duster to a large Chinese urn. She bobbed at Fingal. "Nice to see you home, Doctor O'Reilly."

"Thank you, Bridgit." He smiled at her use of his title. Her elevation of him from Master O'Reilly to Doctor had been instantaneous the moment he'd qualified.

The County Antrim woman from Portglenone had been working for the family since they'd lived in Holywood in the north and had accompanied her employers, Professor Connan O'Reilly and his wife, Mary, and their two young sons to Dublin so their father could take the chair of classics and English literature at Trinity College.

"I'm a bit late. I got held up," he said. "Where's Mother?"

"In her studio, sir. The professor's sleeping, so he is." She inclined her head to the closed door that led to Father's study. It had recently

81

been converted to a ground-floor bedroom to save him the effort of climbing stairs, something he was no longer able to do.

"I'll not disturb him," Fingal said. Father slept a great deal now as his condition worsened. "It's important he gets his rest."

Bridgit's voice quavered as she said, as if to herself, "Sleeping's all very well, but me and Cook wish he'd eat more. The poor professor has no' got the appetite of a stunted wren these days, so he hasn't."

Fingal's stomach growled. It seemed unkind after what the maid had said, but he was famished. "I've missed lunch. I'm sorry, but do you think Cook could make a quick snack? Something that's not too much trouble?"

Bridgit cocked her head and said, "There's tomato soup, and would you like a sandwich, sir? There's a brave wheen of cold ham left over."

"Soup and a ham sandwich would be grand," he said. "Thank you, and please thank Cook for me. Could you bring it along to the studio? And maybe a pot of tea, Bridgit?"

"I'll see to it, sir." Bridgit bobbed a curtsey and left.

Fingal let himself into what had been a guest bedroom before Ma converted it into a studio in 1928. He stood just inside the doorway. On bright days like today, the room was filled with light, and now the mid-

82

afternoon sunshine streaming in accentuated how pale she had become. The tan she'd brought home in May from her and Father's long visit to Greece and Egypt, their wintering over in Cap d'Antibes, had faded, and her eyes were sunken, bleary. He knew she was sleeping badly, but being Ma she refused to admit to any tiredness.

The room was heavy with the smell of oil paint, turpentine, and linseed oil, overpowering the perfume of a huge bunch of red roses Ma'd brought from the garden yesterday and set behind her on a broad windowsill. "Fingal, you're back." She turned from her easel close to the window, upon which was a canvas prepared with a russet wash of diluted oil paint. "Have you had lunch?"

He knew his mother well enough to know she would have been fretting about his lateness, but rather than asking for an explanation she worried he hadn't eaten. "Not yet, but Bridgit's getting Cook to make me some soup and a sandwich. I told her to bring it here. I thought we could chat while you were working."

She indicated one of a pair of folding wooden chairs. "Have a seat then."

Fingal did, and watched his artist mother. Her paint-stained smock was in scruffy contrast to the immaculately dressed woman she usually was. She held a palette with swirls of coloured oils that recently had been squeezed from their tubes. A metal dipper clipped to the palette's edge held linseed oil, and she darted the brush into the dipper and began to soften a dark blue paint with drops of the oil. He knew better than to ask her what the subject would be. Ma never liked to discuss her paintings until they were finished, although she didn't mind Fingal or Father watching as she worked. "I saw Doctor Corrigan, but we were called out to an accident," he said. "That's why I'm late. Some poor divil got hit by a tram. Broke his ankle."

"Not nice," she said.

"He'll be all right," Fingal said. "Pity about his job though."

"Why?"

"The chap's a cooper. He'd just landed a place at Guinness's. He'll be hors de combat for quite a while. They'll find someone else now." For a moment Fingal hoped Ma might say she knew one of the members of the famous brewery family and might be able to pull strings.

"So many out of work. It is a very hard world out there," she said, put the brush aside, and lifted a palette knife, "and none too easy here." She sighed. "You knew Doctor Micks was coming this morning. He said he was sorry to have missed you."

Father couldn't have a better specialist than Fingal's old mentor from Sir Patrick Dun's

Hospital. He attended Father at least once a week.

"He spoke to me in private." There was a catch in her voice. "He doesn't think — He's not confident that Connan is going to live much longer. Doctor Micks offered your father another blood transfusion, but he declined. I think it was the right decision." Her gaze was fixed on Fingal's eyes.

The worry that was never far from the front of Fingal's mind gnawed at him. He was no stranger to death, but watching his own father being wasted by acute myelogenous leukemia was harder than anything he'd done in his twenty-seven years. It was typical of Father's iron will to refuse a transfusion that could only delay the inevitable. Fingal would like to have touched his mother's hands but both were occupied. All he could do was say, "It was the right one. And Father's not in any pain and has all of his wits about him." It was the only comfort he had to offer.

She smiled and braced her shoulders as rigidly as he'd seen old Queen Mary doing in a Pathé newsreel of her husband King George V's funeral in January. Mary O'Reilly née Nixon, was like Her Majesty, a woman of the Victorian age. Sometimes Fingal wondered what went on behind those seemingly reserved façades. He was aware of the door opening behind him.

Ma smiled and said, "Connan. You're

awake. Fingal's home."

Father was leaning on a blackthorn walking stick.

Fingal crossed the floor. "Take my arm." He felt his father's hand on his forearm and together they walked slowly. Fingal helped him onto the other folding chair.

It took Father a while to catch his breath before he could say, "Thank you, son." He'd been a tall man, but now he was stooped. His once black hair was thinning and silver. The tartan dressing gown he wore seemed to have been made for a man twice his size. The skin of the hands folded in his lap was alabaster white and onion-skin thin. Veins coursed beneath. A bruise the size of a half crown disfigured the back of the left hand. "Good to see you home." He looked at the canvas. "Please don't stop, Mary. You know how much I like to watch you work."

With the edge of the palette knife she started applying paint a third of the way up from the bottom of the canvas, drawing it across in a gently ascending thin line.

Fingal knew that as a boat builder begins with the keel on which the skeleton of the vessel is laid, so Ma started her 'scape pictures with the horizon. With so much space left above it, this one was going to be a skyscape. She had a knack for capturing those moments when nature wrought a summer sky of such perfection that the viewer half-

86

expected to see angels in one corner, or those of agony when Boreas the north wind piled up the thunderheads of Armageddon and made mortal man feel tiny and afraid.

"Fingal's just come in. Would you like a cup of tea, Connan?" Ma asked as if it were just another workaday afternoon.

"No, thank you, dear." He turned to Fingal. "Do please sit. How did the interview go? Are you going to take the job?" There was no hint of approval in his voice.

Fingal frowned. His father had a deeply held belief that his younger son should specialize, a desire fostered by his friends Doctor Victor Millington Synge, nephew of the playwright, and Mister Oliver St. John Gogarty.

"Doctor Corrigan, the principal, seems like an interesting man." Fingal smiled. "I must say initially he put me off. Seemed arrogant and bullying, but we had a tête-à-tête. I could grow to like that man a lot, I think. You would, M— Mother." Father hated Fingal calling her "Ma." He had told him often that it was "common," and perhaps he was right. Still, he always thought of her as Ma. "He worried a lot about the poor when he was about my age and is still committed to helping the underprivileged."

She stopped in the middle of softening the edge of part of the horizon. "Good for him. I've seen the living conditions in the Liberties. The sooner they're razed the better. The city fathers have plans to pull down whole streets and put up seven thousand four hundred new dwellings by '38, but that's still a long time away. They should be moving faster."

"I'm sure Doctor Corrigan would agree. He has a more direct approach, looking after the people despite their surroundings, trying to help them one case at a time," Fingal said, thinking of the little doctor and Manus Foster, his skin pink from coal gas poisoning. "He is very committed to his work. I could learn a lot from him."

"Corrigan graduated in the same year as Doctor Micks," Father said, then a cough clutched him and he bent over but soon righted himself and continued. "They attended Doctor Steevens' Hospital together for some of their training. Doctor Micks says the man's a very good doctor." Father coughed again. "For a G.P."

"I can have the job if I want it."

"And do you?" Father asked, and coughed, this time deep in his chest, a moist sound. He gasped twice. "I'm sorry," he said, and worked at getting his breath back.

The disease had spread to Father's lungs. Fingal gritted his teeth. He'd been seeing patients for long enough not to be surprised by the random unfairness of how illnesses struck, but it was unjust how this abomination had afflicted Father — bloody unjust. He was still a relatively young man — only fifty-seven. Fingal clenched his fists, then let them relax, waiting for him to speak.

"I'm all right now," Father said. "I asked if you were going to take the job, Fingal."

"I want to discuss it with Charlie Greer. See if I can persuade him to come and work there too. There are two vacant positions. I'm hoping to see him tomorrow afternoon, and," he hesitated, torn between a feeling of filial duty and a selfish wish to see Kitty O'Hallorhan, "then I'm taking Kitty out afterwards."

"The lovely nurse with the grey eyes that you brought here for dinner on the night you got your Finals results?" Ma said. She had finished the preliminary sketch of the horizon and was blocking out cloud shapes and patterns above using a broad brush loaded with purple-grey paint. Already the sketches were giving Fingal a sense of foreboding, but thinking of Kitty banished it.

"That's her. I'm looking forward to seeing her." Kitty was indeed lovely, soft and very kissable. She was also good fun to be with, and God knew Fingal would appreciate that right now. But despite a longing to see Kitty, he turned to his Father and added, "If it's all right with you."

"You must do both, son," Father said. "There's absolutely no need for you to haunt this place like Banquo's ghost. Mother and I will be perfectly all right."

"Thank you both," Fingal said, "and about my decision. I didn't accept on the spot. Said I'd like a bit of time to think about it. If Charlie says no, the hours will be pretty brutal and I hadn't realised there was going to be a fair bit of paperwork."

Father smiled. "There always is. I should know." He nodded. "I'm glad you're taking your time, son. There's a lot of truth in the adage, 'Accept in haste. Regret at leisure.' "

Father and his words to live by. "The clinical work would be in the Liberties, the Coombe. I know my way around a lot of the district already. I was out there often when I did my midwifery." He smiled. "There's even a chissler named Fingal Flahertie O'Reilly Kilmartin, poor child. If he learns to write he'll have a time of it filling in forms." He remembered how flattered he'd been when the baby's parents had told him they were going to name the wee one in Fingal's honour. "I do like working with the people there. You feel that you're making a difference. Doctor Corrigan said much the same, and if Charlie would agree to come too, the workload wouldn't be so very heavy. I'll not decide until I see what he says."

"Sensible," she said. "Very sensible." She smiled. "I know from the stories you told us about your time at Sir Patrick Dun's you'll enjoy working with the less privileged. If you do decide to accept, I'm sure it will be rewarding work. I'm so very proud of you, son."

Father remained expressionless.

"And, if it's not out of place to say it, so's Cook and me." Bridgit had come in pushing a tea trolley. "Where will I put this, ma'am?"

"Just leave it there, please. Fingal can eat off his lap and we can talk more about the job when you've finished."

Father seemed to be content to sit quietly as Ma worked while Fingal polished off his lunch. "That," said Fingal, holding on to his second cup of tea, "was just what the doctor ordered."

Father smiled and started to say something, but his words were strangled by more coughing. Ma transferred the palette knife into her left hand, leant forward and patted Father's hand. "It's all right, dear. Don't try to talk. You'll tire yourself out."

Fingal watched his father struggle for breath, knowing exactly what the leukaemia was doing to his body. The proliferation of the blood's white cells was suppressing the production of red cells that carried oxygen. It wasn't the same mechanism that had made Manus Foster unconscious, but the result was the same. Oxygen starvation of the tissues. The disease, now having invaded his lungs, accounted for Father's breathlessness and his cough.

"You know my feelings, son. I'd like to see you specialize, but . . ." He managed a weak smile. "Once I thought you should be a nuclear physicist."

"You may have been right, Father," Fingal said. "I'm not going to become a Rockefeller working in the dispensary system."

"No," said Father, "no you're not, but I believe you could be a contented man, and you have your health." Fingal detected no hint of bitterness or envy in his father's words, then he was wracked again. Ma looked at Fingal, who rose and cradled his father's head, as Professor Connan O'Reilly must have cradled his infant sons'. Fingal held on until the coughing stopped, released his father, and said, "All right now, Dad?" The time for the formal "Father," which had until very recently been the only way Fingal and his brother Lars had addressed the man, was over, although Fingal would always think of him as Father. "All right?"

Father nodded. "You have the Gailege, the Irish, Fingal." He swallowed. *Is fearr an tsláinte ná na táinte.*"

"Health is better than riches," Fingal said, and thought, how true. Father and Ma had never been attracted to extravagance, seemed to have everything they needed. He glanced at Ma's canvas. Already the cloud outlines had been formed and she was using a thick impasto to give one a foreboding body. He

92

felt a goose walk over his grave and thought, No wonder the ancient Norse believed that the Valkyries, the goddesses who decided who would die in battle, careered on wild horses through the Heavenly maëlstroms.

Father reached for Fingal's hand. "I may have my opinions." His voice had a feathery quality, but then he pulled himself upright in his chair and said, as firmly as ever Fingal remembered, "I may think specialisation is right for you — but I've always taught you and Lars, 'To thine own self be true.' "

Fingal smiled and cleared his throat. "Unless it was in conflict with what you thought was best for us. As you said a few moments ago, you initially thought I should go in for nuclear physics. But you've softened a lot —" He hesitated. "— Dad."

"I was wrong. Then." Father smiled. "Apparently on occasions some old dogs can be taught new tricks. Do it, son. Try general practice, even if Charlie doesn't. If it's what you want, stick at it. If it's not, think about my opinion, after I'm gone."

If Fingal had any remaining reservations about taking the job, Father had put them to rest. The lump in Fingal's throat was threatening to strangle him. He stared at the floor, then at his father's pallid, wasted, but smiling face. "Thank you," he said. "Thank you, Dad." And as he poured more tea for himself, Fingal O'Reilly wished he could ignore the social convention that prohibited grown men from embracing. "And I will remember."

"Good," said Professor O'Reilly. "And now, if it's still warm, I think I will have that cup of tea."

8

WITH ACHING HANDS
AND BLEEDING FEET

O'Reilly listened to the rain hammering against the surgery windows at Number One Main Street. Bloody Ulster summer squalls. He headed for the waiting room, but Kinky, holding the hall telephone, stopped him. "Before you see your next patient, sir, his lordship's on the line."

"Fine. Thanks, Kinky." He took the receiver. "John?"

"Fingal. Glad I caught you. I've just discovered I'd made a ghastly oversight. I do apologise."

O'Reilly frowned. "Oversight?"

"Yes. Myrna's accident and all that. I muddled up the guest list for tomorrow. You and Kitty should have been invited. It's the opening day of grouse season."

Indeed it was. O'Reilly, who frequently was invited to shoot on the marquis's moor in County Antrim, had been disappointed not to have been asked this year, but understood how his lordship had to share his favours throughout that county too. "Don't worry about it, John."

"Myrna usually handles these things. I'm glad we got her home yesterday . . ."

Despite his good intentions O'Reilly had not been able to make time to visit her in hospital, but Cromie had kept O'Reilly up to date on her progress.

"I found your invitation wedged under a pile of tack catalogues this morning, so needless to say it didn't get posted," he said with a laugh. "Any chance you two could still come? I'd love to have you both there, and Arthur's such a help with pushing up birds and the retrieving."

"I think so. I'll have to arrange cover, but I'm sure Doctor Bradley will oblige. She's out now. I'm not sure about Kitty. She's off today, but I think she's on duty tomorrow. I'll phone you after lunch."

"I'll look forward to hearing."

O'Reilly replaced the receiver. It would be a splendid day out on the moors near Loughareena, County Antrim, and, he thought as he marched along the hall, no distance from Ballymena. He wondered if Barry might be free for dinner that evening. It would be good to catch up with how he was getting on.

O'Reilly opened the door to his waiting room and admired the roses on the wallpaper. Their bright hues always managed to make him feel cheerful even on the greyest day, like today. He said to the remaining patients, "Is it Colin or yourself, Lenny?" as he bent and scratched the droopy ear of Murphy, Colin's new puppy.

Lenny Brown pointed at Colin's bare and grubby left foot. "Colin again. Sorry, Doc. He cut his foot a few days ago, but it's getting worser, so it is. It was all right this morning when he went over to Gerry Shanks's place so Mairead could mind him. The missus had til go til Belfast and I've my work. Mairead brung him til the building site half an hour ago because he said it had started to hurt like bedamned. I took one look at his foot and brung him right here, so I did."

O'Reilly shook his head. "In the wars again, eh?"

"Yes, Doctor," Colin said, and sniffed.

"Come on then, let's have a look at you, but leave Murphy here. He'll be all right if we shut the door."

"Be a good dog, Murphy," Colin said.

Lenny bent, then lifted and carried Colin. "He was getting about rightly at brekky time, but he can't walk on it now." As O'Reilly led them to his surgery he remembered how the last year had gone for Colin Brown. Cut hand Barry'd sutured last summer, ringworm of his scalp, greenstick fracture of his ulna and radius this year, and now this? The little lad was accident-prone. "Pop him up on the couch, Lenny" — Mister Brown deposited his son — "and have a pew."

Lenny took one of the hard-backed chairs and adopted the splay-legged posture common to all who sat there and on its twin. Patients had to brace themselves because years ago O'Reilly had sawn off a couple of inches from the front legs so patients would slide forward, be uncomfortable, and not be tempted to stay too long.

"How'd you do your hoof, Colin?" O'Reilly asked.

"You knows Donal Donnelly? Him that has the gru-dog Bluebird, like?"

O'Reilly laughed. "Indeed I do. And I know his greyhound. I've made a few bob on her."

"Well, I was out at his place three days ago with Murphy, my new wee pup. We'd went out on the bus. Donal —" He glanced at his father as if expecting a reprimand. Small boys did not call adults by their Christian names. "He likes me to call him Donal, Daddy, honest to God."

"I'd call that impertinence. Weans should respect their bloody elders and betters, so they should."

"Och, come on, Daddy. Donal says it's all right and he's helping me train Murphy."

"I suppose." Lenny shrugged. "All right, but you try calling me or your mammy that way." He turned to O'Reilly. "I blame it all on that there American TV."

"Train Murphy? That's very decent of him," O'Reilly said. "Donal's a good man with dogs."

"Aye, he is that, and I'm helping him with his dog too, so I am." O'Reilly heard the pride in the boy's voice. "He's got all kinds of plans for her." Colin dropped a wink and for a moment O'Reilly could have sworn he was looking at Donal Donnelly. He knew Donal was planning on doing a bit of "flapping" at an unregistered track, and as O'Reilly remembered it, Donal had said owners' kids often presented the dogs to the stewards. Since Donal's own child was far too young to help him with his schemes, it looked as if Donal had found a suitable kid for whatever he was planning. "And he says he's mentioned it til youse, Doctor, but I've to keep my trap shut with everyone else." The wink again. "There's never nobody out at Dun Bwee to see me and him together with the dog."

O'Reilly chuckled and said, "Crafty bugg —" and cut himself off. Not in front of children. He wondered how much Lenny and Connie Brown knew about the dog scheme? "And you and Connie don't mind, Lenny? Colin's not a bit young to be working with racing greyhounds?"

"Not at all, Doc," he said with a laugh. "Kids do it all the time. And Donal's a sound man. We all know he's a bit of a schemer, but there's no real harm in him. Him and me has a wee understanding about this. I'm helping a bit too — and if a bookie loses a few bob, you'll hear no weeping and wailing and gnashing of teeth round here. Colin's not going to get hurt and he has a new interest. He's certainly doing a great job with Murphy — with Donal's help. You should see the wee pup sit when he's told to."

O'Reilly shrugged. It was true youngsters were often involved with the training of racing dogs and horses, and if it was all right with Lenny and Connie Brown then O'Reilly could wonder all he wanted about the exact nature of the upcoming plot, but for now could afford to turn a blind eye. "So what happened to your foot?" he said.

"It was a dead brill day and there was dew on the grass so I took my shoes and socks off for til run through it." He grinned. "Feels lovely on your bare feet, so it does." His grin fled. "But there was something sharp and I cut my foot. Miss MacAteer, I mean Missus Donnelly, was wheeker, so she was. She cleaned it, put on some iodine — it stung like blue buggery —"

O'Reilly glanced at Lenny but Colin's language didn't appear to upset the man, probably because Lenny's own was hardly snow-white.

"Then she put on a great big Elastoplast. It was a bit sore, but I could hirple about on it right enough until this morning when I was at the Shanks's. Mrs. Shanks took off the plaster about half an hour ago and the whole thing was beelin' so she brung me to my daddy and he brung me here."

"Let's have a look." Indeed it was "beel-ing." Pus was coming from a two-inch-long cut in the middle of the sole. It was a nasty sight now, an eighth of an inch wide and showing no signs of healing. Julie Donnelly's iodine clearly hadn't been effective as a disinfectant, or perhaps Colin had got more dirt into it. The cut probably should have been sutured, but it was too late now because it was the same rule today as it had been when he was a student: "If there's pus, drain it." The wound would have to heal by what was called secondary intention, after the inflammation settled down, but that would be rapid in a healthy youngster like Colin and antibiotics would make short shrift of the infection.

"All right," said O'Reilly, "we'll get that fixed soon enough for you, Colin."

In a very short time, O'Reilly had shown Lenny how to clean the wound with hydrogen peroxide and put on a gauze dressing. "Do that twice a day until it stops weeping, and keep a clean dressing on it until you bring him to see me this day week. Don't let it get dirty or wet and no walking on it until the skin's grown back. In a young fellah like

Colin that should be two or three weeks. I'll see if I can get crut—"

"Buggeration. You mean we'll have to lift and lay him for three whole weeks?" Lenny didn't wait for O'Reilly to finish.

"Buggeration's right, Daddy," Colin said, eliciting no response from Lenny and making O'Reilly wonder why he'd bothered to moderate his own language earlier. "It's my summer holidays. All gone. Can youse do nothing, Daddy?"

Lenny frowned. "If I made him a crutch, could he hop about, Doc? It'd be awful hard for a wee lad to have til sit around all day."

"No reason not to, Lenny. You'll be going round like a bee on a hot brick, Colin, and you'll be fit in September for —" O'Reilly remembered Colin's antipathy to school so didn't finish the sentence.

It was mandatory for anyone who had cut themselves where there was soil in which the spores of the causative organism might lurk — even if their immunisation schedule was up to date — but Colin wasn't impressed with the tetanus toxoid jab. He yelled at the top of his voice and was answered by a loud *woof* then whining from the waiting room.

"We'll get you back to your dog in just a minute," O'Reilly said.

Colin soon cheered up when O'Reilly gave him half a dozen jelly babies from a bag of sweeties in his jacket pocket. Carrying sweeties for young patients was a trick he'd developed back in his Sir Patrick Dun days.

"Here you are, Lenny." O'Reilly handed over a prescription for the cleanser, gauze pads and bandages, and penicillin V. "Give Colin four tablets as soon as you get home from the chemist, then 125 milligrams, that's one tablet, four times a day for a week," he said, "and count yourself lucky we've got antibiotics these days. They're the greatest things since Noah ran the Ark aground." He well remembered another infected foot back in 1936. He'd never ever forget a boy called Dermot Finucane.

"Thanks, Doc," Lenny said. "Connie'll bring him in next week."

Colin piped up, "Thank you, Doctor O'Reilly — and don't you never say nothing about Donal's dog."

"I'll not," O'Reilly said, and chuckled. He wondered if Ballybucklebo was big enough for two tricksters.

Kitty was sitting in her usual chair to the right of his own at the dining room table. He sang in his soft baritone a snatch from the song "Have I Told You Lately that I Love You?" He'd first heard it twenty years ago. "Well, I bloody well do, even after being married to you for five whole weeks and four days today." He inclined his head. "I could get very used to it."

"Me too," she said, then stood, made sure no one was near, and kissed him so forcibly he was no longer aware of the pelting of early-August raindrops on the bow window.

"And I wish I'd had the wit to do it back in '36, but —"

"Now, Fingal," she said, "you've told me that regret is the most useless emotion. What's done is done." She lowered her voice. "I've always been sure we were meant to be more than a short romance, and God bless you, you great inarticulate bear, so did you, you just didn't recognise it or know how to express it. You slipped up back then, boy, but there's no need to plough the same furrow twice." She held up her left hand with her solitaire diamond engagement and simple wedding ring on the third finger.

"Thank you, love," he said, "thank you," and the growth of his heart in his chest nearly choked him.

"By the way," she said, "I was passing and heard a funny noise in the waiting room. Someone had left a pup there. Looked like Colin Brown's dog."

"It was," O'Reilly said. "Colin'd cut his foot, but a bit of penicillin'll see him right."

"Poor wee lad." She pursed her lips. "Fingal?"

"Yes?"

"When was the last time you decorated your waiting room?"

He frowned. "Dunno. Why?"

"I have never in all my days seen anything as gaudy as those roses."

"My roses? I like 'em."

She sat, cocked her head, and said, "Och well, I suppose there's no accounting for taste," then glanced to the hall and clearly decided not to pursue matters with Jenny Bradley in the hall hanging up a sodden raincoat.

"Hello, Jenny. Grab a pew," O'Reilly said as she came in.

"Fingal. Kitty." She took off the jacket of the navy blue suit she often wore when working and put it on an empty chair. "It's bucketing down out there."

At five foot six with blonde bangs, bright blue eyes, small nose, well-filled white silk blouse, and slim waist, Jenny Bradley was a most attractive twenty-six-year-old, Fingal thought. "Busy morning?" he asked.

She parked herself on his left. "Not much," she said. "Little lad up on the council estate with hay fever. It's that time of year and the rain bringing pollen down doesn't help. He settled down after I gave him nought point three milligrams of adrenaline, one in one thousand solution subcutaneously. I popped in with Mister Devine like you asked me to. He's sad, but it's six months since his wife died and he seems to be managing. I'll be going out again after —"

"Lunch," said Kinky, appearing in the doorway. "Pea and mint soup with a shmall-little bit of fresh cream and finely chopped mint garnish, so."

"After lunch," Jenny said. "Youngster up in the hills. Sounds like out-of-season whooping cough, but," she took a deep breath in through her nose, "that smells delicious, Mrs. Kincaid. I'm sure he can wait a little longer."

Jenny Bradley's settling well into the routine and seems to have a well-honed sense of who can wait for a little while and who needs instant attention, O'Reilly thought. I'd have made the same decision of lunch before whooping cough. Even Kinky's soup, though, would have had to wait for chest pain or bleeding.

Kinky had set the steaming bowls in front of each diner. "I had planned to serve it cold, it being summer, but it does be coming down in stair-rods so I thought you'd all, especially Doctor Bradley, appreciate something warm, and it does be very, very —"

"Jasus Murphy," O'Reilly roared, spitting out soup and clapping his hands to his mouth, "I'm marmalized, scalded like a butchered pig."

Kinky sniffed as only she could and said distinctly, "Very hot, so."

"Thank you for warning us, Kinky," Kitty said, clearly trying to stifle a smile. "Now, Fingal, there's no need to shout. Try to remember what our mothers used to say. Blow on it and eat it round the edges like a little pussycat does."

O'Reilly guffawed. "And did your mother tell you that too, Jenny?"

She nodded.

"And it does be sound advice, sir," Kinky said. "It stops a man burning his mouth and keeps his tie clean too."

"I don't think," Kitty said with a smile, "that pea green goes with Trinity College stripes." She looked up. "If Doctor O'Reilly gives you his tie would you sponge it, please, Kinky?"

"I will, so. I always do."

It was a matter-of-fact statement, O'Reilly recognised, not a hint that Kitty might mind her own business and leave Kinky's doctor's laundry and clothes cleaning arrangements up to Kinky.

She held out her hand. "But ties do be the divil to wash. Maybe the dry cleaner's?"

"Please," O'Reilly said, feeling like a chastised six-year-old as he undid the knot and handed her his tie. "Thank you, Kinky." He smiled at Kitty.

"Now," said Kinky, "after all those shenanigans, please eat it up before it gets cold." She left muttering to herself, "More haste, less speed."

Fingal didn't blow on his plate, but was more circumspect as he took his first mouthful. "Nectar and ambrosia," he said. "Food of the gods."

"And," said Jenny, "if Homer is to be believed, used by Tethys to prevent Achilles' recently deceased body going off." She must have seen Kitty's raised eyebrow because Jenny said, "I'd not have mentioned it in nonmedical company."

Kitty laughed and gave a dismissing wave with her left hand. "Good heavens, you won't hear anyone saying 'not while we're eating' around here, Jenny. We've about sixty years of medical experience between us."

Fingal's second spoonful stopped halfway to his mouth. *"Mirabile dictu,"* he said, "wondrous things are spoken. The woman knows her Homer." And without hesitation, Jenny replied, "Virgil. *Aeneid.*"

Fingal ignored the ringing of the telephone, Kinky would answer it, and said, "I'll be damned. You're right. Twice. Well done." He smiled inside. He'd thought he'd not be able to play his duelling trivia game now Barry had left, but this wasn't the first time Jenny Bradley had matched him. In the nearly seven weeks she'd been here, four working in harness with him, she'd been willing, hardworking, clearly had a sense of fun, and so far medically had shown that she knew her stuff. "You're fitting in nicely here," he said.

"Thank you, Fingal." She hesitated, then said, "With most of your patients. At the

108

beginning quite a few left the waiting room when they saw I was doing the surgery. Even after six weeks some still do."

"Oh?" he said. "Why do you think that is?"

"There's not many of us 'lady doctors' around. It just takes time to let people get used to seeing a woman who isn't a nurse with a stethoscope."

"Does it not bother you?" Kitty asked.

Jenny shook her head. "I had to get used to 'But girls don't do medicine' from the time I was sixteen and announced I wanted to go to medical school. I'm sure that nice Helen Hewitt who got the marquis's scholarship'll find the same thing. You ignore it, shrug it off . . ." Her eyes hardened. "And if you want to get even, do better than everybody in the class."

"And did you?" Kitty said.

Jenny coloured. "Only two of us out of a class of ninety-one graduated with first-class honours."

O'Reilly whistled. "First class? You never told me."

Jenny laughed and said, "You never asked me."

"Well done you," O'Reilly said. He chuckled. "I was happy enough to pass." He pushed his empty soup plate aside. "And you'd settle for G.P.? Most honours winners specialize."

"I wasn't sure what to do," she said, "so I decided to give G.P. a try. I love it, and," her blue eyes lit up, "this is the best practice I've ever been in. So far anyway."

"Glad you like it here," O'Reilly said. She'd told him at the wedding, and in no uncertain terms, that she'd be looking for a full-time position. O'Reilly had made a promise to Barry Laverty that if, within six months, he still wanted it, he could have his job back. Time would tell, O'Reilly thought, but to avoid any premature discussion of the future he said nothing of his thoughts. He hoped, because he was so impressed with the young woman, that he'd not find himself in a difficult position when it came to keeping his promises to young Laverty should the need arise. It would be good to see Barry tomorrow if it could be arranged. O'Reilly finished his soup, then remarked, "I wonder what culinary delights Kinky has in store for the next course?"

"That soup, Kinky, was out of this world," Kitty said when she appeared.

"Thank you." Kinky beamed and said, "And I do hope you will enjoy your Scotch eggs and salad, so." She served, the women first, then O'Reilly. "And you needn't worry about burning your mouth on these, sir. They do be cold."

O'Reilly laughed. "Fair play, Kinky, and the soup was lovely." He waited for her to tell them who had been on the phone. Oh well, if it was a patient needing a home visit, Jenny would take care of it.

Kinky stood stiffly and took a deep breath. "I wonder, sir, if I could ask a very great favour?"

"Fire away!"

"That was Mister Archie Auchinleck on the telephone."

O'Reilly smiled at Kitty. So the romance with the milkman that had started when Kinky had come home from hospital was still in full flower.

"There does be a Saturday matinée at the Tonic cinema . . ."

"*The Sound of Music*'s playing," Kitty said. "We should go sometime, Fingal."

Over my dead body, he thought. He'd heard the songs on the radio. Saccharine rubbish. But O'Reilly said, "And Archie's invited you?"

Kinky blushed and nodded. "Someone will need to be here to answer the phone if Doctor Bradley is out on a call, so."

"We'd be happy to do that for you, Kinky," Kitty said. "Wouldn't we, Fingal? We've no special plans."

"Of course. You go and phone him right back, and there's no need to rush home when it's over."

"Thank you, sir. Thank you." Kinky's grin was vast. "I'll phone at once, but I will be home to make tea, although I might invite Mister Auchinleck to dine with me in my kitchen if that would be all right?"

"Of course, Kinky."

An even stronger gust hurled rain against the windowpane, rattling the glass and sending a flying column of draughty chargers through where the sash was ill-fitting.

"And," he said, "I hope by tomorrow it'll be a better day, because ladies, do you know what tomorrow is?"

Jenny frowned. "Thursday, the twelfth of August."

"And?" He saw Kinky, who certainly knew what he was driving at, grinning.

"Beats me," Jenny said.

"The Glorious Twelfth."

Jenny's frown grew deeper. "That's in July."

"No," said O'Reilly, and chuckled. "July the twelfth of 'glorious and immortal memory' is the day of the Orangemen parade, and the 'immortal memory' applies to Robbie Burns. August the twelfth is much more important than either. It's the opening day of grouse, that's *Lagopus lagopus scotica,* or possibly *hibernica* — some ornithologists think the Irish bird is a different species. First day of grouse season and the marquis phoned me this morning —"

"And you want me to cover?" Jenny said. "Poor wee birds."

"I'll do Friday," he said, hoping she wasn't going to refuse.

She shrugged. "Fine by me, but I do feel

sorry for the grouse."

He didn't know how to answer that, so said, "Any chance you could get a day off, Kitty? The invitation is to you as well."

"I'll ask Jane Hoey," she said. "It's my normal day off today and Jane's working, but she's pretty decent and I'll make it up to her next week. I'll give her a call." She stood.

"Better and better." He rose. "Once you know, I'll phone Waveney Hospital, see if Barry can get free tomorrow evening, and you, Doctor Bradley, you are now off duty until 0800 hours tomorrow. I'll go and see your little fellow with whooping cough and look after the shop for the rest of the day."

9
COME, MY LAD, AND
DRINK SOME BEER

"So, you're going to take a job as a dispensary doctor, Fingal?" Bob Beresford said as they scurried through a rain shower. The smell of fresh coffee beans roasting at Bewley's café on nearby Grafton Street was heavy on the air. They pushed through the door and into the front of the long room that was Davy Byrnes pub.

Fingal thought he detected a faint note of condescension in his friend's voice. Robert Saint John — pronounced "Sinjin" by his Anglo-Irish Ascendancy family — Beresford was his usual dapper self. His fedora was tipped at a rakish angle and Fingal was quite sure that under Bob's Burberry raincoat was one of his bespoke drape-cut suits. Tapered trouser cuffs were obvious under the coat. "That's my plan," Fingal said as they walked through the bar. "It'd not be your cup of tea, Bob."

Bob shuddered. "I tried when we were students, but I'm really not excited about dealing with lice and scabies. And the smells . . ." He nodded to an acquaintance leaning on the bar. "Mind you, to tell you the truth, Fingal, I'm not cut out for a Merrion Square practice either. I really don't like working with sick people."

Fingal laughed. "We've known that ever since we started at the hospital. I reckon doing microbiology research with Prof Bigger is right up your street. How are you enjoying working with Trinity's new dean of medicine?"

"It's all very new to me, but he's teaching me the scientific method. He's got me plating out — you remember the old experiments we had to do with bugs on agar jelly plates? He has me at it, and putting pellets of a new compound called red prontosil on the agar of half the plates to see if it will inhibit bacterial growth there while the undrugged plates flourish."

"Interesting," Fingal said. "You'll let me know how it all turns out?"

"If you want to know, sure." Bob grinned. "Actually it's fascinating. I never really thanked you for suggesting I consider research."

"We had to get you doing something, you idle waster." Fingal shrugged. "And even if you don't want to admit it, you've always had what the ancient Greeks prized most —"

"The figure of Adonis?" Bob raised an eyebrow.

Fingal shook his head. "No, you buck eejit — an enquiring mind."

"Oh, that? Well, I suppose so, and seeing I do have one, may I enquire if you are serious about wanting Charlie to work with you too?"

Fingal eyed Bob, but he was lighting a cigarette. His face was a blank. "Charlie? That's right. I've asked him. Phoned him yesterday. Gave him all the details. He said he'd think about it. There he is, with Cromie."

The two men sat at a table at the far end of the room. The ginger-haired Charlie Greer, and Donald Cromie, who preferred to be called simply "Cromie," held straight, nearly full glasses of Guinness. Fingal went to the bar. "The usual, Bob?"

"Please."

"Pint and a Jameson, please, Diarmud."

"Right you are, Fingal." The barman's form of address was not undue familiarity. The four friends had, since they'd started medical school together in 1931, frequented Davy Byrnes pub, where the fictitious Mister Leopold Bloom in James Joyce's *Ulysses* had once enjoyed a gorgonzola sandwich. Diarmud was a friend more than a barman. He started to pour the Guinness from the barrel that had been broached the longest. The stout in it would be going flat. He'd let that settle, then add more from the new barrel where the ale would be too fresh to be drunk by itself. The resulting blend should be a perfect pint, smooth, creamy, bordering on sweet. "I'll bring dem over."

"Come on, let's join the lads. I'm anxious to hear what Charlie thinks." Fingal was dying to hear what Bob really thought too, but for now he'd let the hare sit. They nodded hellos at other regulars who leant on the counter or sat at tables. Fingal thought, as he passed through the crowded bar, that this city was special, the energy of its people, its history, the gems like Phoenix Park, the Abbey Theatre. And he knew — he knew — how much he wanted to work with the Dublin poor. Father's earlier opinion had sealed the decision for him, but damn it all, he was doing this for himself. He also realized he wanted very much to get to know Doctor Phelim Corrigan better. Fingal reckoned he could learn a lot from the older man who'd enjoyed his work in the tenements enough to keep him at it for twenty-nine years. Besides, it would be a daily puzzle as to which way the parting of his toupee might be facing on any given morning. Fingal smiled. He hoped Charlie would come too.

Pipe and cigarette smoke and beer smells filled his nostrils. He overheard scraps of conversation.

"Do youse t'ink dere'll be a war in Spain?"

a man in a duncher and raincoat asked his companion. "I hear the country's in an awful mess since they chucked out the king. The Fascists and their bloke General José Sanjurjo keep havin' a go at the Republican government and their leader, that Manuel Azaña —"

"Let dem get on with it," the man's companion interrupted. "We've enough trouble here wit' our own fascists. Call demselves Blueshirts. Fellah called Eoin O'Duffy's in charge. Another feckin' Adolf Hitler. Strutting round giving each other straight-arm salutes. De Valera declared dem illegal in 1933, but I hear dey still meet. Maybe O'Duffy'll send dem to Spain to fight if dere is a war."

Fingal smiled. Dubliners were not people to ignore the world around them. He fetched up at the lads' table in time to hear Bob say, "Move over in the bed," and Charlie and Cromie, while making greeting noises, shifted their chairs to make room.

Fingal sat next to Charlie but deliberately didn't look at him. This was his decision.

"Fingal O'Reilly, don't ever play poker," said Charlie with a laugh. "I know what you're thinking and before you ask me if I've made up my mind, I've thought it over and yes, I'm ready to give this dispensary practice a go if they'll have me."

"Grand," said Fingal, grinning as he stuck

118

out his hand, which Charlie shook. "That's the berries. We've to see the boss, Doctor Corrigan —"

"Here y'are." Diarmud set the whiskey and Guinness on the table. "One and tenpence please."

Fingal handed Diarmud a two-shilling piece and accepted his tuppence change. Tipping was not customary in a Dublin pub.

Fingal lifted his glass. "To us in practice, Charlie. I'm looking forward to it."

Charlie drank. "Me too."

"And we've to see this Doctor Corrigan at twelve tomorrow," Fingal said. Charlie's agreement was the icing on the cake. "I'll meet you at the corner of West and North Saint Stephen's Green at eleven thirty," he said. "It's only a doddle from there."

"Great," said Charlie. "That's no distance from my digs on Adelaide Road. Eleven thirty it is and we'll beard this Doctor Corrigan in his lair."

Typical Charlie. Never able to be serious about anything for long — or at least never willing to appear to be taking something seriously.

Bob smiled. "Good luck to you both, and please don't forget, there's always plenty of hot water in my flat."

"What are you on about, Beresford?" Charlie asked.

There was the tiniest of curls to Bob's lip.

"I'll get in some carbolic soap just for you. Kills fleas, I hear, and masks unpleasant smells."

Charlie threw a mock punch and said in a thick Northside accent, "Feck off, you toffee-nosed swank. Away on back to yer manor house and leave us culchies to do the real work."

Fingal took a deep pull from his pint. That exchange had answered his question about how Bob Beresford felt about Fingal and Charlie's choice. Bob did not approve. Oh well, being close friends didn't mean that they all had to like each other's job choices. Bob was entitled to his opinion, as long as he didn't make a thing of it.

As far as Fingal was concerned, not only was it going to be fun to work in harness with one of his best friends, with three doctors in the practice there would surely be time for his other interests. He'd come so close to playing rugby for Ireland last season and he wasn't getting any younger. He was determined to give it everything he had to try to realise his dream of representing his country this season, and of course, there was Kitty. Lovely Kitty. He'd be seeing her later today.

"So," said Bob, sipping his whiskey and lighting another Gold Flake, "that's three of us decided. What about you, Cromie?"

Cromie took a long drink, leaving a creamy tidemark three-quarters of the way down the glass. "Me?" He ran a hand through his thinning fair hair. "I'm going home back up to Ulster tomorrow. Stay with my folks. Do a bit of sailing. I'll be starting as a surgical houseman at the Royal Victoria Hospital in August. I'm going to develop a special interest in bones."

"Good for you, Cromie," Fingal said. "I know fractures are treated by general surgeons, but I reckon one day we're going to have doctors who only do bone work. You could be one of the first."

"More interesting than working with the great unwashed, I should think." Bob finished his whiskey, glanced at his friends' glasses, and called, "Same again please, Diarmud."

Fingal wished that his friend would let the matter drop. He'd made his point.

Diarmud interrupted Fingal's thoughts by calling, "Right y'are, Bob."

"We will miss you, Cromie, you great bollix," said Bob, "but you'll keep in touch?"

Cromie ignored the friendly insult. "With you lot? After what we've been through together for five years? Damn right. And sure it's only a few hours away from here to Belfast. The train goes from Amiens Street Station."

"Seems we're all pretty well set," Fingal said, and fished out and lit his briar. "Will you be keeping your flat on Merrion Square, Bob?"

"I hope so. It's a bit pricey, but I still have dear old auntie's money and I see no reason not to be comfortable."

"All very well for some," Charlie said, "but I don't imagine too many dispensary doctors have places on the French Riviera. How about you moving in with me, Fingal? Save a few bob splitting the rent."

Fingal sighed. "Maybe later, Charlie." He let go a blast of blue smoke. For the immediate future he was needed at home. "You all know that my old man has acute myelogenous leukaemia," he said.

Three heads nodded. No one spoke until Cromie finally blurted out, "You feel so bloody helpless," then took a quick swig from his glass before noticing it was empty.

Charlie's shoulders rose and fell as he inhaled and exhaled down his nose.

"Aye," Fingal said, "you do." He glanced down at the tabletop then back up to his friends. "My old man's not going to last much longer." Funny how easily the words slipped off his tongue. Was it his training that let him sound rational, accepting, despite having one fist so tightly clenched under the table that his arm shook? "My brother Lars is miles away in Portaferry, and my mother's a brick, but I know she appreciates having me about the place. I'll be staying at home for a while." And maybe he needed Ma as much as she needed him.

"Is there anything we can do?" Charlie asked. "Anything at all?"

Fingal shook his head. "Not really, but thanks for offering. I think my family are resigned to things. It's . . . it's really just a matter of time now." He felt his nails digging into his palm and forced his hand to relax.

No one spoke. What could anyone say that wasn't trite?

"Here y'are," Diarmud said, setting fresh drinks on the table and accepting Bob's ten-shilling note. "I'll get your change in a minute."

The sadness of the mood was lifted by Diarmud's prattling. "Did you have anything on the horses last T'ursday, Bob?" Diarmud, who must have been unaware of the atmosphere, was grinning fit to beat Bannagher.

Bob's weakness for the horses was legendary. He shook his head. "Actually for once I wasn't able to get to the races last week. Big family do at home."

"Bejasus, it was hold the feckin' lights for me. I got a daily double at five to one and then ten to one. Five bob bet on the first horse, let it and the winnings ride on the second, and dat bugger came in first too. I took away fifteen quid. You should have seen the look on the bookie's face, fellah called 'Rags' Rafferty. I'm on the pig's back. Rich as yer fellah, King Creases."

Fingal smiled. Diarmud meant Crœsus.

"Good for you, Diarmud," Bob said. "Everybody deserves a bit of luck." He avoided looking Fingal in the eye.

Diarmud spoke more softly. He pulled a scrap of tatty grey fur from his pocket. "You can't beat the oul' rabbit's foot," said he, and winked. "I wasn't eavesdroppin' nor nuttin' but I overheard you discussing careers. Youse've been bloody good customers here since '31." He held up the bunny's hind foot. "It would please me greatly if every one of you would give my oul' foot a rub so you'll all have luck in your new jobs." He solemnly handed the talisman to Bob, who rubbed it and passed it to Cromie. Fingal, who was last, smiled as he took his turn. Scientifically trained as he was, the old Irish superstitions died hard. He stroked the soft fur and was grateful to Diarmud for sharing his talisman. "Good luck to all of us," he said. And he meant it. He returned the charm to its owner. "Thanks, Diarmud."

"My pleasure," he said, and shoved it back in his pocket. He headed for the bar. "Sing out if you need another jar."

"No more for me after this," Cromie said, his words slightly slurred. "Two's my limit."

Fingal was pleased his friend had come to recognise the weakness of his head when it came to the drink and glad that the lighter mood had returned. He glanced at his watch and said, " 'Fraid it's my last too, lads. I'll see you tomorrow, Charlie. Bob, we'll get together soon, and, Cromie, you stay in touch."

Nods of assent.

"Sorry, but if I don't get a move on, I'll be late. I'm taking Kitty to the movies and then for a bite."

"And," said Charlie with a deadpan expression, "where exactly do you intend to make this dental attack on the lovely Miss O'Hallorhan?"

"Scary," said Caitlin "Kitty" O'Hallorhan as, hand in hand, she and Fingal left the three-thousand-seat Savoy Cinema on Upper O'Connell Street and walked through the late-evening crowds toward Nelson's Pillar. She laughed and tightened her grip. "I wonder who did Elsa Lanchester's silver lightning streaks at the sides of her hairdo? *Bride of Frankenstein.* What'll they do next? Son of Frankenstein?"

Fingal recalled the warmth of Kitty's kisses and the softness of her in the back stalls after the house lights had gone out, her clinging to him in faked terror, which gave her an excuse to snuggle up. He chuckled and said, "Thinking of changing your style, Kitty? I like it the way it is." Her hair was ebony, shiny, and rippling against her shoulders as she tossed her head.

"Only if you get bolts put in the sides of

your neck like the Frankenstein monster." She cocked her head to one side. "You're nearly as big as Boris Karloff."

"More articulate, I hope," he said, "but I concur with his opinion," and in an imitation of the monster's speech announced, "Fooood, goood."

The restaurant was a small room, simply furnished. The sound of murmured conversations rose and fell. A waitress said, "For two, sir?"

"Please. In the window." He followed Kitty, as always admiring the sway of her hips, the curve of her calves. He waited until she was seated.

"I'll bring the menus. Would you care for a drink?" Her accent was Dublin, but not as thick as that of the folks from the Liberties.

"Kitty?"

"White wine would be nice. No, are we having red meat so we'll have a red?" Kitty never had paid any heed to that convention.

"Bottle of —" He frowned. "Which is the one you like?" He'd only drunk wine with Kitty once since they'd parted a year ago. They'd had a good claret at his folks' house last week on Graduation Night, the night of their reconciliation. Father had managed to eat at the table and meet Kitty, but had retired to his bed in his study shortly after. For a moment, Fingal felt guilty that he was not at home now, then remembered his father's words: "There's absolutely no need for you to haunt this place like Banquo's ghost." Bless you, Dad.

"Entre-Deux-Mers," Kitty said. "If you've one chilled."

"We do, ma'am." The waitress left.

Kitty leant forward. "I did enjoy the film, Fingal. Good escapist nonsense. Not a patch on Mary Shelley's original *Frankenstein* novel, but it was fun. Thank you for taking me," she pointed out the window, "and I love O'Connell Street. I'd hate to leave Dublin. Just look."

He did and saw a Dublin United Tramways tram clattering along the centre of the street, a blue flash leaping between the top of the pole and the overhead electrical wire. Cyclists were everywhere, and for a moment he cast a thought to John-Joe Finnegan and wondered how his ankle was mending. Sir Patrick Dun's was no distance from Lansdowne Road; maybe Fingal would pop round and see how the cooper by trade was getting on.

Motorcars crept along the congested thoroughfare. Fingal noticed a cream Hillman Minx Deluxe 4 and a dark green open Bentley-Rolls V12 Tourer among the numerous Fords and Morrises. Well-dressed people thronged the sidewalks, and on a street corner a man, probably an Italian immigrant, ground the handle of a barrel organ while his monkey, wearing a red waistcoat and fez, held out a tin cup for coins from passersby. And against walls and on street corners raggedy men, women, and children, the halt and the cripples, hands outstretched in supplication, Dublin's battalions of beggars.

Two streets away people, throngs of people, eked out an existence in the tenements. Out of sight. Out of mind. Well, they weren't out of his or Ma's. "O'Connell Street," he said. "It used to be Sackville Street, you know, until they changed the name. It's still where the toffs go, but Dublin's not so pretty a few streets over."

"I know," she said. "And it bothers you, doesn't it?"

He nodded, but smiled. "I've saved up telling you 'til we got here, but I'll be starting work next week, not too far from your flat. In the dispensary in Aungier Place in the Liberties."

"That's not Parnell or Merrion Square," Kitty said.

"I'm not looking for the carriage trade. Neither's Charlie Greer. He'll be working with me."

She touched his hand. "I'm not surprised, Fingal. I still remember you with the patients at Sir Patrick's. I think you're going to be happy with your choice."

"I hope you're right." He hesitated. Even with his closest friends, he'd been reticent about explaining exactly why, but he felt completely at his ease with Kitty. "I think it's because of Ma. As long as I can remember she's worked for the less well-off. I've always admired her for it. I love medicine and all the time I was a student working with the poor I've felt I was doing something really useful. And, Kitty? It's a good feeling."

"I know. Nursing at Baggot Street Hospital's like that too. You know I got all worked up about the poor in Tallaght, my part of Dublin, and that's why I picked nursing when I realised after a couple of years at art school I couldn't make a living as an artist. I've never regretted that choice, so I do understand what you're saying, and I respect you for it," she said. "I think it takes someone special to want to do it." Her smile was broad. "And I think you're special, Doctor O'Reilly."

Fingal glowed. "Thank you," he said quietly. "Thank you very much."

He felt the pressure of her hand and knew she was telling him, as she had last year in a tearoom on Abbey Street, that she loved him. He started to apologise again for sending her away, readied himself to make the leap and tell her he loved her. "Kitty, I'm sorry —"

"Your wine, sir. Will you taste it?"

Blast. He'd tell Kitty his feelings later. There was no real urgency. He felt — he felt comfortable with her. "No, thank you. Please let the lady try it." He ignored the waitress's raised eyebrow as she poured. So what if women never sampled the wine? Kitty knew her stuff in the oenophile department.

"Perfect," Kitty said.

The waitress poured, shoved the bottle in an ice bucket, and produced two menus. "Here you are," she said. "I'll give you a minute."

"Cheers." Fingal sipped. Cool, crisp, fruity — and not a patch on a well-pulled pint of stout, but tonight was Kitty's night. "Here's to your bright eyes." Grey flecked with amber. He drank again.

Kitty smiled and said, "Thank you," and consulted the menu. "Choices," she said, "decisions, decisions."

Fingal read the table d'hôte menu, didn't fancy roast lamb tonight so turned to the à la carte.

A discreet cough drew his attention to the waitress, who now stood by the table, pencil and order pad in hand. "Have sir and madam decided?"

"Sorry," Fingal said. "Give us a tick."

The waitress sniffed and said, "Take your time. God keeps makin' plenty of it, but Chef's not the Almighty and he wants to close the kitchen."

"Kitty?"

"I'll have the lamb chops please, and mash."

"Sirloin, rare, and chips. We'll get veg?"

"You will."

"Terrific," said Fingal, "and sorry to keep Chef waiting."

The waitress tutted and tossed her head. "Sure aren't all chefs the same; believe they're no goat's toe, but see our one? Our one t'inks he's a philosopher. Profound, like." She shook her head and curled her lip. "He's about as deep as a feckin' frying pan — and twice as dense." She left.

Fingal laughed. Slapped his knee. "Did you hear that? 'Deep as a frying pan.' I can't help liking Dubliners. Where else in the world would you hear the likes?"

"Probably," she said, "nowhere outside the city, but definitely in a practice at Aungier Place."

He laughed. "As they'd say in those parts, 'True on you, Kitty. True on you.' " He exaggerated the first syllable of true so it sounded like "tuhroo."

Her grip on his hand tightened. "Good Lord, Fingal," she said, "you are half a Dubliner even if your folks did bring you here from the wee north, and now you're sounding like a Northsider at that." And she laughed. "I know when you get settled into this job you're going to love it."

"And if Charlie comes in I'll only have to work one weekend in three and I'll have evenings off midweek —"

"And that'll leave plenty of time for," she hesitated, "your family."

He nodded. Kitty needn't say any more. He knew she understood.

"And," she said, "I hope there'll be some left over for us," and puckered a pretend kiss.

He tingled at the "us." "There will," he said. "All the time in the world." He grinned. "And I'm not like the chef. I'm happy to take all the time the Good Lord sends — for us." He looked into those smiling grey eyes and knew he meant every word. "And, by the way," he said, lowering his voice. "I love you."

10
Upon the Heath

"I didn't know you'd been invited, O'Reilly," Bertie Bishop said, pulling the stock and barrels of his twelve-bore from a leg-o-mutton gun case he'd taken from the boot of his Bentley. The councillor was wearing plus-fours, a Norfolk jacket, and a deer-stalker.

He reminded O'Reilly of a rotund, Edwardian Mole in an illustrated edition of *The Wind in the Willows*. Ostentatious, O'Reilly thought, not a bit concerned that his own outfit was scruffy. Wellington boots, old tweed pants, a gansey knitted by Kinky years ago worn under a patched hacking jacket, the ensemble topped with a Paddy hat.

"And it's nice til see you, Mrs. O'Reilly." Bishop favoured Kitty with a wintry grin.

To O'Reilly's dismay, the man had been included in today's opening day of grouse season on the marquis's County Antrim moor. This despite his gaffe on his lordship's pheasant shoot back in January during which Bertie'd nearly shot Kitty.

"And you, councillor," Kitty said, and favoured him with a dazzling smile.

Hypocrite, O'Reilly thought, barely hiding a smile himself. Or perhaps, more charitably, Mrs. O'Reilly was just being diplomatic. She was dressed for the day in a headscarf, plain waterproof jacket, Donegal tweed skirt, ribbed woollen stockings, and laced brogues. Fingal approved. Simple and practical gear for a day out tramping the moors. She carried a shooting stick. And she looked lovely.

He tucked his own gun under his arm. "Keep an eye on Arthur, would you, please? I want to have a word with Myrna. Doctor-patient stuff. Stay, Arthur." He wandered across to where the marquis had parked his shooting brake at the side of the road. Myrna was sitting nearby on a camp stool, a portable easel set up in front of her, and her water-colours open on a folding table. "How are you, Myrna?" O'Reilly said. "Sorry I didn't get a chance to come and see you in hospital. I hope Sir Donald took good care of you."

"Fingal, lovely to see you. And I'm sorry about nearly losing your invitation."

"Never worry," he said. "How's the hind leg?"

"Remarkable," she said. "It's only three weeks since the stupid thing was fixed. Your friend Sir Donald said he used something called a Kuntscher nail and explained how in the old days I'd have been in hospital for months."

Like my friend John-Joe Finnegan was back in 1936, O'Reilly thought.

"I'm not allowed to bear too much weight yet. Not up to tramping with you lot, but I love it up here and it's a marvellous day for a few watercolour sketches."

She was a keen watercolourist, but her work tended more to the Grandma Moses primitive school than the lush paintings of the Mourne Mountains by Percy French. "Just wanted to make sure you were all right," he said. "Don't hesitate to call if you're worried."

"Of course. Enjoy yourself up there."

Myrna was right. It was a great day for the shoot and her art. Overhead in the blue heavens, small clouds drifted high above County Antrim and out across the distant enameled waters of the North Channel. Further north, a summer shower was tumbling over the purple bulking masses of Scotland's Mull of Kintyre and further still was the island of Islay, where in the town of Lagavulin they distilled a damn good single-malt Scotch whisky.

"Glad you could make it, Fingal," the marquis said when O'Reilly arrived where Kitty stood with Arthur. The marquis was instructing Bertie and the other three guns, a local farmer and his wife and another landowner. The two Antrim men had springer spaniels at their feet, and the marquis's liver-and-white Jack Russell terrier, Buster, sat by his master.

"Thank you, sir," O'Reilly said.

"Fingal, I want you to anchor the left end of the line."

"Fine."

"Then, at twenty-five-yard intervals, Edna, you beside Doctor O'Reilly, please." She was the wife of Richard Johnson, who farmed near Clough Mills, and she was a crack shot. O'Reilly had met Ned Falloon, a local land-owner, and the Johnsons on previous shoots.

"Then you, Richard, then Ned. Bertie, you'll be beside me and I'll anchor the other end of the line."

O'Reilly understood that Bertie was being put next to John MacNeill so the marquis could keep an eye on the councillor.

"Questions?"

A shaking of heads.

"Right," said the marquis. "Ned, if you'll take Richard and Edna and the springers in your brake, I'll bring the Ballybucklebo contingent in mine. See you at lunchtime, Myrna."

"Have fun," she said.

The marquis held open the passenger door for Kitty, leaving Bertie and O'Reilly to get in the back, and put Arthur and Buster, who were old friends, in the rear compartment. The shooting brake jounced and rattled along the rutted lane that climbed through a mile of cultivated stepped fields until it reached the border of the moor.

O'Reilly couldn't make out the conversation from the front so he sat quietly, looking forward to the day's sport, delighted that Jenny had been so accommodating in changing on-call days so he could be here — another reason she'd be a distinct asset if Barry didn't want to come back. Maybe they'd find out more about that at dinner tonight. He smiled. All was right with the world and —

"What's all this rubbish I hear? You've brung in a lady doctor, O'Reilly?" Bertie leant closer and said over the noise, "Bloody great waste of taxpayers' money, women in medicine. I know all medical students pay something, but the government pays a lot more per student. I hear tell the marquis give a scholarship to Helen Hewitt too. Load of bullshite. They should never let women into medical school, if you ask me."

"I don't believe I did, Bertie," O'Reilly said. His euphoric bubble had been pricked and he could feel his nose tip blanching. "But by God if Jenny Bradley's good enough for me, and she is, she'll be good enough for you."

"Hey on, Arthur. Hey on out, boy," O'Reilly roared. "Push him out." By the time the marquis had aligned the guns, O'Reilly's choler over Bertie's remarks had subsided. The man had sputtered a bit after O'Reilly's riposte, but had uncharacteristically lapsed into silence. He was quite simply a solid-gold twenty-four-karat gobshite and nobody would ever change him. To do so would need a Road to Damascus experience, and as far as O'Reilly knew, Damascus was about three thousand miles away. Forget him and enjoy the day, he'd told himself. And he was. This was the fifth beat. "Hey on, boy."

As if the gundog needed encouragement. The big Labrador quartered the ground, completely in his element, nose down hunting for scents, tail erect but barely moving. Sunlight made his coat shine.

O'Reilly carried his shotgun across his chest, muzzle pointing safely up, butt ready at the instant to be tucked into his shoulder. From the surface of the barrels came a faint whiff of three-in-one oil. Wildfowling on Strangford Lough's salty shores was hell for making gunmetal rust. The smelly oil was preventive.

With Kitty slightly behind and to his left, he followed Arthur as the shooting party climbed a rise, all ears, human and canine, alert for any hint of grouse breaking cover. "Hey on, boy. Hey on."

The two springer spaniels as well as Arthur were working the cover ahead and he could hear their owners' cries of encouragement.

O'Reilly caught the toe of his boot, stumbled, and regained his balance. Watch where you're going, eejit, he told himself. You know well enough about the gnarly twisted roots of the heather up here. The group had already covered a broad strip of such territory as they walked toward Ballypatrick Forest. When they reached its fence, they'd rest for a few minutes, maybe have a smoke, then wheel and retrace their steps over a new beat for a mile to the heights above the valley of Glendun, one of the famous Glens of Antrim. He murmured a few lines of an old song,

Where the gay honeysuckle is luring the
    bee,
And the green Glens of Antrim are calling
    to me.

O'Reilly, a County Down man who thought Strangford Lough was as near to Heaven as mortals could get, had no difficulty understanding why folks from these parts, folks like Ballybucklebo's schoolmistress, Sue Nolan, who came from Broughshane, felt just the same about their glens. He wondered how Barry's romance was progressing. He'd find out at dinner tonight.

O'Reilly was nagged by an ache in his calves. Not as fit as you should be, he told himself. He'd know about sore muscles tomorrow, but then you couldn't make a kipper without killing the herring. If you wanted a day's rough shooting that meant lots of hiking where the guns and their dogs covered the ground on foot, starting the game in front of them. There were no gamekeepers, no beaters, no pickers-up like at the driven grouse shoots, which were now too expensive for all but a very wealthy few. There the guns were accompanied by loaders and waited in butts. When beaters drove the birds, usually in groups of five, over the butt, the hunter would fire the first gun's two barrels, hand it to the loader, take the second gun of the matching pair, usually of James Purdey & Sons manufacture, use the next two barrels, and if necessary accept the first gun reloaded. King George V was reputed regularly to kill five birds out of five. The names of those of the aristocracy who usually missed with all six barrels was, tactfully, not recorded.

O'Reilly's ruminations were cut short, and the second he heard the alarm call of a sharp *Goback, goback, goback,* he raised his gun to his shoulder. With a rapid whirring of stubby wings, four red grouse broke cover immediately in front of Edna. Her shot. He'd not poach until she'd fired twice, but he slipped off the safety catch and covered the bird nearest to him. From a corner of an eye, he admired how in one effortless motion she brought her weapon up, sighted, fired at a bird, and as it collapsed in a puff of russet feathers, she took the next with the left barrel before the first had hit the ground. She'd taken her chance well.

His bird was now in a rapid downward glide. The butt thumped his shoulder when he squeezed the trigger, his ears rang, and the smell of burnt smokeless powder tickled his nose. The fourth grouse, calling, *Chut, chut, chut,* curled away to O'Reilly's left to land safely in the heather well outside the paths of the approaching sportsmen. Good. Breeding stock for next season.

At the sound of the shots, Arthur stopped in his tracks, marked the falls, and looked back at O'Reilly.

He heard Kitty say, "Good shot, dear."

He smiled at her and said to Edna, "Nice right and left."

"Thanks, Fingal." She broke her shotgun, ejected the spent cases, and reloaded. When the party had assembled this morning and parked on the Loughareena Road, he'd admired the walnut stock and blued barrels of her new Boss twelve-bore. Those gunmakers had been supplying sporting weapons to the gentry since 1812, the year Napoleon Bonaparte had defeated the Russians at Borodino, which Tchaikovsky had commemorated in his famous overture. "Hi lost, Arthur," O'Reilly called and, pleased with his own shooting, sang a few cheerful bars. "Pom tiddle iddle tiddle om pom pom, Pom tiddle

iddle iddle om pom pom," with great stress on the "om pom poms."

The dog ignored the mangled music. He took his line and sped ahead. A springer was heading in the same direction. In moments, the Lab had returned, sat at O'Reilly's feet, and offered up a cock grouse with russet plumage, white legs, and a black tail. There were white stripes under the wings and a red comb over each eye. "Good boy. Hi lost." O'Reilly took the bird and slipped it into a game bag slung over his left shoulder. It didn't matter who collected the birds. At the heels of the hunt, the marquis would give each gun a brace — O'Reilly happily imagined Kinky roasting his to make a tasty snack for him and Kitty. The rest of the day's bag would be sold to Belfast restaurants to help defray the costs of the shoot.

In a short time, Arthur returned with a second bird, was relieved of his burden, complimented, and sent out to a new command of "Push 'em out now."

O'Reilly noticed that the springer was once again quartering the ground, so it must have retrieved the third bird and, like Arthur, was hunting again. The line of guns advanced with several more shots fired before they neared the boundary of the coniferous forest, its piney smell drifting on the breeze. He saw the marquis hold up a hand, and as the other guns reached the rusty barbed wire, they

142

walked along it to join him. "Good sport, so far," his lordship said. "The reports that it's been a first-class breeding year are true."

"I'm not so sure Jenny Bradley would agree about sport," Kitty murmured.

"She's not backward in coming forward with an opinion," O'Reilly said, wondering if he was altogether happy with Jenny's propensity for questioning, then remembered how Phelim Corrigan had responded to Fingal's challenges back in '36. The young woman had every right to speak her mind. It showed spunk.

"They're such pretty little things, the grouse," Kitty said, "I could feel sorry for them myself, but I do know how much you love your shooting." She looked down at a grinning Arthur. "And so does he."

"Don't you worry about the grouse. As I told Jenny, grouse rear large clutches every year so their populations soon recover. Conservationists like my brother Lars carry out annual counts. There are five thousand breeding pairs in all of Ireland alone and another two hundred and fifty thousand in Britain. Their greatest threats are from natural predators like martens and kestrels, and possibly a nematode worm."

"Not from hunters like you, Nimrod, then?"

"A grandson of Noah, I believe," he blew her an imaginary kiss, "and, 'a mighty hunter before God,' to quote. No, we really don't do

143

much damage to the population."

"I'm glad." She laughed and said, "And I love to see you so happy, Fingal, taking a bit of time off. It's beautiful up here and we couldn't have had a better day for it. That sun's wonderful."

Not everyone bred and used to living in cities like Belfast or Dublin, as Kitty had been, thought highly of trudging over hills and through bogs. He smiled at her. A remarkable woman, Mrs. Fingal O'Reilly, and dressed more sensibly than he. O'Reilly lifted his hat and drew a sleeve across his forehead. "I," said he, feeling a bead of sweat roll down his back, "am baking." He stopped, made sure the safety catch was on, and handed his gun to Kitty. It took only a few moments to take off the game bag, get out of his jacket, and strip off his gansey, which he handed to her. "Carry that for me, will you, love?" He didn't wait for a reply, redressed, and took back his gun. "We'd better catch up," he said, and lengthened his stride.

"Wait for me." Kitty trotted after.

"You've shown us good birds this morning, sir," Richard Johnson was saying as O'Reilly and Kitty joined the party. "Thank you very much."

"And I hope the next beat will be profitable too," the marquis said. "It'll take us back to the cars and —" He looked sideways at O'Reilly. "I think we'll break for lunch."

144

On cue O'Reilly's gut rumbled. "Good idea, sir," he said.

"Fingal," Kitty said sotto voce, "behave." She smiled at him.

"Sorry, but John always puts on a marvellous spread and we breakfasted early."

"One change," the marquis said. "I don't think Edna's had her share of birds yet. I'd like her and Bertie to change places."

"Certainly," said Bertie. Etiquette called for the councillor to comply without demur.

The line formed and off they set down the gentle slope, Bertie walking on O'Reilly's left.

He looked ahead to where the heather moor ended, and narrow, stepped, cultivated fields ran steeply down to the Glendun River as it meandered to the coastal village of Cushendun, meaning the bottom of the brown river. If memory served, *Glendun* was the name of the boat Barry had raced on this year. O'Reilly grinned. He was looking forward to dinner tonight with the young man. Barry'd said he'd made reservations for six thirty at the Ballymena Arms Hotel.

All around them the air was filled with humming as honeybees toiled in the early heather blossoms, making their prized pure heather honey. He pointed downhill to where the dogs were approaching a neat row of narrow vertical white boxes. "See those hives, Kitty? The apiarists bring them up here every August so their bees can work in the heather.

145

The hives are taken back to the valley in the autumn."

"I remember my mother getting heather honey. I loved it, but I never really stopped to think where it came from. Now I can picture it coming from these beautiful purple moors."

A long-eared brown form leapt from the ground a few feet in front of Arthur, who stopped and looked expectantly at Bertie Bishop. It was his shot.

O'Reilly swung his gaze along the line Bertie must take to hit the hare, gasped and yelled, "Don't, Bertie. For God's sake —"

Boom.

O'Reilly watched the action play out, as if in slow motion, as the hive directly in front of Bertie exploded.

"Kitty. Quick. Wrap my gansey round your head and lie down facedown."

Once he was sure she had obeyed, he lay down and pulled his jacket up over his own head, lay prone, but kept his head sufficiently high that he could see what was going on.

What looked like a curl of smoke rose from the hive and made a beeline, O'Reilly smiled at the unconscious pun, for where Bertie stood. A high-pitched "Yeeeow" came across the moor and Bertie Bishop, arms flailing like a demented windmill, took off at a gallop downhill, heading for the shelter of the marquis's shooting brake a hundred yards past the hives. The swarm of enraged bees

146

followed in hot pursuit.

"Are you okay, Kitty?"

"All right so far," she said, peeking out from the gansey. "The bees seemed to know who was responsible."

O'Reilly shook his head. "The man should not be allowed within six feet of a gun. I've my bag in the Rover." He made sure no insects were heading their way, then stood. "And I've got the blue bag to ease the pain of stings, and adrenaline and cortisone if I need them. I'd better get the marquis to run me and Bertie down there. Bring Arthur, will you?" He unloaded and set off trotting behind the line of guns to the marquis, leaving Kitty to make her own way. Multiple beestings could be life-threatening, and she, if anybody did, would realise that the patient must always come first. With a bit of luck, Bertie wouldn't be too badly stung and they might get in a few beats after lunch. From the steeple of a church somewhere near Cushendun he heard, borne on the breeze, a clock's bell chiming two.

11
ONE . . . COMES TO
MEET ONE'S FRIENDS

"I like the look of this place," O'Reilly said, rubbing his hands and peering around as he walked with Kitty along a carpeted hall in the Ballymena Arms Hotel.

Motes caught the evening light spilling in through mullioned windows and there was a hint of a certain aroma, a combination of old plaster and furniture polish, that he always associated with establishments of elegant, long-standing permanence. The original manor house had been designed and finished in 1846 by the same architect who had drawn up the plans for the 1849 additions to the campus of Queen's College, later the Queen's University of Belfast.

Here the panelled walls were hung with nineteenth-century sporting prints of fox hunts and shooting scenes, probably originals. Two red grouse, exemplars of the taxidermist's art, stood proudly in a glass case set on an antique bog oak sideboard. A flintlock fowling piece with a single barrel of

Damascus steel was mounted on the panelling above. He knew the gun had to be at least 250 years old.

He nodded to a well-dressed couple coming in the opposite direction, silently thanking Kitty for brushing aside his assertions that in a country town like Ballymena his shooting gear would do rightly. She'd ever so tactfully insisted that he bring a jacket, shirt, tie, pants, and dress boots. He would have been horribly out of place here if he hadn't listened to her. They'd changed in a secluded spot where the road from Loughareena passed through Glenariff (Glen of the arable land) Forest Park, laughing like guilty teenagers when an unexpected farm lorry had appeared and a half-dressed Kitty had had to hide behind a tree until the vehicle passed.

Beside a pair of doors, a polished brass sign read LOUNGE BAR. Dinner guests, while consulting the menu, usually had their pre-prandial drinks in the bar. He made a small bow, opened one door, and said, "Madam?" As she passed him, he marvelled at how, by exchanging her waterproof jacket for a well-cut tweed one, removing her silk headscarf and arranging it around her neck, and substituting sheer nylons and high heels for her woollen stockings and brogues, Kitty had transformed herself from an outdoors woman to this elegant creature.

"You're looking lovely," he said quietly.

"Thank you."

Muted conversations came from several occupied tables. He spotted Barry and Sue sitting on a sofa, facing two armchairs. The furniture was grouped round a massive stone fireplace large enough for a lord of the manor to roast a stag. Although laid, the fire had not been lit. How cosy, O'Reilly thought, it would make this room on a winter's night.

Barry, who, O'Reilly noted with pleasure, was holding Sue's hand, must have spotted them because he let go of it and started to rise as was proper for a gentleman when a lady joined the company. O'Reilly, who couldn't ignore more than thirty years' training and experience observing people, was concerned to notice dark circles under Barry's eyes.

"Please sit down, Barry," Kitty said, and took her place on the sofa, crossing her legs and smoothing her skirt.

Once the introductory pleasantries were concluded, O'Reilly said, "I see you two have drinks and menus. Kitty, what'll it be?"

Her answer of "Gin and tonic, please" coincided with the arrival of a dinner-suited waiter who, with a small bow, offered O'Reilly two leather-bound menus and the wine list.

"Are your pints in good order?" O'Reilly asked.

"Yes, sir."

"Pint and a G and T for the lady."

"Certainly, sir." He left.

"Now," O'Reilly said, sitting beside Kitty and giving her the *carte des vins,* "you pick the wine, please, and before we go any further, Barry, Sue, tonight's our treat —"

"But —" was as far as O'Reilly let Barry go before fixing the young man with his "quell a mutiny" gaze. "Ours."

"Thank you, Fingal," Barry said.

"Very much," Sue said, and she lifted her copper plait from behind her back and re-arranged it to fall over one shoulder of her bottle-green mini-dress. Despite himself, O'Reilly couldn't stop making a quick comparison, and in his unbiased opinion Kitty had better legs. He rubbed his own calf and hoped hers weren't aching as much after all that earlier scrambling over the grouse moor.

"So how're things at —"

"How was Rhodes — ?" Barry said, having started to speak at the same time as O'Reilly.

All four laughed. "Right," said O'Reilly, "Kitty and I had a wonderful time in the Med." He smiled at her. "I didn't know she could swim like a fish, and," he spoke to Barry and Sue, "if it wasn't for Kitty, bless her, I'd have starved before I could work out which Greek dishes were half-edible. I simply cannot get excited about vine leaves or feta cheese."

"Can't you imagine him, Barry?" Kitty knotted her brows, scowled, and said gruffly

151

in her deepest voice, "What the hell do you mean I can't have a Guinness and you've no John Jameson? Jasus Murphy. Cradle of civilization, my" — She dropped her voice so it wouldn't carry. — "cradle of civilization, my arse."

Sue laughed. It was a melodious sound. "Oh dear," she said between chuckles. "Oh dear."

Barry glanced at O'Reilly, then started to laugh too. "I seem to remember you, Fingal, saying something about not poking alligators in the eye with blunt sticks. Seems to me, Kitty, not having a decent pint or a half-un available would have the same effect."

She sucked in her cheeks and nodded. "Uh-huh."

"But have you ever tried that God-awful retsina? And ouzo?" O'Reilly feigned gruffness. "Like drinking bloody tar."

"Do you drink tar often, Fingal?" Kitty asked in her most innocent voice. "I didn't know that. I do know you can be a fire-eater sometimes."

O'Reilly was pleased to see how Sue's hand had crept back into Barry's. "Wait 'til I get you home, Mrs. O'Reilly." Dear God, he thought, Kitty did make him laugh, and he loved her for it.

"Excuse me, sir, your drinks." The waiter had reappeared.

"Thank you," O'Reilly said. "We just need

a little longer."

"Sir."

"Sláinte," O'Reilly said, and took a deep pull on his Guinness. Kitty could say what she liked. This stuff beat retsina into a cocked hat.

"Anyway," Kitty said, sipping her gin and tonic, "apart from some culinary difficulties — and come on, Fingal, you took a real shine to calamari and *tiramisu* — we've had a wonderful honeymoon."

And for a moment, Fingal O'Reilly could picture himself standing, holding her hand, and dropping a kiss on her lips as a full moon shyly slipped from a burnished silver sea and rose over the acropolis at Lindos. The moon had seemed particularly bright that night, dimming the stars that had burned and danced like fireflies on a polished ebony sky.

He knew he was grinning and didn't care. "We did," he said. "Wonderful, but it's back to porridge now. The weary walking wounded of Ballybucklebo still need attention." He looked at Barry. "Young Jenny is doing extremely well." Let's see if Barry rises to that. "But I want to know, even if it has only been six weeks, how are you enjoying obstetrics?"

Barry yawned and covered his mouth with his hand. "Very much," he said, "and I'm not complaining, but I'm on call every other night. It can be a bit hectic — but very

153

satisfying."

"I'm pleased to hear that," O'Reilly said. And he was. Primarily for Barry's sake, much as O'Reilly would like to have him back. But perhaps too, there might be no need to have to disappoint Jenny Bradley if she did work out as a potential partner and wanted to stay. Time would tell.

He became aware that Kitty and Sue were pursuing their own line of conversation. "You know," he said to Barry, "I flirted with specialising and spent time as a junior at the Rotunda in Dublin in 1937. Doesn't seem so very long ago. I really enjoyed obstetrics but —"

Barry lowered his voice. "You weren't so excited about gynaecology?"

It was O'Reilly's turn to nod as Barry said, "The difficult cases are interesting, very interesting, and I'm starting to learn surgery — and I like that — but the outpatient clinics are a bit — a bit dull."

O'Reilly understood. The routine complaints, although critical to each woman, were not medically very challenging, and worse, as far as he was concerned, you never got to know your patients as people, hardly ever. "Painful periods? Discharges? Itches? Contraceptive advice for Protestants?"

"Fingal, it's 1965," Barry said. "A lot of Catholic women are ignoring their priests. They're too shy to go to their G.P.s, it's a sensitive subject, but they come to our outpatient clinics asking for help. Ulster is part of the United Kingdom. It's not like the Republic."

O'Reilly sighed. "I know. I saw them in the Liberties in Dublin, fourteen to a room, the married women dropping babies once a year like farrowing sows. Poor creatures." He shuddered. "You keep up the good work." He swallowed a mouthful of Guinness.

"I will." Barry leant forward. "And never mind my work, how are things in Ballybucklebo?"

So he hadn't lost interest in the place. O'Reilly laughed. "A patient from the village even followed me to the grouse moor today." He explained about Bertie's apian attack. "He was lucky enough to get away with only about a dozen stings. I got the stingers out of him in no time. Bit of blue bag, a few aspirin, and, fair play to Bertie, he reckoned he could carry on. Most of the stings had worn off by the end of the shoot."

"If he had arthritis, it might even have been a good thing," Barry said. "The rheumatologists still use beestings for pain relief."

"True." O'Reilly pursed his lips. "I could kick myself for letting an opportunity go for teaching Bertie an object lesson, though. Earlier he'd been less than flattering about female doctors. I'm sure he'd have been delighted to know that male bees don't have stingers and that every one that nailed him today was a worker bee — a female."

"Pity you missed the chance. I'd love to have seen the look on his face," Barry said. "I miss Ballybucklebo, you know, even our having to interfere with Bertie's schemes." He looked down then, back at O'Reilly. "And what about the other folks there?"

"Kinky sends her love. She and Archie Auchinleck are becoming an item. Sometimes I wonder if I might lose her."

"Good God. I hope not," Barry said. "She's as much a fixture at Number One and in the village as you are, Fingal."

"You, young man, make me sound like my rolltop desk. Fixture indeed."

"I'd have thought it's a pretty comfortable feeling, being well known and respected. Knowing everyone."

And are you missing it, Barry? O'Reilly wondered. "You're right," he said. "And you know Donal and Julie had a wee girl? She's thriving. Donal's up to no good with a greyhound, and he's roped young Colin Brown in to help. That pup you got him is growing like a marrow in August. And Aggie Arbuthnot's getting on well in her new job as a stitcher." He patted Barry's knee. "You left your mark, Barry."

There was something wistful when Barry said, "I know."

O'Reilly carried on. "Helen Hewitt's burst-

156

ing at the seams ready to start her studies in September . . ."

"And how are the folks in the Duck? Willie and Mary and Helen's dad and . . . ?"

"No idea." O'Reilly shook his head. "The public bar's men only so I haven't been in since we got back. Some night when Kitty's out with her friends I'll nip over. I've been missing the *craic* there."

"I do too. Tell you what," Barry said. "I'm still racing yachts and Sue's switched allegiance. She's crewing with us now."

O'Reilly saw how their eyes met and Barry squeezed Sue's hand.

"Next time we're at Ballyholme why don't we pop in at Number One? You and I could —"

"Nip across for a quick pint? Brilliant."

"Is sir ready to order?" The waiter had reappeared.

"I'm sorry," O'Reilly said, "but," he took another pull on his stout, "Doctor Laverty and I could use another. Ladies?"

"I'm fine," Kitty said.

"Thank you, no." Sue shook her head.

"And we'll be ready to order the minute you come back."

"There's no rush, sir. The kitchen's not too busy tonight." The waiter left.

"Not like a chef, do you remember, Kitty, in a restaurant on O'Connell Street who was in a rush and according to our waitress

157

thought he was a philosopher?"

"I'll never forget what the lass said, 'He's about as deep as a frying pan — and twice as thick.' "

Everyone laughed.

"Och," said O'Reilly, "that was back in Dublin City, dear old Dirty Dublin on the banks of the Liffey. Sometimes it seemed like everyone in Dublin had a way with words. I think it was Brendan Behan who said, 'James Joyce made of this river the Ganges of the literary world.' "

12
ANY MAN'S DEATH
DIMINISHES ME

The Liffey at low tide on July 17, 1936, stank as badly, Fingal reckoned, as the Ganges must. He'd experienced the noisome Hoogli, one of the distributaries of the great Indian river, when his freighter had called at Calcutta back in 1928.

Here in Dublin, the light summer northeasterly wafted the whiff of drying mud flats through the open windows of the Aungier Street Dispensary.

He and Charlie were into their second week as dispensary doctors. Charlie was out making calls, Phelim Corrigan was working next door, and at almost one o'clock the waiting room was practically empty.

Fingal could see one man sitting there. His arm was in a sling, his index finger was strapped with adhesive tape to his middle finger, and they stuck out past the sling's end. His head was swathed in bandages. Phelim must have patched him up, and Fingal wondered, only for a moment, why the man hadn't gone home.

A woman in a shawl had a grubby boy by the hand. She stood. "I'm next," she said.

Fingal took the pair into his surgery. It was the work of moments to determine that both mother and child had scabies; the symptoms of constant burning itching and the dark lines under the skin creases between the fingers where the itch mites had burrowed were diagnostic. The couple were the eighth, or was it the tenth case this week? He'd lost count.

"The pair of you have scabies, mother," he said.

"And me udder four chisslers, too. Can you fix us?"

"Your best bet is to take the whole family to the Iveagh Public Baths where the sulphur in the water will kill the mites," he said, "and if you can wash all your bedclothes with boiling water, and not let your family share towels, combs, or brushes." He sighed. For all the likelihood she'd be able to comply, he reckoned he might as well advise her to walk across the surface of the Liffey for good measure, but she surprised him.

"I'll see to it," she said. "Believe it, sir, I feckin' well will."

Fingal was impressed with her determination.

"T'anks very much, sir. Come on, Donnacha."

As Fingal followed them into the hall, Phelim's surgery door opened and a patient came out. Beneath his greasy duncher a bandage held a patch over one eye, a bruise extended down over his cheekbone, and a sticking plaster on his cheek probably covered sutures.

He ignored Fingal, went into the waiting room, and growled at the man there, the only one there, "Come on, Joseph Mary Callaghan, you great bowsie, let's get the feck out of here. I've enough to buy us a couple of jars."

They left, arms around each other's shoulders.

Fingal smiled. That's why the man had been waiting. Fingal let himself into Phelim's surgery.

"Afternoon," Doctor Corrigan said from his raised stool. "Take a pew."

Fingal noticed, as he took one of the cane-backed chairs, that the parting in the little doctor's hairpiece was no longer central, but more on a northeast to southwest axis.

"And if ye're curious, the lad who left was in a ruggy-up last night on Golden Lane, just round the corner."

"Pardon?"

"Ruggy-up. Fight. National pastime in the Liberties. Soon as one starts you hear the women screeching, 'Ruggy-up, ruggy-up.' Gets the whole neighbourhood out for a free show. Better than the cinema. Good clean fun. And they don't do each other too much damage." He laughed and said, "That's 'Jam Jars' Keegan who just left, but ye should have seen the other fellah."

"I did," Fingal said, "in the waiting room."

"Joe Mary Callaghan," Doctor Corrigan said. "I'd to put twelve stitches in his head and he'd bust his finger on Jam Jars's skull. The bones weren't displaced so all I needed to do was strap the busted finger to the one beside it."

Fingal hadn't heard of that. He made a mental note.

"The pair of them came in together today like a couple of long-lost friends. It's always the way of it. Get into a fight. Beat the tar out of each other, declare a winner, and go back into the pub for a pint and a singsong, sober up, the next day usually, and come here. Desperate what the drink does."

The wall-mounted phone rang.

Phelim answered. He offered the earpiece. "It's for you."

"O'Reilly?" Fingal said.

"Fingal, dear, can you possibly get home soon?"

It was Ma and there was no need for her to elaborate. "Of course."

In moments, he'd explained to Phelim, who agreed to hold the fort. Fingal called a taxi — to hell with the expense.

Father had been very low when Fingal had left that morning. He'd debated with himself about staying at home. Doctor Micks had been round yesterday while Fingal was at work and had suggested to Ma that Lars should be summoned from Portaferry. He'd arrived at teatime, and because he was there and Ma would not be alone Fingal had decided to carry on. He wasn't sure whether his sense of duty had brought him or if his reluctance to sit through a deathwatch had driven him out.

The taxi ride home had seemed interminable, particularly when a dray blocking the Mount Street Bridge forced the driver to make a detour by way of Grand Canal Street. Fingal sat in the backseat muttering, "Come on. Come on."

When they arrived, Fingal paid and took the steps two at a time. The front door was unlocked.

Ma was sitting in the lounge studying a pattern and saying quietly to herself, "Knit two, purl one." For as long as Fingal could remember, whenever something upset Ma, she either painted furiously or turned to her knitting. She said she found the need to concentrate and the rhythm of the needles soothing.

She looked up. "Fingal," she said. "Thank you for coming." Her eyes were red-rimmed.

He crossed the room and dropped a kiss on his mother's head. "How's Dad?"

"Very weak." She sighed. "Lars is with him. We've been taking it in turns to keep him company, but I don't think he knows. He's been sleeping since you left."

"Good." As Fingal well knew, there was a great kindness in sleep. "Are you all right?"

She shook her head. "Not really, but I'm managing." She produced a tiny smile. "I have to. Bridgit and Cook are dreadfully cut up." She frowned. "Have you had any lunch, son?"

Fingal shook his head and smiled. Ma. "It's fine, thanks," he said, and for once it was. His appetite had fled. "I'll go and see how Lars is." As he crossed the room, he heard the steady clicking of her needles.

Lars sat in a small armchair beside Father's bed. He turned as Fingal came into what had been Father's study but was now a bedroom. As the rogue white cells interfered more and more with the bone marrow's ability to manufacture red cells, the blood's oxygen-carrying capability declined. The slightest effort now made Father horribly short of breath. He'd no longer been able to walk to the dining room, and for the past five days had taken his meals in bed. "Finn," Lars said. He did not smile, but stood. "Have a pew. I'd like to stretch my legs." He moved aside and stood in the window, the one through which Father was able to see his belovèd birds at the bird table.

Fingal sat and looked at his father, the once powerful paterfamilias, professor of classics and English literature at Trinity College, expert on the works of MacCaulay and Wilde, friend of the Who's Who of Dublin society. He'd shrunk to a low mound under bedclothes that barely moved with each of his panted breaths. Even Father's head seemed to be smaller, his once dark hair wispy on the pillow, his lips, except where a cold sore disfigured the lower one, were as white as the linen pillowcase. His forehead, relaxed in sleep, was smooth and care-line free. His nostrils flared with each indrawing of breath and his pale thin hands fluttered and twitched on the counterpane.

Fingal took his father's pulse. It was barely palpable, fluttery, with no more strength than the wings of a trapped moth. Father muttered something that sounded like a snatch of ancient Greek. Fingal swallowed. "I'm glad you came last night, Lars, and were able to talk to Father." He stood, pursed his lips, and lifted his shoulders. "I've seen this before. Dad's not going to last much longer."

"I understand." Fingal had explained to Lars and Ma that there was nothing more even Doctor Micks could do, except, and Fingal had kept this thought to himself, sign the necessary papers when the time came. "Should we call Ma?"

Fingal nodded.

Lars left and Fingal was alone with the father he'd loved, respected, and come to dislike yet never hate. Finally a rapprochement had been made. "I don't know if you can hear me, Dad, it's Fingal, but thank you, thank you for everything." He knelt and kissed the pale forehead. "I love you, Dad."

Fingal stood as Lars returned with Ma. "Here," he said, "sit here, Ma."

She did, and took Father's hand.

"Would you like us to leave you alone with him for a little while?" Fingal asked. Ma too, was a woman of Queen Victoria's time who would find it hard to display deep feelings in front of anyone, even her grown children.

She frowned, cocked her head as if considering the matter, then said, "Please. I should like that. For a minute or two."

Fingal inclined his head to Lars and together they left, closed the door behind them, and waited in the hall. No words were spoken. A grandfather clock that Fingal could remember from his boyhood in Holywood ticked and tocked, measuring the minutes, the hours, and the days of people's spans. "Man," Fingal thought, "that is born of woman hath but a short time to live," but this was too bloody unfair. Too damn short. He thought he heard a sob coming from the study and glanced at Lars.

"You go, Finn," Lars said, his voice cracking.

Fingal opened the door slowly. Ma was sitting regally erect. She had dashed away a tear with the back of one hand. She held Father's with the other. "I think your Father's gone, Fingal," she said. "Thank you for letting me be with him, but I'm sorry I kept you and Lars —"

"Ma," Fingal said, "it was right and proper you were here, and Lars and I have both had our chances to say our good-byes." He stood behind his mother and squeezed her shoulders. "Bear up. We're both here."

She managed a smile and patted one of his hands. "Thank you," she said. "My boys are such a comfort to me." She stood. "I know it's a great deal to ask, but . . ." She inclined her head. "Could you?"

"Of course." Fingal understood that she was asking him to confirm Father's death. He moved past her. The skin was icy, the pulse gone. Fingal bent his head to Father's mouth but there was not the slightest current of air. He looked at the white face, soft in repose. Father's eyes were open, and already they had the blurry opacity that had become familiar to Fingal. Death was no stranger to Dublin's hospitals, where half the patients had consumption and precious few recovered. He closed the eyes and, as was the Irish custom, found two pennies to lay there to keep the lids closed. "I'm sorry, Ma," he said. And while Doctor Fingal O'Reilly, the dispassionate professional, steeled himself to be strong for Ma and Lars, inside — and he hoped well hidden — an emptiness filled his soul. "I'm sorry. He's gone, but Dad didn't suffer. You need to know that."

"Thank you, Fingal. I do understand," she said. And a tear glistened. "Please go and wait in the lounge. I'll join you in a minute or two, then we must tell Cook and Bridgit."

Fingal inclined his head and Lars left. "I'll phone Doctor Micks," he said. "There are formalities."

"I know. Thank you, son."

Fingal closed the door behind him and walked to the telephone. He'd phone Doctor Micks and between them they'd take care of the statutory notifications that Fingal himself had had to learn at Aungier Street in his capacity as registrar of births, deaths, and marriages. It was a good thing Lars was a solicitor. He'd understand all the morbid intricacies of arranging funerals, having wills probated, placing death announcements. Together they'd need to comfort Ma and Bridgit and Cook while the hurt in them all healed over time.

13
HIS PERSONAL PREJUDICES

"Styes don't take too long to heal," O'Reilly said to seventeen-year-old Peter Dobbin. The wiry, fair-haired labourer worked on farms in the Ballybucklebo Hills, and if O'Reilly had his way with the selection committee, he would be playing lock forward for the Bally-bucklebo Bonnaughts Rugby Football Club this coming season. The young man was as strong as a Shire horse. He had a nasty hordeolum, an infection of the follicle of an eyelash, on his left upper eyelid. It was red and swollen and beginning to point. "You'll need to —" There was a sharp rap on the door and O'Reilly spun and stared.

Who in the blue blithering blazes was knocking? Kitty had left for work. Kinky should be telling Jenny Bradley if there was an emergency, not him. She was on call today and Fingal had last seen her heading upstairs after breakfast. No patient would ever have the temerity to by-pass Kinky and try to be admitted to the sanctum sanctorum when

O'Reilly was consulting. The waiting room was packed and he did not wish to be held up.

Before he could yell "Go away," the door opened and Jenny Bradley, paying no attention to Peter, said very calmly, "Will you come here please, Doctor O'Reilly," and went back into the hall.

Jasus. Sounded like himself commanding Arthur. At least she'd said please. O'Reilly snatched off his half-moon spectacles, lumbered to his feet, and headed for the door. Was the house on fire? Was she unable to deal with some life-threatening emergency? Damn it all, he had thought the woman was absolutely on top of her work. "I'll just be a minute, Peter."

"Pay me no heed, Doc," Peter said, and managed a smile. "I won't run away, so I won't."

O'Reilly strode to the door and closed it behind him.

"What — ?"

Jenny was on the phone. "That's right. Twenty-six Shore Road. Doctor O'Reilly will meet the ambulance there."

She'd called an ambulance for the Bishops' house. And he was to meet it? Jasus.

"Thank you." She replaced the receiver, and none too gently.

"What in the name of Beëlzebub's blazing pitchfork is going on, Jenny? An emergency

170

and I've to go? Can't you cope?"

She inhaled before saying, "Perfectly well, Fingal, medically." Her face was flushed. "I was on my way out to start my home visits and the phone rang. I answered it to save Kinky the trouble. A Mrs. Bishop was calling and sounded hysterical. I got her calmed down. Apparently her husband —"

"Bertie Bishop." After the conversation in the marquis's shooting brake, O'Reilly had a premonition of what was coming.

"— has had a sudden chest pain that went into his arm —"

"Good lord." O'Reilly tensed, his mind racing. "That's either angina or a full-blown myocardial infarction." He frowned. Ordinarily Jenny should have raced to the Bishops, leaving Kinky to send for the ambulance. Anyone with chest pain, especially radiating to an arm, must be admitted to hospital at once. Angina, pain brought on by narrowing of the coronary arteries interfering with the oxygen supply to the heart muscles, wasn't life-threatening, but a heart attack was. Only the recently introduced electrical defibrillation, the passage of an electrical shock through the heart, could save the patient's life. And that had to be done in hospital.

"Apparently Mister Bishop flatly refused to see a woman doctor. Demanded your presence." He could tell by the tenseness in her jaw she was struggling to control her own

171

temper. "I wasn't going to waste time argu-
ing. I asked for their address, got you, phoned
the ambulance —"

"And you did right." Stupid, pigheaded,
bloody Bertie Bishop. O'Reilly felt the tip of
his nose grow cold, a sure sign it was blanching, partly because he was cross with himself
for not warning Jenny about the man. "I'll
go. I'm sorry about Bertie, Jenny. You'll have
to do the surgery. I'm off. We'll sort out the
home visits later." He headed for the surgery,
grabbed his doctor's bag, and said to Jenny
as he passed her in the hall, "Peter Dobbin's
in there. He has a stye so tell him to use a
warm saline eyebath three times a day and
no —"

"No penicillin ointment because it might
excite allergy — I'll see to Peter and the rest."

O'Reilly knew he should apologise for getting irritated with this self-assured and
competent young doctor, but patients with
chest pain weren't like ones with whooping
cough. Chest pain couldn't wait. He ran for
the back door and sprinted through the
garden. Angina required glyceryl trinitrate.
O'Reilly knew he had some in his bag. He'd
not need it if the pain had passed, but if it
hadn't, the vasodilator and morphine for the
pain were all he could offer — and a damn
quick trip to hospital.

He fired up the old Rover, took off the hand
brake and, with a clashing of gears, rammed

his foot on the accelerator and took off like Juan Fangio behind the wheel of his Formula One Alfa Romeo. Chest pain couldn't wait. He spared not a thought for any cyclists who might be on the road.

"Thank God you've come, Doctor O'Reilly," said Flo Bishop. "I was making him a wee cup of tea in his hand, like, when you arrived. I have him in his study in his chair, so I have. The pain's gone now, you know. I'll take you through til him." She swallowed. "Do you think he'll be all right?"

O'Reilly followed Flo along the hall. "It's a good sign that the pain's gone." It had probably been an anginal attack, he thought. If the cardiac muscle had been infarcted, seriously damaged, the pain would have persisted. Bertie'd probably need neither the nitrate nor the morphine today.

"Thank God for that," she said. "Bertie'd me worried silly. I thought he was going for til die." A tear glistened in the corner of her eye. "He's all I've got." She sniffed and dabbed her eyes with the backs of her hands. "After we was married in '29 I had four miscarriages. Doctor Flannigan sent me to a specialist who said another pregnancy would kill me and I needed me tubes tied, and . . ." She sniffed. "Bertie wouldn't adopt."

That had been before O'Reilly had started working here. Love, he thought, knows no

173

boundaries.

She took a very deep breath. "Please make him better, Doctor, sir."

"I'm sure, even sight unseen, Flo, he'll get over this attack." Still, angina in such a relatively young man was worrying for his doctor, but there was no need to alarm Flo.

"I'm awful sorry about him not wanting til have the nice wee lady doctor."

Flo, like many terrified relatives whose anxiety had been allayed, was prattling out of a sense of relief. He said gently, "We'll let that hare sit for now, Flo. Let's get a look at the patient." And let's get you better, Bertie Bishop, before I pop round and read you the Doctor Fingal Flahertie O'Reilly Riot Act on courtesy to the medical profession — regardless of the sex of the physician.

They passed the open lounge door. "In here," she said, ushering O'Reilly into a room where a jacketless Bertie Bishop sat in a swivel chair, his left elbow on a flat-topped desk strewn with papers and builders' catalogues. "About bloody time, O'Reilly," he said. The man's collar was open and stuck out to the sides, still attached to the back collar stud.

"I'll go and see to the tea," Flo said. "And Doctor O'Reilly says you're going to get well, Bertie." She patted his hand and smiled at him as she left.

"Bertie," O'Reilly said. "Chest pain, was

174

it?" He grunted, stood over Bertie, and reached for his wrist. As he counted the beats, ninety-six per minute and perfectly regular, just a little fast, he noted that although Bertie was pale, the normal flush was returning to his cheeks.

"Aye, bloody ferocious so it was for a minute or two. I couldn't hardly get my breath, but it's away there now."

"What were you doing before it happened?"

"I was on the phone reaming out a buck eejit of a supplier."

"You'd lost your temper?"

"Wouldn't you have? Me with a whole crew on a site getting paid by the hour and the headcase that's supposed to have delivered the bricks has run out of stock? He's costing me an arm and a bloody leg, so he is." Bertie's voice rose and he banged a fist on the desktop.

"Bertie, unless you want the pain to come back, calm down," O'Reilly said. "Take some deep breaths and look out the window at this beautiful view." His desk was beneath a picture window that looked out over a rolling lawn and across Belfast Lough to the coastal Antrim villages of Greenisland and Carrickfergus — the rock of Fergus — with its twelfth-century Norman castle built by John de Courcy. Bertie glanced out the window, sighed, then stared down at his desk.

"Has it ever happened before?"

"That your man's let me down? No, and he'll not never again neither, so he'll not. Not when I'm done with him."

O'Reilly shook his head. The man would wrestle a bear for a halfpenny. "No, Bertie. I meant, have you ever had a pain like it before?"

"Not at all. And you'd've known, for I'd've sent for you, not some bloody woman."

The last thing O'Reilly wanted to do was incite another anginal attack, but . . . "Bertie," he said as gently and as firmly as he could manage, "Doctor Bradley is not as experienced as me, but she is as well qualified. People with chest pain can die and every second counts. She's working with me. In future, I may not be available to you. Am I clear?"

"Look. It was bloody sore, so it was. I was scared. Flo was going out of her mind fluttering about. I wanted the best. I always get the best, even if it's only you, O'Reilly, and I don't trust no female doctors." Judging by the colour of his cheeks, Bertie's choler was rising, and O'Reilly decided not to press matters — for now. But even if his years in practice had taught O'Reilly that worried patients could be bloody rude, he had to make an effort to hide his desire to go up one side of Bertie and down the other. The man needed a good talking-to — later.

O'Reilly's immediate concern was to determine if Bishop had experienced a series of what were known as "warning pains" for a few days before this bout. They could presage the onset of a full-blown heart attack. Their absence was a promising sign.

O'Reilly fished out a portable sphygmomanometer, set it on the desk, pushed up Bertie's shirtsleeve, and wrapped the cuff round his upper arm. Blow it up, stethoscope to the front of the elbow, slowly let the cuff down, and listen for the sounds of the pulse to reappear then disappear. "Blood pressure's up a bit," O'Reilly said.

"So would yours be, O'Reilly, if you was losing money hand over fist."

O'Reilly shook his head. "Open your shirt." A quick listen with his stethoscope gave no further clues. O'Reilly removed the earpieces and shoved the instrument into his jacket pocket. "Do up your shirt," he said, "while I give Flo a roar and then I'll explain to you both what's happening and what's going to happen." He strode to the door, called, "Can you come here please, Flo," and returned to Bertie's side.

"You can tell me," Bertie said. "Flo'd not understand anyroad."

"Do you do the cooking, Bertie?" For a moment, O'Reilly remembered noticing an advertisement in the paper for a builder's business for sale up in Portrush — sixty-odd miles away. Perhaps Bertie might decide to buy it, move, and torment some other G.P.

"Me, cook?" Bertie's lip curled. "I've Flo. You don't buy a dog and bark yourself. Why'd you want to know that anyway?"

"Patience, Bertie," O'Reilly said, and sighed.

Flo reappeared and stood beside her husband. "How is he, Doctor?"

"All right," said O'Reilly. "This time. I'm certain Bertie's had what's called angina of effort. Exercise or an emotional upset can bring it on and it goes away fairly quickly. It happens because the blood vessels that supply the heart have become narrow."

"How?" Flo asked.

"Too much fat in the diet, not enough exercise, and we're beginning to think smoking may contribute. You know how a kettle or a water pipe gets furred if the water's too hard?"

"Aye."

"If somebody eats too much fat for too long, the arteries get furred with what we call plaque — fat."

Flo frowned. "You mean I've not been feeding him right, like?" She glanced at Bertie.

"Hardly your fault, Flo. Everybody in Ireland likes a good fry-up, deep-fried battered fish-and-chips, properly marbled beef, but we'll have to change that, Bertie."

"You mean I'll have for til give up rashers and Denny's sausages? No more fried bread?"

178

Bertie looked like a little boy who'd lost his last marble. "You're a cruel man, O'Reilly, but then all youse doctors are forever going on about giving up this and giving up that."

"To tell you the truth I don't know about what you might have to forgo, and anyway, eventually the choice will be yours, not mine," O'Reilly said, "but Doctor Bradley's sent for the ambulance and —"

"He's for the hospital?" Flo said, and gasped. "That's ferocious, so it is. I thought it was just a wee pain, like, and he's better now, you know."

O'Reilly shook his head. "The attack's over, but you need some tests and long-term treatment. You'll be going to ward Five in the Royal, Bertie. Doctor Pantridge is the senior cardiologist there. You'll need an electrocardiogram and some blood work to confirm my diagnosis. You'll be given glyceryl trinitrate tablets to put under your tongue —"

"Now, just a minute, O'Reilly. I'm a bleedin' builder. I know what that is. That's what makes dynamite explode, so it is. No way I'm putting that stuff under my tongue, so I'm not."

"You needn't worry, Bertie. The tablets are quite stable, and the dose is very small, Half a milligram. You take one if you feel the pain coming on again. They make blood vessels dilate. Let more blood through."

"Huh," said Bertie, sounding unconvinced.

"The staff at the Royal'll make an appointment for you, and you should go too, Flo. That's why I wanted you to hear this. A dietitian will tell you all the stuff I don't know about special diets. She'll tell you what Bertie can and can't have." And maybe, he thought, if Flo eats the same kinds of meals, she'd lose a bit too. He wondered if her childlessness had led to using food as a way to comfort herself. But he put the thought aside. Bertie was the focus today.

"Yes, Doctor," she said.

He glanced at Bertie's waistline. "My guess is that you'll need to shed about two stone."

"By God, I'll starve," Bertie said in such tones that O'Reilly could almost feel sorry for the man.

"No, you'll not. I'll not preach, Bertie," he said, "but in a way you've been lucky. You could have had a real heart attack, but this is a warning. If you heed it, do as you're bid about your diet, take a bit of exercise, and stop getting yourself worked up to high doh, you'll probably live to a ripe old age."

The doorbell chimed. "That'll be the ambulance," O'Reilly said.

"I'll let them in." Flo left.

"You have been lucky, Bertie, but I don't want to talk about the future in front of Flo. Any one of us could get hit by a lorry tomorrow. There are no guarantees in this life. You have angina, that means narrow heart vessels, so you could have a heart attack at any time. We can't widen them or replace them. But if you pay attention to what the dietary people tell you at the Royal, keep your temper under control, have pills handy at all times and get one into you if you feel even a twinge, you've probably got another good fifteen years ahead of you." The textbook said ten to fifteen, but why not err on the side of optimism?

"By God, I hope so," Bertie said. He hung his head. "In soul, I do indeed, so I do."

"And let's hope," said O'Reilly, "this'll be your last trip to hospital for quite a while."

14
I Was Sick, and Ye Visited Me

Fingal climbed the Grand Staircase toward Saint Patrick's Ward, opening the door to the familiar sights and sounds of the place he'd lived in for practically two years. The black walls, the painting of Saint Patrick preaching to Oisín, the rows of beds where men moaned, coughed, snored, or chatted with a neighbour. It hadn't changed. His nostrils were filled with the fumes of strong disinfectant struggling to overpower the stronger smells of sick and dying humanity.

"Fingal, or should I say Doctor O'Reilly?" said Sister Daly, the senior nurse on the ward. "And to what do we owe the pleasure of your company at Sir Patrick Dun's?" Her grin was broad. "Nice to see you, young man."

"And here I thought we were friends, Mary Daly," Fingal said with a chuckle. "We don't need the titles."

"True on you. How are you, Fingal?"

"I've been worse," he said, and smiled. "Professionally I'm happy as a pig in you know what. I'm working with Charlie Greer at a dispensary practice in the Liberties, and today, Saturday, August the first, 1936, is my first weekend off."

"And so you're here, uh, at the hospital? Not out gallivanting?" She smiled, shook her head, and crossed her arms over her chest. "Uh-huh. So the new job's going well?"

"Like they heard the fellah say when he jumped off the Wellington Monument in Phoenix Park, 'So far so good.' Three weeks in and it's grand. The work is just as satisfying as I'd hoped." And the nights on call, staying in the dispensary, gave him some respite from the funereal sadness that, despite Ma's best efforts, pervaded the big house. For a moment he thought about telling Mary about Father, but why? She didn't know Fingal's family and it was only with his very close friends that he was willing to show his grief.

Mary cocked her head. "Mind wandering, Fingal? I thought I'd lost you for a moment, there. And how's the fair Kitty O'Hallorhan?"

"Fine. In fact, she's splendid. She's at Baggott Street Hospital. I'm seeing her tonight. I'm on call a lot but the redoubtable Doctor Corrigan is taking call until Monday morning —"

"Phelim Corrigan, at Aungier Place?"

"The very one."

She laughed. "Don't let him too near Kitty. He's a bachelor man, and a terrible one for the ladies." She winked at him. "He's only ten years older than me and, eejit that I am, I let him squire me around for a few months about nine years ago." Did Fingal detect a wistfulness in her voice?

"I didn't know that," Fingal said. The more he found out about Phelim the more human the man became. "I'll remember it."

"How do you find working with him?"

"I wasn't sure about him at first, you should have seen the way he lit into one of his patients . . ."

"Who'd done something awful to a child?"

Fingal startled. "How did you know that?"

"He's daft about kiddies. Hates to see them hurt."

"I could tell, and he likes to play the old gruff ogre. He bade farewell to us on Friday afternoon with the cheery admonition, 'Enjoy yer weekend, but be sure the pair of ye's back by nine on the button on Monday morning or I'll dock ye a day's pay.' "

Mary laughed. "That's Phelim."

"He's a damn good doctor, and it's a comfort to consult him on the difficult cases. Or the kinds of problems unique to the tenements. Charlie and I didn't see a lot of that stuff here in Dun's. It's mostly handled by the chemists and G.P.s."

"I can imagine. And was it wanting to see more of the 'stuff at Dun's' that brought you here on your weekend off instead of being out flying your kite?" She tilted her head to one side.

"No." He laughed. "Three weeks back I saw an accident, gave first aid until the ambulance came. They brought him here with a Pott's fracture . . ."

"Mister JJF," she said.

Still this nonsense of only referring to patients by their initials. And why should it have changed in only a month?

"Don't tell me you're the Big Fellah?" She looked him up and down. "I should have guessed."

" 'Fraid so." He laughed and so did she.

"He's doing as well as can be expected," she said. "Mister Kinnear did a closed reduction and put a plastercast on it. We've been doing weekly X-rays and the surgeons are pleased with the alignment of the fragments. The patient's in the OTC Commemoration Bed." OTC stood for officers training corps.

"Oh," said Fingal, and felt a little shiver. He remembered the first time he'd read the brass plaque beside the bed. . . . *Endowed by the citizens of Dublin in recognition of the gallant defence of Trinity College. Easter 1916.*

"I know," she said, "it hit you hard when KD died. My heart bled for you."

"It did hurt," he said, thinking of Kevin Doherty, who two years before had lain in the same bed, "and thank you for that, Mary."

"Och," she said, "everybody felt it except

185

that one there." She lowered her voice to a whisper. "Heartless gobshite." She inclined her head to a gangly figure in a white coat who was halfway down the multiple-bedded ward. He had gold pince-nez and a protuberant Adam's apple. "Your old friend Fitzpatrick's our new houseman."

"Good God," said Fingal. "Ronald Hercules. How do you put up with him?" He remembered the arrogant man who had been in Fingal's year.

"With great difficulty," she said, "but needs must. Go on now and see your patient. I've a report to write, but I'll make you a cup of tea before you go."

"Thank you. I'd like that." He headed off between the rows of beds.

"What brings you here, O'Reilly?" Fitzpatrick demanded as Fingal passed the bed where Fitzpatrick was turning back the bedclothes preparatory to examining a young man.

"I know one of the patients. He got hit by a tram. I saw him then."

"Still the same O'Reilly. Don't think anyone but you knows how to treat people." He sniffed.

"*Au contraire,* Hercules" — Fingal knew the man hated to be called Hercules — "just curious about how he's getting on." He kept walking.

He passed a bed with a metal gantry at its

186

foot where bandages from a man's injured leg had been twisted into a rope that ran over a pulley-wheel and were attached to a twenty-pound weight. The end of the bed was elevated nine inches and the patient lay head down. That was how fractured femurs were treated. The traction kept the broken ends aligned and reduced the damage to the surrounding muscles. Fingal's nostrils were assailed by the stench of Sinclair's glue, a substance made of glue, water, thymol, and glycerine with powerful adhesive properties and a ferocious stink. The compound was applied to the skin once a fracture had been reduced, and the bandages, which would be used to exert traction to keep the bone ends in place as they healed, stuck firmly to the glue. Its smell, and all too frequently that of decaying flesh in cases of infected compound fractures, were the olfactory hallmarks of orthopaedic patients. The man would be there for three months.

"Jasus Murphy, Doctor O'Reilly. What brings you here?" said John-Joe Finnegan from the next bed as Fingal passed the gantry. He put down the *Irish Times* and smiled. Fingal glanced at headlines that screamed, *Adolf Hitler Opens Berlin Olympics Today,* and a smaller one announcing, *Command of Nationalist Forces Split Between Generals Franco, Quipo del Llano, and Mola*

Vidal. The Spanish Civil War had broken out on July 17.

"I used to work here," Fingal said. "Sister Daly's an old friend. I pop in to see her once in a while and I knew they'd brought you here so I thought —"

"You'd see how I was doing. Fair play to you, sir. Fair play." He grinned. "Mister Kinnear, the surgeon, he says I'll be here for at least another six weeks til the bones have knit." He sighed. "Even den I'll have a funny-looking joint, but I'll be able to hobble around. It was good of you til come to see me, sir. Did you get the job with Doc Corrigan?"

"I did," said Fingal, "three weeks ago yesterday."

"Dat's grand altogether."

"And are they treating you well, John-Joe?"

"Couldn't be better. At least I get my three squares a day in here. Jasus, but the grub's great."

Fingal, when he'd been a resident student here, had been fed from the same kitchen. "Great" was not the adjective he'd have used, but he supposed that when your diet was mostly potatoes, vegetables, and beef parings that could be bought for fourpence, the variety of the hospital meals would seem pretty good.

John-Joe sighed. "It's tougher at home. I've a plot out at Dolphin's Barn where I grow some veg. A fellah I know's looking after it for me." He forced a smile. "Anyroad, my Ailish and the two weans are managin'. She gets the 'Relief' money on Wednesdays and dat pays the rent, the neighbour's granny looks after our two while Ailish makes a few bob as a cleaner, and she's always been brilliant on Saturday nights at the nine thirty auctions."

Fingal frowned. "I'm sorry, I don't understand."

"Bless you, sir, and why would you, a toff like yourself?"

Fingal had never exactly thought of himself in those terms, but he supposed in John-Joe's eyes he would be.

"Every Saturday night at nine thirty the butchers auction off all the meat they couldn't sell during the week. She gets some not bad leavings. Makes great stews. You might not t'ink much of dem, but och, sure, sir, for the likes of us, when you never get a salmon you're happy wit' a herring."

Fingal smiled.

John-Joe's face fell. "The trouble is when dey let me out we'll have another mouth til feed — me — and it'll be hard looking for a job."

Fingal wished he could say something comforting, do something practical, but he knew he was powerless. "I wish . . . well, anyway," he said, "I'm delighted to see you're

189

doing well."

"And t'ank you for comin' til see me. If you're working in Aungier, I'll likely see you round the place, sir."

"Indeed you might," said Fingal. "You take care. I have to trot." He half turned, then remembering, shoved his hand into his jacket pocket and fished out a packet of Woodbine cigarettes. "Here," he said, giving them to John-Joe and, ignoring the man's thanks, headed back up the ward only to meet Doctor Micks going the other way.

"O'Reilly," he said, "what brings you here? I thought you were working in a dispensary."

"An orthopaedic patient, sir. Pott's fracture. One of Mister Kinnear's." Fingal smiled. "He's doing well, I'm pleased to say."

"Good." Doctor Micks stared down at his highly polished black shoes then straight at Fingal. "I'm so very sorry about your father."

"It was decent of you to come to the funeral, sir. My mother appreciated it."

"I wanted to come. Your father was a good man and I enjoyed getting to know him, even under the circumstances. It's a pity we can't do more." He pursed his lips. "Sorry I couldn't make the interment and graveside service, but Holywood's a long journey for me from Dublin."

"It's all right, sir. We understand. It was my father's wish to be buried there. He was born there and he wanted to — well, to go home."

"Yes, of course. Please," said Doctor Micks, "give my regards to your mother."

"I will," said Fingal, and after a moment's embarrassed silence said, "I'd best be going, sir." He headed down the ward, angry for the plight of John-Joe Finnegan, sad for his father, and suddenly in need of a comforting cup of tea with Sister Mary Daly.

15
BRING EQUAL EASE
UNTO MY PAIN

"I'd've come out to the farm to see you, you know, Brenda," O'Reilly said.

The pale young woman before him had curly auburn hair under a rain-spotted plastic hood and dark eyes behind National Health Service granny glasses. She was clearly having difficulty breathing, and, judging by the way she screwed up her face, each breath hurt. "Och, Doctor, dear," she said, and grimaced, "I'm not altogether at myself, but I'm not at death's door neither. There's no need for anyone to come traipsing out into the Ballybucklebo Hills on a day like the day."

He heard rain pattering on the surgery window. It hadn't been the greatest summer, and here in early September yet another disturbance had come in from the Atlantic. Och well. They say in Ireland, "Rain at seven, fair by eleven," and it was pretty well true. Four hours was about the spacing of the small low-pressure systems that tore across the isle bringing rain squalls — and kept it emerald.

"Not at yourself? You're not just a bit unwell, Brenda Eakin, you're sick. I could have come, or seeing it's my turn in the surgery today, I would have sent Doctor Bradley."

"Doctor Bradley?" Brenda lowered her voice. "Och, sure, haven't you seen me ever since I was wee and don't you know all about me? I'd be daft to swap horses in the middle of a gallop, if you know what I mean, like? I'm happy for til see yourself, so I am."

O'Reilly pulled off his half-moon spectacles and peered at her. Bertie Bishop's strong re-action to a woman doctor four days ago and now Brenda. Jenny still had failed to convince some of the practice that she was to be trusted. He tried to persuade himself that it was the usual reactionary response of country folk to anything new . . . "Better the divil you know, that it?" he said, and smiled. But he was concerned. Was it merely because she was new, and young? Barry had taken a while to be accepted. He'd almost forgotten how he'd had to help young Laverty when a patient of his had died and it seemed the whole village had lost faith in him. O'Reilly would help Jenny all he could too, but it was also up to Jenny, who'd been here for more than two months, to keep working hard to al-lay local suspicions. But she could hardly change her genetic makeup.

After having taken an instant liking to the young woman, he was also becoming increasingly impressed with her clinical acumen. And during the dinner in Ballymena, Barry had expressed no interest in coming back. If he didn't, Fingal would be happy to work with Jenny Bradley as his partner, if she could fit in here. Worry about it later, he told himself. Get Brenda sorted out first.

"You're no divil, Doctor O'Reilly. You just —" She gasped. "— only pretend to be as tough as oul Balor."

In Irish mythology, Balor was the king of the Fomorians, a race of giants. His gaze could turn men to rock. O'Reilly harrumphed. Pretend indeed? She'd not seen him having that little chat with Bertie a couple of days ago. The doctors at the Royal had confirmed O'Reilly's diagnosis of angina. Bertie had had no more attacks, and as O'Reilly had instructed the good councillor on the subject of manners to all doctors, he'd fixed Bertie with a glare that bloody nearly turned the man into a lump of Mourne granite. Balor? When his ire was up, O'Reilly would have made the ferocious giant look like an edentulous pussycat, but he needn't dwell on it. The problem of the moment was to get Brenda better.

"Now, let's be getting you seen to. The last time you were in was last October. For painful periods." He'd been confident back then that the twenty-six-year-old wife of farmer Ian Eakin was suffering from primary dysmenorrhoea, periods that occurred in ovulatory menstrual cycles and were caused by contractions of the uterine muscles. It was unrelated to any organic disease. The exact cause was not known. It often disappeared after a first baby was born. "You didn't come back," he said, "so I imagine the medicine worked?" He'd told her to use a combination of aspirin and paracetamol, which did not require a prescription. They were to be taken four times a day on the first day of her period when the pain was worst and twice a day thereafter until the pain went away as the period diminished.

She rubbed the right side of her chest. "Pretty well. Ever since then the minute my monthlies start, I get a wheen of pills into me like you said til and I'm able til thole the cramps and get on with —" She caught her breath. "Mother of God, that smarted." She inhaled, but it was shallow. "Like I was saying, it takes me and Ian and a bit of help from young Peter Dobbin til keep the farm going — Peter's eye's better by the way. So I'm able for til do my work, so I am. I didn't need to bother you, sir, and sure don't most women have cramps anyroad?"

"Sad, but true," he said. Although there was some evidence that as the repressive strictures of the Victorian era were being cast aside, the numbers were falling, and a good thing too. There was precious little medicine could do. Most approaches were either to treat the symptoms medically with painkillers or resort to dilating the cervix under anaesthesia and curetting, that is scraping out the uterine lining, known as a D and C. Some heroic surgeons removed a plexus of nerves from the pelvis and claimed a 70 percent success rate, but similar results had been reported using psychotherapy.

"The new contraceptive pill does work for painful periods, Brenda." Because, he knew, it suppressed ovulation, which clearly was a prerequisite for primary dysmenorrhoea to occur.

"Aye, but me and Ian want a family so it's a no-go, so it's not," she said. "Anyroad, I have my monthlies right now. They're a bit niggly, but . . ." She screwed up her face. "This thing in my chest, that's a different kettle of fish."

"When did it start?"

"This morning about six. I'd just got up and I was feeding the chickens when I took this stabbing in my side every time I breathed in. I have it still. For a wee minute there now I thought I was going til keel over I felt so —" She gasped and said, "Excuse me, sir," before continuing. "— faint."

"I see." In fact he didn't, not precisely anyway. Her symptoms sounded as if she had irritation of the pleura, the double membrane that sheathes the lungs. There were a number of causes. "Did you hit your chest on anything?"

She shook her head.

That ruled out traumatic haematothorax, blood between the pleural layers caused by a blow. "I remember giving you a TB test in 1946 when you were seven."

"And it come up in a red bump and you said that meant I was immune til TB."

It did, so one obvious cause was excluded. O'Reilly never saw a patient with chest troubles without remembering the high rate of TB in the tenements in the 1930s. Many people were infected as children, were unaware and shook off the disease, leaving them immune for life. Her red lump had been a positive immune response to the Mantoux test. Other causes? She was far too young for lung cancer. "You've no pains in your legs?"

"No, sir. If I didn't have this pain in my chest, I'd be going round like a liltie."

Not long ago Barry had been worried about Aggie Arbuthnot's deep venous phlebothrombosis, but it didn't sound as if Brenda could have had a pulmonary embolism from such a source. He was narrowing his suspicions. "And you were perfectly all right up until this morning?"

"Fit as a flea, sir."

Heart failure, nephrotic syndrome, a severe

197

kidney disease, and cirrhosis of the liver could all cause fluid to enter the pleural cavities, but such patients would all have been very ill for a long time and both sides of the chest would be affected.

"Do you feel hot or are you having chills?"

She pursed her lips, grimaced, and shook her head.

She certainly looked pale and sweaty. He leant forward and put the back of his hand on her forehead. A bit damp, but he was confident she wasn't running a fever. "Have you a bad cough?"

"No, sir."

It didn't look as if she had pneumonia, either viral or bacterial. O'Reilly blew out his breath through semi-closed lips. He was coming to the end of the possibilities he knew. "Better have a look at you, love," he said, rose from the swivel chair, and helped her onto the examining couch.

By the time he had finished a thorough examination, the only unusual thing he had been able to find was a small area of dullness to percussion over the base of her right lung in the same place that she was feeling the pain. He'd been unable to pick up any sounds with his stethoscope of breath entering the lung there, but immediately above the dull part of the lung he had noted a strange phenomenon. When he'd asked Brenda to whisper "Ninety-nine," he'd heard the words through his earpieces as if she was speaking directly into his ear. The effect — with the musical name of whispering pectoriloquy — was often heard over a lung that was badly inflamed. It could also appear immediately above a collection of fluid in the pleural cavity.

He stuffed the stethoscope back in his jacket pocket. "Put your clothes on, Brenda," he said, stepping outside the screens, "then I'll try to explain." If he could.

O'Reilly was frowning and scratching his head when she called, "I'm all dressed now, Doctor."

When he went back she was lying down, doing up the last button of her amber blouse.

"You have a small collection of fluid round the bottom of your right lung," he said. "It's a kind of pleurisy." Most folks knew what that was.

"Pleurisy?" she said. Her eyes widened. "Is it serious, like?" Her voice trembled. "When I was wee, my auntie Norma died of pneumonia and you was our new doctor then, sir, after Doctor Flanagan passed away. You told my da that his sister had pleurisy as well."

O'Reilly nodded. He could picture the woman even now, twenty years later. And despite all he'd seen in his younger days in Dublin, regardless of having had to deal for six years with the carnage of naval warfare, he'd been saddened by her death. Norma

199

McCausland had been a bright and high-spirited young woman — and much too young to die. No wonder Brenda was frightened now. "I remember Norma well, Brenda. It was 1946, and I'd only been here a few months. We knew about penicillin, but it was just after the war and I couldn't get my hands on any."

"She was awful nice, so she was."

"I know, but what happened to her isn't going to happen to you. In the first place, I can promise you you don't have pneumonia."

"Are you sure?"

"Positive."

She smiled. "Thank God for that."

Even after thirty-four years in medicine O'Reilly still marvelled at the absolute faith of most of his patients in his pronouncements. "And in the second place, if you do develop a fever and it starts to look like pneumonia, we've antibiotics galore. Fix you in no time flat." Not quite true if the cause was a virus, but there was no need to worry her. "But we will have to get to the bottom of it," he said. "You'll need a chest X-ray."

"Now? Like today?"

"I'll send you to Bangor Hospital. They can do it there. Could Ian run you down?"

She sat up and took a breath. He could see how she was trying not to show that it hurt. "Doctor O'Reilly, could it maybe wait for a few days? Please?"

O'Reilly was sure he knew why she was asking. She was a farmer's wife and it was September. "Harvest?"

"That's right. Ian and Peter are at it from dawn 'til dusk. They should have it in in another few days, but they need me too, so they do." She pointed at the window. "Now the rain's stopped Ian'll be reaping the barley and Peter'll be driving the lorry that catches the grain that's been threshed out." She smiled. "Ian reckons it'll be a wheeker crop, so it will — if he can get it in time. And there's no time to waste." O'Reilly heard the urgency in her voice. "He rented a new CLAAS Herkule combine harvester, one with a self-cleaning rotary screen."

"A rotary screen?"

"Aye. It's a new whigmaleery, you know. Stops grain dust from clogging the radiator so the engines never overheat like they used to and you can keep reaping nonstop. It's hard, dry, dusty work, so it is, with all that chaff in the air, and they need me for to feed them, make cups of tea because they eat on the run, bring them plenty of water. And the cows need milking." He saw the pleading in her deep brown eyes. "Please, sir. I always wrap a hanky round my face when I'm near the combine. Keeps the dust out."

"Give me a minute," he said. He couldn't understand why she had this small pleural effusion and an X-ray might give some answers.

But the truth was, it probably wouldn't help him decide on any different treatment than he could offer today. "Brenda," he said, "I'd like to get an X-ray —"

"But —"

He held up a hand. "I'm pretty sure one of two things will happen. Either the accumulation of fluid will get absorbed and you'll start feeling better soon, or it might just get bigger, in which case, it's the Royal Victoria for you." To have the fluid removed, he thought, but kept the thought to himself. "You have a phone?"

"Aye."

"If you can stick the pain and promise, and I mean promise, to call me the minute the pain gets worse or you're having more trouble breathing —" He made a rapid calculation. "— I can be at your farm in fifteen minutes."

"Oh, thank you, sir," she said. "I promise. Honest to God. Cross my heart."

"And," he helped her down, "go on using the painkillers I gave you even after your monthlies are over. They'll help the pain in your chest a bit. Have you enough?"

"Aye. I bought a clatter last month to do me for six months."

"Good," he said. "Now, try not to overdo it." And take a short trip to the moon while you're at it, he thought, knowing from experience how tough and hardworking Ulster farmers' wives were. "Get as much rest as

202

possible, and try to keep warm. Lots of fluids."

"Yes, Doctor."

"Sit down for a minute," he said as he helped her to a chair. "How are you getting home?"

"Mister and Mrs. Houston live not far away. Sonny's a real gentleman. He give me a lift in his motorcar, you know, and he's waiting for me, so he is, in the waiting room."

As she spoke, he sat at his desk and filled in an X-ray requisition form. "If you get worse," he said, rising and giving it to her, "you'll not need this. The hospital doctors will see to it. But if you're getting better, and I'm fairly sure you will, the minute the harvest's over I want you in Bangor Hospital for a chest X-ray, then come in and see me the next day." O'Reilly wasn't quite sure what it might show if the fluid had gone, but it was better to be safe than sorry. "Right," he said, rising. He offered his arm.

"I can manage, sir," she said, and he knew she was trying to prove to him, and probably to herself, that she could cope unaided.

In the waiting room, all eyes turned toward him. He nodded a greeting to the other patients and as always admired the roses on the wallpaper. He wondered why Kitty thought they were gaudy. That's what she'd said the day Colin Brown had an infected foot.

Cissie Sloan grinned back. She'd be in to get her thyroid pills and, he sighed, a good blether. Sonny Houston stood.

"Morning, Sonny," O'Reilly said, "how's Maggie?"

"Right as rain," Sonny said. "She's home making a plum cake for Brenda and Ian, and seeing to the dogs. We've six now. We couldn't find a home for the last of Missy's pups, but I saw Colin Brown yesterday. He's making a good fist of his dog Murphy."

"Good for Colin," O'Reilly said, wondering how Donal and the boy were getting on with Bluebird and when Donal was going to race the animal. "And it was kind of you to bring Brenda in."

"It was really no trouble." He looked expectantly at her. "If she needs to go to the —"

"Doctor O'Reilly's for letting me go home," she said.

"Wonderful. I'm delighted to hear it." Sonny offered his arm, which she took.

"And don't forget, Brenda, if you're worried at all, *at all,* phone. Either myself or Doctor Bradley" — That provoked a few subdued mutterings among the other patients — "will be out in a flash."

He barely heard her "Yes, Doctor," as he said, "Right. Who's next?"

"Me, sir," said Cissie, lumbering to her feet. "I need more of them wee thingys Doctor Laverty prescribed. They're doing me a

204

power of good, so they are. I'm brisk as a bee
—" She was still talking on the intake of
breath as he closed the surgery door behind
her.

16
SKILL IN SURGERY

"Jasus, Doctor, I hope it works. The back's still feckin' killin' me." Lorcan O'Lunney, the Dublin tugger, shook his head. "I'm like a toad with a broken leg dragging meself and the cart about. Last time I was here some pregnant woman told me to try her granny's bog onion poultice. And she gave me her granny's prayer too." He made a derisive snort. "About as much use as a fart in a high wind."

He was clearly aggrieved but held out his callused hand to take the prescription. He was the last patient of the Monday morning surgery as Fingal began his fourth week working at the Dublin dispensary. He'd enjoyed the rest of his Saturday after he'd left John-Joe Finnegan at Sir Patrick Dun's. Thanks to Phelim Corrigan's flexibility with the on-call schedules, he and Charlie were now bona fide members of the Wanderers Football Club and would have their chances to earn their places on the first fifteen this season, the first step toward that much-longed-for Irish cap. Turned out Phelim had played Gaelic football at the county level in his youth, and despite the prohibition by the Gaelic Athletic Association of its members attending "Garrison" or "English" games like rugby and cricket, he took a keen interest in the fortunes of the Irish Rugby team.

And the evening spent with lovely Kitty? He told himself to stop grinning and concentrate on Lorcan O'Lunney's aching back. He had to show the sympathy he felt for the man. Fingal took a deep breath, pursed his lips, and said, "It can be miserable, I know."

What Lorcan needed was a long rest, but Fingal might as well suggest the man take a Mediterranean cruise. Pulling that cart hour after hour, day after day was all that kept a roof over Lorcan's and his family's head and put stale bread on their table. "Here," Fingal said, handing over a scrip', "Take that to Mister Corcoran, the apothecary. He'll make you up a strong liniment with oil of wintergreen" — it contained a salicylate, as did aspirin — "and he'll also compound these tablets." Although Fingal had never seen it used for backache, the Atophan he was prescribing was effective for another joint disease, gout. It was worth a try. "Break one up, mix it with water and baking soda, take the same dose three times a day, and come and see me next week."

"All right." Lorcan shrugged, took the paper, clapped a duncher on his balding head, and headed for the door. "I'll give her a go, but I'm not expectin' to be yellin', 'whoa, hold the fecking' lights because I've had a miracle cure.' You'd need to go to Lourdes for dat and where'd a man like me get the money for the fare?" He shrugged. "But t'anks anyway, sir, for doin' yer best."

He'd barely closed the door when Phelim and Charlie came in.

"Great," said O'Reilly, rising and lifting a small picnic hamper that Cook filled every morning. "Lunch." He was aching for today's cold poached salmon and mayonnaise sandwiches and hard-boiled eggs with a big slice of her Bramley apple pie to follow.

"Will ye wait a minute?" Phelim held up one hand like a policeman on traffic duty then adjusted his toupee. "Charlie's agreed to do the afternoon visits, Fingal. One of my few paying patients seems to have twisted or ruptured an ovarian cyst. She's in a lot of pain."

"And you sent her to hospital? Don't see why that should hold up lunch," Fingal said as he opened the hamper and lifted out a sandwich wrapped in greaseproof paper. A woman as sick as that needed surgery.

"I did not." Phelim reached over, removed the sandwich from Fingal's hand, and returned it to the hamper. "I asked Doctor

208

Andrew Davidson, a gynaecologist from the Rotunda, to make a domiciliary visit. He came straight out and agreed with my diagnosis. He's sent for his team and they're setting up her bedroom as an operating theatre. It'll take an hour to sterilize everything, longer to set up the portable operating table and get everything ready. He's going to operate as soon as it is. I'll give the anaesthetic. I've come back to get my gear. You'll assist Doctor Davidson. Clear?"

"Yes, yes, of course." Fingal looked longingly at the sandwich but had to admit it would be an interesting way to spend the afternoon. He knew that surgery was often carried out in wealthy patients' own homes, but he'd never seen it done. He felt a momentary twinge of nerves and then relaxed. Surgical assisting had been part of the routine of his student days and he'd discovered that he had a talent for it.

"One thing," Phelim said. "You and I, Fingal, when we get our fees we'll pool them and divide by three. No reason Charlie should be left out."

"That's very generous, Phelim," Charlie said.

"No, it is not," Phelim said. "But it is fair. It'll be the same when it's Charlie's turn to come with me. Now, leave yer posh grub behind, Fingal, and follow me. Ye'll not starve. If I can do without my rasher sand-

209

wiches you can do without your poached salmon."

Fingal followed his senior colleague along a corridor to a storeroom and waited as Phelim picked up a walnut carrying case and a bottle labelled chloroform. "Right," he said, "off. And in case ye're wondering where I got patients like these, I've known Jane Carson since she was a little girl in Roscommon. Her father was a resident magistrate. She married a toff, but not too far up from her class. Her husband Robin's a director of more Dublin companies than ye could count on yer fingers and toes."

Phelim parked near the junction with Baggot Street on Mount Street Upper. At its far end Fingal could see the pillared portico and domed cupola that gave Saint Stephen's Church the nickname the Pepper Cannister. The thoroughfare was as broad and sunlit as Aungier Place was narrow and dark. This part of Dublin had been developed in the 1770s and '80s. Fingal could imagine top-hatted coachmen driving the barouche-landaus and coaches of the gentry, each carrying ladies with lace bonnets and parasols while young bucks trotted on prancing thoroughbreds. It was a street on which the characters in a Jane Austen novel would not have been out of place — except for their English accents.

He and Phelim crossed a wide pavement to

the red sandstone arched doorway of a four-storey terrace house. When his senior colleague knocked on the glossy black door, a uniformed maid answered. They were expected. "Mister Carson will receive yiz, Doctors," she said. "Follow me."

Fingal found himself in a spacious drawing room. The Regency striped fabric of armchairs and a love seat made him wonder if the furniture was indeed of the period. Most likely.

"Robin," Phelim said, "meet my partner, Doctor O'Reilly. He'll be assisting."

The tall man, well dressed in a morning suit and highly polished shoes, offered a hand and said, "Thank you for coming, Doctor."

Fingal guessed he was in his mid-twenties. "How do you do, sir." They shook. Fingal knew that the Carsons were one of the remaining families of the Anglican Ascendancy, the landowners who were more English than Irish and who had been the aristocracy before the Potato Famine and the subsequent land wars. Their old family seat had been out in Mayo, not far from Roscommon, where Phelim had said Mister Carson's wife had come from. "You two will take care of my Jane, won't you? And Doctor Davidson — he's the Master of the Rotunda, isn't he? So he must be good." There was a quaver in Carson's voice and rightly so, Fingal thought. Major abdominal surgery was not risk-free.

"Try ye not to worry, Robin. I'm sure she'll do very well," Phelim said. "And if ye'll excuse us, Doctor O'Reilly and I should go up. But we'll come and explain when it's all over."

"Of course. I'd appreciate that." Robin Carson tugged on a nearby satin bell pull, there was a faint jangling in the distance, and soon the maid reappeared and bobbed.

"Please show the doctors the way."

Fingal followed Phelim into the wide hall and up two flights of deeply carpeted stairs. "In dere please, sirs. Doctor Davidson and his nurses are waitin'."

Fingal followed Phelim into a room where the curtains were drawn back and every light was burning brightly. Surgeons needed to see what they were doing. He noticed at once that most of the furniture had been moved out, and saw the patient, an auburn-haired young woman, lying under a blanket on a portable operating table. She appeared to be very drowsy and had probably been given a dose of chloral hydrate as a sedative, although a larger one than Phelim had prescribed for the teething Aidan Curran.

Phelim went over to her, laid a hand on her shoulder, and when she slowly turned her head to him and blinked, he said, "Soon be over now, Jane, and we'll have you tucked up in your own bed." He nodded to a single bed against one wall. Fingal could see the bumps of hot water bottles under the blankets. The patient would be popped in there postoperatively.

Two uniformed nurses bustled about, preparing towels and basins of water.

A tall man in pinstripe trousers, their braces crossed over his shirt, was washing his hands, his sleeves rolled up above the elbows. "Ah, Doctor Corrigan. And young Doctor O'Reilly. I recall you from your time in the Rotunda. You had a good pair of hands in surgery."

"Thank you, sir." He remembered Doctor Davidson's report about an outbreak of puerperal sepsis, childbed fever, at the Rotunda Hospital in 1935. The senior man was presently investigating the bacteriostatic properties of a new medicine, red prontosil, in that disease. Prontosil, an aniline dye, was the subject of Bob Beresford and Professor Bigger's research in the laboratory too.

Fingal's nose was assailed by the smells of the antiseptics perchloride of mercury, carbolic acid, and absolute alcohol. In one corner of the room, a cylindrical drum standing on three feet gurgled and hissed. A steam gauge on top indicated ten pounds of pressure. Fingal had never seen one but guessed it was a portable steam sterilizer for their overalls, masks, gloves, instruments, and towels.

He watched while Phelim opened the walnut case and withdrew a device with a face mask attached to a thick rubber tube. A similar tube on the other side was attached to a glass bottle which Phelim was filling with chloroform. Fingal recognised it as a Vernon Harcourt apparatus for controlling the rate of flow of chloroform vapour. The fluid level rose in the glass. Two beads, one blue, one red, floated in the liquid, and by noting their level, Phelim would decide if the patient was getting too much or too little chloroform. He used a strap to hang the device round his neck. "I'm ready," he said.

"Come and scrub, Doctor O'Reilly," Doctor Davidson said. "Doctor Corrigan, please start the anaesthetic."

Fingal washed his hands in three successive basins, carbolic soap and water, clear water for rinsing, and biniodide of mercury 1/1,000 solution. A nurse, herself already dressed antiseptically, helped them into their sterile masks, overalls, and gloves.

"She's under," Phelim said. "Pulse is fine, respiration's regular."

Fingal was impressed. The little doctor sounded so unconcerned he might have been reading a weather forecast, and yet he had the patient's life in his hands.

"Thank you." Doctor Davidson moved to the right side of the operating table. The patient was hidden beneath sterilized towels. An exposed strip of abdominal skin glistened.

Fingal knew that Doctor Davidson preferred to use absolute alcohol to sterilize the skin.

Fingal took up his position on the patient's right, facing Doctor Davidson and the nurse who would hand the surgeon his instruments.

Phelim sat on a wooden kitchen chair at the patient's head, holding the rubber mask over her nose and mouth. "Ye may start anytime," he said.

"Good. Scalpel."

Doctor Davidson made a midline incision from umbilicus to pubic symphysis, and Fingal mopped away blood and used artery forceps to clamp bleeding vessels for Doctor Davidson to ligate with silkworm gut. He talked as he worked. "First chap to remove an ovary was Ephraim McDowell in 1809 in a log cabin in Kentucky. No anaesthesia and the patient was making her own bed by the fifth day. Tough folks, the old hillbillies."

Fingal saw the smile behind the mask when the gynaecologist continued, "I'm glad we have you and your chloroform, Phelim." Fingal knew that titles were often dropped in operating rooms once the patient was asleep. "I'd not have the guts to operate with the patient conscious."

Nor me, Fingal thought, and shuddered. He wondered if the senior man's banter was carefully planned to camouflage the butterflies he must be feeling inside. Slicing open a fellow human was not a natural thing to do.

"My pleasure," Phelim said. "And ye may be wrong, Andrew. There's some evidence that a Robert Houston of Glasgow successfully removed an ovarian tumour in 1701. I study medical history. Ye can learn a lot from it."

Something else Fingal had not known about Phelim Corrigan.

"Anyhow, young O'Reilly, now we have her open," Doctor Davidson said, "if you could retract?"

Fingal lifted a stainless steel instrument with a long narrow handle and a broad deep blade mounted at ninety degrees. He put the blade into the nearest side of the wound and pulled, then did the same with the far side, thus giving the surgeon better access to the abdominal and pelvic cavities.

"Keep it like that." Doctor Davidson slipped his right hand inside and slowly brought out the ovary. A healthy ovary should be about the size of a walnut, but Fingal could see how this one was as big as a small orange. The Fallopian tube that ran on top of the diseased organ was distorted. Both were a dusky red due to an obvious twisting of the ligament that suspended the ovary from the corner of the uterus. Torsion. Phelim had been right in his diagnosis.

"Now, young O'Reilly, if you were me, what would you do?" Doctor Davidson asked.

"The safest and easiest thing would be to

remove the tube and ovary, sir." God, it was like being back in class.

"That's right, but watch." Doctor Davidson rotated the organ and relieved the twist in the stem. Immediately the colour began to improve. "I think," he said, "we can preserve this ovary and tube. She's no kiddies — yet."

Fingal watched as his senior split the ovarian tissue, which although fully intact had been turned from a solid organ into a sheet and compressed into a thin envelope by the tumour growing inside. The effect was rather like the thinning of the rubber of a child's ballon when it was inflated by air. What had once been a solid, healthy ovary was now no more than an outer thin skin covering the tumour beneath. The technique was first to dissect the skin from the underlying cyst. Doctor Davidson gradually worked the blunt handle of his scalpel between the ovarian tissue and the cyst until it was completely free, then dropped the mass into a stainless steel dish. In what seemed like no time, he had placed rows of sutures and reconstructed the ovary. "It's amazing," he said, "how that ovarian tissue will reconstitute itself in a couple of months."

Only a tiny amount of blood seeped from the repaired ovarian incision. "Now," he said, and pushed his hand gently inside the pelvic cavity. "Uterus feels normal. Other ovary and tube fine. Let's put this back." Fingal watched

217

as the now untwisted and repaired ovary and its tube were replaced in the pelvis. "Retractors out."

Fingal complied.

"Closing in a minute, Phelim," Doctor Davidson said. "You can start bringing her back." He leant over the dish containing the tumour and sliced into it. "Look at that," he said as oily sebaceous material oozed out. Strands of hair appeared. "Dermoid cyst. Benign. No worry about cancer." He started to sew, closing the peritoneum first. As he worked, he said to Fingal, "Interesting tumours. Nobody is sure how they grow, but they often have identifiable structures in them, like hair or teeth." He laughed. "My old prof, Doctor Henry Wilson, used to tell us students that the diagnostic sign for a dermoid cyst in a patient was to put an ice pack over the lower abdomen, then listen with your stethoscope. If you heard —"

"Teeth chattering because of the cold," Phelim said, "ye knew what ye'd got."

Fingal, who had heard the same old joke when he was studying gynaecology, thought it politic to manage a small laugh.

"Will you close the skin, O'Reilly?" Doctor Davidson arched his back. "My back's killing me."

"Yes, sir." Fingal frowned. In the teaching hospitals, juniors were usually left with the routine job of closing wounds, but this was a

218

private patient. He wasn't sure if it was a sign of Doctor Davidson's faith in his assistant's technique or simply that the man's back really was hurting from bending over the patient. Davidson would be able to stand more comfortably when his only task was cutting the ends of Fingal's stitches. Fingal felt a twinge in his own lumbar regions. He looked at the consultant, still arched, teeth bared in a grimace of pain. Just like poor old Lorcan O'Lunney. For a mischievious moment, Fingal wondered about suggesting a bog onion poultice. He bent to his work, stitching and knotting as carefully as he could so Jane Carson would be left with as unobtrusive a scar as possible. "Finished, sir," Fingal said.

"Good," said Phelim. "She's almost awake." He took the mask from her face.

Doctor Davidson cocked his head to one side and regarded the wound. "Neat," he said. "Very neat. And swiftly done. I knew I could trust you to do a good job. You do have good hands, young man."

Fingal was glad his toque and mask hid most of his blush.

"If you ever get tired of working with the old bog-trotter there —" Doctor Davidson took off his mask and grinned at Phelim, who smiled and shook his head. "Come and talk to me at the Rotunda. I'm always on the lookout for promising young trainees and I have special moneys." He arched his back again and rubbed the small of it with one hand.

I wonder, Fingal thought, watching the doctor continue to knead his back, if a trip to the massage department at Sir Patrick Dun's might help Lorcan?

17
THE LITTLE FISHES
OF THE SEA

"Morning, Archie," O'Reilly said as he went into the kitchen looking for a blouse of Kitty's that Kinky was to have ironed. "Back still behaving itself?"

Archie Auchinleck was sitting drinking a cup of tea at the kitchen table, his tweed jacket draped casually over the back of his chair. He smiled and rose. "How's about you, Doctor? The back's rightly, so it is, dead on, like, and thanks for asking."

O'Reilly took it as normal that he could at any time ask anyone in the village a specific, concerned question about their health, not the usual "How are you?" For a second he wondered about Brenda Eakin's chest. It was four days since she'd been in and she hadn't phoned nor had the hospital sent a report of her X-ray. He must assume she was no worse, possibly better, and still helping with the harvest. "Sit down, Archie," he said, "and finish your tea." If O'Reilly had heard nothing from Brenda by Monday, he decided, he'd try to drop in on her while he was out making his home visits.

Archie sat, crossed his legs, and lifted his teacup. O'Reilly noticed the way the man held the handle delicately and extended his little finger in a fair imitation of how Ma's upper-crust friends would have back in the '30s. "I just popped round for til see Mrs. Kincaid for a wee minute, like," Archie said.

His "poppings in" had become an almost daily event, and if it was after his milk round and Kinky wasn't too busy, the "wee minute" could stretch for quite a while. O'Reilly suspected he was going to lose his friend and housekeeper soon and yet was delighted for her. Like himself, she'd been alone for a long time. Too long.

"Lovely day out, so it is," Archie said, "but there might be rain later for I'm getting ferocious stoons in my thumb, so I am."

Archie's thumb's sudden shooting pains were regarded locally as being as good as the BBC weather forecasts, so much so that he had staunchly refused O'Reilly's offers of treatment. "Hope not," O'Reilly said. "Seeing it's Saturday and we're both off duty, Mrs. O'Reilly and I will be having an outing after lunch. What do you know about greyhounds?"

Before Archie could answer, Kinky appeared from the door of her quarters, said, "Doctor O'Reilly," beamed at Archie, and said to him, "Is your tea all right, dear?"

The "dear" was not lost on O'Reilly. Kinky had changed a lot since her surgery, and her growing attachment to Archie Auchinleck was clear to see. She seemed younger, was given to occasional moments of what he could only think of as girlish giggling. He'd been surprised by the depth and timbre of her contralto when he'd heard her singing "My Favourite Things." That she could yodel so well when she moved on to "The Lonely Goatherd" as she polished the silver had come as a total surprise to him, and he'd known her for going on twenty-six years. It looked like *The Sound of Music* had taken her fancy.

"Just a wee taste more, please." Archie held out his cup. "I often go to the oul gee-gees with Donal Donnelly, but I don't know nothing about racing dogs, sir. That's Donal's corner, so it is."

"Hmm. Just wondered," O'Reilly said happily, watching the cosy scene of domesticity.

Kinky lifted a teapot and poured, added milk, two teaspoons of sugar, and stirred the tea before handing him the cup.

"You like sweet things, Archie?" O'Reilly asked.

"In soul I do, sir. Indeed I do." He glanced at Kinky, smiled, then said, "I've never tasted nothing in my life like Maureen's raspberry

223

Pavlovas. They're sticking out a mile, so they are."

There was no greater accolade in Ulster, and Archie was right. "They are that," O'Reilly said. "Spectacular." He envied Archie, who was tall and angular. In local parlance he'd be described as being "only as fat as a hen across her forehead." He apparently could tuck into his blooming Pavlovas till the cows came home and with no apparent ill effects. Maybe it was because of the exercise he got trotting up people's drives every day carrying full bottles of milk from his electric milk float and back down with yesterday's empties. O'Reilly really missed Kinky's desserts, creamier sauces, and the magical things she used to do with the humble spud, but there was no doubt that the diet she had instituted for them after her discharge from hospital in May was finally working wonders for his waistline. Soon she'd be asking Alice Molony the dressmaker to take in the waistband of several pairs of his pants. Kinky herself must have lost at least a stone and looked much better for it.

He waited as Kinky went over to the ironing board.

Perhaps Flo Bishop was having the same success at the Bishop house? O'Reilly knew he really should call on the councillor again, but their last meeting had been less than friendly. As he had promised himself he would, O'Reilly had demanded the respect due to Doctor Jennifer Bradley be accorded by Bertie. He'd told Jenny about it and for now would let the hare sit. Fingal's visiting the councillor would not prevent another anginal attack. That was up to providence — and Bertie Bishop.

"Here it is, sir." She handed him Kitty's blouse, ironed and neatly folded.

"Thanks, Kinky."

"Could I ask you a shmall favour, sir?"

"Sure."

"Would yourself and Mrs. O'Reilly" — Kinky was always formal in front of other people — "be able to answer the phone if Doctor Bradley has to go out this morning? I need some things from Belfast and —"

"Of course."

"Archie can run me to town, can't you? It will save me having to take the smelly old 'covered wagon,' so."

O'Reilly smiled at her use of the locals' name for the one-carriage diesel train that ran from Bangor to Belfast and back with stops along the way.

"Aye, certainly," Archie said.

"And we'll be home in time for me to get lunch ready by twelve, so."

"Off you go, Kinky. We'll not be leaving for Kirkistown until one. We're meeting my brother Lars, then going to see how Donal and young Colin Brown and a certain greyhound do at an unofficial meet."

"Is it Donal's dog then?" she asked.

O'Reilly remembered the need for secrecy. "I'm not sure. I don't think it's Bluebird. He said he's finished racing her. She's a pet now." He marvelled at himself, how easily the little lie had rolled off his tongue. He'd always enjoyed a bit of intrigue — for a good cause.

She looked at him sideways, head tilted. "No matter. If Donal's racing one, that's good enough for me. I've another shmall-little favour to ask, sir. If you'll excuse me?"

He nodded.

She went to her quarters, came straight back, and offered him a ten-shilling note. "To win, for me please. Donal's dog."

O'Reilly chuckled and took the money. He already knew how fond she was of the horses, and how successful. "What have you seen, Kinky?" he asked. After all, the whole village and townland knew that Maureen "Kinky" Kincaid was fey.

"With the sight? Nothing." She lowered her voice. "But I do know Donal Donnelly." And to his surprise, she winked. "Now you run along, sir. Archie and I will get going right away, and don't worry, lunch will be on the table at twelve noon, so."

And it was.

"That smells wonderful, Kinky," Kitty said

as the Corkwoman served up grilled plaice garnished with lemon slices and parsley, green peas and mint, and boiled new potatoes, limiting O'Reilly to one spud. The peas and herbs had been grown in the back garden.

"I'm sure the fish is fresher than anything I used to buy in a Belfast fishmonger's."

"I bought it on my way home," Kinky said. "Archie drove me to the sea wall on the Shore Road. There's a local fisherman, Jimmy Scott, you know him, Doctor O'Reilly."

"I do indeed," Fingal said, thinking about how the man had had a nasty bout of contact dermatitis last spring that only cleared up when Doctor Hall, the dermatologist at the Royal, was able to identify the cause. Jimmy was sensitive to the zinc in the pieces he bolted round the propellor shaft once a year. Because of a peculiar electrolytic effect that O'Reilly didn't quite understand, the salt water tended to corrode the quaintly named "sacrificial anodes" rather than the boat's propellor shaft and the propellor.

"Jimmy goes out into the lough at the crack of dawn and he's usually selling from the sandstone slabs on the top of the wall by eleven. I bought a string of six, so that's your ones and three more for Archie and myself too, that we'll have for our tea this evening."

Damn it, O'Reilly thought, the man's practically moved in here — he smiled — and

227

I'm delighted for Kinky.

"That's what I mean by really fresh," Kitty said.

"You'll get none fresher than Jimmy's unless you cook them on the boat, so." She smiled and said softly to herself, "There's nothing better than a herring straight from the sea, gutted, dipped in flour, and thrown straight into butter in a pan on the galley stove. When you're married to a fisherman, you can do that. I remember it well." O'Reilly heard no sadness in her voice. He was gladdened that after all these years she was able to let go of her drowned husband, Paudeen. He knew how she'd felt about the loss in the past.

"Thank you, Kinky," Kitty said. "Ouch." Lady Macbeth was standing on her hind legs, front paws on Kitty's thigh, tensing to leap onto her lap, clearly attracted by the smell of the fish. She pushed the animal away. "You're sweet, your ladyship, but you've got very sharp claws and you'll ladder my stockings."

Kinky scooped the animal into her arms. "You come with me now, you wee dote, and leave the doctors and Kitty in peace. I'll find you a nice bit of plaice skin later, so."

"Aaaargow," said Lady Macbeth, who had long ago learned, as is the way with felines, that the big, comfortable Kinky Kincaid had been placed on this earth primarily to minister unto the needs of one small white cat.

"I'd wager," said O'Reilly, "that you'd be hard-pressed to work in a practice that feeds you half as well, Jenny."

"I think," she said, smacking her lips and keeping her fork hovering over a now half-destroyed plaice, "if the *Michelin Guide* gave stars for home cooking, Mrs. Kincaid would be top of the list. You are a very lucky man, Fingal. You've Kitty, the marvellous Kinky, and apart from the odd snag, you run the best practice a young doctor could hope to work in."

Fingal stopped in mid-chew. Snag? He looked at her. She was obviously enjoying her lunch, looked relaxed and happy and, if he wasn't mistaken, was possibly teasing him a little. He liked that. But he knew what she meant. "Are you still having trouble?" He hadn't been able to observe anything first-hand. After a very short time showing her the ropes, Fingal and Jenny had worked independently, just as he and Barry had when the young lad started. She'd not said anything to him lately about any difficulties she might be having, although he knew very well about Brenda Eakin's and Bertie Bishop's opinions.

"Not enough to bother anybody with."

"Sure you don't want to tell us?" Kitty asked.

Jenny seemed to be deciding what to say and O'Reilly knew that Kitty was wise enough to let the young woman take her time.

Jenny Bradley in her own way was becoming part of the Number One Main Street family — and O'Reilly liked that. In the couple of months she's been here, Jenny had dined often with him and Kitty and, in Jenny's own words, liked to "help them watch TV" if there was something worth watching. Jenny had become very good about giving Arthur his walks when O'Reilly was busy, and often, if he came home early in the afternoons, he'd find her in the lounge curled up with Lady Macbeth on her lap reading J. G. Ballard or Ray Bradbury or Isaac Asimov, her favourite science fiction authors. There wasn't much for youngsters here if she went out. She was a golfer, liked to swim in Bangor's saltwater Pickie Pool, had tickets to the symphony for the next season, and had her own circle of younger friends up in Belfast. And he'd begun to suspect, by the number of calls from a Terry Baird, that she had a boyfriend too.

And she was careful not to intrude too much on O'Reilly and Kitty's privacy. When they were together as two off-duty doctors, it was like the old navy mess ashore. "Talking shop," discussion of professional matters, was taboo. He could understand why she'd said nothing.

She set her napkin on the table and said, "I'm not complaining, Fingal. Simply letting you know. My father used to tell me and my big brother, Stanley, 'You're both big enough and ugly enough to look after yourselves.' "

"I've never seen your brother," Kitty said with a laugh, "but I'd hardly call you ugly." O'Reilly looked over at Jenny in her open-necked white silk blouse and red Stewart tartan mini-kilt, as bright and pretty as a rosebud.

"Thank you." Jenny laughed. "Figure of speech. Dad had his sayings . . ."

Just like my father, O'Reilly thought.

". . . and he wanted both of his children to be able to fight their own fights. I truly appreciate you speaking to Councillor Bishop, Fingal, he was the worst, but I've met men like him before. He's not going to change his mind."

O'Reilly nodded. "You may be right."

"I am. It'll take a miracle. And if you're not here and he has more angina — which he will sooner or later — I'll look after him whether he likes it or not."

"Good for you." O'Reilly clenched a fist and waggled it in a gesture of encouragement.

"And I do understand why some of the other customers want to see you — it's a question of comfort with the familiar. I know it takes time to build trust. I've seen it in other practices."

"Exactly what I thought when I saw Brenda Eakin on Tuesday. She wanted to see me, but they're not all like that. They can't be." He sliced off another piece of fish. "Just how bad is it?"

She shrugged. "It's only a few folks — funnily enough, mostly women — but it's been that way since I started seeing patients years ago." She took a long drink of water. "They'll get used to me. I'll not get a better job anywhere. I mean that. And if Barry doesn't want to come back —"

"The job's yours." O'Reilly had made his decision with barely a thought. She was a damn good doctor, he knew because he'd seen a lot of her patients in follow-up, and he admired her feisty attitude. "And whatever I can do to help."

She smiled. "Thank you. Thank you very much, but there's another thing my dad used to say when we were little: 'The Lord helps those who help themselves.' "

"Wrongly thought to be biblical," O'Reilly said, "frequently attributed to Hezekiah, King of Judah, who defeated Sennacherib, the King of Assyria, somewhere around 700 BC if anyone's interested."

"Not really," said Kitty, and laughed, "but we know it amuses you." She puckered a pretend kiss.

"You wait, Mrs. O'Reilly." He puckered up himself, then said, "Pay no attention to us, Jenny. You keep plugging away. I'll do what I can, and we'll have to wait for Barry's decision." If he wanted to come back, having to let Jenny go was going to make Fingal O'Reilly very uncomfortable.

Kitty looked at her watch then at O'Reilly. "Come on, Fingal. Time's moving. Eat up and let's get going."

Jenny grinned, raised an eyebrow, and said, "And if anybody is looking for you both while you're away I'll tell them that Doctor and Mrs. O'Reilly are — going to the dogs."

18
THE CLOUDS YE
SO MUCH DREAD

"Come on, Kitty. Let's get going," Fingal said as she locked the door to her flat on Leeson Street. He took her hand. "We've to be at Bob Beresford's at one thirty if we're going to get out to the course for the first horse race. He'll go daft if we're late and make him miss the two thirty." And, he thought, I'll be very happy to get into the bar tent for a pint or two. He grinned. "Never mind old Omar Khayyám and his loaf of bread and jug of wine and thou beside me in the wilderness. I'm up for a pint of stout, a big *cruibin,* and thou beside me at the paddock." He kissed Kitty and she kissed him back.

"Behave yourself, Fingal Flahertie O'Reilly," she said, and pretended to slap his face. "And I don't like stout." She smiled up at him from under her eyebrows. "But if you're as sweet to me as Bob usually is, I'll let you buy me a chicken sandwich and a glass of claret."

"To you? I'll be sweet as honey." He swung

their hands in exaggerated arcs like a couple of schoolkids might and grinned as she laughed.

They'd strolled to the corner and turned onto Fitzwilliam Place in the sunny August afternoon, surprised by the number of pedestrians hurrying in the same direction. "Busy today," he said. "They'll be heading for Ringsend or Sandymount. It's only a couple of miles from the middle of the Liberties. Lots of those folks go to Ringsend on weekends to watch the Gaelic football, kick a ball around, row, or swim in Dublin Bay. It's the poor man's Lido."

"I'm not so sure," she said. "A lot of the men are wearing blue shirts and dark ties."

"Maybe supporters of some club?"

"I don't think so, Fingal. They could be Blueshirts." She sounded concerned and was frowning deeply. "I wonder what they're up to? Maybe there's to be a meeting of some sort?"

"No idea." He'd known of the organisation formed from men who'd fought on the Irish government's side in the 1921–22 Civil War. They'd called themselves the Army Comrades Association and in imitation of Hitler's Brownshirts and Mussolini's Blackshirts had chosen to wear the colour blue. They gave the Roman salute and flirted with Fascism, but they were mostly anti-Communist and pro–Catholic Church. "They pretty well

235

folded up in 1933," he said. "I think they amalgamated with some other small groups and formed Fine Gael, one of the new political parties." And that was enough about that. The last thing he wanted today was to become involved in anything political. He agreed wholeheartedly with Phelim Corrigan's opinion of politicians. A curse on all their houses. "Do you know," he said, itching to tell her about something that had been at the forefront of his mind for days, "I saw something astounding last week that could have come straight out of a Victorian novel. Much more interesting than a bunch of eejits in pretty shirts."

"What?"

"You're a nurse. You've seen diptheria."

"Yes. Bad cases in kids are horrid. Poor wee mites." She tightened her grip and stopped him from swinging their hands. "Gasping for breath. Scared skinny."

"Phelim says we're seeing a lot less because we've had a vaccine since the early '20s."

"And that's a very good thing," she said.

"But kids do still get infected. Some mothers refuse to have them immunised. We saw one last Tuesday. Sick as a dog. You know how in bad cases a membrane forms over the larynx and upper trachea and blocks the airway?"

"I've only seen it once."

"Me too, and it reminded me of that scene

in *Tom Brown's Schooldays* where the head-master saved the life of a boy who was badly afflicted, but at risk of his own."

She stopped walking, forcing him to stop. "How?"

They stood like a small rock as the tide of pedestrians swept by.

Fingal smiled to himself. He'd certainly got her interested and clearly willing to drop the subject of political rallies.

"The mother brought the wee boy to the surgery. I made a diagnosis, gave him anti-toxin just the way they'd taught me, but he couldn't breathe, he was cyanosed and getting bluer. I didn't know what to do." He'd been terrified. "The next step was a trache-otomy, but I've never done one."

"It must have been awful for you too," she said. "I know how helpless nurses and doc-tors can feel. What did you do?"

"I got Phelim from next door. I've never seen anything like it. He didn't hesitate. He had me hold the kiddy tightly, grabbed a thin metal tube, put it into the boy's mouth, God knows how far into the throat one end went, and then he started to suck on the other end."

"Dear God," she said, her eyes wide. "Suck?"

"It was a repeat of the novel's scene. After a minute or two he pulled out the tube and there was a sheet of grey membrane hanging off its end." Fingal recalled the moment with absolute clarity. "And the wee lad was hauling in great whoops of breath and the blue colour was leaving his cheeks."

"That is astounding," Kitty said.

Fingal nodded. "Phelim Corrigan, in my opinion, saved that boy's life at no small risk of infecting himself. But the incubation period's two to four days so he's out of the woods now."

"And you admire what Phelim did, don't you, Fingal?" she said quietly.

He nodded. "Phelim's the kind of doctor I want to be. Always, always puts his patients first."

"I wonder," she said, and he detected a wistful note in her voice, "if that's why he never married?"

"I've no idea," he said, and to bring a smile to her face, added, "and once the kiddy was clearly going to be all right, do you know what he did?"

"No."

"He gave the mother a bollicking for not having had the child vaccinated, and to make his point — and he's very good at pretending to be angry — he ripped off his toupee and hurled it across the room. He's bald as a coot. I nearly ruptured myself trying not to laugh." And to Fingal's delight the thought must have hit Kitty's funny bone. She dissolved into helpless laughter. When she'd pulled herself together, she finally managed to say,

"I love the way you make me laugh — and I love you, Fingal O'Reilly." Not waiting for a response, she started walking, bringing Fingal along with her.

As they continued up Fitzwilliam Place East he rattled on about the other interesting cases he'd seen since they'd last been together two weekends ago. Juggling his on-call schedule, her often unpredictable off-duty times, and catching up on sleep, often took a bit of doing. Ma needed to be kept company too, although she seemed to be brightening. She was talking about selling the house on Lansdowne Road and moving to Portaferry to be near Lars.

As Fingal and Kitty neared Merrion Square, she pointed ahead. "Hang on a minute please, Fingal. I'm sure we've plenty of time and I do want to see what's going on over there."

"It sure as hell is something." As they passed the east side of Merrion Square Park, it was clear to Fingal where the crowd was going. The lawns were filling up. In the mid-'30s, Dublin was frequently the scene of political rallies with parties forming, dissolving, reuniting in different configurations. Not his cup of tea. He'd been too busy studying for years and now was fully occupied and enjoying working.

Fingal and Kitty arrived at the crossroads where Merrion Square South continues as

Mount Street Upper. For a moment he spared a thought for Jane Carson in her big house there. She'd had her surgery nearly three weeks ago, had made a remarkable recovery, and only two days earlier, he and Phelim had stopped taking it in turns to make daily visits. One of them would call in in a week or so. Fingal had discovered that he and her husband, Robin, shared an interest in rugby football. Decent chap, Robin. He and Fingal had taken sherry together in the drawing room.

He was distracted by a roar of cheering and deafening applause coming from the throng gathering in the park. More political haranguing was about to start, not something that appealed, but Kitty was tugging at his hand. "Fingal, please. I want to hear."

He glanced at his watch. "All right," he said. "We can afford ten minutes." In truth he would find it nearly impossible to deny her anything. "But I think we should move along to the north side of the square. We'll be able to hear better there, and it's closer to Bob's flat. Look." He pointed to a raised platform against the hedge halfway along the park's north boundary. On each side of the dais, loudspeakers were mounted on poles, and a lectern stood in the middle facing into the park. From one pole flew a blue flag with a red Saint Andrew's Cross.

"Good Lord," said Kitty. "That's the old

flag of the Army Comrades Association. They are Blueshirts. I was right."

Fingal and Kitty turned left and walked along with the park to their left, the four-storey redbrick terraces behind low wrought-iron railings to their right. Judging by the number of drawn curtains, most of the wealthy Merrion Square folks were not interested in the doings across the road. A few faces peered out of open windows.

"We're nearly at Bob's place," Fingal said, and stopped, "but you know if we go further and turn left again we'll be on the same street where Arthur Wellesley, the Duke of Wellington, was born. May the first, 1769. Dublin is steeped in history to her marrow."

"And we're seeing history over there." Kitty pointed at the park. "It's filled with Blueshirts. William Butler Yeats lived on Merrion Square too, you know, and he wrote marching songs for them. He thought they were true Irish patriots."

"I like his poems.

Two girls in silk kimonos.
Both beautiful, one a gazelle.

You're my gazelle."

"Fingal. Thank you." Her smile was radiant, but very quickly she turned back to look at the park.

Fingal could see the official party mounting

the dais. A Tannoy loudspeaker buzzed and whistled, then a man wearing a blue shirt, dark tie, and dark beret stepped forward and stood at attention before a microphone. He tapped it with his finger, making loud clicks.

Silence fell.

"Good afternoon," he said, his words amplified and tinny. "My name is Patrick Belton, I come from County Longford, I fought with Michael Collins, God rest his soul, and I've been in prison for my beliefs in a free Ireland."

The crowd applauded, whistled.

"Although never a Blueshirt myself, I wear their uniform today in admiration of what they stood for and in sympathy with their cause, which I believe will become our cause." He gave a Roman salute by raising his right arm stiffly at forty-five degrees from his shoulder, and was instantly imitated by all the blue-shirted men in the audience.

Fingal flinched, so loud was the cheering, and he shuddered. He'd seen Pathé newsreels of Nazis and Italian Fascisti. And to see the same salute, here in Ireland? Appalling. Fingal remembered a scrap of conversation he'd overheard in Davy Byrnes pub a few weeks ago. "Blueshirts? Fellah called Eoin O'Duffy used to be in charge. Strutting round giving each other straight-arm salutes. Maybe O'Duffy'll come back and lead dem to Spain to fight if dere is a war." Was that what this was about?

When the noise faded, Belton continued. "Before getting on with the business of this meeting, I call on Father Eamon O'Sullivan to bless us and our deliberations." He stood aside and a robed cleric in cassock, stole, and biretta stood before the microphone, raised his right arm above his head, fist closed and the index and middle finger extended.

The crowd knelt.

Fingal, out of respect, bowed his head while Father O'Sullivan intoned a blessing and finished, "*In nomine Patris, Filii, et Spiritus Sancti* . . . Amen." His Latin was not improved by his thick Kerry accent.

He was answered by a chorus of amens and stepped aside to be replaced by Belton. "My friends," he said, his voice reverberating from the speakers, "as you all know, a civil war has been raging in Spain since the seventeenth of July."

The crowd communally drew in its breath. So, Fingal was right. This was about the war in Spain. It was hard not to know about it. It was never out of the headlines.

"Come on, Kitty," said Fingal. "It's none of our business."

The Tannoy continued distorting Belton's speech, which quavered as he spoke about massacres of clerics in Spain by troops of anti-Catholic government forces.

Fingal tugged at Kitty's hand. "Come on,"

he repeated. "I've had enough." He started to walk. "I want no more discussions of war on such a lovely afternoon."

"I agree, but . . ." She had to step aside to avoid a boy in a brown uniform riding a bicycle with a full wicker basket slung on the handlebars. A metal plate on the frame announced, *Beirne's Butchers. Fine meats and poultry. We deliver.* Fingal knew the lad's wage for delivering choice cuts of meat to the big houses on Merrion Square was five shillings a week.

He waited for Kitty outside Bob's door.

She held up a hand. "Fingal, before you ring the doorbell —"

"What?" He knew he sounded curt, but he was hoping she'd leave matters alone now. The prospect of a day at the races with his old friend Bob Beresford and Kitty was far more enticing than an afternoon spent trying to solve the world's problems.

"No," she said. "I'm going to say what I have to, Fingal."

He sighed. "Go ahead." This was an entirely new side of her and not one he was sure he liked.

"I don't care about the politics in Spain. I worry about something else. You were upset by one boy with diptheria, rejoiced that Doctor Corrigan was able to save his life."

"True."

She pursed her lips. "The city of Badajoz

fell to the Nationalists last Friday. They rounded up hundreds of defenders and locked them in, of all places, the bull ring. By reports coming out of Spain, they were machine-gunned, bayoneted. We don't know how many were killed." There was a catch in her voice, a glistening at the corner of her eyes. "I can't help wondering . . . how many children have been left without parents. I keep thinking about them, about the orphans, about who looks after them?"

The Tannoy intruded, "— we must support the Spanish government forces because they are our Spanish Catholic brothers and sisters against the forces of evil. We will form a committee to be called the Irish Christian Front. Who is with me?"

"Shut up," he muttered.

"Fingal." Kitty took a pace back.

He shook his head. "No, Kitty, not you. I understand how you're feeling. I do. It's the loudspeaker. I just don't want to hear any more. Not today." He hadn't a clue what to do to comfort her. It pained him to see the woman with whom he'd fallen in love concerned so fiercely with a matter over which neither of them had the slightest control.

"They're going to need nurses —"

"What?" Fingal's eyes widened. "Kitty, you don't mean —"

"No," she said. "No, I'm not going to volunteer. Don't worry, but . . ." She sighed.

"All those children. God have mercy."

A cloud must have crossed the sun because a shadow fell over Merrion Square, and when Fingal, seeking refuge from the blaring loudspeakers, the mindless cheering of the mob — and from Kitty's sadness that he couldn't take away — pushed the bell of Bob's flat, it wasn't with his customary cheerful jab.

19
LIKE A DOG HE HUNTS IN DREAMS

"I liked Jenny's *craic* about us going to the dogs today, Fingal," Kitty said, and chuckled. "That girl's sense of humour can be very dry." She settled farther back into the passenger seat. "Donal Donnelly and young Colin Brown and an 'unofficial' greyhound? Quite the combination."

"She's a good head, Jenny. And Donal? You'd never know the minute with that one. Unpredictable as a feather in a hurricane."

O'Reilly'd had to slow down to get through the town of Kircubbin, which was often busy on a Saturday. But he was intent on making up time on the last few miles to the disused military airfield at Kirkistown where the unofficial greyhound racing was to be held. "I'm dying to see what Donal's up to this time with that dog with no name."

"No name? I thought the dog's name was Bluebird. We saw her the day we went to visit the new baby, didn't we?"

"We did and it was, but not today. You see,

Donal is —"

"Don't —" said Kitty, raising her hand. "Don't tell me. I don't want to know." She rolled her eyes at O'Reilly and chuckled. "I have a feeling the less I know the less I will have to conceal, and I've never been a good liar. You'd think I should be as used to Donal Donnelly's antics by now as you. Remember when he was a patient on my ward in April? Three days after surgery and he was running card schools and trying to make book on the time the tea trolley would arrive. He bribed the tea lady, you know, to come at two thirty-seven on the button, not her usual three o'clock."

"So that's how he was sure he was going to win. I'll be damned." O'Reilly chuckled, changed down, and took a sharp right-handed bend. The tyres screeched. He raced the car up the face of a small hill, one of the many drumlins that studded County Down, crested the rise, and for a brief moment became airborne before touching down with a shuddering of the suspension.

He felt her hand on his arm. "Fingal. Slow down. I nearly lost my lunch."

"Sorry, love." He eased his foot on the accelerator and let ten miles an hour bleed away.

"Thank you."

They settled into a companionable silence. He glanced up. Overhead, a low cloud, darker

248

than the grey cumulus behind it, had rolled in from the west. A ragged vee of geese, too large to be Brent so probably very early winter migrant Greylags down from their breeding grounds in Spitzbergen, were flying from his left to right. He knew they would be crossing nearby Strangford Lough and heading for one of her many grassy islands strewn carelessly like green confetti on a ruffled blue gown. A series of harsh *ho-onks* drifted in on the light westerly coming through his open window. "Greylag," he said, their cries confirming his suspicions.

"That's nice," she said, "but please concentrate on driving."

O'Reilly smiled. Kitty was a decent driver herself. He'd noted this on the few occasions when he'd been driven by her in her tiny Mini. But she was a little too cautious for his tastes.

He looked ahead. The narrow road was empty, not a vehicle in sight. Beneath the stubby blackthorn hedges, fuchsia bushes, and dry stone walls, the grass of the verges looked tired after a long summer. They were studded with yellow tansy and purple common mallow. The lowing of a herd of Friesans in a pasture was punctuated by two sharp bangs. He glanced right and saw the skein of geese flare and with frantic wingbeats claw for altitude. Not a bird fell so the wildfowler had missed with both barrels.

O'Reilly smiled. He enjoyed wildfowling but was always happy for the ones that got away. "The season's been open since last Wednesday, September the first. I'll maybe get a day out with Arthur soon." The big dog had been left at home today. Jenny loved walking him and the beast had taken an immediate liking to her. No need to risk him getting embroiled in a fight with one of the highly strung racing dogs when he was in good hands at home.

"How about the Saturday after next when Jenny's on call again? It's time I looked for some outlets up here for my paintings. There's a group that was founded eight years ago by a Gladys MacCabe, the Ulster Society of Women Artists. They're having an exhibition. I'd like to go, perhaps join so I can get a venue to exhibit here in the north. I'd still sell my work through Dublin, but USWA could be a good *entré.*"

O'Reilly slowed, made the left turn onto the Rubane Road, accelerated, and said, "Fair play to you. Bloody marvellous idea. Now hang on, it's only about another mile." He climbed a gradual slope. The Ards peninsula, from the Irish *ard* meaning high ground, was about three miles across and stretched from the Irish Sea to Strangford Lough. The airfield was at the top of the plateau and had been an RAF satellite of the main aerodrome at Ballyhalbert on the east coast. After the Battle of Britain it had housed 504 Squadron's Hurricane fighters before becoming a Naval Fleet Air Arm Station called HMS *Corncrake II.*

"Here we are," he said, turning left onto an access road. Up ahead he could see many vehicles parked in a field. "We'll nip in there," he said, and tried to, but the way was closed by a five-bar gate manned by a large man wearing a duncher, brown grocer's coat, and a leather satchel slung over one shoulder. O'Reilly spoke through the open window. "Yes?"

The man tugged at his duncher and said, "Two adults, two quid and ten bob for the parking, sir, so it is."

"King's bloody ransom," O'Reilly said, fishing out three notes. "Here."

The man stuffed the money into his satchel, opened the gate and, as O'Reilly passed, pointed to the end of a row of cars. "Put you her fornenst thon blue Ford Consul. Reverse in. It'll be easier for til get out after, like."

The car bounced over the ruts.

"That's one of the new E-Type Jaguars," Kitty said, pointing to a low-slung, long-nosed, British-racing-green painted sports car. Large glass-covered headlights were recessed into each wing, and the driver and passenger accommodation was well to the rear under a curved hard top.

"Is it? Racy-looking yoke," O'Reilly said, "very sporty, and by all that's holy, the fellah getting out of it is my brother, Lars." O'Reilly stopped, stuck two fingers in his mouth, and let go a whistle that would have done the locomotive of the Belfast to Dublin Enterprise train proud.

Lars turned, saw the Rover, and waved.

"Be with you in a minute," O'Reilly yelled, moved on, and parked. "Come on," he said, opening Kitty's door.

The turf underfoot was springy, and he took her hand and led her to where Lars Porsena O'Reilly stood beside his motorcar.

"Kitty. Finn. Great to see you. You're both looking well."

"Thank you." Kitty inclined her head.

O'Reilly admired her raven hair with its silver tips tucked in under a silk headscarf. "You look fit and well yourself, brother," O'Reilly said. "New chariot?"

Lars grinned. "My little extravagance. I bought her secondhand from a client." He stroked the bonnet gently and said, "She's a late '64 Series I, four point two litre, six cylinder, XK6 engine —"

"Lars." Fingal held his hands in supplication. "Have mercy. I know you're daft about cars. I still remember your side-valve Morris Cowley back in '35. But I'm not sure Kitty needs all the specifications."

"Oh," said Kitty in her most innocent voice, "I have to say I prefer the two-door coupés to the convertibles, Lars. Good choice." She whistled. "Those four-point-two litre engines are quite a step up from the original 1961 production models."

O'Reilly's jaw dropped once, then a notch farther when she said, "Enzio Ferrari called the E-Type 'the most beautiful car ever made,' you know, Fingal." She turned to Lars. "You will take me for a spin in her, won't you, Lars?"

"My pleasure," Lars said. "A beautiful car for a beautiful woman."

O'Reilly shook his head, harrumphed, and fixed his brother with his best Balor glare. Dear God, the woman never ceased to amaze him. He fished out his briar, lit up, and took Kitty's hand. "Come on," he said, "to the dogs."

"How's about ye, Doctor O'Reilly?" Lenny Brown asked. "Say hello nicely to Doctor and Mrs. O'Reilly, Colin."

Colin was dressed for the important occasion in uniform blazer with the crest of Mac-Neill Memorial Primary on the breast pocket, and short grey pants above woollen stockings, one of which was crumpled round his ankle. He snatched off his school cap, grinned, and said, "Nice til see youse, sir, and Mrs. O'Reilly."

He and his father stood beside a nondescript-looking builder's van. O'Reilly noticed that there were no windows in the rear compartment.

"Hello, Colin," Kitty said. "Your foot's all better, is it?"

"Dead on," said Colin. "Healed up in no time flat." He pulled a face. "I've for til go back til school on Monday with all the other kids," then he smiled, "but I'll be in Miss Nolan's class again. She's a wee cracker, so she is." Ten going on eighteen, O'Reilly thought, but knew Sue Nolan would have no difficulty managing the little scamp. He wondered for a moment if Barry would be popping up to Ballybucklebo to see her. Might be a chance for that trip to the Duck the young man had suggested over dinner in Ballymena last month, see if he was still liking specialising. O'Reilly realised he'd let his mind wander and was forgetting his manners. "And this is my brother, Mister Lars O'Reilly from Portaferry," he said.

"Pleased til meet you, sir," Lenny said. "Grand day for the races, so it is."

"It is that," Lars said.

O'Reilly looked round. From this elevation he could see the coast, the dark waters of the Irish Sea, and in the distance the shores of Scotland's Mull of Galloway. Not a cloud in the sky. Not to the east. He turned west. The dark cloud he'd noticed on the drive up was still hanging over Strangford, and if anything, seemed bigger. It would probably blow over, although there was still the small matter of

Archie's weather-forecasting arthritic thumb. "The first race will be starting in about fifteen minutes," he said. "We want to get a good place at the finish, so if you'll excuse us?"

"Trot youse on, sir," Lenny said, and moved closer to O'Reilly. He lowered his voice. "Donal's in the van, so he is with, ahem, Buttercup."

"Buttercup? Nice name," O'Reilly said, knowing very well it was Bluebird in the van. He was aching to see the dog but knew he must be patient.

"What race will Buttercup be in?" Kitty asked.

"The second," Colin said. "My daddy'll take her til the start over thonder." He pointed across the flat ground to a narrow area of concrete. It must have been the perimeter track for taxiing to and from the dispersal hardstands during the war. He could imagine the airfield shuddering to the roar of the Hurricanes' Merlin engines, a sound O'Reilly knew from experience that once heard was never forgotten. The track ran in an oval shape round the outer border. A set of starting stalls were set up across the far limb.

"A fellah'll drive a car to pull the fake hare round the track til the finish." He pointed to a spot directly across from the start. A line drawn between start and finish would have made the racecourse look like a large concreted U. O'Reilly guessed it was about five hundred yards, twenty-five less than the distance at an official track. "And," O'Reilly could see the little lad's chest swell, "that's when I'll get ahold of Buttercup, she's well used til me, and I'll put on her leash and take her til the stewards, so I will. They always take a good gander at the winning dogs, so they do." He winked. For the second time, O'Reilly could have sworn it was a younger Donal winking. "They need til make sure there's been no hanky-panky, like."

"Indeed," said O'Reilly, struggling to hide his grin.

"How can you be sure she will win?" Lars, who was not in on the plot, asked with a frown.

Colin said, "No harm til you, sir, but a policeman wouldn't ask you that."

O'Reilly laughed. "In other words, 'Mind your own business' — sir."

"Oh," said Lars. "I see. It would appear our young friend is well versed in the power of positive thinking."

"I need to see to Buttercup for a wee minute," Colin said. "Mebbe I'll see youse all before the finish of the second. I have to come here for til be ready til collect her." He fixed Lars with what O'Reilly could only describe as a pitying smile and said, "That'll be after she's come first, you know."

20
SO WHITE! O SO SOFT.

"It's nearly twelve, Doctor O'Reilly." Phelim Corrigan stuck his head round the surgery door. His parting was running fore and aft today, but some of the strands of his toupee, which Fingal had long ago assumed was horsehair, were sticking up like the prickles of a hedgehog.

"Nearly finished, Doctor Corrigan," Fingal said. It was Saturday, September 12, and he and Charlie had been in post for nearly nine weeks. Enormously enjoyable weeks professionally, and this was Fingal's weekend on call. "These are my last patients. I'm just starting with them." He smiled at a woman of twenty who stood at the examining couch where a nine-month-old baby wearing nothing but a clean vest and a nappy lay. She'd brought him in wrapped in her shawl. "Be with you and Jack in a sec, Dympna," then he turned back to Phelim. "Shouldn't be more than ten minutes."

"I'll take over from ye then. I'll be upstairs.

Give me a call when ye go." The door was closed. Fingal got off the stool and as he crossed the floor thought how very decent it was of Phelim to agree to work from noon until tomorrow morning so Charlie and Fingal could play rugby together.

"Sorry about that," he said as he stopped at the couch and gave Dympna Dempsey a smile. "Let's start at the beginning about young Jack here? I don't suppose you're any relation to —"

"We are, sir. Jack Dempsey the boxer is me oul' one Casey's dad's second cousin." Dympna was a strong-featured woman who had obviously washed and brushed her long glossy chestnut hair before putting it up in a bun. She was wearing what was probably her best blouse and long skirt for the visit. She smiled. "We never seen him, mind you. The family moved to America. But do you remember him, sir? They called him the 'Manassa Mauler.' He was world heavyweight champion from 1919 'til 1926."

"You're related to Jack Dempsey? He was my hero when I started to box. Took the title from Jess Willard in 1919. Lost it to Gene Tunney."

"If you don't mind my asking, sir, is that why your nose is a bit out of kilter?"

"Guilty as charged." O'Reilly guffawed and his laughter made baby Jack start mewling. She picked him up and rocked him, crooning, "Wheest, wheest, wee one."

"Sorry, Jack," said O'Reilly. "And what seems to be the trouble with young Jack?"

"Well, sir, he's been getting awful gurny lately."

As if to confirm her statement, baby Jack's little noises moved up in volume to hoarse crying interrupted by sniffs and an occasional yell.

"Probably just teething," Fingal said, hoping he was going to be able to reassure the young mother.

She frowned. "He's nine months and my granny says he should have his front ones by now." She held him to Fingal. Jack screeched and as Fingal peered into the open mouth, Dympna said, "See? Toothless as a feckin' oyster."

Fingal frowned. By nine months the lower central incisors and the upper central and upper lateral incisors and even the lower lateral incisors should have, in correct medical terminology, erupted.

"And I could wash his nappies in the sweat coming off his poor wee head."

That wasn't simple teething. Jack's mother had lost a tooth, often a sign of poor diet. "Where do you live?"

"Back Lane off High Street," she said.

Probably subsisted on the usual appalling diet, and hardly ever saw the sun. A diagnostic idea was beginning to germinate, and her ad-

259

dress had made him wonder about something else. As Fingal began to examine the baby's head, he said, "Do you by any chance know a fellah called John-Joe Finnegan?"

"The cooper? Got hit by a tram? Him and my Casey both have plots at Dolphin's Barn for growing spuds and a few veggies . . ."

At least, Fingal thought, they'd be getting iron from the greens.

"Casey looked after John-Joe's plot while he was in Sir Patrick Dun's."

"I saw him in hospital about a month ago. John-Joe told me someone was taking care of his allotment. That was your husband? Small world," Fingal said as his fingers noted how hot and sweaty the baby's scalp was. He gently pressed against the parietal bones situated in front of and above the ear. Fingal felt them sink and when he suddenly let go, he noticed how they snapped back into place as a ping-pong ball might if he'd handled it in the same way. That was called craniotabes and happened because the bones were unduly soft. If he was right about the diagnosis he was refining, craniotabes usually appeared in the eighth or ninth month of life of those afflicted. One or two more signs and he'd be sure. "Could you take off his vest, Dympna?"

She did, to the accompaniment of much crying.

"When did he start to sit up?"

"Couple of months ago." She frowned. "But

he doesn't crawl about much."

Babies should sit at six months, be crawling by nine, but if their back became sore from sitting, they'd find the most comfortable position and not budge. Another clue. Fingal inspected the ribs, easily visible under the pale skin of the skinny chest. Everyone from the tenements was pallid from lack of sunshine. It wasn't diagnostic, but the paleness was another hint. A series of rounded bumps ran in an arc from below each nipple to near the tip of the tenth rib halfway to the child's back. He was looking at a rachitic rosary, knobs caused by a fault in the way new bone was laid down. He'd first seen a picture of it in a most useful little textbook, *Hutchinson's Clinical Methods,* originally published in 1897. Treatments might have changed since then and more diseases could be recognised, but the signs and symptoms of many, and how to elicit and recognise them, were still useful today. "Get him dressed, Dympna, and come and sit down while I give you a note and a scrip'. I'll tell you what's wrong in a sec. And don't worry." He crossed the floor, climbed up onto the high stool, and started writing. With a bit of luck, Mister Corcoran, the apothecary, who usually worked until noon every Saturday, would still be in his room.

Dympna, with an unhappy Jack wrapped in the fold of her shawl, sat and looked at Fingal expectantly.

"I'm glad you brought him in when you did, Dympna —"

"Is it bad?" Her eyes were wide, her voice high-pitched. She snuggled Jack to her.

"Not yet."

"It's not — it's not . . ." She glanced around and lowered her voice to a bare whisper. "It's not consumption?"

"Certainly not."

"Thank the Lord Jasus." She crossed herself.

Tuberculosis was rampant and so feared in the tenements that even its name was only uttered in a whisper, and women would swear blind that their husbands were in "The Joy," the Mountjoy Gaol, rather than admit he was in the Pigeon House sanitarium at Ringsend, staffed by nuns and often the last stop for what were described as "terminal sufferers."

"He's got rickets, and you've caught it early before it gets any worse."

"Rickets? It gives people melodeon legs and funny-shaped heads, doesn't it?"

"It does," Fingal said, knowing that when fully opened, the bottom of the bellows of a button accordion, a melodeon, was markedly curved, making it an apt description of bowed legs. "And sometimes they get what we call kyphoscoliosis, but that's a fancy name for a hunched back."

"Like your man Quasimodo in that there

262

film about the one in Notre Dame in Paris? I seen it at the Carlton Cinema on O'Connell Street, but it's gettin' knocked down and a new one built." She looked down at a now-sleeping Jack and dropped a light kiss on his forehead. "What can I do, Doctor?" She smiled. "Mrs. Costello, she lives across our street, boils the backbones of skate fish and uses the water to rub on her kiddies' legs to keep them straight."

"I think we can do better than that," Fingal said, knowing that that home cure was utterly useless, but recognising that it didn't help to criticise. "Rickets," he said, "is caused because the bones need calcium. We get most of that from dairy products."

"Milk and cheese?" Her lip curled. "About as plentiful as feathers on a feckin' frog where I live."

"I know," O'Reilly said, "and we need vitamin D to help us absorb the calcium. The sun helps us make the stuff in our bodies."

"Sun? In the Coombe? The houses is so close together you'd get more feckin' light down a coal mine."

He sighed. "I know that too. And I'm sure you'll not be eating salmon and trout much either, nor egg yolks, and they all have lots of calcium too."

"Salmon's for the toffs who can afford to catch dem or spend a week's wages for the likes of me at the fishmongers."

He thought guiltily of the poached salmon sandwiches he'd left uneaten the day Doctor Davidson had operated on the now fully recovered Jane Carson.

"We do eat fish on feckin' Fridays, the church says we have til, but it's mostly herrin's or salt cod."

Neither provided the necessary nutrient. "Ah, but," he said, "there's more ways of killing a cat than drowning it in cream." He handed her a prescription, a form, and a letter. "That's for cod liver oil. It's stuffed with vitamin D and has vitamin A too. All you need to do is give wee Jack three teaspoonfuls every day. And I've put some calcium tablets there too, and if you could manage to buy some condensed milk? Not all Jack's bony changes that have already begun will go away, but it will prevent any more happening."

"Wonderful, sir. And we could stretch to a few cans of Carnation every month." She smiled. "Do you know the poem about Carnation, Doctor?"

"No."

"Carnation Milk is the best in the land," she started in a singsong voice,

Here I sit with a can in my hand
No tits to pull,
No hay to pitch,
You just punch a hole in the son of a bitch.

O'Reilly's guffaws started young Jack mewling again.

"My daddy learned that from an American doughboy in France in 1918."

"I think from what I read," Fingal said, "we're soon going to be learning more than just funny ditties from the Americans. They're a very resourceful lot." He returned to the immediate task. "Now let's get you seen to. Give the scrip' to Mister Corcoran if he's still here, or come back on Monday if you've missed him. Another couple of days won't make any difference. This here's," he handed her the form, "so Jack can have an X-ray at Sir Patrick Dun's, just to be sure I'm right." And to establish a baseline so if Jack's condition deteriorates, I can assess by how much, Fingal reasoned. "They'll send me the results. And this," he gave her the letter, "is so he can have weekly sun-lamp treatments for a month in the Light Department at Temple Street Hospital. It'll build up the vitamin D in his body too."

"T'anks very much, sir," she said. "And I know you're in a rush so we'll be going."

He slipped off the stool, bent, and picked up his hold-all full of his rugby gear. "Don't hesitate to bring Jack back if you're worried. Otherwise, take him to see one of the midwives in a couple of weeks."

"I will, Doctor."

He held the door for her and Jack and

pointed to the apothecary's hatch, which was still open. "You get the cod liver oil and calcium into him and in another twenty years maybe he'll be as good a fighter as the other Dempsey. If I'm passing Back Lane in the next few weeks I'll pop in. See how he's doing."

That brought a smile. "T'anks again. Do you know, John-Joe was right? You are a good skin, Big Fellah."

Fingal nodded, accepted the compliment, yelled up the stairs, "I'm off, Phelim," and headed for his bike. As he crossed the yard, he recognised how in a very short time he'd stopped railing about the God-awful conditions in the tenements that brought on diseases like Jack's rickets, a completely preventable disease. He thought he'd come to terms with his own role; fighting a rearguard action, patient by individual patient, and letting the city fathers get on with the necessary slum clearance. And he wasn't going to worry about it today.

Today was the first chance he and Charlie had to show what they were made of in a friendly rugby match between two carefully selected Wanderers' teams. It would test fresh club members against old stalwarts to see if the new boys should play for the second fifteen, the not-quite-excellent-yet squad, or at the highest level, the first fifteen. There was no doubt that Charlie, who was already an international player, would be picked, but Fingal would have to prove himself. When he'd asked Phelim if they could swap week-ends, the little doctor had refused. But before he could be reminded of his promise, he'd said, "We don't need to swap. I have a dispensary committee meeting Saturday morning, but I'll take over at noon for ye. Play a good game and see yer lady friend in the evening and ye do Sunday on call from nine." He'd brushed aside Fingal's thanks with a curt snatching off of his wire-rimmed glasses and a snapped, "Och, wouldn't ye do the same for me if I asked ye? Wouldn't ye? Course." A decent man, Doctor Phelim Corrigan.

Fingal pulled his secondhand Raleigh from the bike rack, slung his leg over, and pedalled away. It wasn't far, a little over two miles, to the grounds on Lansdowne Road. He joined the ranks of other cyclists, motorcars, and drays, taking pains to avoid the tram tracks. The sun, weaker now in September than it had been on some of August's sweltering days, warmed him, and inside Fingal Flahertie O'Reilly felt a warm glow too. He'd just finished another week of doing a job he loved and now he was off to pursue his other loves. Rugby with Charlie, popping home to see Ma, and an evening with the delightful Kitty O'Hallorhan. For no very good reason, he started pedalling faster and gave a great "whoop" that so startled a nearby cyclist that the man had to stop and put one foot on the ground. Fingal ignored the man's yell of "Watch where you're going, yeh feckin' big bollicks" and tinkled the bike's bell long and loud to clear other riders from his path.

21
In a Slither of Dyed Stuff

"Excuse me, sir. A wee word please?" The voice was low and vaguely familiar.

O'Reilly turned to a small, grey-bearded man with a Homburg pulled low over his grey hair and green eyes. "Yes?" To secure a good spectator's spot here at the finish line O'Reilly had left Kitty in the car park with Lars, chatting to a local Portaferry friend. Already, race-goers were jostling for positions because the first race would be starting soon. O'Reilly frowned. "Do I know you?"

The stranger grinned and exposed a set of buckteeth.

O'Reilly started. "Thundering Jasus, Donal?"

"Aye, but keep your voice down, sir. I want for til see the fun, but I don't want anybody til recognise me. Me and Bluebird's here indognito, like."

O'Reilly grinned. Was Donal making a clever play on words or was this yet another example of what Fingal, in deference to

Sheridan's Mrs. Malaprop, was beginning to think of as Donalapropisms. "Where did you get the —"

"This get-up? Aggie Arbuthnot. You know she's in the Ballybucklebo Strolling Players?"

"I saw her in *Philadelphia Here I Come* last month. They were very good." O'Reilly remembered how Aggie's usually auburn hair had been done up in a grey bun for her part as the middle-aged Madge.

"She give me a taste of gum arabic for til stick on the beard and moustache like, and what she calls a grey rinse that actors use for til put in my hair." He lowered his voice. "And she done me a special brown one for Blue — Sorry, Buttercup. Aggie says it won't hurt the wee dog and I'll be able to wash it out as soon as I get her home. A bit of a brown touchup on her face, flanks, and backside and you'd think she was a brindle, not a blue, so you would." He held a finger to his lips. "I already fooled a couple of my doggy friends when I done her up last week, said she was a new dog I was thinking of buying. And Aggie was right. The rinse washed out a treat. And Aggie?" He grinned. "That one has a mouth like a steel trap when it comes to secrets. Just like you, sir. Mum's the word, so it is."

"You, Donal Donnelly, are definitely one of a kind." With a follower in your footsteps in young Colin, O'Reilly thought.

"Och, well," said Donal, "it's only for a bit of *craic,* like. Maybe we'll make a bob or two, but sure them bookies can afford it." He turned and said, "I see Mrs. O'Reilly and your brother coming, sir, so I'll just take a wee dander, lose myself a bit in the crowd, you know. I'll see you back here for the second, but don't let on youse know me, all right?"

"Off you go," O'Reilly said, still chuckling.

"Who was that?" Kitty asked as she and Lars arrived to stand beside Fingal.

"Just one of the dog fanciers." He bent and whispered in her ear, "Donal Donnelly, but pretend you don't know."

"Know what?" She laughed.

Someone started bellowing into a handheld megaphone. "Ladies and gentlemen, the first will begin in five minutes. Five minutes."

The distorted voice took Fingal back to an August day in 1936 and a man talking over a Tannoy in Merrion Square Park about the Spanish Civil War. He banished the thoughts and paid attention instead to the goings-on on the far side of the track where handlers were putting their dogs into the starting traps.

The *bang* of the starter's pistol grabbed his attention. He looked across to the far side where eight lean dogs, each wearing a coloured numbered jacket, began tearing round the track following a stuffed hare towed by an old Morris Minor. Racing greyhounds

271

could reach top speeds of more than forty miles an hour.

The noise was deafening as the punters cheered on their dogs. He watched a black one take the lead, each stride as powerful as the sudden unleashing of a fully wound crossbow. On the top of the curve, a white dog put its narrow muzzle in front. O'Reilly decided to cheer for the black, which was challenging strongly. "Run, black dog," he yelled. "Run." Even though he'd decided only to bet on Donal's Buttercup today and had no money on this race, he still wanted the black to win, and as they came into the final straight, it nosed ahead. "Go on," O'Reilly yelled, "go on," only to subside as a fawn dog slipped past on the outside and crossed the finish line first. "Phew," said O'Reilly, well aware that his pulse was racing, "you can pack a lot of excitement into thirty seconds."

"I noticed," Kitty said. "The last time I saw you as worked up at a sporting event was at last season's Ireland, Wales rugby game."

"Didn't win that time either. Bloody Wales did, fourteen to eight."

The cheering faded. A squat man wearing an open-necked shirt and a V-neck sleeveless pullover stood beside O'Reilly. The stranger tore off his duncher and yelled as the last dog, by a wide margin, crossed the line, "Was your dam mounted by a bloody snail? You couldn't catch a flaming cold, never mind a hare. Keep going round the track. You might come in first in the second race." He turned away, ripped up his bookie's ticket, and said to O'Reilly, "That's the trouble with these here unofficial tracks. Nobody knows the dogs' form. Half of them aren't good enough to run at places like Dunmore or Celtic Park." Then he smiled. "Och, but sure I'd only five bob on. Losing it won't break the bank. Me and the missus come down from Belfast, so we did. Great way for til spend a Saturday afternoon, so it is." He turned to an equally squat woman wearing a floral dress and floppy hat. "Stay you there, Maisie. Keep our places, like. I'll go and put a few bob on a dog in the second race. Will I bring youse a shandy?"

"Aye," she said, "and don't put as much lemonade in the beer this time." She looked up and O'Reilly followed her gaze as she said, "And bring my Pac-a-Mac. I don't like the look of thon cloud."

Certainly the cloud O'Reilly had noticed earlier had grown, but it was still over the Lough, and the Ards Peninsula was bathed in sunshine.

A cheer rang out. O'Reilly looked to a roped-off area just past the finish on his side of the track. Four men wearing long brown cotton coats with red armbands stood in a tight group, one holding aloft a blackboard upon which were chalked the names and

273

numbers of the winning three dogs. He twisted it from side to side so everyone could see. O'Reilly presumed they were the stewards, though certainly not members of the Irish Coursing Club that regulated official greyhound racing in Ulster like its counterpart Bord na gCon, the Board of the Hound, did in the Republic of Ireland.

Six of the eight finishers had already been collected by their handlers. The eighth dog, number six, which according to the blackboard was called Broggle Billy and was the winner at two to one, was being led away after having been examined by one of the stewards to make sure, as Colin Brown had been at pains to point out, there'd been "no hanky-panky."

Out of the corner of his eye, he saw a streak of gold and turned to see the owner of the last-place dog chasing his animal, which was now running like a liltie across the field. The dog's burst of speed was too little, too late. Good luck to you, he thought. I hope you catch the beast — and I hope young Colin will have no difficulty collaring Buttercup after the next race.

He felt a tug on his sleeve and looked down. School cap askew, dog leash in one hand, Colin Brown smiled up at O'Reilly.

"Think of the divil and he's sure to turn up," O'Reilly said, and smiled.

"Aye. Not be long now," Colin said. "My

daddy's got Blu — Buttercup over for the start, so he has." He lowered his voice. "And thonder," he pointed to an open gate in the hedge surrounding this part of the old airfield, "my daddy'll bring the van over til there so we can all get home. I'm til take the dog for a once-over by a steward after the race." He put a finger against his nose. "And my daddy'll come up and get the prize."

"Good for you, Colin," O'Reilly said, thinking, You little scamp. "Now stay with Mrs. O'Reilly and my brother. You can wait for the race with us." He winked at Colin. "I just want to have a word with a bookie." He spoke to Kitty and Lars. "Keep an eye on young Colin here. I'm going to have a flutter for us and Kinky." Her ten-shilling note was in his pocket. "Do you want anything put on, Lars?"

Lars shook his head. "I think I'll hang on to my cash today, thanks, Finn. E-Types do cost a penny or two."

"Ladies and gentlemen," the megaphone intoned, "the second will begin in five minutes. Five minutes."

"Good luck," Kitty said. "Make sure you're back in time to see the race."

O'Reilly made his way through the crowd of strangers to where queues had formed in front of five men, each with a slung satchel. Every one had a small blackboard on an easel, and on it in chalk the names of the dogs in the second race were displayed, and their

275

odds. O'Reilly joined a line and waited his turn. There was no sign of the likes of Honest Sammy Dolan or Willie McCardle, the bookies from Ballybucklebo. In fact, he'd seen virtually no one from home.

A grey-haired, bearded punter wearing a Homburg was in the next line. O'Reilly heard him say, "Aye, Buttercup to win at ten to one. Here's a fiver," which would be nearly two weeks' wages for Donal. The dog had better win — and Donal had better not get found out.

O'Reilly stood in front of a tall, rangy man with an eyepatch over his left eye. His bowler hat was tipped at a rakish angle and he had a cigarette stuck to his upper lip. "Wot'll it be, guv'nor? Fancy one of the bow-wows?"

Good Lord. The man was English, Cockney at that by the sound of him. "Five pound ten on Buttercup to win, please."

The smile was lopsided. "Right, chum." The intonation in those two words said, "There's one born every minute." He licked the end of a stubby pencil, scribbled in a book, tore off half of the page along a perforated line, took O'Reilly's money, stuffed it into the satchel, and handed O'Reilly his half of the ticket. "The best of Donald, me old garden. Oo's next then?"

O'Reilly stuck the ticket in his pocket and headed back to where Kitty and Lars would be waiting. Donald? Garden? Cockney rhyming slang. He chuckled. Got it. Donald Duck — luck. Garden gate — mate. And folks thought the Ulster dialect hard to understand? Good thing two of Surgeon-Commander O'Reilly's sick berth attendants on HMS *Warspite* had been Cockneys and had taught him the intricacies of rhyming on occasional quiet days during the war. "All set?" Kitty asked.

"Mmm."

"See way over there, now?" Colin said. "That's my daddy and Buttercup, so it is. She's number three."

"I can see her," O'Reilly said. "It's almost time."

"Aye. I'll away on down to the judges' enclosure, so I will," Colin said. "Be ready til get her after the race."

"Just a minute," Kitty said, bending down to straighten his cap and pull up the sock that was round his ankle. "Let's have you looking your best for your big moment."

O'Reilly noticed that Donal had found a place at the finish line too. He winked at O'Reilly, who winked back.

A shadow fell over the course and O'Reilly looked up. The cloud was drifting over the Ards Peninsula on its way to Scotland.

One of the stewards in their enclosure picked up the megaphone. "Ladies and gentlemen. If I can have youse's attention? The dogs is at the start, and —"

There was the sharp crack of the pistol.

"They're off."

The Morris Minor rushed past the starting gates dragging the lure and eight dogs burst out, every muscle and sinew stretched to breaking point as they tore after. Even before the pack reached the top of the curve, O'Reilly could see the brindled Buttercup leading by a head, but a black was edging past her. "Move it, Buttercup," he roared in his best quarterdeck voice, making damn sure she'd be able to hear him over the yells of everyone else.

He glanced to see Donal ripping his hat off his head.

The dogs came closer, closer. "That's her, Kitty, the brindle in third place," O'Reilly said. "Come on Blu — Buttercup."

Maybe his yell had helped, but it was as if one of those boosters Americans used to fire their rockets into space had been ignited. Buttercup tore down the straight and crossed the finish a length ahead of the other leading dog.

O'Reilly, delighted to have won for himself and Kinky, saw Donal hurl his Homburg into the air, catch it, and start heading for the bookies. A line from the song "Kelly the Boy from Killane" flashed into O'Reilly's mind: "Fling your beavers aloft and give three ringing cheers."

"Hooray!" he roared. "Hooray! Hooray!"

278

"Look, Fingal," Kitty said, "there's Colin."

Colin was having no difficulty catching the animal. The lad proudly clipped on the dog's leash and led her to the place, not ten yards away, for one of the stewards to examine her. By the way the man was smiling, all was well. Donal's psychology — knowing that adults instinctively trust children — was going to pay off.

A lightning bolt tore to the earth silhouetting the round tower of nearby Kirkistown Castle against a sky of black, and in a second the thunder crashed and echoed. Huge raindrops came pelting down. O'Reilly ripped off his jacket and threw it over Kitty's head. "Run for the car," he said. That bloody cloud had arrived with a vengeance.

Kitty needed no further bidding and took off.

O'Reilly looked back to the makeshift paddock. "Oh Jasus," he said. As the crowd scattered, he had a clear line of vision to the field. The steward attending Buttercup was holding up a brown-stained hand and frowning. Brown drops fell from the animal's muzzle and the brown patch on her flank was leaching into the surrounding grey-blue fur. Donal had said he would easily be able to wash the rinse off the dog at the end of the day. The rain was saving him the trouble. The steward grabbed for the scruff of Colin's jacket. "C'm'ere you, you wee —"

Colin ducked, narrowly missing the man's grasp, and with Buttercup/Bluebird cantering by his side charged for where his father had parked the van and was opening the back doors.

"Go on," O'Reilly yelled. "Run."

The steward was in pursuit and gaining. He was shaking his fist and yelling, "Come back here, you little bugger. Come back."

He'd have collared Colin if a small, grey-bearded man in a Homburg hadn't managed to stick out a leg and send the steward on a slithering belly flop into the mud. Donal jumped over the man and raced after Colin and the dog.

"Go on, you-boy-yuh," O'Reilly said in encouragement, noticing that three more stewards had joined in the pursuit, a rotund one lagging behind his fellows. One of the spectators who had turned to watch yelled, "Two to one on the wee lad."

O'Reilly watched as Colin, the greyhound, and Donal charged through the open gate and piled into the van one after the other. Lenny Brown slammed the doors and rushed to the driver's seat. The van's engine started with a roar and a blast of blue exhaust smoke, and the vehicle sped fishtailing away toward the main road. O'Reilly noticed that the rear number plate had been covered in mud.

The stewards' posse reined in, clearly admitting defeat, the fat one wheezing like a

280

set of clogged bellows, and O'Reilly heard one say, "Crafty buggers. I wonder who the hell it was?" and another reply, "No idea, and we've about as much chance of finding out as hearing a fart in a tornado."

Twenty minutes later, O'Reilly, Kitty, and Lars were in the Mermaid pub in Kircubbin. Mrs. MacDowell had lit the fire and each was holding a hot whiskey in still chilled hands, having a good belly laugh at the notion that for once the biter — arch-schemer Donal Donnelly — had been well and truly bitten.

"Och well, no harm done," said O'Reilly, taking a sip. "The punters who put their cash on number three backed a disqualified dog. They were unlucky, but it happens. It's just the same as if their dog hadn't placed."

"Seems to me Donal was probably the biggest loser of the day. Didn't you see him betting five pounds?" asked Kitty. "He'll have a bit of explaining to do to Julie. I'll bet she keeps a pretty tight rein on the Donnellys' finances."

"I'm out a fiver, but I can afford it, and I'll just tell Kinky I decided not to bet so she can have her ten shillings back."

"It might teach young Colin Brown that the power of positive thinking is no match for the power of an Irish cloudburst," said Lars, taking a sip of his drink.

"It might," said O'Reilly, "but I doubt it."

22
TO PUT UP WITH
ROUGH POVERTY

Fingal fiddled with the tuning knob of the radio. The console, with its highly polished walnut veneer, stood waist-high against a wall in the lounge where he and Ma had gone for their after-breakfast tea. She sat in one of the armchairs, teacup in hand. It had become a little ritual, listening to the BBC morning news together before he left for work.

Crackles and hisses came from the Philco's pair of moving coil speakers. Father had insisted on getting the best when he'd bought it for eight pounds, a considerable sum of money. He'd wanted a set that could receive broadcasts not only from the local state-run Radio Éireann based here in Dublin, but also from the BBC.

The crackles faded and were succeeded by a series of high-pitched short pips. The BBC time signal.

"Got it," Fingal said, adjusted the volume, lifted his cup, and settled into the other armchair.

A man's precise, clipped, Oxbridge voice coming from the speaker said, "This is the BBC Home Service. Here is the news for Monday, October the fifth. Yesterday after fierce fighting, the government troops in Spain recaptured Maqueda, a town between Toledo and Madrid which fell to Generalissimo Francisco Franco's troops on September the seventeenth. This is a setback for his Nationalist armies, which have been trying to capture the capital city since August . . ."

Fingal wondered if Kitty had heard. She was still deeply concerned about events in Spain. "Lord Halifax, in a speech in the House of Lords, affirmed Great Britain's position that in company with France they would continue their policy of nonintervention."

"It is truly horrible," Ma said. "I'll never forget the Great War. I hate war." And Fingal heard vehemence in her voice he'd rarely heard before. "The British Prime Minister, Mister Baldwin, supports the League of Nations," she said, "but they seem powerless to stop the trouble in Spain. All those young people." She sighed and shook her head. "And Irish people volunteering — for both sides. Mister Eoin O'Duffy is organising an Irish Brigade to fight for Franco. Completely idiotic. You'd think there'd have been enough Irishmen killed in the War of Independence and the Civil War here at home." She shook her head.

The calm English voice continued, "In England later this morning two hundred unemployed men and their Member of Parliament Miss 'Red' Ellen Wilkinson, bearing a casket with more than eleven thousand signatures, will leave Jarrow on Tyneside to walk the three hundred miles to the Palace of Westminster in London in protest against unemployment in the shipyards. The diminutive, red-haired Miss Wilkinson and the men will be carrying banners with the slogan 'Jarrow Crusade' and will be accompanied by a harmonica band. They will stop for their first night in the town of Chester-le-Street on the River Weir . . ."

"Poor men," Ma said. "I believe eighty percent of them are out of work in Jarrow."

"Terrible," Fingal said, and their plight pricked his conscience about someone else who had lost a job. "I know you'd no luck back in September trying to help my unemployed cooper to get a job here, but I don't suppose there's anyone else you could ask, Ma?"

She frowned. "It's important to you, isn't it, Fingal?"

"It is."

She sighed. "I do have one or two contacts in manufacturing. I thought they were forlorn hopes then, but I'll make some more enquiries."

"Thanks, Ma." Fingal rose, finished his tea, and said, "I'd better be trotting on. I'm doing home visits and I'm on call tonight so I'll see you tomorrow."

"Take care, son."

As he left, he heard, "And now the weather. A deep depression over the Irish Sea will drift slowly southeast, bringing clearing skies to Northern Ireland."

"Well, did you hear w'at happened to Jingles Murphy on Saturday night?" The woman looked middle-aged but Fingal knew she was probably younger. She stood beside her friend pegging a shirt to a line hanging like a loose bowstring on a pole. It stuck nearly vertically from a ground-floor window in a row of houses where similarly festooned poles jutted from most windows.

"Go on, Enya. I'm all ears. Wa't?" Her companion smoked a dudeen, a short clay pipe, as she hung socks on her own pole.

Monday was universally washing day in the tenements, and this was a good drying day with the October sun doing its best. The depression in the Irish Sea must have moved quickly. Fingal had stopped his bicycle. He stood easily, one foot on the cobbles, the other on the far pedal. He wanted to ask directions but couldn't help delaying for a minute or two to hear the women talk.

"The feckin' bowsey got himself paralytic

on red biddy in Swift's Pub on Francis Street. Refused to go at nine thirty, chuckin'-out time as you well know, on a Saturday. He started effin' and blinding, offered to fight any man in the bar. Jingles? Dat bugger'd fight with his own toenails when he's drink taken. The publican gets hold of Garda Jim Brannigan, the biggest feckin' Peeler in the Liberties. 'Jasus,' roars Brannigan, 'I know you, you feckin' bollicks. Behave yourself.' Comin' from Brannigan, dat's usually enough to cool a scuttered gurrier down, but wa't do yis t'ink Jingles does?" She stooped and picked up a pair of patched, but well-washed knickers.

"Go on." The pipe smoker bent backward and put a hand to the small of her back.

"He swings at Jim's head."

"He never?" Her mouth opened so wide she nearly lost her pipe. "Buck eejit. Did Jim destroy him utterly?"

"Not at all, and it's true because my oul' one was there and seen it wit' his own eyes. Jim ducks, drops his paw on Jingles's shoulder, clamps on — and lifts your man about a foot off the floor. One-handed. Lifts him. Says Jim, 'I could charge you with drunk and disorderly, you bollicks . . .' My Fintan seen Brannigan's knuckles whiten as he squeezed your man's shoulder. 'I could beat the livin' feckin' tar out of you, but, Jingles?' 'Ah Jasus, put me down, sir.' He's wriggling like an eel on dry land. 'I'll be good, honest til God. Put me down. You're breakin' me bones.'

" 'You'd better be good, Jingles Murphy,' says Jim and sets him down. Oul Jingles was out of the door like a whippet with its arse on fire. W'at do yiz t'ink of dat?"

"Och, he's a sound skin, Jim Brannigan. One of the best Peelers in the Liberties. Never summons nobody unless he really has to. Settles most t'ings wit' a clip round the ears. He's a well-respected man." The pipe smoker noticed Fingal. Her eyes narrowed. "Yes? Can we help you?"

"Excuse me —" he said.

"Are you a gombeen man?"

Fingal had expected to be greeted with suspicion if not open hostility on a street in the Liberties he'd never visited before. Strangers didn't venture in here unless they were gombeen men — Irish moneylenders looking for unpaid debts.

"I'm not," he said. "I'm a doctor."

"Oh," she said, clearly relaxing. "Well, all right."

Fingal already knew that priests in their cassocks were recognised and tolerated, as were the occasional dog-collared ministers "Protestantising," that is, looking for converts from Catholicism in exchange for money. The men who worked for the Saint Vincent de Paul charity would be known and welcomed, but that was about it until the tenement dwellers got to know you.

"I'm looking for a Mrs. Dempsey. She lives here on Back Lane."

"Mrs. Dempsey? Dympna Dempsey?"

"Dympna. That's right."

Two doors up the possessions of a family — chairs, tables, pots and pans — were piled higgledy-piggledy on the street where a woman surrounded by children wept as two brawny men carried a sofa. An eviction. He realised he was fiercely clutching the grips on the handlebars, but there was absolutely nothing he could do. He made his hands relax.

"You're the Big Fellah," the woman said, taking the pipe from between her lips and pointing at him with the stem. She put a hand on her hip, grinned at him, and said, "Sure, don't our friends like Roisín Kilmartin over on Swift's Alley talk about you — you on your oul' bike working day and night? You know him, don't you, Enya?"

"Only of him, Clodagh. It's the first time I've had the pleasure," said Enya from under a straw boater adorned with a tri-colour ribbon, "and begod there is a size til you, boy. You could likely get a job as Goliat' at Duffy's travellin' circus. Or take on Jim Brannigan in a fair fight." She and the pipe smoker roared with laughter.

"Is it Jack you've come about?" Enya said when she'd collected herself. "Dympna said you was quare and nice about him, getting him artificial sunshine and all. Maybe you could get a couple of days in the Sout' of France for Clodagh here and meself?"

"France's not on prescription," Fingal said. Not here in the tenements, but the wealthy were forever rushing off to European spas and taking sea cruises for their health. "Sorry." He hesitated. He wasn't meant to breach patient confidentiality, but it seemed that these two and probably the whole street knew everything about the boy's condition. "I am looking for Jack, though," he said, and blushed with pleasure at the compliment.

"I'll tell you, Doctor," said Enya with a grin, "you'd better get a bit tougher. If you'll blush because a body said something nice, w'at the hell'll you do if you comes to see a patient and catch the likes of Clodagh in her bath on a Saturday night?"

He could feel his face getting even warmer but was saved from having to answer by two little boys emerging from an open doorway and tearing along the lane, one yelling in a birdlike shriek after the other, "Come back here, Skinny Flynn, you wee gurrier. I'm goin' to feckin' marmalize you."

"Jasus Murphy," said Clodagh, shaking her head. "The language of the feckin' young wans dese days." She turned back to Fingal, who was trying hard not to laugh. "It's six doors down on your left. First landing on your left."

"Thank you." He hesitated, then pointed to where the bailiffs were setting the sofa on the pavement. "Can nothing be done for those folks?"

"Ach," Clodagh said, "not anudder t'ing. The street's taken up collections in the pubs to pay her rent — twice — but her oul' one? Feckin' bowsey. He spent the lot on the drink — twice — and us folks here aren't made of money, you know."

He did know, and he knew of the customs of either passing the hat in the pubs for neighbours in trouble or passing a black sugar bag around to raise money for the wake before a funeral in the poor people's graveyard in Glasnevin.

"Aye, but Clodagh," Enya said, "dat one's got family in Wexford. Dey're going to take her and hers in. Dey'll be here later. It's what she told me, anyroad."

It was a relief to Fingal. "I'm glad to hear it, and thanks for the directions." He dismounted and wheeled his bike to the door of Dympna Dempsey's building.

He'd come from seeing a little boy with tonsillitis over in Ross Road, just around the corner. This could have been his last call, but as he'd cycled over to Aungier Street from home this morning the plight of the Jarrow marchers had made him resolve to go and see John-Joe Finnegan today after the home visits were done. Find out how he was managing. And it had been a month since Fingal'd promised to pop in on Dympna Dempsey. She and John-Joe lived no distance from each other.

23
He Wept Full Well

Fingal propped his bike against the crumbling, whitewashed wall of a terrace house. Moss grew in the cracks in the mortar and great flakes of whitening had peeled off to reveal the grimy, yellow, two-hundred-year-old bricks beneath. He was reminded of a colour photograph he'd seen of a leprosy case. He took his doctor's bag from a wicker basket attached to the handlebars, went through an open doorway into a dimly lit hall, and climbed a creaking, carpetless staircase. He had to step round a raggedy man sleeping on the landing. He probably had nowhere else to go. The landings and hallways of the tenements were full of what were locally called "dossers" and "knockabouts."

Fingal rapped on the door, which was immediately answered.

"Doctor, dear." Dympna Dempsey was all smiles. Her chestnut hair hung to her waist, and she carried a nappy-wearing Jack in her arms. A floppy-brimmed hat was perched on his head. "It's lovely til see you." She opened the door wide. "Come in. Would you like a cup of tea?"

Fingal shook his head as he followed her inside. "Not today, but thanks. I'm in a bit of a hurry. How's Jack?"

"Look at him," she said, holding him out for Fingal's inspection. "The cod liver oil and calcium, and the sunlamps at the Children's Hospital? You're a feckin' miracle worker, sir."

"Hardly, but he certainly seems much brighter," Fingal said, noting the boy's tan, lifting the hat, and putting a hand on Jack's head. He wasn't sweating. Good. When Fingal grasped the front sides of the head and squeezed, the bone resisted. Better. There was no evidence of the previous craniotabes, so the bones were starting to calcify properly. Fingal put the hat back.

Jack, perhaps resenting having his head squeezed, frowned and said crossly, "Da da da da da da . . ."

Fingal could see upper teeth in a mouth that a month before had been toothless.

"And watch," Dympna said. "You remember I said if I set him down all he'd do was sit?" She put Jack down on her shawl, which she'd spread like a rug on the otherwise bare, but well-scrubbed wooden floor. "He goes like a liltie now."

He took off crawling at high speed until he came to a scarred dresser that stood against a

293

wall. Above was a framed picture of Jesus holding a shining red heart, the Sacred Heart, in his left hand. Jack grabbed the side of the dresser, hauled himself upright, turned, grinned at his mother, and, looking determined, took two steps into the room. The boy then stopped, wobbled, grabbed the brim of his hat with both hands — and sat down forcibly on his bottom. His mouth opened, assumed a square shape, and he howled.

Dympna rushed to him, gathered him up, and rocked him, all the while crooning softly.

The little lad's tears stopped and after a few curt indrawings of breath, he nodded off. She kept rocking and whispered, "T'anks, Doctor O'Reilly. T'anks very very much." She dropped a kiss on Jack's forehead.

"My pleasure. You just keep giving him his medicine, Dympna, and you know where to find us if you're worried about anything." Fingal said the words softly, bending to look at the little face, the rosebud mouth, the thin black hair. Seeing the love in Dympna's eyes for her son, rendered, for that moment at least, the bareness of the room, the man sleeping on the landing, and the all-pervasive tenement smells unimportant. Suddenly it didn't seem to matter. "Take good care of him." Fingal turned. "I'll see myself out."

He stuck the bag back in the basket and cycled off whistling "It Ain't Necessarily So," a big hit last year. And why shouldn't he be cheerful? He'd been working full time here for only three months and already was recognised and treated with affection by the people he served. Seeing Dympna and Jack was simply good for the soul. Sure, there were a lot of things like TB, syphilis, and many other infections that he and his profession were virtually powerless to help. But how lovely it was to effect a complete cure, assure a child a life free from bandy legs, a hunchback, and in the case of little girls a pelvis so misformed that when they grew up, normal deliveries were impossible. And to do it with things as simple as fish liver oil, calcium, and artificial sunshine. It was like a miracle, but a miracle based on painstaking research. He pictured Bob Beresford, a lit Gold Flake cigarette in one hand, the other adjusting the focus of a microscope, and wondered how his inquiries into the effects of red prontosil on *Streptococci* were going. He'd be seeing Bob on Saturday and would ask him then.

Fingal turned onto the busier, much wider High Street and as he looked for number ten, sang,

. . . he fought big Goliath who lay down
   and dieth
Little David was small, but Oh my . . .

It was probably Enya's teasing him about his height that had brought the song to mind.

He stopped, pushed his bike over the curb, across the pavement, leant it against the wall, and went into number ten. John-Joe had said he lived in the front parlour. Fingal knocked on the door and heard an uneven tread and the door opening.

"Doctor O'Reilly," John-Joe said. "W'at brings you here, sir? Come in. Come in." His sleeves were rolled up and his forearms covered in soap suds.

Fingal followed into what in the old Georgian house's glory days had been a spacious front parlour. There was much more room here than in Dympna's single front. "I knew it was time for you to have been discharged so I thought I'd drop by. See how you were."

John-Joe held up his arms. "I hate bein' idle. Ailish is out up O'Connell Street cleaning in Clery's department store, the chisslers are wit' the neighbour's granny. I had for til go to Sir Patrick Dun's for my last X-ray. Mister Kinnear says he can do no more for me. I'm fixed . . ."

"I'm glad to hear that," Fingal said.

John-Joe pulled up his trouser leg. "You can see for yourself it's not quite straight, but I'm gettin' about grand. No more crutches. Not even a walking stick. I'm just a bit gimpy." He laughed then said, "I'll not be winning any races like your man Jesse Owens at the Olympics in Berlin back in August."

Fingal could see the deformity and swelling, but for an ankle that had been so badly smashed, Mister Kinnear at Dun's had done a fine job. And he admired John-Joe for being able to accept his handicap with such seeming good humour.

"I'm home about an hour, but I thought I'd leave the kiddies a while longer and get a bit of peace 'til I get the washin' done." He nodded to a galvanised tub full of sudsy water. A corrugated washboard stood at one side. A pile of recently washed clothes was stacked on the shelf where the tub sat. He grabbed a towel and said, "It's woman's work, but it gives me something to do. Have a pew, sir. I'll just dry meself."

"I will." Fingal sat on a simple wooden chair, one of four that surrounded a plain wooden table. He noticed how the front bow windows shone and had curtains. An old Welsh dresser against one wall was decorated with Delft plates, and a plaster statuette of the Blessèd Virgin stood on the dresser's top. At the far end of the room, a double mattress lay on the floor against the wall. It was covered by an eiderdown. Not a typical tenement room by any means, but then John-Joe had had a trade. Fingal fished in his pocket. "Are you still smoking?"

John-Joe shook his head. "The oul' doh-ray-mi's a bit tight. I had til quit, but some days I'd still kill for a feckin' fag." He limped over and took a chair opposite Fingal.

297

Fingal left the ten Woodbine where they were in his pocket. "So you're sure you're getting around all right on that ankle?" he said.

"I am, Doctor. And God bless you for bein' dere the day I got banjaxed. I owe you one, sir. Can I get you a cup of tea?" The man's smile was open, wide.

"It's our job," O'Reilly said, warming to the man. "Tea? Not at the moment, but thanks."

"Dat's all right. And if you don't mind me saying, sir, you have a job. Not like some."

"No luck?" Fingal was glad he'd asked Ma to try to help, but he had no intention of telling John-Joe unless there was something concrete to offer.

"Not yet, sir, and it's not for want of trying. I applied at Beamish's and Murphy's breweries in County Cork, two Dublin distilleries, Jameson and Powers, and Paddy in County Cork, and even Bushmills up in the Wee North." He sighed. "Not a feckin' sausage."

"And you'd've been willing to leave Dublin," Fingal said. "Uproot and go? Even up north?"

"Sir, if I'd the money I'd get on a feckin' steamer and try America, but, och." He stared at the tabletop.

"I'm impressed," Fingal said.

John-Joe straightened his shoulders, looked

298

straight into Fingal's eyes, and said levelly, "Doctor, I know most of the men here are out of work, but my da, and him a cooper by trade too, God rest him, he brung us up that if a man married it was his job to provide."

Which was highly unusual, Fingal thought. He remembered a conversation he'd had with a sixty-year-old female patient. "The men've no feckin' responsibilities," she'd said with resignation. "The men are the *men*. Everything has to be done for dem." And he knew it was how things were in tenement Dublin. "I think your da was right, John-Joe," Fingal said, and he wondered if he could do anything else. "If you don't mind me asking, how are you managing?"

John-Joe sighed. "Well, dere's Ailish's wages, and the Relief does come on Wednesday, though it breaks her heart to take it. Monday's not only washday here, it's trip to uncle day . . ."

John-Joe smiled. "Him as runs the people's bank — the pawnbroker."

"I know," Fingal said. "I found out about that when I first started working here."

"I've given up the fags and I only have one pint of porter a week, on Saturday."

Two big sacrifices for a Dubliner, Fingal knew.

"We won't use a Jew-man, although most folks round here have one."

Fingal had learnt that there were many of

299

the race who were moneylenders or rag-and-bone men who'd buy used clothing, rags, old bones, just about anything they could resell at a profit. The term was universal in the tenements and not derogatory, and the moneylenders were wholly admired for their scrupulous honesty, lower interest rates than those charged by the native Irish in the same business, and for being forgiving to a fault if a borrower was in truly dire straits. They were an integral and respected part of Dublin tenement society.

"Nah, we'll not use one," John-Joe said. Fingal heard a crack in the man's voice when he continued, "Ailish t'inks I don't know, but she's been dippin' into the diddley club money."

"Diddley club?"

"Aye, Mrs. O'Higgins runs a shop further up the street. Ailish and some other mas give her a half-penny a week starting in January, den it goes up to a penny, and up to t'ruppence, sometimes as much as a shilling. Mrs. O'Higgins holds the money until early December and gives it back so the mas have a few pounds to get Christmas treats. There's clubs like ours all over the Liberties and the Coombe." There was a catch in his voice when he said, "I don't like to t'ink w'at the chisslers'll do if we've nuttin' for dem dis year."

Fingal turned away. He could see how

John-Joe's eyes shone and that a tear was on the verge of falling. He heard the man sniff. When Fingal turned back, John-Joe was sitting rigidly, dry-eyed and taking a deep breath.

"I'm sorry, sir, but it destroys me utterly to t'ink of it."

"I hear you," Fingal said, knowing full well that any suggestion of "I'm sorry" would be a further wound to the man's already tattered pride. He didn't want sympathy. "John-Joe, please don't take this the wrong way. Please. What would you say if I was to offer to lend you five pounds at Christmas."

He recoiled. "By Jasus, I won't take —"

"Charity? It's not charity, man. It would be a business transaction, man to man. I'd charge you, as the only interest, a pint in the pub of your choice, to be taken when you've got a job and can pay me back."

John-Joe took a deep breath, exhaled through tight lips. "Are you serious, sir?"

"I am."

"Dear God." This time the tears flowed freely. "I'll take it, sir, but only for Ailish and the kiddies."

"Good man," Fingal said. "It's a promise then. I'll be round with the money in the first week in December."

"I don't know how to say t'anks." John-Joe's voice sank to a harsh whisper. "And I wish I'd not to take your money, sir. I only wish

— I wish to Christ I'd a feckin' job."

Fingal sat silently thinking how smug he'd felt after seeing wee Jack Dempsey and congratulating himself on what a good job he was doing. What about Lorcan O'Lunney? Have I helped his back with lotions and pills when he doesn't need medicine. What he needs is to get rid of his bloody cart and have something worthwhile to do. I'm only scratching the surface. Sanitation, clean water, dry houses, proper diets, and jobs — jobs for the menfolk would do more for the people of the tenements than him and all the other 649 dispensary doctors in Ireland put together. For the first time since he'd started at Aungier Place, Fingal wondered if he'd made the right choice. Was he happy fighting a rearguard action one individual case after another? And back at the Dempseys, he'd thought he was willing to accept how powerless G.P.s were against so many diseases. Was he really?

He looked at John-Joe's tear-streaked face. His needs were more immediate. The man had to have work, but he should be comforted at this minute too, Fingal thought, and became all doctor now his own uncertainty was dismissed. John-Joe shouldn't be left alone. "Tell you what, John-Joe," Fingal said, rising and putting a hand on the man's shoulder. "Show me where the makings are"

— he could see the kettle near a coke-burning stove — "and I'll get us that cup of tea."

24
WE WILL PARDON
THY MISTAKE

"Who's next?" O'Reilly said as he scanned the half-full waiting room. He frowned when he spotted Brenda Eakin and frowned even more when she stood slowly and said, "Me, sir," in a thin voice. She turned to her husband. "I won't be long, Ian." Her left hand clutched the right side of her chest. She was having trouble breathing.

Had she been sick all through the harvest or had she recovered and had a relapse? O'Reilly waited for her to join him in the doorway. She'd neither come back since her last visit a month ago nor had the hospital sent him an X-ray report. Strange. But while O'Reilly was good at following up with his patients, he did expect a certain amount of effort from them on their own behalf. He waited for her to go into the surgery.

The front door opened and Jenny Bradley came in carrying her doctor's bag. "Just finished this morning's home visits," she said, heading for the staircase.

"See you at lunch," O'Reilly said, then went into the surgery and closed the door. "Right, Brenda," he said, "let's get you lying down." Before he helped her onto the examining couch he moved a T-shaped rod along notched tracks so the hinged upper end of the table was held at forty-five degrees to the horizontal. "There, I think that will be more comfortable for you."

"Thank you, Doctor. You're right," she said. She winced with each indrawing of breath. "It does get worser when I lie flat."

O'Reilly frowned. He'd thought it would be easier for them to talk if she was sitting up a little but had no idea why the pain would be worse when she was flat.

"And I fainted this morning, so I did."

Chest pain and fainting? People who had heart attacks could pass out, but whatever had caused what he assumed was her pleural effusion seemed to have recurred, and it was on the right. Heart attack pain was central, and besides she was far too young to be having one. He shook his head. This was puzzling. Most doctors were usually able to hazard an informed guess at the most likely causes of a patient's complaints within the first thirty seconds of a consultation's beginning and spend the rest of the questioning and examination following the trail by seeking confirmatory symptoms and signs. But for once in many years, he was completely at a loss. The clues didn't add up. "Let's start at the beginning," he said.

"I hope you aren't cross with me, sir, but after I seen you last month I did like you said, and in about three days the pain had went away so I didn't need to come here. I thought I was going to be rightly from then on, but it's come back, so it has."

She'd done the same thing last year when he'd diagnosed primary dysmenorrhoea, taken his advice and the pills he'd suggested, and had never come back until she'd developed a new ailment. Country women were a self-sufficient lot. Given the arduousness of life on a farm they had to be.

"Did you go for the X-ray?" If she had it might be a help. He could phone the hospital. Get the report.

She took a shallow breath, gasped, "Ah," hung her head and said, "No, sir. I'm sorry, but I was well mended so I thought it'd not show anything anyroad."

"Yep," he said, "you're probably right." If she felt completely better the cause of her illness had probably resolved and nothing would have shown. No help there. He remembered a case he'd seen years ago in Dublin when he was flirting with becoming a specialist obstetrician and gynaecologist. Fainting and shoulder pain could be the clues to a tubal pregnancy, and an old adage of one of his profs that "Every woman is pregant until proved otherwise" had saved O'Reilly and his patient on more than one occasion. "When was your last period?"

"Which one, sir. The one I had last time I come in, or the one that started three days ago right on time?"

"And is it normal?" If she had conceived in the previous cycle it was just possible for her to be having problems with a very early pregnancy fourteen days from conception, and bleeding because of it. But he doubted it very much.

"Same oul' achy, crampy soreness, but them pills still help."

"And what else is wrong?" He pursed his lips. He knew he was fishing, hoping she'd say something that would point him in the right direction, but he was at a loss.

"Just —" She stopped in mid-breath, grimaced, then said, "Like last month, a pain here in my chest and it's hard til breathe, so it is."

Nothing to help him. Nothing. He'd bet his boots that she had another pleural effusion. But why? "Let's have a look at your chest," he said. "Just sit forward, tug your blouse out of your skirt at the back."

He examined her upper back. Self-same findings as last time including the whispering pectoriloquy. O'Reilly pursed his lips. He was completely foxed. He allowed himself a small smile. Nobody had said doctors had to be right all the time, nor was he ever reticent about admitting when he was stumped. "I'm pretty sure you have fluid round your lung again, Brenda, but I'm damned if I know why."

"Maybe it'll just go away again, like last time?" She peered at him through her granny glasses.

"It might, but we need to get to the bottom of it, find out what's causing it. It's you for the Royal today." She needed the opinion of a specialist physician, a discipline he knew was referred to as internal medicine in America. "Can Ian run you up? Or —" Why not? O'Reilly asked himself. "Or I could get a second opinion here. Ask Doctor Bradley to take a shufti at you."

Brenda frowned. "I dunno. She's awful young, so she is, and she's a lady . . ."

"Doctor," O'Reilly said. "I understand, but female or not she's been to medical school much more recently than me, and I'm sure there are new things she knows. What do you say, Brenda? Will we give her a try?"

"Welllllll . . . if you say so, Doctor O'Reilly, and you'll be here too, won't you?"

"Of course. You wait and I'll be back in a couple of minutes."

And he was, having interrupted Jenny's reading of Isaac Asimov's recent book *The Rest of the Robots.* He explained the complaint and his physical findings on their way downstairs, but not the patient's reticence about seeing a female physician. Jenny had been particularly interested in the fact that lying down made the chest pain worse.

"Good morning, Mrs. Eakin," Jenny said, and smiled as they went into the surgery to stand beside the examining couch. "I'm Doctor Bradley."

"Pleased til meet you, miss," Brenda Eakin said, not quite looking Jenny in the eye.

"I'd like to ask you about your periods. Is that all right?"

Brenda looked at O'Reilly for reassurance.

He nodded.

"They're regular?"

"You could set your watch by them."

"Please tell me about the pains. Doctor O'Reilly says you have cramps."

"Aye."

"Do the cramps get easier or worse as the period goes on?"

O'Reilly leant forward. He'd assumed that it had been a routine case of primary dysmenorrhoea, so common was the complaint, and hadn't paid a great deal of attention to the nature of the cramps.

Brenda sighed. "They get worser until it's over then they tail off, like."

Worse? Bugger. O'Reilly's initial diagnosis had been wrong. In primary dysmenorrhoea — pain caused by uterine contractions with no underlying disease — the pain always eased as the period progressed. He hadn't considered secondary dysmenorrhoea caused by an underlying condition like inflammation, and particularly the ill-understood endometriosis. In those cases, the pain got worse as the period progressed — and both causes of secondary dysmenorrhoea could delay or inhibit conception. Brenda and Ian had been trying for eighteen months. He took a deep breath. But how did that information help understand her pleural effusion?

"And is the pain in the middle of your tummy?"

Brenda shook her head. "Mostly on the right."

"Thank you, Mrs. Eakin," Jenny said. It was only a hint of a smile before her face went expressionless, but it was enough to tell O'Reilly that she was sure she'd solved the problem. "I think," she said, "I can spare you another examination."

Which was considerate, and Jenny had been, given the clinical findings.

"Could I have a word with you in the hall, please, Doctor O'Reilly?"

O'Reilly smiled. A professional thing to do, because Jenny was going to have to correct him and didn't want to do so in front of the patient. "Not at all," he said, turning to Brenda. "You remember I told you last year you'd the kind of period cramps that a lot of women get? Nothing unusual?"

"Yes, Doctor." She looked at him.

"I may have been wrong . . ."

She looked at Jenny.

"And I'm going to ask Doctor Bradley to explain." He watched Jenny's face. He'd certainly taken her by surprise, but hadn't he promised that he'd do everything he could to help her gain the patients' respect? Damn it all, he wasn't infallible and hadn't he had a father who'd taught, "If you're wrong, admit it?" "Go ahead, Doctor," he said.

Jenny nodded. "Mrs. Eakin. I believe I know exactly why you've got painful periods and why you've got the fluid in your chest."

O'Reilly frowned. Was she thinking there was a correlation between the two? If there was, it was something he'd never heard of.

"I believe you have a condition called endometriosis."

"Is that a cancer?" O'Reilly saw how Brenda's eyes widened as she expressed the usual, but unspoken fear of every patient. She was paying rapt attention.

"I promise you it's not," Jenny said. "It's a women's disease. When we have periods . . ."

Nice, thought O'Reilly. A subtle hint of "us women together."

". . . the lining of the womb bleeds and is shed. Some women develop islands of the special womb lining outside their womb, but inside their tummies. The lining is called endometrium, 'endo' for inner, and 'metrium' for of the womb. The condition you have is called endometriosis. When it's period time, the tissue that shouldn't be in there bleeds too. It causes pain like yours down below and in some extremely rare cases when the woman lies down, the blood runs up from her pelvis and gets into her chest and that hurts too."

So that's why that symptom had been Jenny's initial clue, and one that had eluded him.

"When pelvic endometriosis causes pleural involvement it's always right-sided, just like yours, Mrs. Eakin." Jenny turned to O'Reilly as she said, "And I only know about it because I saw a case two and a half years ago in the Royal. Mister Gavin Boyd, who has been a specialist for years, said it was the first case of endometriosis causing haematothorax he'd ever had and that most doctors had never even heard of it."

Graciously done to ease any wounds to my reputation, O'Reilly thought, and she was right, he had never heard of the condition.

"We all make mistakes, Doctor O'Reilly. There'll be no side taken," Brenda said.

In other words, she wasn't going to blame him.

She looked at Jenny. "I tell you, I was quare and disappointed to be took sick so soon after I thought I was better, but if I did have to see a doctor I think I'm powerful lucky you're here, Doctor Bradley. I'll be happy til see you any time, so I will."

You don't know how lucky, O'Reilly thought. He would have sent Brenda to a specialist physician and no internist would even have heard of haematothorax caused by endometriosis, which was a condition that fell within the purview of the gynaecologists. It could have taken forever to sort her out.

"I don't need to examine you because it's usually impossible to feel endometriosis. We have to look at it," Jenny said.

"And would that mean an operation?"

"In a way. If Doctor O'Reilly agrees I'd like us to send you to Dundonald Hospital."

Why the hospital on the outskirts of Belfast on the way to Newtownards? O'Reilly wondered.

"The specialist there, Mister Matt Neely, sent one of his staff to Oldham, a place in England, to learn a new technique from a Mister Patrick Steptoe."

This too, was news to O'Reilly.

"Normally your gynaecologist would have to open you right up to diagnose and remove the out-of-place endometrium and cure you," Jenny said, "but Mister Steptoe has been working on techniques developed in France by a Doctor Raoul Palmer and in Germany by a doctor Hans Frangenheim. The gynaecologist makes a tiny cut below your belly button and puts a telescope in your tummy —"

"Honest to God?" Brenda's eyes were wide.

"A telescope? That's powerful, so it is." She even managed a weak smile. "Will they see any stars?"

"No stars," Jenny said, and chuckled, "but if they see bits of endometriosis, they'll make another tiny incision and put in an electric probe and cauterise the abnormal bits to get rid of them. So instead of being in hospital for weeks after a big operation, you'll be out in one day. Once the cause is gone, your chest will heal up in no time."

"I never heard the like," Brenda said. "Wait 'til I tell Ian, and wait 'til I tell my granny. Thanks ever so much, Doctor Bradley, and thank you too, sir. You're still my doctor, but I know if you ever get stuck you've a one here with a right head on her shoulders, so she has."

O'Reilly knew Brenda's granny, Edie Carmichael. She was the best friend of Cissie Sloan's grandmother. Which meant that three days from now Doctor Jenny Bradley's stock would be blue chip in Ballybucklebo and the townland — and it would be even more difficult to let her go if Barry wanted to come back.

25
Ev'n Do as Other Widows

"You look very well this morning, Ma," Fingal said when she came down to join him in the dining room for breakfast. Today, Saturday, was one week short of three months since Father's death. She had worn nothing but black since then, Bridgit and Cook had put on black armbands, and Fingal a black tie. Convention decreed the uniform of mourning, but its duration was no longer a dismal four years for widows. He rose, pulled out her chair, and saw her comfortably seated.

She glanced at her lavender blouse and grey skirt. "I miss your father dreadfully, Fingal, but I am not going to parade my grief in public by staying in widow's weeds forever. These colours have been acceptable as half-mourning since Victoria's reign and I don't intend to be in them for more than a month. By Armistice Day, I shall be back to my usual clothes."

"I'm delighted to hear it," he said. "I miss

him too," and Fingal did, "but I agree. Grief should be a family matter."

She rang a small bell. "Now," she said, clearly considering the subject closed, "what are your plans for today?"

He hesitated. He knew that if she'd any news for him she would have told him at once, but he couldn't help himself. He had to ask on behalf of John-Joe Finnegan. "I don't suppose you've had any luck yet?"

"With finding work for your friend?" She shook her head. "I'm sorry," she said. "I have tried. You're like me, Fingal. You take the plight of those less fortunate to heart too much."

Bridgit appeared, carrying a tray. "Here's breakfast. Sideboard as usual?"

"Please, Bridgit," Ma said, and rose.

"Nice til see you out of black, Mrs. O'Reilly," Bridgit said, "and what I have here'll cheer you up even more. Porridge, kippers, and toast and marmalade." Bridgit started unloading the tray and putting the covered plates of kippers on a warmer.

"Thank you, and please thank Cook," Ma said. "And, Bridgit?"

"Yes, Mrs. O'Reilly?"

"Both you and Cook can take off the armbands. Thank you for wearing them, I know you both miss the professor." Ma smiled. "We all have to be moving on, all of us have to start cheering up, don't we?"

"Yes, we do, Mrs. O'Reilly, thank you, and we will, so we will." Bridgit left.

A brace of kippers was just what Fingal needed to start his day. Ma having found a job prospect for John-Joe would have been an even better way. Damn. Ma was right. He did take his patients' problems to heart. And he knew he was too old to believe that no matter what the problem was, Mummy could fix it, but he had hoped.

"These are very difficult times, Fingal," Ma said, starting to serve. "Why in heaven's name, with the whole world trying to recover from the Wall Street Crash of '29, would our dear 'president of the executive council' . . ." Fingal heard the tinge of sarcasm at the cumbersome term that really meant prime minister. "Why Mister de Valera in his infinite wisdom would start a trade war with Great Britain, I'll never know. Talk about a mouse taking on an elephant. That was in '31, and it has only got worse, as you know. Particularly among the farmers. And it's thrown even more people out of work. I asked the rest of the folks I know, but I'm afraid no one can help. I'll be speaking to Mister John Jackson when he gets back from the Continent next month. He has a shoemaking factory out at Chapelizod, but I'd be none too hopeful that he has any work either. I am sorry." She handed him a plate of porridge. "Please start."

"Thanks," he said, "and thanks for trying. I do understand."

Ma brought her own plate and sat. "At least," she said, "and I've been working on this for a few weeks — at least I've been able to solve our own employment problems. Trying to find places for Bridgit and Cook after this place is sold hasn't been easy. Most big houses are reducing their staffs. It's simply too expensive now. But things have worked out for us, and just in time too. The estate agent sent round a nice couple yesterday when you were at work and I haven't had a chance to tell you. They were very keen on buying. They'll be making an offer today. If I accept, I'd like to have the sale completed by December the first. Lars will handle the conveyancing and help me find something suitable near him. You did say that when I leave to go to Portaferry you could move in with your friend Charlie?"

"I will, Ma. Any time it suits."

"Good." She rose, lifted his now-empty porridge plate, and gave him his kippers. "Eat up," she said, took her own helping, and sat. She sighed. "I shall miss Dublin. We had quite the social life when your father —" She coughed and looked away, out the window to the redbrick walls covered in Virginia creeper. "But this old mausoleum's far too big for me alone and there are just too many memories. I'd like a change. We were originally from the north, I'd like to go back there, and I can buy something suitable in Portaferry and have some money left over from this sale."

"And you'd rather be in the country? Won't you be bored? All the work you've been doing here for slum clearance . . . ?"

"Heavens, there are plenty of folks involved in that here now." She shook her head. "You'll probably not remember Eunice Greer . . ."

"Husband had something to do with Mackie's Foundry?"

"That's right. She runs a charity for unwed mothers. She's already approached me and I've agreed to help. I'll certainly not be bored, and remember, Fingal, the north is where we're from, and it's not as if I don't still have friends and family up there. I don't expect Lars to lift and lay me, but his work seems less demanding than yours, son, so I'll be able to see a bit more of him." She chuckled. "And I'm not too old a dog to learn new tricks. Lars is going to teach me to drive so I'll be able to come down here and see you and my friends too. I can stay at the Shelbourne when I come."

"You have it all planned," Fingal said. He'd not doubted for one minute that Ma would take charge and organise her life as she deemed fit, but with her usual concern for the servants.

She said, the catch of sadness in her voice, "I've had time to think about it. Perhaps too much time."

Fingal laid his left hand on hers. "And Bridgit and Cook?" he said, squeezing the juice from a slice of lemon over the fish.

"I told Bridgit she can come to Portaferry with me if she wishes." Ma smiled and said, "She and I aren't getting any younger, you know." She stopped, her fork halfway to her mouth. "She's been with us," Ma inhaled a deep breath, as if to help correct herself, "with me, that is, for so long she's more of a friend than a servant. I should have missed her very much so I'm delighted that she's agreed. I think between us we can handle the cooking."

"I'm glad she's going with you," Fingal said. "She's certainly one of my earliest memories. I think she'd be a bit lost in a new position. And Cook?"

"I'd have liked her to have come too, but she'd rather stay in Dublin." Ma shrugged. "I can understand why, she's Dublin born and bred. But I've had a piece of luck," Ma said. "I didn't know you knew Robin and Jane Carson. I was at their home two days ago."

"Originally it was professional, but I've got to know Robin quite well. He's a decent bloke. Great rugby fan."

"Their cook is getting married next month to the butler of some very well-off folks who live between Blackrock and Dun Laoghaire and she's going there with him. Cook has an interview on Monday with Jane Carson."

"I hope it works out," he said. "I'm sure Mrs. Carson will be easy to work for, and their place is close enough to here for Mrs. Kernaghan to be able to visit her friends without having to travel too far." The kippers had been grilled to perfection and Fingal regretfully pushed away his plate and helped himself from a silver toast rack. He would miss Mildred's cooking and chuckled to himself about all the times Ma had corrected him. She was to be addressed either as "Cook" or "Mrs. Kernaghan." It was convention that cooks were called Mrs. even if they, like Mildred Kernaghan, were single women. "And you asked me what I'm up to today?"

"I did," she said.

"First," Fingal said, spooning up Frank Cooper's Vintage Oxford Marmalade from a cut-glass jar. He loved the thick strips of orange peel in it. "First, I'm going to finish Cook's excellent breakfast." He spread the marmalade. "Then I've letters to write. Then I'm having lunch with Charlie and after we'll go to Bob Beresford's place. Bob's our chauffeur. He's the only one of us with a car."

"I like your friend Bob," Ma said. "I like all your friends."

"Bob always did have an eye for attractive ladies," said Fingal.

"What nonsense," she said, blushing. "So will Bob drive you all to Donnybrook Rugby

Grounds?"

"Sure, he likes to watch the matches. We're playing Bective Rangers there at two thirty. They share the facilities with Old Wesley. It's a great place down on the banks of the Dodder River. Father used to take Lars and me there, remember?"

"How can I forget? I thought you were catching pinkeens in the Dodder, but you were watching that awfully rough game. I think that's what got you interested in the first place."

"Come on, Ma, it's not as bad as that. And you know I love it. Charlie and I are playing together for the first time today on the senior team. Charlie was selected after our first trial for the club in September but I'm afraid I had to settle for a place on the second fifteen. Last week a decent lad by the name of Willie Gibson, one of the forwards, broke his collar bone . . ."

Ma shuddered. "Not rough? I do hope you'll take care."

"I promise," Fingal said, "and today's really important. I've been called up to take Willie's place on the senior team."

"Fingal, that's wonderful news." Mary O'Reilly clapped her hands together lightly and then suddenly dropped them to her lap with a sheepish grin. "Well, of course, it's not good news for Mister Gibson and I am sorry he's hurt himself. But really, this is just the chance you've been waiting for, isn't it?"

"It is, Ma, and I intend to make the most of it because I know full well that it's from the senior clubs' first fifteens that the Irish International Team members are selected."

"You will be careful, son?"

"I will, Ma. Promise." She always worried, bless her. "After the game, I'm taking Kitty to the early showing of *City Lights* at the Lighthouse Cinema in Smithfield." He started to rise. "She loves Charlie Chaplin."

"So do I. You have fun, my dear," she said. "The more I hear about this Miss O'Hallorhan, the more I like her. Why don't you bring her round for dinner some night?"

"I will, Ma. Soon, but if you'll excuse me now?" Fingal walked round the table, dropped a kiss on her head, and strode for the door. "I haven't time for the news this morning, sorry. I'll not be too late home," he said, "but please don't wait up."

26
I WANT WORK

"Helen, come in. Come in." O'Reilly stood smiling in the hall with the front door half open. Early October leaves, brown, sere, and rustling bowled along the gutters blown by a chill northeaster.

"I hope you don't mind me coming til the front," Helen Hewitt said. Her emerald green eyes sparkled. "I seen — sorry — I saw Mrs. Kincaid on the street and she told me the waiting room door would be locked, it being late afternoon, like, and just to ring the bell."

"I'm delighted to see you," he said, and he was. "But come in out of the wind and let me take your coat." He hung it, a navy blue duffle complete with hood and wooden toggles, almost certainly bought at the Army and Navy Store in Belfast, on the hall coat-stand. The coats were becoming the unofficial winter uniform of Queen's undergraduates. Her heavy duffle bag, also de rigueur in that group, he set on the floor. "The weight of learning," he said. "Textbooks?"

"Aye, and notes, and I remembered what you told me about doing more reading than medical stuff too. I've been working my way through those collected works of Shakespeare you gi— gave me the day the marquis told me I'd got the scholarship. We had to do *A Midsummer Night's Dream* at school, but I never knew about his tragedies. That there *Julius Caesar*? It's amazing. I go up to Belfast and back on the train every day. It's a great time to read, so it is."

"And my upstairs lounge is a better place to sit and chat," he said, turning. "Come on up. Have you seen the film with Marlon Brando as Marc Anthony?"

"No, sir. Actually, I just popped in to ask you a question, a favour, like, and —"

"Helen Hewitt," O'Reilly said, and pretended to glower at her, "I'm much better at granting favours when I'm sitting down, preferably with a Jameson's in my hand. It's that time of the day." He glanced at his watch, quarter to six. "Come along." O'Reilly started to climb the stairs. "Kitty'll be home soon. I'm sure she'd like to see you too. Jenny's off tonight. She's up in Belfast seeing her beau, a Terry Baird. Have you met him?"

"Not yet," she said.

"Just wondered."

"I don't mean to impose —"

"Helen." He shook his head. "You are not imposing in the least and I'm delighted to see you. Let me explain something. You don't work for me anymore. We're practically colleagues, or will be soon. You're not coming to see me as your doctor, are you?"

She frowned, looked dubious for a moment, then smiled and said, "No, sir, I'm not sick nor nothing, and I suppose I am going to be a doctor."

"Damn right you are. Just like me."

"Thank you." She gave a contented little sigh then said, "Now the reason I came about —"

"Tell me —" He turned, climbed down, took her elbow in his hand, and pulling her along with him said, "Upstairs."

She laughed. "Fair enough."

Once in the lounge he said, "Have a pew. What would you like?" and headed for the sideboard. He poured himself a whiskey.

Helen took one of the armchairs in front of the fire Kinky had lit. "Would you have anything like a Babycham?"

O'Reilly frowned. He'd seen the "genuine champagne perry" advertised on TV in a campaign specifically targeting women. "I'm sorry. Kitty usually drinks gin and tonic. Would that do?"

"Lovely," she said, "and hello, Lady Macbeth." She fondled the white cat's head as the animal purred and made herself comfortable on Helen's lap.

O'Reilly gave her her drink and settled in

his chair. *"Sláinte."* He drank. A whiskey by the fire after a long day. Lovely.

"Cheers," she said. "How's Doctor, I mean Jenny, how's Jenny getting on?"

"Splendidly," O'Reilly said. "Bit of trouble at first."

"Because she's a woman doctor?"

He nodded, then fished out and lit his pipe. "At first, but folks are getting used to her. There are one or two of my women patients who are asking for her specifically now."

"I'm glad to hear that," she said. "And I'm sure it'll be even easier by the time I'm qualified." She leant forward and said seriously, "A couple of the girls in the class have been reading a book by Betty Friedan."

"The Feminine Mystique," he said. "If that stuff interests you, you should try *The Second Sex* by Simone de Beauvoir. I read it when it first came out in 1949. Interesting ideas. I reckon, judging by reports from America, there are changes coming for women." He half-smiled. "And I'm not convinced us men are necessarily going to like them." He wandered over to the bookshelf, took down the volume, and gave it to her. "See what you think."

"Thanks very much," she said, studying the book's cover photo of de Beauvoir. "But she wasn't the first one going on about women's rights. I've read about the suffragettes."

"I think you'd have to go farther back than

that. Mary Wollstonecraft was agitating back in the eighteenth century." He blew a smoke ring. "You still smoking?"

"Aye, certainly."

"Feel free."

She lit up.

He noticed that she was now smoking Gallagher's Greens, a step up from her earlier cheap brand.

"I came to ask you if —"

"Later, Helen. I want to hear how you're getting on."

"I love it," she said, "and a lot of the work's just like what we did for our school exams. Physics, chemistry, botany, and zoölogy." She exhaled, the smoke curling up. "But it's a whole new experience," she said. "There's fifteen of us girls and about a hundred men, and in first year the dental students take the same classes as us so the lectures're always filled." Her eyes widened. "The teachers treat us like grown-ups."

"You are one," he said.

She laughed. "Some of the boys don't behave like it."

"Ragging the teachers, are they? We once had a skeleton called Gladys that could be lowered on a rope from the rafters. Three of my class dressed her in ladies' undies and put an alarm clock in the hollow of her pelvis. It went off in the middle of the class. Great fun."

"I don't suppose you'd have been one of the three?"

He chuckled, winked, and blew another smoke ring.

"Bad divil," she said, and laughed. "I don't think it's changed much. When we started, the professor of physics, Doctor Emelaeus, told us that he was conducting very important experiments in a sonics laboratory under the lecture theatre and that loud noises from overhead could ruin years of work." She sipped her gin. "We were quiet as mice for six weeks, definitely not normal for medical students now, or in your day either, Doctor O'Reilly, I'm sure."

"We could be a pretty rowdy lot," O'Reilly said, "but what the hell? People used to give students fools' pardons for a bit of high spirits."

"They still do. Anyroad, one day one of the boys took a look. There was nothing down there but old storerooms."

"So Doctor Emelaeus had pulled off his own con trick?" For a second O'Reilly wondered if the learnèd professor had taken a postgraduate class from Donal Donnelly.

"Aye, but about a week later, in the middle of his lecture about the Van der Graaf generator, there was a crash from the back row. You know those tiers of benches in lecture halls? 'What was that?' he says. Another crash from the next tier down. Then a crash from the third tier." She laughed. "It would have made a cat laugh to see the prof's face. Crash from tier four. We found out later one of the lads in the front row had half-filled a tin can with marbles, set it on the floor on the top tier and run a string down to where he sat. Every time he pulled the string —"

"Crash," yelled O'Reilly, startling Lady Macbeth. "Och, that's brilliant. Wish I'd thought of it."

"By now everyone was laughing, clapping, stamping their feet." Her grin faded. "I'd started feeling sorry for the wee prof. He gave up. Slammed his textbook, gathered up his notes, and stamped out. We never got to hear the rest of the lecture, but the next time he lectured he did say all was forgiven."

"Mmmm," said O'Reilly. "When's your physics exam?"

"December."

"Elephants aren't the only ones with long memories. If I was you, Helen Hewitt, I'd make sure I knew all about the Van der Graaf generator."

"Do you think so?"

"Wouldn't hurt," O'Reilly said.

"I'll do that, sir." She took a drink. "Now, I didn't want to disturb you, but I did come to ask a wee favour."

"Fire away. It'll be yours if I can do it."

"Cooo-ee, Fingal." Kitty's voice from below immediately preceded the slamming of the back door. "I'm home."

"Upstairs," he called, and rose. "Excuse me, Helen. It's been a long week for her. She'll need her, um, medicine." He went to the sideboard and started to pour a gin.

Kitty came in. She carried something in her hand. It looked like a peculiarly shaped large book. "Helen. Lovely to see you. Don't get up."

Helen, who had started to rise, subsided back into her chair, along with a somewhat chagrined-looking Lady Macbeth. "Mrs. O'Reilly."

"It's Kitty," she said. She accepted her gin and tonic. "Thanks, darling. Lifesaver."

"Sit here," O'Reilly said.

"Thanks again. My feet are killing me." Kitty took the armchair.

"Helen popped in," he said, moving to lean against the mantel, "to let us know how she's getting on at medical school, and it sounds as if she's doing very well, and she wanted to ask me a favour. Go ahead, Helen."

Helen looked from Kitty and then to O'Reilly. "It's about money, and I hate asking for any more favours because the scholarship takes care of all I need, but it would help at home . . ."

O'Reilly was surprised. Was Helen going to ask for a loan?

". . . if I could earn a few bob in the summer holidays next year. A lot of the boys go to England and freeze peas and other vegetables in season. They can make as much as a hundred pounds, but it's heavy physical work."

"I'm sure it is." O'Reilly was relieved that the question of borrowing was not to be raised.

"I came to you, sir, because a girl in the year ahead told me that sometimes country hospitals would take on medical students in the summer as orderlies. Pays thirty pounds a month. But she said you had to be recommended by someone who knows the staff at the hospital."

O'Reilly frowned. "My contacts are at the Royal."

Helen's face fell.

"But," said Kitty, "your friend Cromie's great pals with Mister Walter Braidwood, the consultant surgeon at Newtownards Hospital. We could ask Cromie to ask him."

"Begod we could," said O'Reilly, "and begod, we will." He grinned at Helen. "I can't make you any promises, but we'll try."

"That's wonderful," Helen said. "It would be a great help."

"Grand," said Kitty. "That's settled. Now, how'd you like to help us, Helen?"

Fingal frowned. "What with?"

"Come and see this, Fingal." She set the book on a coffee table and opened it. "We need to look at these samples of wallpaper.

I'm sure you could help us pick one, couldn't you, Helen?"

Helen was leaning over already, turning pages. "I like that light turquoise one with the pinstripe," she said. "What's it for?"

O'Reilly choked on his drink when Kitty looked him straight in the eye, smiled her most beatific smile, and said, "The waiting room. Those God-awful roses really have to go."

27
Do Not Trust the Horse

"That's some motorcar, Bob," Fingal said, admiring a red four-door saloon with a long nose and huge headlights parked outside Bob's flat on Merrion Street. "New, is it?"

"It's well for the wealthy," Charlie said. "What make is it?"

"I got it three weeks ago from a new company," Bob said. "Jensen. It's their 1936 S-Type. Hop in." He held a back door open for Charlie.

Fingal got in the front passenger seat and inhaled that new car smell.

"Won't take long to get there," Bob said, driving away from the kerb. He made a right turn onto Fitzwilliam Place, the same street Fingal and Kitty had walked along in August when they stumbled upon the Blueshirt rally. She'd not been as vocal about the plight of Spanish orphans since that day, but the damn war kept cropping up in their conversations. He hoped she'd let that hare sit tonight. It had been an intense week at the dispensary,

and he wanted to forget about it for today.
He had to be back at work tomorrow.

"How's life abusing you both?" Bob asked.

"It's good to be off work and heading to
play rugby at Donnybrook, I can tell you that
for free," Fingal said.

"Big game for Fingal," Charlie said.

"I know," Bob said. "Seeing Kitty tonight,
Fingal?"

"I am."

"Give her my best," Bob said.

"And mine," Charlie said.

"And how's the job going?" Bob asked.
"Still having fun?"

Fingal hesitated. "I love the clinical work
with the patients, but once in a while not being able to offer much treatment and not being able to do anything about the poverty can
get you down. I'd a rough week. Two patients
I'd got to know died of tuberculosis, there's a
fellah I've come to like who's lost his job . . .
Och, the blazes. I'm trying to put that behind
me and enjoy today."

"Having second thoughts?" Bob asked.

Fingal detected no "I told you so" tone to
Bob's voice but remembered his disapproval
the afternoon in Davy Byrnes pub when Fingal had announced his intention to join a
dispensary practice. "No. I keep watching
Phelim Corrigan and telling myself, if he can
still be happy at his work after twenty-nine
years, so can I." And yet, he had wondered in

335

John-Joe's tenement room, and had worried about it since. Of course he could be like Phelim, Fingal reassured himself. "Charlie, what do you reckon?" Fingal didn't see a lot of Charlie in the day-to-day working of the practice but had assumed that because he'd said nothing to the contrary he was enjoying his work. He certainly hadn't mentioned it at lunch, but they'd had other things to talk about on their day off, like what Charlie thought of Fingal's prospects for an Irish cap, the opening of a brand-new film studio by J. Arthur Rank at a place called Pinewood in England, and Charlie's love life with a country lass from near Maynooth, which seemed to be getting a bit rocky.

"It's a job," Charlie said as Bob passed the intersection with Mount Street Upper.

"You don't sound too enthusiastic, Charlie," Bob said. There was still no hint of smugness. Sound man, Bob Beresford. Fingal frowned and turned in his seat. "Are you not enjoying it? I thought you were."

"It's all right. After three months I've got a feel for the work. You know how much I enjoyed working with my hands when we were students. But apart from lancing a couple of carbuncles and putting in a few stitches now and then, there're no real surgical opportunities. I miss that. And I hear what you're saying about being so bloody helpless most of the time, Fingal. At least if you take out an appendix or sew up a bleeding stomach ulcer you're really curing the patient. I miss that too."

"So are you thinking of moving on?" If Charlie said yes, Fingal would be disappointed, but he would not try to influence his friend.

"I honestly don't know, but I may well be," Charlie said. "I went up to Belfast on my last weekend off and stayed with Cromie. Now there's a man who's happy at his work. Sends his best, by the way. Made me wonder, but don't worry, Fingal. Please. If I do decide to specialise in surgery, I'll let you know long before I say anything to Doctor Corrigan. Anyway, we agreed to stay for six months and then give three months' notice. I've lots of time."

"It's your decision, Charlie," Fingal said. "Of course I'll not say anything to Phelim." But Fingal sensed that his friend would be moving on. He turned back to stare through the windscreen and recognised the corner of Leeson Street, where Kitty had her flat.

"Thanks, Fingal," Charlie said. "I appreciate that, and I will let you know one way or the other in good time. I don't want you working one in two weekends, so I'd give Phelim lots of time to get someone else."

"Fair enough. One other thing. Ma's moving to Portaferry in December. I'll be a homeless waif. Any chance of taking you up

337

on the offer —"

"Of sharing my flat on Adelaide Road? Of course. Any time, Fingal. Less rent to pay, more for a pint or two."

All three men laughed.

Fingal watched the houses go by and frowned. Charlie was having serious second thoughts and, come on, Fingal, he told himself, so are you. Admit it. It hadn't concerned him back in July that Bob had picked research and Cromie surgery. He'd been perfectly confident in his choice of general practice with its opportunities to do some medical good and be accepted by the patients and the community as they got to know and trust him. Now he was questioning just how much good he was actually doing. With Charlie now considering surgery as well, was Fingal going to end up like that old joke about the boy marching in Belfast where one woman says to another, "That's desperate, so it is. Everybody's out of step — except our wee Willie"?

And yet Fingal knew he'd always marched to his own drummer, was always confident in his decisions. Hadn't he stood up to his own father and realised the dream of becoming a doctor? Why the hell now was he challenging his own choice about the kind of doctor he wanted to be?

He jerked forward in his seat when Bob braked suddenly. A Clydesdale horse hauling a Guinness dray coming from Dartmouth Walk had, for reasons best known only to the beast, stopped dead in the middle of the intersection. He could hear the driver yelling, "Och, for God's sakes, Rosebud. Get a move on. I'll give you yer feckin' nosebag when we get til Lannigan's pub and we're unloading the barrels."

The horse whinnied and shook her head, making the polished horse brasses on the heavy collar sparkle in the sunlight.

The driver must have seen Bob looking at him because he touched the brim of his bowler hat — all Guinness drivers wore them, and white aprons — and yelled, "Sorry about dat, sir. Me feckin' horse is working to rule today." He lightly flicked his whip on the beast's large rump. "Now get on up, girl." She snorted, lifted her tail, deposited a heap of horse apples, as much as to say, "Stuff you, mate," then the dray rumbled forward.

Bob Beresford, who earlier in his student career had been pathologically work-shy, laughed and said, "That was living proof of what I used to say, 'The only animal that works is the horse — and it thinks so little of it you know what part of its anatomy it turns to its task. Its arse.' "

Charlie and Fingal laughed. "I know I don't want to be like that horse when it comes to my job," said Fingal, "plodding along until I can put on the nosebag. It's critical that

339

whatever we finally choose we enjoy. We could be doing it for another forty years."

"Not me," said Bob, steering with one hand and lighting a cigarette with the other. "I intend to marry a beautiful heiress who's too proud to let her husband work."

Fingal turned to Bob and studied his face, but couldn't decide if he was serious or not. It was hard to tell with Bob.

"That's one approach," Fingal said with a laugh. "But medicine isn't like laying bricks or — or making barrels like a cooper." He searched for what he was trying to express. "It's getting up in the morning with a smile on your face knowing that you aren't really going to work. I agree entirely with something Phelim Corrigan said after he'd had a long night on call. I suggested the man was pushing himself too hard. 'Rubbish, lad,' he said, 'I wasn't working. Work is what ye do for money when ye'd infinitely rather be doing something else, and what the hell else would I rather be at?' " And that's how I want to feel too, so why these nagging doubts? He wondered how Bob's research was going. "So," Fingal said, "that's two of us. How are things with you, Bob? How are you getting on with Professor Bigger?"

Bob slowed at the intersection where Leeson Street merged with Sussex Road to form Morehampton Road. "At the moment it's frustrating as all bedamned."

"Oh," said Fingal. "Why? You seemed to be excited about your work with red prontosil the last time I saw you."

"I'm excited enough," said Bob, "but I get irritated too. For me to move ahead professionally I have to put papers into research journals, and Prof Bigger doesn't believe in publishing what he calls 'negative data.' "

"Negative what?" Charlie asked.

"Look," Bob said, "let's say I suggest treating earache with, I don't know, garlic oil, and I use it on ten of twenty patients and not on the other ten. And let's say only the treated ones get better. Those would be positive data, a hoped-for result. That report would be accepted by a research journal. But if the garlic oil didn't work? Not worth reporting and no help in a young fellah's career." He sighed and changed down to avoid ramming a large Foden lorry that belched diesel fumes and was creeping along the road ahead. "We can't get the ruddy stuff to work in the lab. The bacteria positively thrive on it."

"Negative data," said Fingal. "Not much use."

"But it's been known since 1931 to work against *Streptococcus* in mice," Bob said. "I don't know what the hell we're doing wrong." The lorry had turned onto Auburn Avenue so Bob sped up for the last lap to the rugby pitch.

Fingal frowned. "Isn't that the same stuff

341

Doctor Davidson is trying to treat puerperal sepsis with at the Rotunda? *Streptococcus* causes childbed fever. He reckoned if Prontosil worked in mice it might cure those women too. There'd been quite an outbreak last year."

"There was," said Bob. "Fourteen cases and four women died because, according to Doctor Davidson, they were getting infected by bacteria he cultured from the noses and throats of the staff. That was the first step in understanding what caused the disease. That's why we had to wear face masks, remember, in the delivery rooms. The next step is to try to kill the bacteria if prevention fails and a woman gets the fever. He's just started the trial. Too early for results yet."

"I hope the Prontosil works," Fingal said. "My God, can you imagine having a drug that cured infections?"

Bob swung through the gates of the rugby club. "It would be an incredible finding, but it should be working in the lab right now, and quite simply it's not. I'm going back to the library next week to see if I can find anything in the world literature that might explain what's going on." He hit the steering wheel with the flat of his hand. "Och well, I'm not in the lab today. I'll worry about it on Monday." He parked. "Come on, Fingal, you said you were going to put work behind you and enjoy today. Stop imagining wonder drugs. Get out there and put your mind to playing the best game of your life. I hear that a couple of Irish selectors, Mister Collopy and Mister Hogan, might be here. They have to find a replacement for Willie Gibson on the Irish team."

A consideration that quite banished from Fingal's mind any thoughts of jobs for John-Joe, being happy at his work, or what his profs had called "magic bullets" — compounds that would selectively target and destroy bacteria. He did remember promising Phelim to get an Irish cap or bust and, by all that's holy, he was going to try.

28
IN THAT CASE
WHAT IS THE QUESTION?

"It's all a matter of priorities, Barry," O'Reilly said, approaching the bat-wing doors of the Mucky Duck, Arthur Guinness walking to heel. "First we'll get our pints on the pour, then seeing that it's been two months since the four of us had that great meal in Ballymena, you and I can have a grand old blether about how the world's abusing you out in darkest County Antrim at the Waveney Hospital."

O'Reilly pushed open the doors and yelled, "Two pints and a Smithwicks for Arthur, Willie."

"Right, Doctor," Willie Dunleavy said, and started to pour. " 'Bout ye, Doctor Laverty."

Barry waved at Willie and said to O'Reilly, "Lord, I've missed this old place." He sniffed the air the way Arthur did at Strangford Lough. "There are lots of pubs in Ballymena, but it's tricky getting to know the locals the way I did here."

O'Reilly surveyed the familar low-ceilinged

room with its dark oak-beamed ceiling, breathing in tobacco smoke fug and the smell of beer. Men in cloth caps, dungarees or waistcoats, and collarless shirts, one or two in suits, were drinking pints of Guinness leaning on the bar. A few sat at tables. There was a chorus of "Evening, Doctors."

"Evening all." He beamed round the room. One regular wasn't here. Archie Auchinleck had last been seen ten minutes ago in Kinky's kitchen drinking tea with her, but most of the usual suspects were; Mister Coffin the undertaker having a jar at the bar with Constable Mulligan, who must be off duty. Fergus Finnegan, the jockey, relaxing with Thompson, the marquis's valet-butler. Dapper Frew, the estate agent, sitting with Father O'Toole. I really, O'Reilly thought, ought to pop in here more often. He'd not darkened the doorstep since before his wedding back in July even though the Duck and its patrons had been part of his life since he'd come to work in Ballybucklebo in 1946. He missed the *craic*. Kitty'd not mind if he nipped in occasionally from now on.

"Sit youse here, Doctors," said Gerry Shanks, the Linfield fan, who rose and motioned to his friend and rival soccer team supporter Jeremy Dunne to get to his feet. "Youse can have our table. We was just finishing up, you know." He smiled when he saw

Barry. "Nice til see you, sir. Down for a visit, like?"

"I am."

"I'll tell the missus I seen you. She'll be that sorry to have missed you, so she will."

"Please give Mairead my regards, and Siobhan and Angus," Barry said, and sat.

"Under the table," said O'Reilly, and the big Labrador obeyed.

O'Reilly sat and lit up his briar. "So," he said, emitting a blue cloud to rise and seek the company of others of its kind, "you've been driving up from Ballymena every second Saturday?"

"I have. I'm on a one-in-two call rota. It's a sixty-mile round trip for me, but —"

"That's a fair stretch of the legs, all those narrow, winding roads, and through the heart of Belfast, but I know it's not to see me. A certain schoolmistress is back teaching at MacNeill Memorial Primary."

Arthur gave a sharp bark, but O'Reilly couldn't see what had disturbed the big dog. "Quiet," he said.

Barry blushed and laughed. "Sue's back living in her flat in Holywood."

'Nuff said, O'Reilly thought, and nodded. Barry and Sue had popped in unannounced today and once Kitty had made sure it was all right with Kinky, they'd agreed to stay for dinner.

"You're looking well, Barry. So's Sue."

While it was a pleasure to be sitting in the Duck chatting with his young friend and colleague, O'Reilly had an ulterior motive: to find out how Barry was making out after three months of speciality training and whether or not he was ready to make a career choice. But O'Reilly was not going to rush headlong at the question. Somewhere between now and the end of the next pint, the opportunity must arise for the subject to flow naturally into their conversation. "She still working with her Campaign for Social Justice?"

"She certainly is, but we've settled our differences over that. She's happy enough to let me get on with my work, and I don't interfere with her civil rights endeavours." He laughed. "She even sent her apologies to a meeting they were having this evening so she could see me. It's been two weeks since we were out together. It was easier seeing her when she was home in Broughshane for the holidays. I've really been looking forward to today." For a moment he gazed into the middle distance with a contented smile on his face.

This boy's smitten, O'Reilly thought, and if she'd not seen him tonight it would be another two before she could see him again. She was willing to forgo something O'Reilly knew was of enormous importance to her to spend time with Barry, so it sounds as if she's falling too. Good for them. Ain't love grand? And I should know. And, he thought, I should also know how duty rotas can play havoc with romances. He said, "I had a one-in-three call system for a while when I started in practice. Busy enough. One in two can be tiring, but you're young." Here was a logical entrée to ask the question. "And you're still enjoying — ?"

"Here youse are, Doctors." A sweating Willie Dunleavy set a tray on the table, unloaded two pints, and bent to put Arthur's bowl of Smithwicks under the table.

"My shout," O'Reilly said, and paid the four shillings and tuppence. "Bring a couple more when you see these getting down, please, Willie."

"Right, sir."

"*Sláinte,*" O'Reilly said, and took a long pull. "Mother's milk." He grinned.

"*Sláinte mHaith,*" Barry said, and drank.

"So, Barry," said O'Reilly. "You're still enjoying —"

"Excuse me, sir," Willie said, "but is your Arthur good with other dogs?"

"As gold," O'Reilly said, tamping down his pipe *and* his impatience. "Why?"

"My Mary's got a new puppy, and I let the wee lad wander around the bar. The customers enjoy seeing him."

"He'll be fine with Arthur. Never worry."

"Thanks, sir. Just thought I'd ask." Willie

headed back to his post at the bar.

"Wonder what kind of beast the pup is?" Barry said.

O'Reilly was more interested in asking his question again without being interrupted but someone was hovering by their table. He looked up. "Alan Hewitt," he said. "How are you? And how's Helen? I saw her a couple of weeks ago. She seemed to be enjoying her work." Pity Kitty had had no word from Cromie yet about a possible position in Newtownards Hospital for Helen next summer.

"Evening, Doctors," Alan said. "Helen's bravely, so she is. She says her first-year courses at thon medical school are wee buns, and she's had time to join something called the Literific Society as well. She's happy as a pig in you know what. I'll tell her I seen you, Doctor Laverty, so I will." He touched his cap and went to the bar.

"She must be even brighter than you thought, Fingal. First-year courses easy? I had to re-sit organic chemistry," Barry said, "and the Literific? That's the interdisciplinary debating society. Been around since the mid-1800s. Very venerable and a bunch of extremely bright sparks in it. Good for her." He took another mouthful.

"I've no doubt that Helen will be able to hold her own," said O'Reilly, then drank, leaving, halfway down his glass, a second white tidemark. "Knowing you've been able

349

to help someone, like finding out about that scholarship she was awarded, is a lot of what rural practice is about. It's not just the medical." All right, so perhaps he wasn't going to let the subject come up naturally in the conversation. He knew he was putting in a not-so-subtle plug for being a country G.P., but the sooner he could let Jenny Bradley know Barry's decision, the better. "Come to think of it, it was the same in city slum practice too —"

"Good evening, sir. I hope I'm not interrupting. Just wanted til say hello til Doctor Laverty." Donal Donnelly stood at the table clutching his duncher in one hand and grinning his moon-calf grin.

"Evening, Donal," Barry said. "Please thank Julie for sending me the birth announcement, and congratulations."

"And thank you, sir, for that blue teddy bear you sent. Wee Victoria Margaret, we call her Tori for short, she never lets it out of her sight. She's growing like a weed. She's cooing and gurgling like a full pigeon loft and she rolls over a lot, so she does."

"Does she? At three months? She's early to be rolling over. Quick developer by the sound of it," Barry said. "Wonderful."

Donal's grin widened. "That's our girl. Takes after her ma."

O'Reilly noticed Donal didn't have a drink, didn't really want to have anyone else at the table until he'd had a chance to find out about Barry's plans, but felt that noblesse oblige. "Can I get you a pint, Donal?"

Donal shook his head. "No thanks, sir. Julie says I'm off them. I've til work it out at saving two bob a pint for every one I don't have and that includes ones I'm offered. I've til save up the five pounds by not spending it, if you see what I mean? It's the money I lost on" — he lowered his voice to an almost inaudible whisper — "Buttercup." He brightened and said in his usual tones, "It's been thirty-five days since the race. I've not drunk enough to have four pound ten in credit, three more days and it's all paid off, and then, by God, I'll be your man, so I will, sir. My tongue's hanging out, so it is."

O'Reilly laughed. "Good for you."

"Aye," said Donal, frowning and lowering his voice again. "Pity about young Colin. They'd suss him out now if he showed up with another dog, but there's a bright wee lad called Art O'—"

"I don't want to know," O'Reilly said loudly. From the corner of his eye he noticed a small brown dog, wandering between the tables. Must be Mary's pup.

"Fair enough," Donal said, "but just so you understand, sir, nobody's come within a beagle's gowl of tracing the mystery dog from Kirkistown. There's a track in County Cavan—"

"Donal," O'Reilly said. "Enough."

"Aye," said Donal. "You're right. Least said soonest mended. I'll be off, sir. I see Dapper Frew over thonder and I need to have a natter with him about Ballybucklebo Highlanders pipe band business."

"Good evening, Donal," Barry said to the man's departing back. "And what was that all about?"

O'Reilly finished his pint, said, "Drink up," to Barry, and waved to Willie. While they waited for the fresh drinks O'Reilly, sotto voce, told Barry the saga of Buttercup, the dog with the coat of many colours.

Barry rubbed the back of his hand over one eye. "No more, Fingal," he said, gasping for breath. "The tears are tripping me. Oh Lord. I've been missing that kind of *craic*. I can't stop laughing."

"Neither could I," O'Reilly said. "He's quite the sprinter, our Donal. And by the way young Colin Brown covered the ground, that infected foot in August was well mended." It reminded O'Reilly of a youngster with an infected foot back in the Liberties, and that memory sobered him.

Barry managed to control himself and said seriously, "I hadn't realised how much I've been missing the Ballybucklebo folks and how much a part of the place I was becoming. Maybe I've been working too hard. I can understand why you've always seemed so

352

contented here. I've been thinking —"

"Your pints, sirs. I didn't bring one for Arthur," Willie said. "His bowl's still half full." He glanced over his shoulder and smiled as he said, "That there's Mary's pup."

O'Reilly looked over reluctantly to where Alan Hewitt was bending over to pat the smallest head of the smallest dog O'Reilly'd ever seen. Alan was feeding it a potato crisp.

"It's one of them Mexican hairless," said Willie. "The customers spoil her, so they do. I don't know what the girl was thinking, calling the wee thing Brian Boru."

"Brian Boru?" Barry chuckled. "Ireland's last *Ard Rí,* High King? Took on the Leinstermen and the Dublin Vikings and beat them at Clontarf in 1014. Hell of a fighter. Might be a name better suited to an Irish wolf hound than a chihuahua."

"He's a scrappy wee lad, so he is," Willie said. "Now, if youse don't mind, that'll be —"

"My round," Barry said, and fumbled for the money. This time, O'Reilly thought, he wasn't going to be distracted by another interruption. This time he was going to see if Barry was close to making up his mind. He waited until Willie had been paid and had left. "Cheers." O'Reilly took a mouthful. "You're right," he said. "I've never regretted my move back here after the war, but I'll tell you, Barry, when I was at your stage I had real second thoughts about general practice."

"Honestly? I never knew."

O'Reilly heard the swing doors open and shut and sent up a silent prayer it wasn't someone they knew. "That," said he, "is because I never told you. I wanted you to make up your own —"

"O'Reilly."

No mistaking those grating tones. O'Reilly looked up to see Councillor Bishop, bowler hat firmly on his head, standing beside the table, legs apart, one hand clutching the lapel of his jacket.

"Laverty."

O'Reilly noted the dropping of the honorific "Doctor." "What can we do for you, Bertie?" he asked.

Bishop leant his head to one side and regarded Barry, but spoke to O'Reilly as if Barry had no corporeal existence. "Young Laverty thinking of coming back here, is he?"

"That," said O'Reilly, "is very much up to him."

"Aye," said Bishop. "Well, if you do, Laverty, we'd not want for til stand in your way, so we'd not."

Barry quickly sat back in his chair. His eyes widened.

Nice use of the royal "we," O'Reilly thought.

Bertie looked O'Reilly in the eye. "And you knows exactly what I mean by that."

354

Lip service only was being paid to the qualifications of a certain "lady doctor," despite the words O'Reilly had had with Bertie on that matter. "How's your chest, Bertie?" O'Reilly asked, changing the subject.

"Grand. No more pains, but see that bloody diet? Jasus." With that he turned on his heel and walked to a table at the back of the bar where a man who O'Reilly knew was the Worshipful Master of a nearby Orange Lodge waited. On his way he passed Mary's pup. "Get away to hell out of that," he snarled. But the little quivering dog held its place.

"I'd not call it welcoming me with open arms," Barry said, "but, crikey, Bertie wouldn't stand in my way?" He smiled.

O'Reilly sighed. "I wish I could tell you it's because Bertie's mellowed and thinks you're a wonderful doctor, but I'm afraid he's still a great gobshite and his remark has got more to do with his total antipathy to female physicians — one in particular." He proceeded to tell Barry briefly about Bertie's angina and his refusal to see Jenny.

"I see," said Barry. "Can the leopard change his spots?"

"Can the Ethiopian change his skin or the leopard his spots, to be exact," O'Reilly said.

"Jeremiah twelve twenty-three," Barry said. And laughed. "I miss you, Fingal. I've no one to play our quotes game with." He sounded wistful.

O'Reilly thought it tactful not to mention that Jennifer had turned out to be as good a verbal sparring partner as Barry, but O'Reilly did say, "Apart from Bertie Bishop, Jenny's been pretty well accepted here by just about everyone now."

"Good for her," Barry said, clearly meaning it. "I remember how tricky it was for me for a while after Major Fotheringham died. But they're pretty welcoming folks here once you get to know them."

O'Reilly hesitated, hoping Barry was going to say more. Instead the lad simply took a long pull on his Guinness and let his gaze roam round the room.

"Barry," O'Reilly finally said, "I don't want to put you under any pressure. I thought when I was newly qualified that I wanted nothing else but to work in a dispensary practice. A few months later I was having serious second thoughts. It's not easy deciding for a lot of us. I do understand."

Barry looked O'Reilly in the eye. "But Jenny's fitting in already. I heard how satisfied you sounded when you told me how well she was being accepted. She wants to stay on, doesn't she? And you'd like my decision soon."

O'Reilly nodded.

Barry inhaled. "I wish I felt certain, but I do miss this place — a lot, and yet I really enjoy obstetrics."

"I understand."

"But you need an answer."

O'Reilly nodded once.

"I'll give you one by December first. Is that all right?"

O'Reilly smiled. "Not only is it all right —" He lifted his almost finished glass. "— I'll drink to it and then I'll have one more while you finish your second. Then it's home for one of Kinky's dinners." Having so enjoyed Barry's company in the Duck this evening, he could only hope her cooking might just add another grain or two to the "I'd like to come back" side of Doctor Barry Laverty's decision-making scales.

O'Reilly took a final swallow of his Guinness and thought that it wasn't an entirely satisfactory way to end the conversation. A clear-cut yes or no would have been helpful, but . . .

One of Arthur's enormous "Wooooofs" rang round the room.

Conversation in the bar died.

O'Reilly looked under the table and soon Barry's head appeared upside down as he too, looked down at the big Labrador. "Did you say the wee dog's name's Brian Boru?" Barry said, grabbing Arthur's collar.

Arthur was scowling at the chihuahua, who, hackles raised, one lip curled, a high-pitched growling coming from his throat, was helping

357

himself to Arthur's Smithwicks.

"It suits him."

29
RISK IT ON ONE TURN
OF PITCH AND TOSS

"I reckon it was pretty brave of Chaplin, making a silent film," said Kitty. "Everybody wants 'talkies' these days." She had her arm linked with Fingal's as they left the Lighthouse Cinema in Smithfield for the mile and a half walk back to the flat she shared with Virginia Treanor on Leeson Street, and the dinner Kitty had prepared. "His Little Tramp character really makes me laugh even if he doesn't say a word."

"I thought Paulette Goddard was pretty good too," Fingal said, and absently rubbed a sticking plaster on his forehead. Somebody's boot studs had gouged a furrow when he and Charlie both tackled a Bective Ranger who would have scored, but for their efforts. It had been a grand game and Wanderers had won. Bob said that Mister Collopy, one of the selectors, seemed to have been impressed. Fingal could only hope so. It would be a couple of months until players were picked to play in a trial match, after which the final

Irish team would be selected.

"She was," Kitty said, "but that scene where he got caught in the cogs of the machine? Absolutely priceless. I nearly wet myself I laughed so much."

Fingal chuckled. Only a girl who was completely comfortable with him would make a risqué remark like that. He liked that. Being with Kitty felt . . . felt right. He removed his arm from hers and took her gloved hand.

They passed the Four Courts on Inns Quay. The new domed rotunda had been patterned on the original. "Started in 1776, opened in 1802, blown to blazes in June of 1922 in the Irish Civil War, one thousand years' worth of archives destroyed. The place was rebuilt and reopened in 1932," Fingal said.

"I only remember the reopening," Kitty said, and looked at him. "You never cease to amaze me, Fingal, with all the tidbits of information you remember." She tapped his head. "Must be getting cluttered in there." She laughed and he laughed with her.

"Having a memory like glue came in handy at medical school."

"I imagine it did. All those facts to learn so you could be a doctor."

They crossed the Liffey. Fingal wondered what it must have looked like before the now oily, scummy waters had been confined to a channel between masonry embankments. A

360

couple of mallard dispiritedly dabbled in the river. "I reckon I'm lucky at my work," he said, trying to dismiss the doubts he'd been feeling. "I know the film was a satire, but it's not too far from the truth about how thousands of people make their livings doing the same tasks over and over, day after day, week after week. Henry Ford's production line may have been a great advancement for his Model Ts, but I don't think it's very good for people. I'd go spare, totally Harpic, working on one."

"Like the toilet cleaner, 'Clean round the bend'?" She chuckled then became serious. "At least," said Kitty, "they do have jobs. I'll bet those poor divils don't." She nodded to the corner of Usher's Quay and Bridge Street where a group of men, all cloth capped, none clean-shaven, some wearing boots, some barefoot, all smoking cigarettes, were gathered round a wall. "That's how a lot of them while away the hours. Pitch and toss."

"Maybe it's because it's Saturday evening and no one's working much anyway by this time," Fingal said, hoping he was right, but doubting it. "At least they're not in the boozers." He stopped and Kitty stopped with him. "Let's watch."

Copper pennies lay on the ground at varying distances from the base of the wall.

One man stood, eyes slitted, and swung his arm underhand, releasing a penny. It landed a long distance from the wall. "Crap shot," he yelled, and walked forward to retrieve his penny.

"You can call that once in a round if you don't like your pitch and want to take it over again," Fingal said.

"Jasus Murphy, would you get a feckin' move on, Payo Quigley," said a freckled-faced youth, "and remember it's the wall over here you're trying to get close to, not the feckin' Liffey." The river was at least two hundred yards behind them. His teasing was greeted by good-natured laughter.

"Quigley," Fingal said, "a surname derived from the Irish, *coigleach.* It means 'unkempt.' "

Kitty said, and not unkindly, "If the boot fits. He certainly could use a haircut."

Payo crouched and pitched again. The penny hit one already on the ground.

Several voices yelled, "Jingle," and men walked forward to retrieve their coins.

"If one coin hits another, it's called a jingle and everybody has to take their pitch over again," Fingal said. "Come on. They could be at this for hours and I'm ready for my grub." He started walking.

"How do they know who wins?" Kitty asked.

"Once all the pennies have been pitched, whoever's coin is nearest the wall picks them up, tosses them in the air, and yells his choice of heads or tails. He keeps all the ones facing up the way he predicted, then whoever was second closest does the same and so on until all the coins have been won. Apparently, a similiar sport was in the original Greek Olympic Games."

"Fingal," said Kitty, "you're at it again, Mister Erudition."

"Just thought it was interesting," he said, and frowned. Ordinarily he didn't mind Kitty's teasing, but had he detected an edge to that comment? He realised they were on High Street and were passing number ten. "I know a man who lives in there. Broke his ankle. Lost his job. Sad."

"Very," said Kitty.

"Ma's going to ask a friend who has a shoe factory if he has any jobs, but she's not very hopeful. It makes you feel so helpless. He's a good man with a wife and two kiddies. He really wants to work but there's nothing for him." Stop it, he told himself. There's no need for self-flagellation. It's not your job to find work for John-Joe even if you are trying. You're on a day off, you're out with a beautiful, vivacious woman, and, his stomach rumbled, you're going for your dinner with her. He looked into Kitty's grey eyes, at her lips, her well-filled cardigan, and hoped her flatmate Virginia Treanor would be out for a long time.

A familiar figure appeared from one of the alleys running between High Street and Cook

363

Street. "Good evening to you, Doctor O'Reilly, sir." Lorcan O'Lunney stopped and set his two-wheeled cart down on its front legs. "I could use a feckin' breather. How are you, sir?"

"I'm grand, Lorcan," Fingal said, "and this is Nurse O'Hallorhan." He saw that the cart was piled high with clothes. Not everybody got Saturday evening off. Clearly Lorcan was at his work.

He politely lifted his duncher. "How are you, miss?"

Kitty smiled. "Very well, thank you." She looked at his cart. "That looks heavy."

He shrugged. "Ah sure, even a hen's heavy if you carry her far enough. But I'm not goin' far. Lamb Alley to deliver these to an oul' one who has a stall in the Iveagh Markets on Francis Street. She'll get them fixed up ready for sale on Monday."

"How's your back, Lorcan?" Fingal said.

"Och, Jasus, sir, it's like a lift at the Gresham Hotel."

Kitty frowned. "It's like a lift?"

"Aye, miss. It has its feckin' ups and downs." He cackled.

They both laughed, and then Fingal said, "Seriously, how is it?"

"Your lotion and pills help a bit, sir."

"I'm glad." And he was, but he wished they helped more.

Lorcan rummaged in his pocket, produced

a packet of cigarettes, opened it, frowned, and said, "Bollicks. I'm out and I'm feckin' well gasping for a drag or two."

Fingal's hand went to his pocket. There was the packet of Woodbine he'd bought as a gift on Monday for the now non-smoking John-Joe Finnegan. "Here," he said, offering the packet, "I don't use these. You have them, Lorcan."

Lorcan stretched out a hand encased in woollen gloves from which the fingers had been cut, smiled at O'Reilly, and said, "Feckin' manna from heaven. Bless you, sir. May you live the life of Reilly and have a large funeral."

Fingal chuckled. In medieval Ireland, the Reilly family, Raghallach, was renowned for their business acumen, and "Reilly" became a colloquialism for money. And only people with lots of friends and admirers had large funerals.

Lorcan opened the pack, removed a cigarette, lit up by cracking the head of a match between his thumb and index fingernails, inhaled deeply, coughed damply, and said, "Grand for the lungs, sir. Keeps them well lubricated." He stooped, lifting the cart's handles off the ground. "I'd better be off, sir, and t'anks a million for the gaspers, Doctor Big Fellah. Nice to meet you, miss." He dipped a slight bow to Kitty and set off on the short journey to Cornmarket and the junction with Francis Street, where, as Fingal remembered, Paddy Keogh, the one-armed sergeant, had lived before getting a job on a building site and moving to a better-class district. He wondered how Paddy was. He'd not seen the man since last year when Paddy had come to the home of his friend Brendan Kilmartin, whose wife Roisín Fingal had delivered of a little boy who was to be named after Fingal. They lived on . . . ? He frowned. Swift's Alley. That was it. "Come on," he said. "Your place," and started walking.

"I take it that was a patient of yours," she said.

"One of my first," Fingal said, remembering meeting the man in Phelim Corrigan's waiting room.

"You never stop worrying about them, do you?"

"Well, I —"

"I remember what you said when you'd had that case of diptheria and Doctor Corrigan sucked the membrane out. You said he always put the patients first — and that was the kind of doctor you wanted to be."

"Within reason," he said.

She stopped, tilted her head to one side, and regarded him. "Occasionally I wonder, Fingal, if some physicians shouldn't be like priests and take a vow of celibacy. Your on-call seems to be making it awfully tricky for us to get together sometimes, and I do miss you."

Fingal frowned. Where the hell had this come from? He revelled in her company, knew she was happy being with him, but he did take his professional responsibilities and his family commitment to Ma seriously. "Are you not happy?" he said. "I know I did turn my back on you last year when I had to work so hard to qualify, but I thought that was behind us. I —" Was Kitty angling for a proposal? He'd certainly never discussed such a thing with her and, anyway, with what he presently earned he could hardly support a wife and children. He shook his head and repeated his question. "Kitty? Are you not happy."

She took a deep breath and sighed. "Truth?"

"Truth."

"I'm happy with you, Fingal, but not with our situation. You're concerned about your friend who lost his job because he has a wife and children. But do you ever think about having those things for yourself? A lot of my friends are married, settled down, having babies. I'm not twenty-one anymore."

So that was it. Fingal looked about in short, jerky glances like a cornered boar looking for a way to escape. "I'm only beginning a career, Kitty. I do love you." And that was as far as he was prepared to go. Please, he thought, let it be enough for now. Until I'm ready — ready to take the plunge. "Look. Ma will be going to live in Portaferry soon, and Charlie's pretty decent about swapping call. I really do want to see much more of you. I'll do my very best to make more time."

She studied his face and sighed. He knew her well enough to know that she was struggling over what to say next. "I love you, Fingal." She frowned. Took a deep breath. "All right. Let's see how it goes." She started to walk briskly and he had to lengthen his stride to keep up. "Come on," she said. "I've a pot roast cooking and I don't want it to dry up."

She had always been able to change the subject quickly if she felt she was on emotionally thin ice. "Kitty," he said as they turned onto Nicholas Street, "Kitty, I love you and —"

"Extra. Extra. Read all about it! International Brigade lands in Alicante to fight for the Spanish Government against Franco!" Kitty had come to a halt, transfixed. "Read all about it." The barefoot newsboy in short, ragged pants turned his attention to her. "Ma'am?"

"Yes, give me a paper, please," Kitty said.

Fingal gave the ragged urchin a copper and accepted a copy of the *Irish Independent.* "Here." He gave it to her.

"I'll read it when I get home," she said, tucking the paper under her arm and striding off again, this time even faster than before. "You know, volunteers from all over have been arriving in Spain since August the first. The ones fighting against Franco's forces are called the International Brigades."

"I know," he said quietly, thinking, Jasus, not bloody Spain again.

"Women have been going with them as part of their medical services."

Fingal's heart jumped. "What? You're not thinking of —"

"I don't know what I'm thinking. I just know that ever since I heard about the massacre at Badajoz, I can't stop thinking about all those children who have lost their parents. It haunts me, Fingal."

"Kitty. Please. I understand how you feel, but there's nothing we can do."

"People always say that. But a nursing friend of mine, Agnes Brady, she's doing something. She joined the Irish contingent, the Connolly Column. I don't know if she'll be with the lot that have just arrived." She stopped and looked into his eyes. "I don't know, but I want to find out. You mentioned the Four Courts — how they were blown up in our Civil War? We know here in Ireland about the horrors of civil war. The one in Spain is just as senseless, but just as important. You worry yourself sick over your unemployed patients here. Permit me to show a bit of humanity, concern for the children of Spain."

And after that Fingal didn't think there was much more to say.

30
THIS IS THE
HAPPIEST CONVERSATION

O'Reilly sat at the head of the dining room table, his jacket hanging on the back of his chair. He watched the play of late October sunlight on the cut-glass chandelier above the table — blue, indigo, and violet — as a beam was refracted through a facet. Illuminated dust motes danced a saraband on convection currents above the sideboard where a warming plate sat under a chafing dish. On it, two shrivelled devilled kidneys remained, the sole survivors of the massacre, largely at his hands, of the original servings. He burped contentedly.

Kitty had left for work, Jenny was in the surgery, and he, Doctor Fingal Flahertie O'Reilly, was temporarily a gentleman of leisure. Not a single solitary sufferer had sought the solace of a home visit.

He spread Frank Cooper's Oxford Marmalade on buttered toast. The stuff had been a favourite of his for years. After several chilly negotiating sessions in 1947, Kinky had given in. Apart from the Lea & Perrins Worcester-shire sauce necessary to the devilled kidneys recipe, Cooper's marmalade was the only bought preserve permitted at Number One Main Street and even then she only served it when she was feeling expansive. Did the fact that Archie had squired her to see *Lord Jim* starring Peter O'Toole last night have any-thing to do with her good mood this morn-ing?

He took a bite, chewed happily, and scanned his *Daily Telegraph.* It didn't look as if the British prime minister, Harold Wilson, was going to prevent his Southern Rhodesian counterpart Ian Smith unilaterally declaring the independence of his country from the British Commonwealth.

Not even a letter from Her Majesty seemed to be having any effect. O'Reilly knew that during the war Smith had survived the crash of his Hurricane, extensive plastic surgery, and later having his Spitfire shot down by German flak. He'd be no pushover if his mind was made up. And O'Reilly was sure it was all very important to Rhodesians.

He supposed he should take more interest in the big wide world, but in Ballybucklebo, as life trundled along with its little dramas, tragedies, and comedies closer to home, things were much more immediate than in — in Belfast, never mind in a country five or six thousand miles away.

And, most important, he, Fingal Flahertie O'Reilly, could not influence affairs in Southern Rhodesia by one jot or tittle. But he could make changes here. Like helping Helen Hewitt. Already Kitty had asked Cromie to speak to his colleague Mister Braidwood about a summer job in Newtownards Hospital for the lass. It seemed Braidwood ran a monthly hand clinic at the Royal, and Cromie would see him there soon. The work of the clinic was critical to artisans, returning their damaged hands to near normal function.

He finished his tea and toast and rose. Kinky'd already tidied much of the stuff away. He'd take the rest to the kitchen. Save her the trip. He lifted the chafing dish and blew out the squat little candles of the warming plate, piled his cup, saucer, plate, and knife on the dish, and headed for the door. He noticed as he passed that the waiting room was packed and wondered why Kitty was still chuntering on about changing his favourite rosy wallpaper. She'd brought the subject up last night.

"Fingal, I wish you'd take it seriously."

"Take what seriously?"

"The waiting room wallpaper. Kinky agrees with me that —"

"It's perfectly fine as it is. My customers don't like changes."

"Honestly," she'd said and had let the matter drop, but that Kitty could be very persistent, he knew from of old.

He went into the kitchen, where Kinky sat on a chair, her back to him. She clearly hadn't heard him come in. She was plucking one of the brace of green-headed mallard drakes he'd shot on Saturday at Strangford Lough. A sheet of newspaper protected the counter nearby where the other bird lay in its full plumage. She had a pillowcase ticking between her knees to accept the soft feathers from the breast. Typical Kinky. Waste not, want not. A few more birds and Number One would possess another down pillow. "Tidied up a bit," he said, putting the dirty things on a counter near the sink.

She looked up. "Thank you, sir," she said, "for I'll be a while plucking and cleaning these birds." She frowned and tutted when she saw that two kidneys had not been eaten. "Was everything all right?"

"We were all stuffed to the gills, Kinky, and everyone said it was grand." To a Cork-woman, there was only one higher accolade than "grand," and it pleased O'Reilly to see the colour rise in her cheeks, cheeks that since her introduction of the slimming diet for the pair of them were still rosy, but like the rest of Kinky, less heavy. "Grand altogether."

"Go 'way out of that, Doctor O'Reilly." She shook her head at him, but her grin was vast.

374

Even after their nineteen years together, twenty if he counted the time he'd spent here as an assistant to old Doctor Flanagan before the war, he could still take pleasure from paying her a compliment.

O'Reilly dragged another chair across the room, set it opposite her, and rolled up his sleeves. Picking up the second bird, he sat. "I'll give you a hand. I've been dressing fowl since our uncle Hedley taught Lars and me to shoot. You know that."

"I do," she said. "And the help's appreciated."

O'Reilly's left hand held the bird by its feet and he let its head fall into the ticking sack. He made his right hand into a loose fist and grasped feathers between outstretched thumb and curved index finger. Pushing his hand away, he tore a tuft of soft feathers free. He dropped them into the sack, then repeated the operation. "I've not lost my touch," he said.

"You do enjoy your shooting, so, don't you, sir?"

"It's more than just shooting, Kinky. It's an excuse to go to a quiet place. Be on my own with Arthur." He let another tuft of feathers fall free. Next to Kitty and his brother Lars, Kinky was the only person in whom O'Reilly would confide. "There's something about our Ireland," he said. "The country places like Strangford Lough, the Glens of Antrim, the

Cliffs of Moher. And I love dirty old Dublin, 'Strumpet City.' " More feathers drifted into the sack.

"And I do be very fond of Béal na mBláth, Clonakilty, West Cork, and Dingle out in Kerry," she said, her arm working in time with his, feathers drifting into the ticking.

He laughed. "We sound a bit like a brochure for Bord Fáilte, the Irish tourist board, don't we?"

"We do not at all. You're like me. You love this country and there's no shame in saying it out loud, so." The entire underside of Kinky's drake was now completely bald, the skin white and pimpled. She turned the bird and started to pluck its back, but this time over a sheet of newspaper. These feathers were too coarse for making bedding.

O'Reilly stopped plucking. "You know, it's not just the places. It's the people north and south of the border. Most of them are hard-working folks. Helen Hewitt wants summer work to earn a few bob for her family."

"Does she now? Good for her."

He shook his head. It seemed that almost since the day he'd started medical school he'd become a one-man job-finder. "I knew a couple of Dubliners, Paddy Keogh, a one-armed army sergeant, and John-Joe Finnegan with a smashed ankle, and they both desperate for work despite their disabilities. They were brothers under the skin to Donal Donnelly."

She laughed. "Donal? A complete skiver if there's money to be made, but I grant you, that man works every hour God provides to take care of his family, so."

"He does," O'Reilly said, and bent back to his own work. He noticed Lady Macbeth sitting on the floor, one paw raised, batting at a single feather that fluttered on the wind of her paw's passage.

"I'm a lucky man, Kinky," he said. "My home's in the best village in all the thirty-two counties. I've a job that is as satisfying as anything I ever dreamed of, and," he bent over and touched her shoulder, "I've got the best housekeeper in Ireland."

"Thank you, Doctor O'Reilly," she said, and he heard how serious she sounded. "I appreciate that very much." She sat back, took a deep breath. "Might you spare a Cork-woman a moment to answer a question?"

"I'm all ears. Fire away." The lower part of his bird's underside was as white as Kinky's now. He continued plucking.

"I think," she said, "I could not have a better employer, sir."

"Thank you, Kinky." A thought struck him. "Or even after all these years would you prefer to be called Maureen?"

"Kinky does be grand, sir, but thank you for asking. That is exactly what I mean. Only a gentleman would ask a thing like that." She frowned and tugged at a single long feather that didn't want to come free. "How a body's called is important to them."

He inclined his head and wondered where this was leading. Perhaps she needed a little prompt. "What would you like to ask me?"

"I'd like to say that apart from yourself, and I don't mean to open old wounds, that I'm the only one here who met your Miss Deirdre Mawhinney before she became Mrs. O'Reilly . . ."

"There's no hurt taken, Kinky." He pursed his lips, inclined his head.

"Poor girl."

He started plucking. "That's very long ago now. I'll never forget her, but the ache has gone."

"And you hurt sore back then. I saw how you still grieved, sir, when first you came back here in '46." She jerked back as the feather came free.

He inhaled. "Aye," he said quietly, "I did." He still couldn't see where this was going.

"And you know my story, my Paudeen, the fisherman, and how he was drowned." It was a flat statement of fact.

"I do, Kinky. And you grieved long and hard too."

"Until Paudeen spoke to me when I had that operation in the springtime of this year, so."

And just as on that day, when she'd told him about her dead husband appearing and asking her to consider remarrying, the hairs on O'Reilly's arms stiffened and he knew goose bumps like the ones on the plucked fowl were appearing. It was generally known in Ballybucklebo that Kinky Kincaid was fey.

"It does seem to me, and I know it's impertinent of me to say so, but if you'll not mind the observation, you've been a different man since Kitty came back into your life."

O'Reilly grinned. "Mind? Kinky? Kinky, why would I mind you saying what's true?"

"Thank you." Her bird was now feather-free. She set it on the counter. "I just need to chop off its wings and feet and clean it, and if you'd like me to finish your bird?"

"I'm fine." He turned his to do its back and waited. He knew she'd come to the point soon.

"The question I need to ask, sir, is if I were to remarry and leave your employ, would you be able to manage?"

He pushed his chair back. His mouth fell open. "Thundering mother of Jasus," he roared. "Has Archie proposed? Has he?" O'Reilly would be tickled pink for Kinky if Archie had, and O'Reilly loved being right. He'd already told Barry of a real concern that they were going to lose Kinky to marriage. "Well? Well?" Lady Macbeth, presumably startled by his shout, leapt up onto the

379

counter, sat down, and began to wash vigorously.

"I'm sorry, sir, but that's not an answer to my question." Kinky's jaw was set.

"You're right, it's not. Manage?" You're on thin ice, Fingal. Say "of course" at once and she'll feel she's wasted all those years here. He frowned. "It would be bloody hard to get used to, but with, I dunno, a part-time receptionist, a lady to come in and clean, I think we might get by, but it wouldn't be the same without you."

"But you would cope? I know I was a bit suspicious at first about Mrs O'Reilly's cooking —"

Suspicious? Closer to feeling persecuted, O'Reilly thought. Thank the Lord she got over that.

"But I know she would not let you starve, sir."

"She'd not." He leant forward, put his hand on Kinky's. "Are you telling me, Kinky, that Archie has said nothing and if I'd told you I couldn't do without you you'd've turned down a proposal if one came?"

She stiffened. "Of course I am, sir. It does be my solemn duty to look after you, so." A tear glistened in the corner of one eye. "Anyway, not a word on that subject has he spoken. Archie does be a very shy man. I simply wanted to know where I stood, in case."

O'Reilly swallowed, inhaled. He said softly, "You'd do that for me?"

"Of course. No need to make a fuss."

He felt humbled and damn near wept himself. He'd been ruminating about loving Ireland, its places, its people. He could add one more person he felt so strongly for. Maureen "Kinky" Kincaid née O'Hanlon. "Damn it, Kinky, I don't know how to say thank you for that."

"And it does not be like you, sir, to be at a loss for words." She sniffed. Took a deep breath.

"And now you know if he proposes you can go ahead and accept."

"Thank you, sir." Bright fire shone in her agate eyes when she said firmly, "Mister Archie Auchinleck doesn't know yet he's going to ask for my hand, so . . ." She grinned. ". . . but he will, bye. He will." Her smile was beatific.

O'Reilly guffawed. "Kinky, you're a marvel. I told you when you were in hospital I'd dance at your wedding, and by God —"

"Excuse me, Doctor O'Reilly." Jenny had come in. "Sorry to interrupt, but I need a second opinion."

"Be right with you, Jenny." He turned to Kinky. "Sorry. You will have to finish plucking —"

A miniature version of the eruption of Krakatoa, but in feathers, covered O'Reilly as

Lady Macbeth, for reasons only known to her tiny feline brain, leapt from the counter and landed on the ticking sack.

"Holy thundering Mother of G —" O'Reilly cut himself off. There were two ladies here. "Come on, you two," he said, "help me get these feathers off me."

As Kinky and Jenny, both chuckling, helped O'Reilly to pluck his feathery self, he wondered. Was Kinky's certainty that Archie was going to propose because the sight had shown her? Or was the self-possessed Corkwoman going to give the hesitant Ulsterman a nudge in the right direction?

31
AND WHAT DREAD FEET

"It's a bloody good thing you learned to cook. Bless you, Charlie Greer," Fingal said, sitting at the table in the upstairs kitchen wolfing down one of the cold sandwiches Charlie had put up this morning from a ham he'd roasted two days ago. Fingal masticated mightily. He'd been doing home visits since nine forty-five and had another call to make this afternoon to see a youngster with something called a "stone bruise." He'd popped in to the dispensary for lunch, and because he hadn't the foggiest notion what a stone bruise might be, he wanted Phelim's advice.

"Bless me?" Charlie, who sat opposite, pretended to grumble. "More like a bloody curse. And here I'd thought sharing a flat would save me money?" Charlie laughed, and shook his head. "You moved in a week ago — I've taken careful note of the date: October 22. The papers were full of Hitler moving something called the Condor Legion to Spain to fight for Franco. I didn't realise the bloody

Vulture Legion was moving in with me at the same time. You're eating me out of house and home, you big lummox." He prodded Fingal's belly. "Where the hell do you put it? There's not an ounce of fat on you."

"Riding my bike burns it off," Fingal said, "and I need the energy for the rugby — and I pay for half of the groceries, so less of your lip, Doctor Greer, you great gurrier. Your perceived imminent poverty, as one of my patients might remark, 'would bring tears to a feckin' glass eye.' "

"And what in the name of the wee man's so funny?" Miss O'Donaghugh the midwife walked into the kitchen as Fingal and Charlie were both laughing.

"Bring tears to a glass eye," Charlie managed to blurt out before dissolving again.

"It's little amuses the innocent," she said, but laughed with them.

"You may be right, Edith. These on-call days tend to make a man feel a bit punchy after a while. But don't you think having a bit of a chuckle with a friend of five years is a good thing?" Fingal said.

"Och, sure," she said, her County Kerry lilt musical to Fingal's ear, "friends are better than gold, so they say. And you're sharing a flat now, are you?"

"We are," Fingal said.

"And it's working well?"

"It would be hard not to get on with this

great eejit. When he's not beating the bejasus out of a sparring partner or on the rugby pitch he's only a cooing dove," Fingal said.

"Away off and feel your head, Fingal O'Reilly." Charlie was still grinning.

Edith shook her head. "Bye, but you northeners are grand ones for the slagging, but we're no slouches out west either with the friendly jibe." She smiled and Fingal thought he detected mischief in her eyes. He'd come to admire her midwifery skills and her no-nonsense approach to life and to two young doctors who were twenty years her junior.

"You're a pair of sound men," she said. "Now I must be running along."

"Bye, Edith," Fingal said.

"She's a good skin," Charlie said. "Saved my bacon last week with an undiagnosed breech. She's a better accoucheur than some of the specialists at the Rotunda."

"Still thinking of specializing yourself, Charlie?"

Charlie nodded. "It's hard making up your mind, but I will give you fair warning if that is what I decide."

"I hear you. I have second thoughts about this job sometimes myself." Fingal took another bite of his sandwich. "Still, it's good to be sharing the flat for the time being. Lots of changes at my old home. Our cook has left to work for the Carson family on Mount Street Upper."

"How's the house sale going?"

"Roaring along. Ma and Bridgit our maid will be out by November the thirtieth. My brother, you remember Lars? He's found a place for Ma to rent in Portaferry while she's looking for somewhere to buy."

"Shouldn't be too hard in a place like Portaferry," Charlie said. "Will you not miss living on Lansdowne Road?"

"I'll miss Cook's meals and I don't mean to be disloyal to my mother, but I can use the extra free time once they've moved."

"For the rugby?"

"Aye. And for Kitty . . ."

Charlie sighed. "I understand. You take care of that girl."

Fingal shrugged. "I'm trying to. She's got a bee in her bonnet about the orphans in Spain."

"And there be more of them now since General Franco started a drive towards Catalonia on Monday."

"I try to be sympathetic, but thank the Lord she'd not said much about Spain on our last two dates." Nor, for which he was grateful, about wanting something more permanent than walking out.

"You pay attention. She's a jewel, that one. You're a lucky man she came back to you." He stared into the middle distance. "Meuros, my Maynooth lassie, blew me out last week."

"I'm sorry. You didn't tell me."

Charlie shrugged. "Och, sure . . ."

And Fingal knew that was all he was going to get out of his friend, a typically reticent Ulsterman. "I am sorry."

"Thanks, Fingal. Now," Charlie said, rising and brushing bread crumbs off his waistcoat, "it's back to the salt mines for me. I'll maybe see you here this evening. I'll go and give Phelim a break so he can get his lunch."

"Fingal, how are ye, boy?" said Doctor Corrigan minutes later. His parting was tending to nor-nor-west today. He came in, poured himself a cup of tea, grabbed a chair, and began unwrapping a rasher sandwich in grease-proof paper.

It seemed to Fingal that it was all the man ever ate at lunchtime. He couldn't help wonder if Phelim had a more varied diet in the evenings. Oh well. The man was too old to get rickets. "Grand, thanks, and yourself?"

Phelim scowled. "More buggering about with the dispensary committee this morning before I could get to the surgery. Talking about redefining the boundaries of some of Dublin's dispensary districts, but they're starting on the North Side so we'll be all right for a while."

"I'm glad you look after that stuff, Phelim," Fingal said. "I hate admin work. Much prefer the clinical."

"And ye're still enjoying it?" Phelim took a bite from his sandwich. "Tasty, by God,"

Phelim mumbled with his mouth full.

"Enjoying the work? Lord, aye," Fingal said, preferring not to let his serious uncertainty show. "I get a bit discouraged that there's so little we can do for so many folks. Sometimes the unemployment gets me down a bit."

"Ye get used to it," Phelim said, and took another bite. "Ye have to or ye'll pack it up like my previous partners."

"No, I'll not," Fingal said, wondering whether he meant not getting used to it or not quitting. "And there's still a fair bit of stuff I'm seeing that we never ran into in the hospital. I've had a request to visit a Dermot Finucane on Bull Alley," he said. "Apparently he's got a stone bruise. I haven't the foggiest notion what that is."

"Not the kind of thing you'd see in hospital," Doctor Corrigan said. "They usually get treated at home unless complications set in." He poured himself a second cup of tea and shoved three spoonfuls of sugar into it. "Ye know the tenements. How many kids wear shoes?"

"When they're in school, the teachers hand out boots from the *Herald* newspaper boot fund, but damn few boys are shod for long after they leave school."

"True. And the streets are covered in animal dung."

"I know," Fingal said. Even with the windows of the kitchen closed, he could detect one of the ever-present smells of Dublin's tenement streets.

"Lad cuts his bare foot, steps in the muck, and what happens?"

"Infection. Inevitable as night follows day."

"If he's lucky it's with one of the simpler bacteria like *Staphylococcus* or *Streptococcus* and doesn't spread," Phelim said, "because the body walls the infection off in an abscess under the thick skin of the sole of the foot. The abscess is known locally as a 'stone bruise.' If it does spread, it's amputation, or septicaemia and a dead kid."

Fingal shuddered.

"If ye're really unlucky and the bug's one of the *Clostridia; tetani,* it'll cause tetanus."

"And *perfringens* gives you gas gangrene," said Fingal. Facts he'd never forget, having been grilled on the very subject of the *Clostridia* family of microorganisms in his final microbiology exam. "The lad's mother came round this morning. Gave me her ticket and asked me to drop in. I thought I'd ask you before I went out what ailed the boy and how I should treat it." He finished his sandwich.

"I'll do better," Phelim said. "I'll drive ye round there and I'll show ye what to do." He finished his tea.

"I'd appreciate that." Fingal waited until Phelim rose, rinsed his cup in the sink, and said, "Come on."

Phelim stuck his head into Charlie's surgery. "I'm going out with Doctor O'Reilly," he said, ignoring a man in a torn undervest who was having a coughing fit. "Look after the shop, please, Doctor Greer, until we get back." He didn't wait for a reply. "Get your coat, Fingal."

Fingal waited while Phelim nipped into his surgery, shrugged into a raincoat, and picked up his bag from its place by the door. "Come on." He opened the front door and strode into an autumn downpour with Fingal in full pursuit. They headed for his presumably once shiny black, now dirt-smeared and rust-pocked, Model T Ford, 1924 vintage.

Phelim opened the driver's door and slung his doctor's bag into the backseat. "Pile in out of this bloody deluge."

Fingal hurried round and heard the springs complain as he clambered into the front. He slammed the door, glad to be out of what Ma would have described as "the kind of rain that wets you through."

Phelim stamped on the starter and to the accompaniment of a strangled wheezing and a backfire like the crack of doom, the engine struggled into life. "It's not far," he said, turning right onto Aungier Street. "Bull Alley's near Saint Patrick's Cathedral."

He braked and waited for a gap in the traffic on Bride Street then drove across onto

Bull Alley.

Fingal peered through the windscreen that the wiper struggled to keep clear. To his left was Saint Patrick's, a medieval Anglican cathedral built between 1200 and 1270. To Fingal the great architecturally ornate house of God, with its precious communion plate, lavish candelabra, lecterns, altar screens, rich vestments, and easy living for the clergy, stood like some rich dowager while the tenements of the Liberties clung round her skirts like so many begging children.

Phelim pulled over and parked at the kerb. "Out." He reached for his bag from the back.

Fingal dismounted and, with his collar turned to the rain, followed, off the street and into a passageway between houses. Their redbrick façades were crumbling. Window sashes needed painting, but on every sill bright flowers grew in window boxes. Inside a half-open window, a linnet in a cage trilled despite the downpour, its red, feathered breast swelling as it sang. Underfoot, dark water overflowed from a single shallow gutter running along one side of the cobbles. It was dammed by the corpse of a cat.

The stink was overpowering but did not come as a shock to Fingal. Three months of working here had inured him to the worst smells the slums could offer, if not to the living conditions of the folks who had no choice but to exist here.

Doctor Corrigan entered a hall and knocked on a shabby door.

The place reeked of human and cats' piss, damp, and stale cigarette smoke. The acrid fumes of the disinfectant Jeyes Fluid, known locally as "Jasus's fluid" hung over all. Someone had tried to hide the permanent stench by sprinkling the stuff in the hall and on the staircase.

The door was opened by a short, grey-haired woman in an ankle-length skirt. She hugged a shawl around her upper body. "Doctor Corrigan, sir. T'ank you for coming. It was the Big Fellah there I spoke to this morning." She looked to Fingal and then back to Corrigan and frowned. "Do you think Dermot needs two doctors to attend to him? Is he dat sick?"

"Not at all," Fingal said. "I'm new at this, and I've never seen a stone bruise. Doctor Corrigan's come to teach me so I'll know what to do with the next one."

She smiled at him, put a hand on her hip. "I'll tell you a t'ing, Big Fellah, you're as honest as a feckin' priest admitting you've more to learn. I like it."

He bowed his head.

"Come in. I have Dermot ready for youse til see." She led them into a single room lit only by light from a cracked but spotlessly clean window, the rays of a paraffin lamp on a mantel, and the guttering flames of a turf fire burning in an open grate. Turf, at two pence for a dozen sods, was cheaper than coal. Fingal had to wait for his eyes to adjust. Plain wooden table, two chairs, one end curtained off with a blanket, from behind which came loud snoring.

Fingal wondered who was sleeping there but knew it wasn't the patient. He was lying on an old overcoat in front of a fire where cabbage leaves and potato skins burned at the back of the grate. The people of the tenements believed that burning them helped keep diseases away. He wished it did, but clean drinking water and proper sewage would keep them away a hell of a lot more effectively.

"Now Dermot," Mrs. Finucane said, "dese are nice doctor men come til look at your foot."

Doctor Corrigan crouched on his hunkers and Fingal followed suit.

"Hello, Dermot," said Doctor Corrigan. "How are ye?"

The lad, who looked to Fingal to be about fourteen, sniffed, wiping his nose with his shirt sleeve. "Me foot's feckin' killing me. It hurts like bedamned. I've a stone bruise the size of County Wicklow."

"I'm sorry," Doctor Corrigan said, clearly paying no attention to the child's language.

"Not as sorry as me. It's not your feckin' foot."

"Dermot." Mrs. Finucane stood over her son. "Be polite to the nice doctor men. They're only here til help."

"My da was going to let it go last night."

"That means drain it," Doctor Corrigan said to Fingal.

"But," said Mrs. Finucane, "he'd won money at pitch and toss and he came home mouldy maggotty drunk. Eejit. It's not like my 'Minty.' " She must have seen Fingal's quizzical look. "Jasus," she said, "we're great ones for the nicknames in the Liberties. There's a 'Rashers' upstairs and 'Duckegg' Brennan across the hall's married to 'Skylark,' her w'at works wi't me at Clery's. My oul wan was christened Cathal, but if you asked for Cathal Finucane round here nobody'd know who the blazes you were talking about. He got 'Minty' because when he was a chissler he was always feckin' peppermints from sweetie shops. The name stuck."

"I see," Fingal said.

"And he's not usually much of a one for the gargle, but . . ." She shrugged and gave a wry smile. "Och, sure, once in a rare while he gets scuttered, and sure wat's wrong wit dat? He couldn't have bitten his own finger never mind let Dermot's bruise out last night. Mind you when Minty went out he didn't know the lad was afflicted." She grunted. "Dat's the snores of himself behind the curtain. The bowsey . . ." And yet Fingal heard affection. "When dat one wakes up he'll be in an advanced state of decomposition." She shrugged. "A bloody great hangover'll remind him dat once in a while I'll forgive him, and I will, but not to make a habit of it." There was a trace of steel in her last sentence.

Fingal hid a smile.

"So ye came for one of us?" Doctor Corrigan said, and stood. Fingal stayed hunkered down.

"Yes, sir. I'm sorry to have to trouble youse, but the poor wee lad's pain's been getting worser. It's not right. He needs help."

"And that's why we're here." Doctor Corrigan turned back to Dermot. "That's why we're here, son."

32
I Hear It in the
Deep Heart's Core

Jenny stopped in the middle of the hallway, forcing O'Reilly to do likewise, and, in the process, to stop speculating about Kinky's marital prospects. "It's not another 'I won't see a lady doctor' difficulty, is it?"

"No." She shook her head. "Nothing like that. The patient has a heart murmur, and —" She grimaced and said, "My sense of rhythm has always been terrible. I'm never entirely sure what I'm hearing. I'm very lucky my internal medicine case in finals didn't have a murmur."

Even twenty-nine years later, O'Reilly could clearly see himself on a ward beside a bed, inwardly trembling, and presenting his findings about a case to two examiners as part of the final hurdle that stood between him and his dream of qualifying as a physician. Being bombed by German Stukas off Crete in 1941 had not been as terrifying as being examined. The same thought had struck him back then as the gull-winged aircraft hurtled down, dive sirens screaming. Taking a direct hit by a bomb was quick and the outcome sure. The finals examination had gone on for three weeks with every nerve screwed up day to day with no guarantee of the outcome whatsoever. He shuddered.

She stood aside, but he indicated that she should precede him into the surgery.

He followed and closed the door behind him. A fair-haired young man, quite unknown to O'Reilly, lay on the examining couch. The patient was stripped to the waist. The room's central heating was off and it was chilly, but it didn't seem to faze the patient. He certainly was not shivering. O'Reilly immediately noticed ruddy cheeks, pallid chest, but deeply tanned forearms and the brown sunburned vee at the top of the man's chest where his shirt would have been left open. Farming? Fishing?

"This is Doctor O'Reilly," Jenny said.

"Pleased til meet you, sir," the patient said. "I'm Hall Campbell, I've just moved here from Ardglass."

"Fisherman?" O'Reilly asked.

"That's right, sir. How did you know?"

O'Reilly chuckled. "What do most men from Ardglass, famous for its herrings, do? And you've an open-airman's tan and," he said, walking to the radiator and turning a knurled iron wheel to the "on" position to the accompaniment of a series of clangs and gurgles, "you're not bothered by the cold. And neither, it seems, is my colleague."

Jenny gave O'Reilly a wry smile and mouthed "thank you."

"Boys-a-boys," the man said. "Is your Christian name Sherlock? I love them detective stories, so I do. *The Speckled Band* was wheeker and see that there *Hound of the Baskervilles*? Absolutely dead on, so it was."

"It's what they teach you at medical school; to be observant and make deductions," O'Reilly said. "Conan Doyle was a doctor and patterned the great detective on one of his teachers —"

"Doctor Joseph Bell of Edinburgh," Jenny said quietly.

"See," O'Reilly said, giving her a smile, "Doctor Bradley doesn't only know her stuff as a doctor."

"She was quare and nice til me, so she was, and dead honest too. Said I'd a heart murmur, but she couldn't make head nor tail of it and was going to get a second opinion." He frowned. "Is a murmur bad, sir?"

O'Reilly said, feeling reasonably confident, "Not necessarily. You look pretty fit to me." Most heart murmurs, caused because the valves were damaged, or the heart or great vessels, the aorta and the pulmonary artery, had been deformed since birth, led to some degree of heart failure. Patients with the condition were, among other signs, usually short of breath and had blue, cyanosed cheeks and lips. "Just let Doctor Bradley tell me your history and then I'll take a look at you, and try to answer your questions."

"Fire away," Hall said.

"Mister Campbell used to crew on a herring boat out of Ardglass, but he got a better offer from one of our fishermen, a Mister Scott."

"That would be Jimmy," Fingal said.

"That's right, sir. Sound man, Jimmy, so he is. He's getting on a bit, wants til retire, so he's letting me buy shares in the boat and one day I'll own her outright."

O'Reilly heard the pride in the man's voice.

"Mister Campbell came in today to see if he could join our practice," Jenny said.

The "our" wasn't lost on O'Reilly.

"You'd told me, when I started, to accept any new patients, so I said of course he could. But that even if he felt fit and well, I'd like to take his history, and examine him so we'd know how he'd been when he came here first and could compare that with what we found if he ever did get sick."

"Just right," O'Reilly said, "and what did you discover?"

"Mister Campbell, who was originally from Donaghadee before the family moved to Ardglass, is a single man. He was born, the youngest of four brothers, at home, three weeks prematurely in July 1940, so he's just turned twenty-five."

O'Reilly noted the prematurity. Babies born early were more likely to suffer from congenital heart defects. Yet the man looked to be in the pink. There was one thing that might be causative . . . O'Reilly concentrated on what Jenny was saying.

"There is no family history of inheritable diseases. He's had the usual children's infections, dropped a weighted lobster pot on his foot two years ago and broke a toe, and doesn't count the number of times he's got a fishhook stuck in his finger or thumb."

"We'll not count them either," said O'Reilly, "but did they teach you at medical school how to get a barbed fishhook out?"

She shook her head.

"They didn't teach me either," he said, "but doctors working in fishing communities do need to know." O'Reilly was careful not to say, "But if you're going to go on working here." That was not finalised yet.

"If youse don't mind me interrupting? It's dead easy," Hall said. "Because of the barb you can't pull it out. You go to the other end where there's an eye for tying the hook on the line. Get a pair of pliers with a wire cutter, cut off the eye, and then use the pliers to shove the hook the whole way through. As the barb breaks the skin on its way out, grab the point of the hook with the pliers, and haul. Bob's your uncle, out she pops."

Jenny was frowning. "Doesn't that hurt?"

"Och, aye," he said, "but you just have to thole it. If you're on a boat, you've to shove your hand in til the sea to disinfect it." He grimaced. "That stings like bug — Sorry, miss."

As if to hide his words and perhaps in sympathy with the man, the radiator rattled and violently shuddered on its cast-iron feet.

"It always does that when it's getting going," O'Reily said. "Pay it no heed." He rubbed his hands. "At least the room's warming up." He asked Jenny, "And was there anything else in Hall's history?"

She shook her head. "That's it, and, oh yes, his pulse is regular and his blood pressure's one twenty over sixty. The diastolic pressure's a bit low."

O'Reilly had already made a shrewd guess, and the low diastolic blood pressure was another confirmatory clue. Hall had been born at home, as was normal practice for second to fourth pregnancies, which were not considered to be as hazardous as first and fifth and subsequent, which should be confined in hospital. His mother would have been attended by a midwife or busy G.P., either of whom might have missed the murmur of a congenital heart lesion, something more likely to be present in a premature. No serious illnesses in the rest of his life so no real reasons for anything but cursory examinations to confirm conditions like measles or whooping cough. No signs of congestive heart failure, which, if O'Reilly was right about the cause of the murmur, wouldn't begin to appear until the late twenties — and Hall was only twenty-five. "I'll take a listen," he said, and did, but confident that he knew what to listen for, put the bell of his stethoscope higher up the chest in the second space between the ribs to the left.

O'Reilly had learnt very early in his studentship that the heart has four chambers. The upper are the auricles and receive blood from the whole body, and the lungs where it has picked up oxygen. The auricles contract and send the blood to the two lower chambers, the ventricles. When the ventricles contract to drive blood to the body and the lungs, the phase of the heart's action known as systole, two valves close to prevent blood being forced backward into the smaller auricles above. That makes an audible *lub,* the first heart sound. Once blood had entered the pulmonary artery and the aorta, supplying the lungs and the rest of the body respectively, the ventricles relax in diastole and the aortic and pulmonary valves close to prevent the blood returning to the ventricles. The closure of those valves produced a *dup,* the second heart sound. All murmurs were classified, depending on their relationship to the heart sounds, as being either systolic or diastolic, or a combination of both. A skilled physician could infer from that timing which valves might be damaged.

In this case, O'Reilly heard a low rumbling that was continuous across both systole and diastole. That was the classic "machinery murmur" he'd been sure he'd detect. He nodded and moved the bell of his stethoscope to the side of Hall's neck. He could hear the murmur over the carotid artery. More confirmation.

He straightened, took the earpieces out, and said to Jenny and Hall, "You did well, Doctor Bradley. Lots of busy G.P.s would have taken a quick history and not bothered to examine Mister Campbell. You are a lucky man, sir — in more ways than one."

Hall was sitting up and listening intently.

"Put on your shirt," O'Reilly said, "and I'll explain." He waited until Hall was dressed. "When you're a baby in your mammy's womb," O'Reilly said, "getting your oxygen from the afterbirth —"

"Excuse me, sir, isn't it oxygen we get from the air when we breathe?"

"It is, Hall, and if we don't get it, as if —" Use an analogy a fisherman would understand, he thought. "Well, like if we're underwater too long, our lungs can't take in any oxygen and we die."

"I know all about that, sir. I was thirteen when the *Princess Victoria,* the Larne-to-

Stranraer ferry, went down near the Copeland Islands. One hundred and thirteen people drowned. My daddy was one of the Donaghadee lifeboat crew, so he was."

"Was he, by God?" O'Reilly whistled. "That's very interesting. All volunteers too. Brave men." O'Reilly pursed his lips. "Terrible day," he said. "The folks of North Down will never forget it."

"I know," Jenny said. "My daddy had a friend who was lost."

"Just about everybody here knew of someone on board her," O'Reilly said, and let a few respectful moments of silence pass. He remembered old *Victoria.* He sailed on her when he'd got leave from the battleship HMS *Warspite* when she'd been based at Greenock in Scotland early in the war. Long ago now. He said, "To get back to your problem, Hall, when we're babies inside our mammy, we're surrounded by fluid. But we don't drown because the afterbirth gives us oxygen. And in order for it to go directly to our bodies, there's a special short blood vessel between the two great arteries of the heart." He saw Jenny nodding. Now she knew what the problem was. "One supplies the body with blood, the other the lungs, but the lungs don't need much blood until we are born and start to breathe. Until then, this short vessel, it's called the ductus arteriosus, lets the blood bypass the lungs. Once we're born, it closes."

He looked at Hall, who was listening intently. "Except in some people, it doesn't close."

"Is that bad, sir? I've never noticed nothing wrong, so I've not." Hall frowned.

"It could be a damn sight worse," O'Reilly said. "Some folks with it get a heart infection, called bacterial endocarditis, but you've been spared that. It can lead to heart failure by the time you're getting close to thirty, but thanks to Doctor Bradley, who took the trouble to examine you, we know about it and can take steps to fix it."

"Honest?" Hall grinned. "That's great, so it is. Thanks a lot, Doctors."

"It's going to mean an operation. I remember," said O'Reilly, "the very first time the operation was done. Back in 1938, a Doctor Gross in Boston fixed the condition for an eight-year-old girl. It was a sensation, operating on the heart — then. Now?" He shrugged. "It's routine. We'll get you up to the Royal to see Mister Bingham, the heart surgeon. He'll have you back on your feet and out fishing again in no time."

"I'll make the arrangements, Doctor O'Reilly," Jenny said.

"I'd be grateful. Good to meet you, Hall." He'd compliment Jenny later. O'Reilly turned to go. As he was closing the door, he overheard Hall Campbell say, "Jimmy Scott told me there was a lady doctor working here" — O'Reilly stopped to hear the rest — "and that there was no need to worry. She was very good." O'Reilly heard a laugh. "Bejizziz, ould Jimmy was right."

O'Reilly's grin was huge as he closed the door behind him.

33
TO COMFORT AND
RELIEVE THEM

"How old are ye, son?" Doctor Corrigan asked.

"Twelve, coming on turteen." The boy's fair hair was cut in a fringe of equal length all round his head. He looked the doctor straight in the eye.

"And do you go to school?"

"Nah. I'm a working fellah. I sell readers. I make ten shillings a week and dat's good money."

When rent for a room like this would be from three to six shillings a week, and a fourteen-year-old girl working in a shirt factory made five shillings a week — and that was reckoned to be not a bad wage — ten shillings from selling newspapers, "readers" in the local argot, would be quite a help to a family's budget.

"And when did you hurt your foot, Dermot?" Doctor Corrigan asked.

"T'ree days ago I was scuttin' on a cart . . ."

"That's, ahem, 'borrowing' a ride by hanging on a tailboard," Doctor Corrigan translated.

Fingal knew all about it. You couldn't walk down a Dublin thoroughfare but some urchin would go by you illegally clinging on to a vehicle.

"When I jumped off, I landed on a feckin' nail and now I've got this ruddy great stone bruise."

"Can we have a look?"

"Go ahead."

"I wonder, Mrs. Finucane, if we could get young Dermot sitting in a chair, and maybe a chair for me?" Doctor Corrigan said. "Doctor O'Reilly will give ye a hand."

Fingal helped rearrange the furniture, and soon Doctor Corrigan was sitting in one chair facing Dermot. "Shove your bad hoof onto my lap, son. Doctor O'Reilly, can ye bring over the lamp, please?"

Fingal did, and peered at the left foot. What looked like a white blister stretched from the ball beneath the big toe to halfway along the sole. A black point stood in its middle, presumably the scab of the nail wound.

"And if I push on it?" Doctor Corrigan asked as he laid two fingers on the lesion.

"You'll hear the gulders of me all the way to Saint Stephen's feckin' Green. Please don't, Doctor."

"I won't, but I'll tell the young doctor it's hot as Hades. Full of pus. Can you twist your

408

foot to the side?"

"Like this?" Dermot rolled his ankle side-ways.

"Good lad." Doctor Corrigan scrutinised the calf. "No lymphatic involvement so we can be thankful for small mercies."

Fingal noted with relief the absence of thin red lines under the skin running up the leg. Their presence, indicating lymphangitis, inflammation of the lymphatic channels, would be a sure sign of spreading infection — and the absolute need for amputation.

"So," said Doctor Corrigan. "What we have is a plantar abscess, better known as a stone bruise." He slowly lifted the boy's foot, stood, and set it gently on his chair. "We'll fix you up in no time, Dermot. Now." He looked over to Mrs. Finucane. "Mother?" He nodded his head to the far side of the room.

While he and Mrs. Finucane talked, Fingal set the lamp back on the mantel beside a plaster statue of the Blessèd Virgin in a blue shawl and rummaged in his pocket. Ever since he'd started seeing young patients he'd carried a halfpenny bag of sweeties. "Dermot," he said, "what would you say to a piece of clove rock?"

"I'd say, 'True on you, sir.' " Dermot, despite his obvious discomfort, managed to grin.

"Here."

The boy popped it in his mouth. "T'anks."

"And if you're a brave soldier while Doctor Corrigan fixes your foot, I'll give you two more later." Fingal knew that because the skin over the abscess was so tightly stretched there would be no sensation when the pus was released. But if Doctor Corrigan followed up with the second step of treatment —

And he was going to. Mrs. Finucane was filling a saucepan with water from a bucket. It would have been brought in from a pump in the yard.

"Give me the bag there, please, Doctor O'Reilly." There was just the slightest hint of emphasis on the "please" and Phelim gave Fingal a wicked little grin.

"Here you are." Fingal handed it over — and smiled back.

Doctor Corrigan took out a square of cloth, a sling, and half a loaf of what looked to be stale bread. He took them to the table, crumbled the bread into the cloth square, folded it over, and rolled it in the sling. "Let me know when the water's boiling," he said to Mrs. Finucane.

"Yes, Doctor." She stirred the fire and set the saucepan on top.

"Right," said Doctor Corrigan. "We'll drain the thing now." From his bag, he brought out a bottle of Dettol, the newest antiseptic, and swabs. "I'll need a bit of help," he said. "Doctor O'Reilly, come with me and we'll wash our hands." They did so over a galvanised tub.

When Fingal returned, he bent to the boy. "How's the rock?"

Dermot mumbled past a still half-full mouth of hard-boiled sweetie, "Grand."

"We'll get through this the pair of us, won't we?" Fingal said.

Dermot looked up to Fingal towering above him. "Aye, because I want d'em other two sweeties."

Fingal squatted so he was at the boy's level, trying to keep him occupied. Waiting for a procedure was often worse than the thing itself. Fingal was relieved to hear Dermot's mother say, "Water's ready."

The boy's gaze left Fingal's face and he stared as Doctor Corrigan set the bread poultice in the saucepan with the two dry ends sticking up above the water.

"Have ye a towel?" Doctor Corrigan said.

Doctor Corrigan lifted the boy's foot, took his seat, and when Mrs. Finucane appeared with a threadbare but well-laundered towel, he spread it over his knees and put Dermot's foot on it.

"Now, Doctor, bring that lamp over here again, and open the bottle of Dettol and pour some onto a swab. This will be cold, Dermot, but it won't hurt," he said, taking the swab from Fingal.

"Promise?"

"I do." Doctor Corrigan swabbed the sole of the foot over the abscess.

Dermot sucked in a swift breath. "It's colder than a witch's tit," he said, but didn't move.

"Now, Doctor, in the side pocket of the bag you'll find a wide-bore hypodermic and a box of matches. Flame the tip of the —" He mouthed the word "needle."

Fingal did. "Here." He handed it to Doctor Corrigan then stood behind the boy, a hand on each of his shoulders. Fingal felt Dermot stiffen. "Youse isn't sticking that feckin' great t'ing in —" The boy's shoulders relaxed. Fingal saw the yellow stream flowing onto the towel and Doctor Corrigan mopping more away with swabs that, as they became saturated, he chucked on the fire.

"Jasus," said Dermot, "it's a miracle. The pain's gettin' better already."

"Doctor O'Reilly, can you fix the poultice?"

"I can."

"Mrs. Finucane, I want you to watch what Doctor O'Reilly does, then when this one's cold you can heat up another one and put it on."

Fingal took the saucepan from Mrs. Finucane, setting it on the table. He was wreathed in steam as he lifted the two ends of the sling and began twisting them in opposite directions. Hot water dripped from the middle as the water-soaked bread was compressed. He kept working until no more drips appeared. "It's ready," he said.

"Could you do that, Mrs. Finucane?"

"I could, sir."

Fingal frowned. More than one poulticing? It was believed that the application of the poultice when the wet bread was almost at the boiling point would sterilise the abscess. He didn't understand why Doctor Corrigan wanted the mother to learn how to do it. Perhaps Phelim used a different approach?

"Doctor O'Reilly," Doctor Corrigan said sharply, "take yer time and only bring it here when ye can stand to put it against yer own elbow."

So it wasn't to be applied at boiling point? Interesting. "It's not quite the way we did it at Sir Patrick Dun's, Doctor Corrigan."

"Don't believe everything your seniors in the hospitals tell you, son," Doctor Corrigan said with a smile. "It's bad enough to have an abscess without getting your foot scalded as well. I believe that a hot poultice, not a boiling one, works by increasing the blood flow to the site and promoting healing. There's no need to roast the poor wee divil, but I think poulticing the way I do it needs to be done more often than only once. If Mrs. Finucane can learn, it saves the nurses from coming round."

"Are youse goin' to boil me foot, sir?" Dermot asked. His voice was quavery.

413

"No, son, I'm not, but I am going to make it warm." Doctor Corrigan tousled the boy's hair. "We want a foot that's better, not a human *cruibín.*"

Dermot managed a smile. "Mind youse," he said, "I'd go a boiled and pickled pig's trotter right now. Dey beat the boiled pig's cheeks we'd for our tea last night. Da bought dem for a treat wit' some of his toss money before he went down the boozer."

"I'm sure they would." Doctor Corrigan turned and asked Fingal, "How's it coming?"

"I think it's about right."

"Bring it here." He looked the boy right in the eye. "Now, Dermot, I'm going to put a hot poultice on your foot."

Fingal stood behind the boy and put his hands on his shoulders, for comfort and to restrain him if he jumped.

Doctor Corrigan laid the middle of the sling containing the hot bread against the abscess.

Dermot whimpered and tensed before saying, "It's feckin' hot."

Fingal said, "Can you thole it, Dermot?"

The little lad looked up. "I could for another couple a bits of clove rock."

Fingal smiled, and as Doctor Corrigan knotted the ends of the sling to keep the poultice in place, he put another hard candy into Dermot's open mouth, just the way a mother bird would pop a worm into a chick's beak. "Good lad," he said. "Now that wasn't too bad, was it?"

"One last thing," Doctor Corrigan said. "Toxoid, please, Doctor O'Reilly."

Fingal rummaged in the bag, found a stainless steel box and a glass ampoule. He went to the table, turned his back to Dermot, and started to draw tetanus toxoid into the syringe.

Fingal ignored Dermot's cries of, "Lie across yer knee wit' me pants down? The feck I will," and didn't even turn to see what was going on.

Fingal held the syringe vertically and pressed on the plunger to expel any air. A few drops of toxoid dribbled from the needle's end.

"Come on now, Dermot," Mrs. Finucane said, "be a good boy."

Fingal concentrated on his own task, not wanting to hurt the child but realising that there was a real risk of tetanus, which could happen anywhere from eight days to several months after an infection began from bacteria in animal faeces. The toxoid had been available since 1924 and its use as a vaccine had reduced the number of cases and was steadily bringing the death rate down. Even if a child had been immunized, it was wise to give a booster dose after an infection when it was possible that the spores of the causative organism had entered the body. It might not prevent the disease, but it could reduce its severity.

He turned to discover that Doctor Corrigan had Dermot over his knee with his pants half pulled down. Mrs. Finucane was holding Dermot's head between her hands. Fingal took a deep breath. It was the work of moments to give the toxoid by intramuscular injection.

Dermot yelled, "Yeeeaagh, youse poxy bollixes. Stop it. Dat feckin' hurts."

Fingal flinched. He knew it did. He finished and withdrew the needle.

Not even Dermot's screeching had any effect on the snores coming from the far end of the room.

Mrs. Finucane said, "Less of your language, Dermot, or you'll get a warm ear."

"It's all right," Doctor Corrigan said, pulling up Dermot's pants and explaining to Mrs. Finucane, "It's to prevent lockjaw."

"You say you're sorry to the nice doctor for that mout'ful of rubbish or I'll wash your mout' out wit' black soap." She was standing hand on hip, lower jaw set.

"Sorry, Doctor O'Reilly," Dermot muttered, rubbing his backside before he sat down.

"Here," said Fingal, giving the boy the whole bag of clove rock. "You were very brave. Keep these."

"T'anks. T'anks a lot." Dermot grinned,

looked at Fingal, and asked, "Did you remember a fellah called Enda from Weaver's
Street? Youse doctors had to take a pea out of
his lug last year? You once give him a bag of
bull's-eyes."

Fingal had to think. "On a Sunday, about
noon?" He and Kitty had taken a walk by the
Grand Canal last June. "He was swimming
with a bunch of other gurriers."

"I was one of dem. He called you the Big
Fellah, remember? Wait 'til I see Enda and
tell him you was here and I got sweeties too,
Doctor Big Fellah."

Fingal laughed. "Say hello to Enda from
me and remind him not to put anything in
his ear bigger than his elbow."

"Indeed I will, and I'll keep him a couple
of bits. He shared wit' us last year."

And that was how life was in the tenements.
The poorest of the poor, sharing, helping
each other out, slow to point a finger, quick
to help a friend.

Fingal waited until Doctor Corrigan finished explaining to Mrs. Finucane how and
when to repeat the poulticing, and to keep
Dermot's foot clean, and motioned to Fingal
that it was time to leave.

Outside the sun had broken through. Someone had removed the dead cat and the gutter
was flowing freely. Fingal sat in the car beside
Doctor Corrigan, who stamped on the starter
and pulled away.

Fingal felt the heat of the sun on the roof of the old car. It mirrored the warmth within him.

"Hot." Phelim wound down the window. "So," he said, "now ye know what a stone bruise is and what to do if ye see another one."

"I do. Thanks for showing me. This is what's really involved, isn't it? Getting a diagnosis right, being able to treat something effectively, gaining a patient's trust and respect."

"I hear ye, and I also saw how ye glowed when Dermot remembered ye." He stopped at Bride Street. "Do ye remember the day we met and ye asked me why I stayed here?" He drove across the road.

"I do."

"I think I said something like, 'I fit in and it's comfortable to be respected.' And that's true. I like being part of this place, part of the lives of the people who live here. But it's more than that. Much more. Are ye beginning to understand now?"

"I think so." Fingal nodded. It was more than just gaining the respect of his patients. He thought of Kitty and what she'd said a month ago. "You said he always put the patients first — and that was the kind of doctor you wanted to be." He'd wondered then if he'd detected a tinge of envy, a worry that she might have to take second place to his work. "I'm beginning to understand that there's more to this than doing a good job. That's not why you put the patients first, is it?"

Phelim stopped at the corner of Aungier Street. "Hang on until I get across the road." The traffic was heavy and he waited for a gap.

Fingal noticed a group of people gathered round a man singing. The words drifted in through the open car window.

> . . . I sat me with my true love.
> My sad heart strove to choose between
> The old love and the new love.

He recognised the song of the United Irishmen of 1798, "The Wind That Shakes the Barley." Strolling balladeers were as much a part of the tenements as beggars, buskers, and Italian organ grinders and their monkeys. A spectator threw a coin into the singer's hat that lay on the pavement. Fingal hoped the man would earn enough for a bite to eat.

Phelim scooted across and made his right turn. "No, I do not put the patients first so I can feel good about doing a good job. Not at all. That would be all wrong. Selfish." He hesitated. "I think there's some things they can't teach ye at medical school." He swung into the dispensary courtyard and parked. "Either ye see the patients as simply yer bread and butter, a job to do when ye're on duty, or God help ye, ye give a damn about them as people. And that's something ye're born with. Ye don't learn it. And that transcends whether or not there's something else ye'd rather be doing if they need ye."

And surely that was something that a nurse like Kitty could understand.

Phelim turned in his seat and faced Fingal. "I see it in ye, boy. Ye care. Ye're going to make a fine doctor."

Fingal blushed. "Thank you, Phelim." The words of the balladeer's song came back to him. "My sad heart strove to choose between the old love and the new love." Was putting the patients first why Phelim had never married? Had his sad heart made a choice? Fingal ached to know, but realized with a shock that he'd only known the man since July. It was too personal a question. "Can I ask you one more thing before we go in?"

"Ye can."

The sun went behind a cloud. Fingal stared out the window, then said, "It's great when we do help someone, but so many of our patients die. You feel so bloody helpless. Does it not bother you?"

"Aye. A bit." Phelim smiled. "So ye have to get to be like Pharaoh."

"Pharaoh?"

"Aye. When Moses said, 'Let my people go,' what did the ruler of Egypt do? I'll tell ye. He hardened —"

"His heart." Fingal nodded. "I see."

Phelim put his hand onto Fingal's shoulder. There was compassion in his voice. "It's a paradox. I do all I can for them, but I'll be no use to anyone if I'm in mourning all the time."

"And so that's what you've done? Hardened your heart?"

"Aye. And ye'll have to too — or ye'll not stick to dispensary practice long."

34
DANCE, DANCE, DANCE, TILL YOU DROP

"It's like Paddy's market in here. Have you ever seen the like?" O'Reilly stopped in his tracks and had to put his mouth near Kitty's ear so she could hear over Sam the Sham and the Pharaohs coming through loudspeakers. The music all but drowned out the steady drone of conversation, bursts of laughter, and kiddies' yells.

Wooly bully, wooly bully, woolly bully.

She laughed and said into his ear, "I saw a travelogue about Carnival in Rio de Janeiro once. That's about as close as I can get. Lots of music, food, and fancy dress." She chuckled. "A lot of it was fancy undress too."

"This, madam," he said, "is Rio's Carnival, the Bahamas's Junkanoo, and New Orleans's Mardi Gras rolled into one." "Madam" was an appropriate form of address to a lesser mortal from Henry the Eighth. The Tudor king's costume — soft shoes, hose, puff breeches with scarlet silk in the slashes, doublet, and neck ruff — had fitted him perfectly when he'd tried it on at Elliott's Fancy Dress Shop in Belfast. And with no extra padding. Kinky's campaign to slim him down had been only partially successful. "The Ballybucklebo Bonnaughts Sporting Club's annual Halloween, or if you prefer Féile na Marbh, the feast of the dead, is a ta-ta-ta-ra of the very first magnitude." He inhaled the smells of a mixture of beer, tobacco smoke, and perfume — someone was wearing Evening in Paris.

"Yes, Your Majesty. I do agree," Kitty said.

"You'd better agree, or it's away to the Tower and off with your head."

She smiled coyly, but didn't curtsey. She crossed her left arm across her tummy, leant forward, and made a leg, as would a sixteenth-century male courtier to his monarch.

And a very well-turned leg at that. O'Reilly wondered how many women in their fifties had the figure to pull off dressing like a pantomime Robin Hood, a part traditionally played by a young woman, with a pheasant's tail feather in her green hat, white loose-sleeved shirt, green jerkin, and tights. Damn few, that's how many. But, by God, his Kitty could, bless her. He tingled.

He scanned the crowd in the function room, saw who he was looking for, and turned to Terry Baird, Jenny's boyfriend of nine months. "Don't think you and Jenny have to spend all night with us old fogies, but the marquis of Ballybucklebo and his sister Myrna will be keeping places at their table for us to use as home port between dances. You'll join us, of course?"

Terry frowned and made a whistling noise as he inhaled. "A peer of the realm? Oh boy." He raised an eyebrow and looked at Jenny, who O'Reilly thought made a most fetching Little Bo Peep, although, from what he remembered, the original's skirts had been much longer.

"His lordship's a pussycat, Terry, a charming, unassuming man," said Jenny. "I've met him twice before. You and he will get on, I promise. He's a keen angler. Play your cards right and you might get invited to fish his beat on the Bucklebo River."

"Really? I'm all for that." Terry laughed, then said, "But I'm not sure a convict," he nodded down at his prisoner's uniform of loose-fitting cotton shirt and pants with large black arrows pointing up and a number across his back, "is absolutely the best company for a noble lord, but what the hell?"

"Robin Hood here will guide you," O'Reilly said. "But you can't miss them. Myrna's the one with the bloodstained surgical gown and a carving knife through her head." She was no longer using a walking stick, he noticed. Wonderful what modern orthopaedic surgery could do. "The marquis is Sir Laurence Olivier's Hamlet, complete, as you can see, with Yorick's skull. I'll get the drinks, and you try not to die of thirst before I get back. A lot of folks will want to say hello to me between here and the bar."

As Kitty and the others headed one way, O'Reilly made his way through the crowd at the edge of the dance floor. He was delighted Jenny had been able to come. It didn't hurt for the villagers to see that someone who might very well be one of their permanent doctors had a human side, and could let her hair down. O'Reilly and she were free tonight because Kinky was holding the fort with Archie at Number One. She could reach O'Reilly here by phone if necessary.

It's been a hard day's night and I've been
    workin' like a dog
It's been a hard day's night. I should be
    sleepin' —

The Beatles' hit roared through a room festooned with fake cobwebs, cardboard skeletons, and cut-out ghosts. O'Reilly's gaze roamed over the tables that surrounded the dance floor. Jack-o'-lanterns carved from turnips were the centrepieces. Fortunately they were not lit. When they were, the stink would gag a maggot.

The window curtains were open and ghoulish scenes had been painted on the panes by someone with considerable skill. O'Reilly wondered who the unsung Michaelangelo might be.

Grown-ups in fancy dress, witches, wizards, clowns, pirates, and cowboys were all dancing. One couple were encased from neck to knee in cubes of cardboard decorated to look like a pair of giant dice. By the way both were sweating, they must have been extremely uncomfortable.

"Hello, Your Majesty." Sue Nolan dropped a curtsey. She was standing by a trestle table set up with a galvanised tub full of water and apples. A line of children waited to take their turns bobbing. "Having fun?" she said.

"Just getting started." He admired her dirndl and pointed white cap with upturned bits over the ears. With her single copper plait, she made a natural Rapunzel. "On your own? No Barry tonight?"

She shook her head. "Duty calls us both."

And for a moment O'Reilly remembered how duty had called him thirty years ago and what it had cost. "Don't you mind?"

Her smile was vast. "Not a bit. He's a good man, Fingal. You know that. He's worth waiting for."

"True," O'Reilly said. "Very true." He hesitated. "I don't suppose —" That wasn't fair. Barry had promised an answer in only thirty more days. Be patient. "Don't worry about it."

She cocked her head and smiled. "If he's made up his mind, he hasn't told me about it. But I know we both want what's best for Barry."

"We do. And we want what's best for this wee lad." O'Reilly gestured to the tub.

Sue followed O'Reilly's gaze, took two lightning-quick paces, and grabbed the arm of a four-foot devil in the form of Colin Brown. His hand was on the back of a partially submerged head. "Colin Brown, you let Art O'Callaghan breathe this very instant. *Now.*"

A soggy clown's head surfaced. His red nose hung askew on its elastic. He hauled in a great lungful.

"Sure, miss, I was only steadying Art's nut so he could get a good bite at the apple, so I was. Isn't that right, Art?" Colin fixed Art with a glare.

"That's right, miss, honest to God," Art said, and shook his head like a retriever shedding water.

And the Mafia thought they'd invented *Omerta,* the code of silence? "Enjoy yourselves, you lot," O'Reilly said. "I'll have to move on."

The high-pitched harmonies of the Beach Boys filled the air as he wove past tables where people were tucking into dishes from a potluck supper, drinking their pints and short

427

drinks, smoking, and chatting.

"Excuse me, Doctor."

O'Reilly felt a tugging on one of his silk sleeves and turned to see Flo Bishop, a perfect Tweedledee, sitting with Cissie Sloan, dressed as an Irish washerwoman, Aggie Arbuthnot as Cinderella pre–fairy godmother, and a stranger. He guessed the glasses in front of each were brandy and Benedictine, which was coming back into its own in Ulster as a drink for ladies. "How's about ye, sir?" Flo said.

"I'm grand, Flo. Ladies," he said, inclining his head.

"And this here's my cousin Sylvia from Ahoghill," Cissie said.

O'Reilly bowed to an apache dancer from Paris's Left Bank. Her beret was tilted on top of shining shoulder-length blonde hair and her horizontally striped jersey was rather well filled. A thick patent-leather belt encircled a narrow waist, and her black skirt was split to expose black fishnet stockings that vanished into a pair of high-heeled black pumps. *"Bonsoir, Mamselle. Enchanté,"* O'Reilly said, bent, took her hand, and lowered his lips to within half an inch of its back.

"Och," she said, "I dinny speak any o' they foreign languages, hey" — her sibilant Antrim accent was pronounced — "but it sounded lovely, bye. Thank you, sir."

Cissie said, "I think Sylvia's quare nor brave

428

wearing that outfit, so I do. And so's Flo with hers. Mind you, she's lost a stone and a half since her and Bertie went on that diet and —"

"You're a buck eejit, Frew."

Fingal turned to see Bertie Bishop, who clearly considered dressing up beneath his dignity, standing red-faced at a neighbouring table, pounding it with his fist. The unfortunate object of his venom was Dapper Frew, full-time estate agent, occasional Highlanders piper, and part-time Count Dracula. O'Reilly was sure that even in the hall's dim light he could see spittle flying from Bertie's lips.

"Doctor, please, could you go til Bertie, get him to settle down, like? I don't want him having no more of them vaginal attacks —"

O'Reilly swallowed his laughter. "Anginal attacks, Flo. Anginal." Flo wasn't the only Ulster denizen to make that mistake.

"Right. Well, maybe you could have a wee word with him? Get him to see sense, like? Calm him down?"

"I'll try," he said.

Bertie was still yelling. "Call yourself an estate agent? Three thousand for my spec-built house? Jasus. You'd probably give ice cream away to a bunch of bloody Bedouin in the Sahara rather than ask a decent market price, so you would. See you, Dapper Frew — ?" Bertie wagged a forefinger.

"Evening, Bertie. Dapper. Great party."

"The hell it is, O'Reilly," Bertie snapped. "Have you seen Flo? She's astray in the head, so she is." His voice grew louder. "There she is, wife of the worshipful master of the Orange Lodge, county councillor —" He fiddled with the gold Masonic fob on the watch chain across his belly. "— senior warden in the Masons. But she wouldn't be told. She says, says she, 'We'd make a lovely Tweedledum and Tweedledee.' 'Away off and chase yourself,' says I. 'I've my position til think of.'" He pounded the table. "And no wife of mine's —"

"Bertie," O'Reilly said, "if you don't calm down, she's going to be your widow."

"What?"

"Have you forgotten what happened the last time you lost your temper?"

Bertie rummaged in his waistcoat pocket. "I have not." He had lowered his voice and produced a silver snuff box. "I've my TNT pills in here, so I have."

"Good," said O'Reilly. "Now take ten deep breaths, sit down, and calm down, Bertie."

As Bertie huffed and puffed, Dapper said, "Thanks, Doctor." He shook his head. "I don't know anybody who can lose the bap like Bertie." He shrugged. "Most of us are used til it by now, but still —"

"Maybe I did get a bit heated," Bertie said.

"Aye," said Dapper. "You did, but I'll forgive you if you buy me a pint."

430

"Buy you a pint?"

"Bertie," said O'Reilly, a warning in his voice.

"Okay, okay, a pint it is."

"Now, if you'll excuse me?" He moved on toward where Willie Dunleavy stood behind the bar hatch.

He rubbed his temple and ran a finger under his ruff. It was warm in here and noisy with conversation, laughter, and the Rolling Stones at full blast, which could hardly be described as a chamber sextet. Och, well. Everybody was having a great time.

"Hello, Doctor O'Reilly."

O'Reilly had bumped into and nearly upset an apparently one-legged Mister Robinson, the Presbyterian minister. "Are you the Reverend Long John Silver?"

"Aaaar, Jim lad," Mister Robinson said in a fair imitation of Robert Newton, then lifted his eye patch and leant on his crutch. "I'm going to have to let my leg down," he said. "I've got the most ferocious pins and needles."

He'd have his left leg strapped up under his frock coat, O'Reilly reckoned. "I would do it sooner, rather than later, if I was you. You must have your harness so tight it's cutting off the blood supply to your muscles. If you leave it much longer, it'll hurt something fierce when you let it down."

"Thanks for the advice. I will." He started

to unbutton his coat.

A vaguely familiar figure danced slowly by in a false silver nose and a black cowboy hat. He must be a Tim Strawn, Lee Marvin's evil twin brother in one of the year's hit movies, *Cat Ballou.* His partner, her long blonde hair loosely round her, wore a simple, flowing, white floor-length dress and a circlet of flowers on her head. O'Reilly had no trouble recognising Julie Donnelly.

The couple stopped. "How's about ye, Doc?"

"Donal," O'Reilly said. "Hello, Julie. You look lovely. Lady Godiva?"

"Aye, before she got up on the ould gee-gee in her birthday suit. There's a limit, you know," Donal said.

"You're getting to be the master of disguise, Donal," O'Reilly said. "A regular man of a thousand faces."

"Like your man Lon Chaney?" Donal winked. "Aye, me and my new dog — er, Brandywine — done good last weekend down in Cavan. That wee lad Art O'Callaghan's nearly as smart as Colin Brown, so he is."

Which may account, O'Reilly thought, for Colin's recent attempt to drown Art. O'Reilly had known since last year's Christmas pageant that Colin did not suffer rivals lightly. O'Reilly lowered his voice. "Still using that water-soluble dye?"

Donal nodded. "Aye," he said, "and a new

432

paint you can wash off, but that's for something different, so it is." He pointed to a window where a painting depicted the banshee holding curled bony fingers over a gaping coffin. "I done all the windows in here for tonight. We'll clean it up tomorrow."

"I'm impressed, Donal," O'Reilly said. "You're quite the artist."

"Och," said Donal, "we'd a great art teacher when I was at school."

O'Reilly shook his head. He never ceased to marvel at the hidden talents of many of his patients. His thought was interrupted when Julie said, "Lord above, would you look at that there?"

O'Reilly had to look twice. Hard to believe, but Sylvia, the slim, sinuous, sexy siren from Ahoghill, was being steered round the floor by a jacketless, sweating Bertie Bishop. He stopped, and with one hand pushed her away to the length of their outstretched arms. She thrust out one leg as might a tango dancer and started to pirouette back.

Fingal watched the scene unfold as if in slow motion; the girl spun, Bertie's gaze — lascivious was the only adjective O'Reilly could think of — ran from the tip of her high heel to the white strip of thigh above the fishnet's welt. He wondered what the sight was doing to Bertie's blood pressure.

Shirley Bassey belted out "Goldfinger."

The man with the Midas touch.
A spider's touch.

Other couples stopped to watch as Bertie, clearly revelling in his moment of fame, cocked his head back like a flamenco dancer and adopted an arrogant sneer. He pushed Sylvia away for a second time, looked puzzled, grimaced, and yelled, "Oh shite." Then he clutched his chest, rolled his eyes to heaven — and crumpled to the floor.

35
LILIES THAT FESTER SMELL

"I know I'm on call today, Fingal," Doctor Corrigan said, "but I need ye to help me out."

Fingal lifted his head from his task of bringing the Register of Births, Deaths, and Marriages up to date, a job he loathed, and looked at Phelim. His parting might have been arranged using a micro-calliper, so precisely was it aligned. "If I can."

"Charlie's gone for the weekend, Miss O'Donaghugh and I have to go out for a confinement, and Minty Finucane from Bull Alley dropped in. They're worried about Dermot, the little lad with the stone bruise we saw yesterday. Says the lad has a fever. Wants one of us to go and see him."

"Fever? That doesn't sound good. I'll go straight round," Fingal said. He shoved the hated paperwork away and went to get his bag, glancing at his watch. Five o'clock. He wasn't seeing Kitty at her flat until six for dinner. He'd pick up a bottle of wine from an off-licence on his way, couple of pint bottles of Guinness. Might even stretch to a bunch of flowers. Ever since she'd said she wasn't pleased with how infrequently they could meet, he'd been trying to keep his promise to see more of her. He'd lots of time to see the patient and get to her place.

"Thanks," Phelim said. He took off his spectacles, *huuuh*ed on them, polished them with a hanky, and stuck them back on his nose. "Probably nothing to worry about, but a bit of reassurance won't hurt." He walked for the door and turned. "I'll see ye on Monday, but I'll be late. Another bloody commitee meeting about dispensary boundaries."

"Monday it is," Fingal said, and followed Phelim into the yard, slung his bag into the bike's basket, and pedalled off standing on the pedals and bowing his head into the wind of his passage, wanting to get to Bull Alley, see Dermot Finucane, and get away as quickly as possible.

Familiar streets now after four months. He'd learnt the shortcuts and indeed so narrow were some of the alleys that linked streets it was often faster getting about by bike if he had more than one call to make. Left from Aungier Street would take him onto Golden Lane, which shortly after changed its name to Bull Alley, which ended in a T-junction with Patrick Street. Places he'd been to as a student like Francis Street, Swift's Alley,

Weaver's Street were not much more than ten-minute rides away.

"Hello dere, Doctor Big Fellah," a woman carrying a wicker basket full of laundry called as he passed her on Golden Lane.

"Hello yourself, Clodagh. Grand October day." He recognised the pipe smoker, one of the Dempseys' neighbours from Back Lane. "In a rush," he called over his shoulder as he sped by.

Fingal swerved to avoid a tugger, wondered for a moment about Lorcan O'Lunney and his back, and paid no attention to several beggars, most of whom now recognised him and didn't waste time importuning him. On the corner of Bride Street and Bull Alley, a man had placed a battered fedora containing a few coppers on the footpath and was playing a slip jig on a penny whistle. Fingal recognised the tune, "Drops of Brandy," played in 9/8 time.

He propped his bike against the wall, grabbed his bag, went through the open front door, and knocked on the Finucanes'.

It was opened by Mrs. Finucane. She looked haggard. "T'anks for coming, sir. He's taken a turn. His foot's festerin'. Come in. Come in."

Festering, Fingal thought, wrinkling his nose. During his time in Sir Patrick Dun's he'd become thoroughly familiar with the stink of infected flesh.

"We bought a mattress from dat poor one who got evicted yesterday," she said, "so Dermot could have a bed of his own." She stood wringing her hands. "And I've changed his poultice like Doctor Corrigan said. But the little lad's been shiverin' and he's burnin' up."

Fingal's eyes were becoming accustomed to the gloom. He saw Dermot lying on a single mattress in front of the unlit fire, crossed the room, and knelt by the boy. "Hello, Dermot."

The boy turned his head. His eyes were glazed, a sheen of sweat glistened on his forehead. He mumbled.

Fingal felt a hot sweaty forehead, took a pulse racing at 120 per minute, and said, "I'm going to take off your poultice."

It wasn't difficult to untie the knots and remove the pus-stained thing. Fingal had to force himself not to turn away from the smell. At once he saw the red streaks beginning to run from the abscess toward the boy's ankle. The infection had reached the lymphatic channels that carried fluid from the tissues, the lymph, back into the general circulation. Dear Lord, not a clostridial infection. Please not gas gangrene. He looked at the wound, now ulcerated and red, but it didn't have the hideous red-purple colour of gangrenous, wet, dead tissue. The leg itself wasn't swollen nor when Fingal gently palpated it could he feel the crackling sensation — crepitation —

438

associated with the presence of gas in the tissues. The boy was drowsy, and gas gangrene patients were usually alert and complaining of severe pain. Fingal put his head close to the ulcer and sniffed. He could not detect the classic mousy odour. He straightened and heaved a sigh.

He'd bet his life, and if he were wrong, the patient's, that this was not a clostridial infection. It was probably streptococcal, in which case, judging by how close to reaching the ankle the red lines were, there was a little time left before amputation of the foot became imperative. But just how much time he couldn't be sure. And what the hell was the future for a boy with one foot? Incongruously, a line from a song ran in Fingal's head, "You'll have to be put with a bowl to beg . . ." Not if he could help it. Didn't red prontosil kill that particular bug in mice?

He stood. "Mrs. Finucane, I'm sorry, but the infection's spreading." Fingal wondered if this was because of Doctor Corrigan's unorthodox method of using a hot rather than a boiling poultice, but simply wasn't sure. It had been meant to be kinder to the patient, was obviously a technique the doctor had used successfully for years, and, anyway, why worry about it now? What mattered was that an infection was progressing, overwhelming Dermot's own defences. It must be stopped.

"Dear Jasus." She clapped both hands to

her mouth and started to weep. "He'll take the blood poisoning. It'll be the deat' of him . . ."

It was true. If the infection spread fast enough and widely enough, the bloodstream would be flooded with bacteria, causing septicaemia, known as blood poisoning. It was usually lethal.

"And him my only one, just Dermot and Minty and me. Dat's all of our family." She wept silently. "Don't let anythin' take Dermot from us, sir."

"It will not," Fingal said. "By God, it will not." He put an arm round her shoulder and squeezed. "I want you to trust me." Fingal inhaled. He'd been anxious enough considering a risky course of action which might save the boy's life and not at the expense of his leg either, but now he was even less confident that it would be the right thing to do.

She stared directly into his eyes.

"We can send Dermot to hospital now," he said. "The surgeons will have no choice but to amputate the foot, but he'll live."

"Take off his foot? Och, Jasus. Do they have to?"

Fingal blew out his breath, pursed his lips, clenched his teeth, and made his decision. "Maybe not," he said.

"Honest to God?" He heard the hope in her voice, saw a tiny smile start.

"I know a doctor at the Rotunda . . ."

"Rotunda? But sure dat's for women and babbies, not wee boys like Dermot." Her face crumpled.

"I know, but Doctor Davidson's treating infections just like the one Dermot has. There's a new medicine that should be able to kill the germ that's infected Dermot. If I can get some —" He debated for a moment about whether to tell her the drug was experimental, that as far as he knew it had worked only in mice. No. It would take too long to explain. If he was going, he had to go — now. "I can be there and back in under an hour. I think it's a gamble worth taking."

"A gamble?" She frowned.

"If I can get the medicine, it might kill the germs in time to save Dermot's foot. Do you understand?"

She nodded.

He glanced back at the red lines. How high the life-saving amputation would have to be would depend on how far they had travelled up the boy's leg. Fingal needed to get going at once. If he wasted too much time it could even cost Dermot his life. "I'll not deceive you, Mrs. Finucane," he said, "there is a risk, but I honestly think it's worth it."

She sniffed, dashed away a tear. "If you say so, Doctor. I want Dermot to have a normal life. I don't want him to be a feckin' cripple. Do what you t'ink best for my boy."

"I'm off," he said. He left his bag and ran

to the door to meet a man who must be Mister Minty Finucane coming in. "Your wife'll explain," Fingal yelled, and grabbed his bike.

He was panting when he propped his bike in a rack and headed for the Rotunda Hospital's front door. The traffic had been heavier than he'd expected when he'd reached O'Connell Street and it had taken him twenty-five minutes to get here. He went through the front door. Now he had to find Doctor Davidson or at least someone who knew about the trial with red prontosil and who might be able to help. If anyone would know it would be one of the senior nursing sisters. Inhaling hospital smells — Dettol, baby puke, and floor polish — he trotted along a familiar corridor to the post-natal ward. That's where any cases of puerperal sepsis would initially be diagnosed, and if anyone would know about the trial of Prontosil, they would be on this ward. Terrific. Sister O'Grady, an old friend, was on duty.

"Hello, Fingal. What brings you here on a Friday night?"

"I need help, Oonagh," he said.

"With a midwifery case?"

He shook his head. "I've a kid with an infected stone bruise. He's going to lose a foot unless I can kill the infection. I wondered how the trial with Prontosil was going."

She glanced round and lowered her voice. "We're not meant to talk about it, but we think it's working. It seems to do the trick in about thirty-six hours." She nodded her head once and smiled. "It's quite miraculous, but hush-hush. Doctor Davidson doesn't want to raise hopes until he's absolutely sure it does work."

Fingal understood. It was rightly considered unethical to trumpet premature news about a potentially revolutionary form of treatment until its efficacy had been proven beyond doubt. But Sister's word was good enough for him to want to try Prontosil for his patient. He clenched his fists and grinned. "That's amazing. Now, how could I get my hands on some tonight?"

Her smile disappeared. "You'd have to speak with Doctor Davidson, the master, but he's in London at a conference."

"No." Fingal nearly shouted the word. Damn it, damn it, he was sure he was so close to being able to save Dermot's foot and now that chance was being pulled away. "Is there no one else I could ask?"

She frowned. "I — I suppose you could talk to Doctor Williams, the resident doctor."

"Where is he?"

"I'll get him." She picked up the earpiece of a telephone, held it to her ear, jiggled the cradle, and spoke into the mouthpiece. "Operator? Connect me with Doctor Williams, please. He's in the common room."

Fingal shifted from foot to foot, inwardly muttering, "Come on, come on."

"John? Oonagh. Doctor O'Reilly's here and he needs to talk to you. I'll put him on."

He took the earpiece in one hand and bent to speak. "Doctor Williams, Fingal O'Reilly here. We met last year when I was here doing my midder."

"I remember. Big lad, got your nose bust in a boxing match. How can I help you, Fingal."

The "Fingal" was very collegial. A promising start. "I've a thirteen-year-old with an infected foot, it's going to have to be amputated . . ."

"But this is a maternity hospital. I don't think we can help him."

Fingal heard the puzzlement in the man's voice. "I don't expect you to, but when I was here, Doctor Davidson was investigating red prontosil. I think it would work for my patient. Save his foot. Can you help me get my hands on some?" Say yes, damn it. Say yes.

Silence.

"Hello. Hello. Are you still there?"

"Doctor O'Reilly, I'm sure you mean well . . ."

The formal Doctor O'Reilly. He's going to say no.

". . . but I have absolutely no authority to

release an experimental drug to anyone, no matter how worthy the cause might be. I'm sorry. I really am."

Don't give up. "Is there absolutely no possible way you could let me have some? Please?"

"I am sorry, Doctor O'Reilly. I truly am."

Fingal took a deep breath. Inside he was yelling, but that would get him nowhere. "I understand. Thanks anyway. Good night." Fingal put the earpiece on the cradle and broke the connection. "Thanks for trying, Oonagh," he said.

"No luck?"

He shook his head. "Looks like I gambled — and lost."

"I'm sorry."

Fingal's mind was in turmoil. Gambled. The word struck a chord. Gambler. Bob Beresford was a gambler, and Bob — Fingal looked at his watch, quarter to six — might still be home and able to get some Prontosil from the research laboratory. "Oonagh, can I get an outside line? It's urgent."

She lifted the earpiece. "Get me an outside operator, please." She handed the earpiece to Fingal.

"Operator here."

"Merrion 385, please."

Pause. Strange noises. "Hello, Merrion 385." Bob's voice.

Glory Hallelujah, he was home. "Bob? Fingal."

"Hello, Fingal. Nice to hear from you. How's life abusing you —"

"Bob. I need help. Wait for me. I'm coming over. It's urgent."

"All right. I'll be here."

Fingal did a quick calculation. Parnell Square to Merrion Square? About a mile and a half. "Be there in ten, fifteen minutes." He hung up the earpiece. "Thanks, Oonagh. I'm off."

"Good luck, Fingal." He heard her words as he fled down the corridor. Maybe Bob could help, just maybe, but Fingal O'Reilly wasn't going to give up without trying everything possible.

36
THE HEART
NO LONGER STIRRED

Sylvia crouched over Bertie, eyes staring, both hands over her mouth.

"Come with me," O'Reilly said to Donal to the accompaniment of Sylvia's high-pitched keening and cries from others of "Oh my God" and "What happened?"

O'Reilly took three paces to Bertie's side, knelt, ripped open his shirt, and felt for Bertie's heartbeat. None. "Blue blazes." O'Reilly pounded his fist against the breastbone, and again. A couple of swift blows might get the heart restarted. No pulse. He put the flat of one hand on Bertie's chest, his other hand on the back of the first, and leant his weight forward to compress the chest. He relaxed and pressed down again. "Donal," he called, "run and get Doctor Bradley, Kitty, and the marquis here on the double. And Sylvia, try to calm down. It's not your fault."

Her moaning subsided and she stood, sniffling and wiping her eyes.

O'Reilly tipped Bertie's head back, pinched

his nose, took a deep breath and, covering Bertie's mouth with his own, exhaled into Bertie's open mouth. Shirley Bassey was singing,

it's the kiss of death from
Mister Goldfinger . . .

"Turn that bloody thing off," he yelled, and bent to his work. He wasn't sure how long he could keep Bertie's circulation going with external cardiac massage and mouth-to-mouth artificial respiration — the kiss of life. But he was going to give it everything in his power, at least until he could get his hands on some medication.

Kitty knelt by his side.

"Cardiac arrest," he said, "can you take over for a minute?"

Kitty, senior nurse that she was, did, and Fingal stood. "Jenny, Bertie Bishop's in cardiac arrest. Run out to my car, get my bag, bring it here. Your legs are younger than mine." Just about the same thing Doctor Corrigan had said to O'Reilly back in 1936.

"Right." She tore off.

The music stopped. People stood in little groups, clearly wondering aloud what was going on. Conversation was muted. O'Reilly said, raising his voice, but keeping it steady, "Can everybody hear me?"

Murmurings of assent.

"Right. Councillor Bishop has been taken ill." O'Reilly was surprised by the number of voices he heard saying, "Och dear," and, "The poor soul" and, "Dear love him."

"I need to give him some treatment. I hate to spoil your fun, but I think those of you with kiddies should collect them up and maybe all of you should go outside and get on with the fireworks display we were going to have later." He yelled, "Who's in charge of the fireworks and bonfire?"

"Me, sir," said Donal, who had returned and stood at the marquis's side.

"Get people moving and you and whoever's helping you get things under way, but leave room for an ambulance to get here."

"Right." Donal left.

"My lord?"

"Yes?"

"You have keys to the office. When Doctor Bradley comes back, take her to the telephone."

"Certainly."

O'Reilly looked down. Kitty was working steadily and Bertie's colour didn't look bad. O'Reilly realised that Flo Bishop and Cissie Sloan were standing at his side. Cissie was holding Flo's hand as if they were a couple of schoolgirls.

"Is he dead, Doctor?" Flo's voice quavered.

"No, Flo, Bertie's alive," O'Reilly said. "But he's had a heart attack."

"Oh my God," she said, "that's desperate, so it is. Och, Bertie." She looked down at her husband, then up at the doctor. O'Reilly laid a hand on her shoulder. "He's very sick, Flo." No need to tell her that the councillor's heart had stopped and that it was touch and go. "An ambulance is coming to take him to the Royal."

"For Doctor Adgey and Doctor Pantridge to look after again, like?"

"That's right."

"They'll do their very best for him, I know that, so I do." She sighed.

"They will." He turned to Cissie. "Take Flo back to her table." He glanced at a tearstained Sylvia. "And Sylvia too. Make sure Aggie's there and stays with them while you get Flo and Sylvia neat brandies. For their nerves. I'll come and talk to you all again as soon as I can."

"I'll do that, Doctor dear, and never you worry your head about it. I'll take good care of her, so I will. Flo and me's been friends since we was . . ."

O'Reilly paid no further attention and was but vaguely aware of folks moving past on their way out. He knelt beside Kitty. "You all right?"

"I'm fine." She compressed the chest before breathing into Bertie's mouth.

"Here." Jenny handed O'Reilly his bag.

"Thanks. Now go with his lordship and

he'll get you a phone. Get an ambulance."

"Right," Jenny said, and took off at a trot.

Found it. The glass ampoule of adrenaline was where he knew it was supposed to be. In seconds he had filled a syringe with 1 mgm. He knelt beside Kitty. "Let me at his chest."

Fingal counted down from the collarbone. He drove the long needle through the chest wall in the middle of the fourth gap between the ribs on the left, injected the stimulant directly into the heart muscle, and withdrew the needle. Work. Come on, work. He put his fingers at the side of Bertie's neck. Fight, Bertie. Come on. You're not the most pleasant of men, but you are a feisty bugger. Fight for your life, Bertie. There it was. Praise be. His fingers felt a pulse in the carotid artery and as Bertie's chest began to move, the man took a deep, shuddering breath.

Bertie's heart had started again, but he still had to be taken to the Royal Victoria at full speed where, if he went into cardiac arrest again, they had the recently introduced equipment for delivering an electric shock to the heart muscles in the hopes of getting the heart to beat normally.

O'Reilly put the used syringe into the bag. When Bertie came to, he'd experience excruciating chest pains. Just as Mister Robinson's bound-up leg muscles were feeling the aching of oxygen lack because the blood flow to them was being interfered with, so Bertie's

451

heart muscle, which had been damaged by the infarction and was also oxygen-deprived, would respond. And anyone whose chest had been repeatedly shoved at by O'Reilly would not think they'd been caressed by a butterfly. He prepared and administered into the deltoid, the big muscle over the top of the shoulder, an injection of a third of a grain of morphine. Bertie flinched, moaned, put a hand onto his chest. His eyelids flickered and his eyes opened. O'Reilly laid a hand on the man's forehead and said quietly, "It's all right, Bertie. It's all right. Lie still."

The hell it was. The man's heart could stop again at any moment. O'Reilly grabbed Bertie's wrist. The pulse was weak but regular — now. But any one of three cardiac arrhythmias — ventricular extra-systoles, ventricular tachycardia, or ventricular fibrillation — could supervene. O'Reilly had never forgotten a patient in Dublin in 1934, Kevin Doherty, who had died of ventricular fibrillation. And it could only be reversed by that recent innovation, electrical defibrillation, at the Royal. Hang on, Bertie, until the ambulance gets here. If the force of O'Reilly's will could do anything, Bertie would survive.

"Well done, Fingal," Kitty said, stood, and put a hand to the small of her back. "I —"

The rest of her words were drowned out by a shrieking whistle and a series of loud bangs. A skyrocket, O'Reilly thought. Flashes flickered through the windows. Donal had got the fireworks going.

Kitty had knelt beside Bertie again and was taking his pulse. "He's holding his own," she said, "and the morphine's working."

O'Reilly glanced at his watch. Eight forty-five. Bertie's heart still had to keep functioning for at least another hour to allow time for the ambulance — he thought he could hear a distant siren — to get here, load the patient, drive back to Belfast, and get Bertie admitted to ward five. If he fibrillated there, it could be corrected, but between now and then? Keep going, heart.

Jenny Bradley had come back. "How's the patient?"

"As well as can be hoped, but —"

"Keep that bloody woman away from me," Bertie said in a slow, husky voice. "Don't want her here."

O'Reilly looked at Jenny and shook his head.

Jenny shrugged. "It's all —"

The row of the siren outside cut off her words and O'Reilly was sure he had heard tyres crunching on gravel. The siren stopped.

Ambulance attendants came racing into the hall pushing a stretcher on wheels. O'Reilly frowned. Why was a nurse in the blue uniform dress and white apron of the Royal Victoria here, and who was the young doctor in a long white coat?

As the ambulance attendants arrived, stopped and waited, the nurse knelt beside and started to question Kitty, whom she obviously recognised. She clearly paid no attention to the fact she was debriefing Robin Hood.

"Doctor O'Reilly," Jenny said, "I'd like you to meet Doctor John Geddes. He's training to be a cardiologist. John and I worked together two years ago. When I phoned the Royal, he was on duty. I spoke to him and asked him if our case was of interest to him. He had to check with his boss, Doctor Pantridge, and he gave the okay."

Okay for what? O'Reilly wondered. No time for that now. From the corner of his eye, O'Reilly noticed the attendants loading Bertie onto the stretcher. "Pleased to meet you," O'Reilly said, "excuse my costume," and offered a hand that was shaken. "We'd better get Bertie aboard."

"Right, Your Majesty, Doctor O'Reilly. No time to lose," Doctor Geddes, a soft-spoken man said with a smile. "Can you give me his history and your findings while the attendants get him loaded? I'll examine him there."

"Of course. Just a tick." He nipped over, asked Kitty and Jenny to go and look after Flo and Sylvia, and as he followed the trolley, O'Reilly gave the young man the clinical details. He finished as they reached the back of the vehicle. It was parked under a velvet

454

firmament, where red and green skybursts hung between the constellations. It looked to O'Reilly as if the body of the Plough was for a few moments carrying a stook of blazing straw, and the air smelled of burnt gunpowder. A chorus of "oooohs" and "aaaahs" rang in his ears.

The attendants and nurse began to load Bertie headfirst into the well-lit passenger compartment.

Doctor Geddes climbed in. "We have to get going. I'll call you. Let you know how he's doing."

"I understand," O'Reilly said, still wondering why Doctor Geddes had arrived with this ambulance. Och well, Jenny could explain. Bertie clearly was in good hands and that was the main thing. He turned to go, but through the still open back doors of the vehicle he heard the nurse. "He's fibrillating."

O'Reilly stopped in his tracks. Damnation. There was nothing he could do but await the outcome. He couldn't make out exactly what was happening, but could see the nurse giving the same resuscitation he and Kitty had while Doctor Geddes made methodical preparations. He flipped some switches — O'Reilly heard a deep electrical humming — then smeared jelly onto two flat metal-plated discs on plastic handles. These were attached by coiled insulated cables to a Heath-

Robinson-looking device with bright lights and dials with needles like those on an ammeter. One attendant called, "Charged."

Doctor Geddes put a padded spatula between Bertie's teeth as might be done for a patient having an epileptic attack to prevent them biting their tongue. "Everybody clear," Doctor Geddes said. Everyone stepped away from Bertie, except the doctor, who put the metal plates directly onto Bertie's naked chest and held them there by pressure on their plastic handles.

Another rocket detonated high overhead, accompanied by the roar of its blast as O'Reilly saw Bertie convulsing like an epileptic. That was what the spatula had been for. Doctor Geddes must have administered an electric current, meant for the heart, but which would also cause Bertie to thrash. When he lay still, Doctor Geddes put his stethoscope to the chest. He smiled. "Sinus rhythm," he said. "His ticker's firing on all four cylinders again."

O'Reilly felt like applauding, dancing a jig. He'd just witnessed the impossible. That weird-looking contraption with the two paddles must be some kind of portable defibrillator. *Mirabile dictu*. Wondrous things are spoken. "Thank you, Doctor Geddes," O'Reilly called.

"My pleasure," the young man said. "Now we'd best get him to the Royal. I'll be in touch. Thank you for asking us to come."

Doors were closed and with siren screaming and lights flashing, the ambulance headed back to Belfast.

O'Reilly went back into the clubhouse. All the lights were on and the once-festive decorations looked tired and tatty. The silence, broken only by the sounds of his boots on the floor, was the silence of the grave that very well might have been Bertie's fate, but for Doctor Geddes and his crew.

The place was deserted except for Kitty, Jenny, and Terry, who were sitting at a nearby table. He joined them.

"Well?" Kitty asked.

"Bloody miraculous," he said. "Bertie fibrillated and they shocked his heart and got him restarted on the spot."

"I don't believe it," Kitty said. "Honestly? I'd heard rumours of a portable defibrillator being developed."

"The rumours were right. Bloody marvelous. I need to tell —" He frowned. "Where are Flo and her friends?"

Jenny said, "Flo and Sylvia were very upset so I gave them each a sedative and Aggie and Cissie took them home."

"Good."

She rose as if to go.

"Hold on," he said. "Tell me about Doctor Geddes and his infernal machine."

She sat. "Doctor Frank Pantridge —"

"I know him," O'Reilly said. "He's got a black Labrador who's Arthur's brother. Sure, I know who he is — Doctor Pantridge, won the Military Cross in Singapore, Japanese POW when the fortress fell in 1942. He studied cardiology in Michigan after the war. Known widely, but not to his face, as Frankie P."

Jenny said, "That's him."

"I remember how excited everyone was when he introduced in-hospital defibrillation in 1964," Kitty said.

"He went one better," Jenny said. "The death rate for people who fibrillated at home was nearly seventy percent. So Doctor Pantridge remarked, 'Then we'll just have to go out and get them, won't we?' He got together with John Geddes, who's making this study his thesis, and then enlisted an electrical technician, Mister Alfred Mawhinney, who rigged up a portable defibrillator using two twelve-volt car batteries and a static inverter. The whole thing weighs about a hundred and fifty pounds, but it works." She grinned. "I was Frankie P's houseman in 1963. That's where I met John, and he's been keeping me up to date on developments." She shook her head. "Doctor Pantridge does not suffer fools gladly. There's been a fair bit of resistance from the medical establishment to his idea for a portable device, but last month he was able to get an ambulance devoted to the project and had a portable defibrillator fitted."

"And a bloody good thing for Bertie Bishop too," O'Reilly said.

"We were lucky, or Bertie was," Jenny said. "The formal study is set up to begin in January 1966 for budgetary reasons. There'll be trained doctor-and-nurse teams and attendants assigned to the devoted ambulance twenty-four hours a day. They're going to call it the Mobile Intensive Care Unit, but already it's been nicknamed 'the flying squad.' "

"The sooner they get it going the better," O'Reilly said.

"Doctor Pantridge apparently agrees. John had mentioned to me that his boss was aching to give the setup an unofficial try before January. The ambulance was equipped and sitting in the garage. There are always a couple of spare drivers in the place. Any ward nurse working in the hospital defibrillation programme could be conscripted to assist."

"I know the nurse who was here tonight," Kitty said. "June Irwin. She's a cardiac nurse with a very good head on her shoulders."

"She has," Jenny said. "I've worked with her."

"And Frankie P wanted to give the thing a test run?" O'Reilly said.

"All it needed was a G.P. who knew about it, someone like me, and John to be on duty when the G.P. called and a final go-ahead from Frankie P — and he carries a walkie-talkie. He's not hard to find."

"That's amazing," O'Reilly said. And it was. "I've never seen anything like it or heard anything about it. It certainly rescued Bertie."

"And if he fibrillates again on his way to the Royal they can give him another shock," Jenny said.

"Do you know," O'Reilly said, "if Bertie survives — and that's not guaranteed, but his chances are a damn sight better now — I'm going to make certain that the councillor will be fully informed about exactly who was responsible for saving him."

"You really think it will make any difference?" Jenny said, picking up her shepherdess's crook. "I still say it's going to take something pretty dramatic to get Bertie Bishop to accept me, or any other woman doctor."

"And practically dying isn't dramatic enough?" O'Reilly chuckled. "Even for Bertie, I think that qualifies. Come on, Bo Peep, Kitty, Terry. The fireworks will be over soon and I don't think the party will survive Bertie's own fireworks display. Home. I fancy a wee half-un and you could probably use one too. Then, when I hear from your Doctor Geddes, Jenny, I'll pop round and see Flo."

Followed by his small entourage, O'Reilly headed for the door, shaking his head. That had been bloody miraculous, a medical-world first, and he was immensely privileged to have been a witness. Nor was it the first time in his life he'd been privy to developments that had revolutionised the way medicine was practised.

37
WHAT MAD PURSUIT?

"Good Lord. Here already, Fingal?" Bob Beresford said, looking at his watch and Fingal's bike. "You got Congreve rockets on that thing?" He took a drag from his Gold Flake.

Fingal, sweating like a galloping horse and breathing quickly and deeply, shoved his bike up the shallow front steps of the building on Merrion Square. "All right to leave it here in the hall?"

"Sure, for the moment. Come on in." Bob indicated the open door of his flat.

Fingal left the bike and went in. "Thanks for waiting. I hope I haven't interrupted anything, Bob?"

"Not tonight," Bob said. "I'm a bit between —" He coughed. "Bette seems to have found someone more glamorous than a humble medical research worker."

"Sorry to hear that. Look, Bob," he said, "I need your help."

"All right, but sit down and tell me about it. Whiskey?"

Fingal shook his head and remained standing. "Red prontosil worked in mice given lethal doses of *Streptococcus,* didn't it? It cured them, and other infected mice that weren't treated died, right?"

"Yes." Bob smiled wryly. "Pretty positive data showing that the stuff's effective — in mice."

"But it won't work in your culture plates?"

Bob crushed out his cigarette, shaking his head. "No, damn it, and it won't — ever. So much for my research project."

Fingal frowned but ploughed on, "But I've just spoken to Oonagh O'Grady at the Rotunda. She told me on the quiet that it is working in Doctor Davidson's cases of puerperal sepsis. I don't understand. Puerperal sepsis is caused by haemolytic *Streptococcus,* the Prontosil seems to be working against it in those women, but Prontosil isn't effective on your culture plates with the same microorganism?"

Bob cocked his head. "Fingal O'Reilly," he said, "you sure as hell didn't come charging over here all hot and bothered at teatime on a Friday night to get a lesson in bacteriology. What's up? And would you for God's sake sit down?"

Fingal shook his head. "I don't have time to sit, Bob. I have a kid with a foot infected with *Streptococcus,* and the infection's spreading. Unless he has the foot amputated, he's going to get septicaemia. I thought — I thought —"

"You thought that you might be able to cure him with red prontosil. That it?"

Fingal nodded.

Bob said quietly, "You might just be right."

"What? Do you really mean that?"

"I've spent hours in the library since the day we went to Donnybrook —"

"And?"

"It's a long story, but there is early evidence that it does work in humans."

"Praise be." Fingal realised he was trembling. "Bob, can you help me get my hands on some? Please?" Fingal waited. Say yes. Say yes.

Bob sucked in a breath through tight lips. "We've got quite a stock in the lab —"

"Do you have a key?"

"Of course."

Fingal grabbed Bob's arm and started hustling him to the door. "Come on. Let's go."

"Hang on," Bob said, and frowned. "It specifically says on the bottles, 'Not for use in Humans.' Professor Bigger will kill me if he finds out. I could lose my job." His nose wrinkled. "I'd have to take a job like yours. Perish the thought."

Fingal exhaled through his nose. Forcibly. Think, man think. How to get Bob to help? A slow smile started. Fingal knew enough about medical researchers to understand their Achilles' heel. "He'll not fire you if it works and you help me cure the kid. I'd call that pretty important positive data. Might even be a prize in it for one of Professor Bigger's top students. And he'd reap some of the glory too. He'd forgive you."

Bob cocked his head. "It would be a gamble, but damn it, at pretty short odds. I've found out a thing or two about Prontosil since I started reading about it." He laughed and said, "Who called you 'the wily O'Reilly'?" He headed for the door. "It'll be quicker in my car. Leave your bike here in my flat."

"God bless you, Bob," Fingal said, grinning from ear to ear and getting his bike from the hall.

"And just so you know," Bob said, "we've been very good friends for a while. I'd have helped you even without the carrot of possible scientific glory, you bollix. To say nothing of the fact that a little chap's life is at stake here. When I started this job it was because you suggested it, Fingal, as a better option for me than seeing patients, but the more I read and the deeper I get involved, I'm beginning to undersand that us drones slogging away in laboratories might eventually do more good than all you hands-on doctors. Now come on."

Both men were quiet as Bob drove away.

"Right," he said, "it's only five minutes to Trinity, but the traffic's bloody so be quiet and let me concentrate."

Fingal looked over at his friend with new eyes. Working with Professor Bigger was changing him. And what had he meant about "pretty short odds"? They were what bookies gave on sure things at the track.

Fingal sat in the passenger's seat clutching a glass bottle stoppered with a large cork. Some traces of paper had stuck to the glass when he'd ripped off the warning label. Inside was a bright red-orange compound. Red prontosil. Bob had brought a glass beaker, scales, a metal spatula, and a glass stirring rod. "And you do think it'll work, Bob?"

He stopped at the junction with Nassau Street to let a tram bound for Terenure pass. "I wouldn't have a couple of weeks ago. All I knew was that it worked in mice, because our profs had told us that when we were students, but it wasn't working in my lab."

"But you said there is evidence that it works in humans."

"There is now, but until June of this year all the tiny hints it might work were reported in German or French. Nobody here had heard of them, and if they had, the medical establishment pooh-poohed the idea that a chemical could kill bacteria." He passed Duke Street with the Mansion House farther down Dawson Street on the left. "There's Davy Byrnes pub. It's time we went back for a pint. See Diarmud."

"Aye," said Fingal. "Soon, but not tonight. Go on about Prontosil."

"A German chap, Gehard Domagk, first showed it worked in mice in '32, and he did a human study, but he didn't publish the combined data until '35. His article was in *Deutsche Medizinische Wochenschraf.*"

"That's a mouthful you'd need to chew twice," Fingal said, "but why did he wait so long to publish?"

"No one's sure. He was working for a pharmaceutical company. They'd applied for a patent in 1932, but the patent wasn't approved until '35. A month later, Domagk's work appeared in print."

Fingal grunted. Three years of lives that might have been saved if the stuff really was effective.

Bob skirted Saint Stephen's Green. "Then a Doctor Foerster reported, in German, that he'd cured an infant with septicaemia. Again in '35." He shook his head. "You've no idea how much time I've spent trying to get my hands on obscure foreign journals and then getting the damn things translated."

Fingal clutched the bottle more tightly. A single case? One swallow does not a summer make, but anything that would cure something that was universally fatal must have some merit. It must. It must, but there still was that question. "So if it's so bloody good, why won't it work in your lab?"

Bob chuckled and turned onto Cuffe Street. "Bunch of Frenchmen led by a Doctor Trefouel sorted that out. By itself, Prontosil is about as much use as tits on a boar, but once inside a body, it's broken down into a number of different compounds. Trefouel's team managed to isolate the main one. It's called sulphanilamide, and when it comes to holding off hordes of *Streptococci,* the thing's like Leonidas's Spartans at Thermopylae." He passed Aungier Street and stopped, waiting for a chance to turn right onto Bride Street. "Naturally they published in French and us insular peoples can't read the bloody language. But it's there in a journal once you know where to look."

"I'm impressed, Bob," Fingal said. "You've certainly been doing your homework." Bob may have chosen research because he had no desire to practise medicine, but he was clearly taking his job seriously. He could be going to the racetrack and finding a rich woman but he's hanging out in libraries instead . . .

Bob chuckled. "Well, I have to 'remain a student,' to justify getting Auntie's bequest, don't I?" He drove along Bride Street. "And the best is yet to come. I'm sorry for Doctor Davidson, but he's been pipped at the post. Priority for curing puerperal sepis with Prontosil will go to two Englishmen, Doctors Colebrook and Kenny. They published their results in the *Lancet* in June. Four months ago." He turned left onto Bull Alley. "It worked. It bloody well worked. I'm sure Davidson's group will know that. They'll be disappointed not to be first, but all scientific studies need to be replicated by other groups before we should take them seriously. It's valuable work going on at the Rotunda."

"Park here," Fingal said, halfway along Bull Alley. "Jasus, Bob." His voice was hushed. "So you think we really do have a chance to cure young Dermot?"

Bob nodded. "I sure as hell hope so." He started to get out. "Lead the way. I'll see where you go, then come back and get a couple of gurriers to keep an eye on my car. It's getting dark and motorcars go better if they still have their wheels and batteries. I'll bring my stuff in a minute."

"T'ank God you're back, Doctor O'Reilly. Dermot's gettin' worser." Mrs. Finucane stood beside her son's mattress. "He's taken a lot of fits of the shudders."

Fingal nodded. Not surprising. As the infection spread, more toxins would be released, the fever would go up, and the body would respond by a series of muscle spasms called rigors. "Where's my bag?"

"Here, sir." Mister Finucane, who had

shaved, handed the bag to Fingal, who set the Prontosil bottle inside and took out a thermometer. He knelt beside Dermot. He was breathing rapidly at a rate of more than eighteen breaths per minute. Merely to touch his skin showed that the half-conscious boy was burning up. Fingal tucked the glass tube under Dermot's armpit, then took his pulse, one hundred per minute. He looked at the infected leg and foot. The ulcer did not seem to have gotten any bigger. He bent and sniffed. Still no mousy odour, but the stink of pus made him gag. The red lines had spread farther up and were now just past Dermot's ankle. The infection was gaining. Would the red prontosil stop it? He was sure that there was still time to save the boy's life by getting him to hospital for a quick above-ankle amputation, damn it all, but what about what Bob had told Fingal in the car? Prontosil worked. He wondered, Do I have the right to decide for Dermot and his family? hesitated, and then told himself that because he was trained to weigh the pros and cons and Dermot's parents were not, it was Fingal's bounden Hippocratic duty to do so. Sometimes being expected to make such decisions on behalf of patients was a heavy load to carry, but it was part of a physician's job.

"Who the feck are you?" Minty said.

Fingal turned to see Mister Finucane blocking Bob's entrance. "It's all right. This

470

is Doctor Beresford. He's a specialist in infections. He's come to help."

"Dat's all right den. Come in, sir. Didn't mean to be feckin' rude."

"Quite all right," said Bob, taking in the shabby room in one sweeping glance, then heading for Dermot's bed.

Fingal turned back to his patient, removed the thermometer, went to the paraffin lamp, and held the glass tube in front of it. The thin column of mercury had stopped at the mark showing 100.2° Fahrenheit. Fingal took a deep breath. Any two of the three findings of a respiratory rate of twenty or more, a pulse faster than ninety, and a temperature greater than 100.4° F were diagnostic of septicaemia, blood poisoning, for which modern medicine recognised no cure. So far only one of Dermot's readings was over the threshold, but how long would that state of affairs last? He stood and said to Bob quietly, "It's Prontosil or bust. I hope to God your English and French doctors are right. What dose do you reckon to start with?"

Bob said, "I think Doctor Domagk used ten grams? Why not? And repeat it every four hours."

"Fair enough. Will you make up the first dose?"

"I will. Fortunately it's water soluble so we can give it as a draught." Fingal retrieved the bottle from his bag and gave it to Bob, who took it and his scales and other paraphernalia to the table. "Mrs. . . . ?"

"Finucane," Fingal said.

"Mrs. Finucane, could you please heat a kettle of water?"

"Yes, sir." She hung one on a cast-iron gallows over the turf fire and turned to Fingal. "Will he be all right, sir?"

Fingal hesitated then decided to do as he'd seen his old teacher Doctor Micks do when death could be imminent. Hide nothing. "I'm not sure," he said. Oonagh O'Grady had said if the stuff was going to work it would do so quickly. "But we'll have a pretty good idea by this time tomorrow."

She sobbed and said, "Please make him better, sir. Please."

"We are trying. I promise."

"Should I send for Father Burke?"

Fingal shook his head. "If I think it's coming to that I'll tell you. I promise."

Mister Finucane put his arm round his wife's thin shoulders. "Come over to the corner, Orla. We'll say the rosary." He looked at Fingal. "We'll let the doctors get on wit' their work."

They moved aside and Fingal, after casting one more glance at Dermot, moved to beside Bob, who now was stirring a mixture of Prontosil and warm water in the glass beaker. The aniline dye swirled like red smoke.

A quiet, "Hail Mary, full of grace. The Lord

is with Thee. Blessèd art thou among women . . ." came from Dermot's parents.

"I've mixed it," Bob said. "Here."

Fingal took the beaker. It was warm. He knelt beside Dermot, lifting the boy until he half sat. He put the glass to the boy's lips. "Drink up."

Gagging and spluttering, the boy choked most of it down. He had a red stain round his lips when Fingal lowered the lad onto his pillow.

Fingal stood and went to a basin of water, washed the beaker, and set it on the table with the bottle of the medication and Bob's gear. "Thanks, Bob. Thanks for everything."

Bob sniffed and wrinkled his nose. "Always glad to help a friend," he said, then lowering his voice, added, "And you work in places like this every day?"

"Pretty much."

"How do you stand the stink?" He scratched his side. "And I do believe I've been bitten by something. Probably a flea, or fleas."

"Holy Mary, Mother of God . . ." the voices droned on.

Fingal frowned. He was perfectly capable of compounding any further doses. Hadn't they spent hours under Doctor Micks's patient tutelage, weighing and measuring grains and minims, ounces and grams? They'd decided to repeat the dose every four hours. How many doctors did that take? "Tell you what, Bob. There's no real need for you to stay."

"Except to keep you company. And to see if — and I hope to God it does — the damn stuff works."

"Aye, but I need you to do some other things." Give him a job and Bob wouldn't, Fingal hoped, recognise that for the sake of his sensibilities he was being chased off.

"Oh?"

"Go home and phone Doctor Corrigan." Fingal rummaged in his inside pocket, scribbled in a notebook, and ripped out the page. "That's his number at home and that's the dispensary number. You'll have to track him down because he was going out on a delivery the last time I saw him. Explain to him what I'm doing and that I'm staying until it's over." One way or the other, Fingal thought, and crossed his fingers. "Tell him I'm sorry, I know it's not his turn, but will he please cover this weekend?"

"I'll do that."

Fingal grinned. "Then have a nice hot bath and use that carbolic soap you offered Charlie and me when we first told you about working for a dispensary," he lowered his voice, "for the fleas, then yourself a nice Napoleon brandy, smoke a Gold Flake or two, and perhaps even send up a prayer —"

"Holy Mary, Mother of God, pray for us

474

sinners . . ." came from the corner.

"And come back here at teatime tomorrow and see if you can get my bike in the back of your car."

"All right, Fingal. If you're sure."

"Go on with you. I'll say your good-byes." He watched his friend leave quietly and went back to sit beside Dermot when a thought struck. Christ. He'd forgotten about Kitty. As Fingal raced for the door to try to catch Bob and ask him to phone her, he heard two supplicant voices, ". . . now and in the hour of our death. Amen."

38
FATHOM DEEP I AM IN LOVE

"Done for the day, Jenny?" said O'Reilly, starting to rise from his armchair as she came into the upstairs lounge. Her blonde hair was freshly washed and set. She wore a single strand of pearls at her throat, a hint of cleavage showing above the neck of a simple but elegant black dress. Black satin opera gloves completed the ensemble. Quite a change from the usually modestly blue-suited working physician.

"Please don't get up, Fingal," she said. "Done for the day? Indeed I am. *Finale. Finito. Finis. Omnino complevit.*"

Fingal chuckled. "*Omnino complevit?* Did you enjoy Latin at school?"

"Mmmm," she said, "I love learning new things. And it helped me to understand my own language better."

"I agree," said O'Reilly, "but I don't think you're going to a Latin class tonight."

She laughed, a musical sound. "Not one

bit. I'm going up to Belfast to fly my kite. It's Friday."

"Kick up your heels? Good for you, but drive carefully. There's more frost forecast." Winter had arrived in the north of Ireland even though it was only the first week of November. The light was gone outside and by six o'clock Kinky had got the curtains closed and a fire roaring in the upstairs grate. Outside the wind growled past the bow windows.

Kitty should be home soon. He lifted his booted right foot to keep the left one company on a footstool and swirled the Jameson round in his glass. "Seeing Terry Baird again?"

She smiled. "We're going for dinner at the Tavern Buttery down by the Law Courts."

O'Reilly whistled. "His law practice must be doing well." The Buttery was a popular and pricey restaurant.

She laughed. "We go Dutch. I'm a salaried working woman, thanks to you, Fingal, and I like to pay my share."

"Can I get you a pre-prandial?" He nodded toward the decanters.

She shook her head. "I'm driving and I'll need to be off in fifteen minutes." She lifted her current read, *World's Best Science Fiction: 1965,* from the other armchair and sat. "Just wanted to tell you about a patient I saw this afternoon. She's one of yours, but, and don't get cross, Fingal, she wanted a woman's opinion."

He roared with laughter. "Why in the hell would I get cross? I think my practice is getting bigger since you came."

"Thank you. Anyway, you know Norma Cochrane."

"Twenty-six. Lives on the Shore Road. Husband's an avionics expert at Short's aircraft factory. He has a face not even the tide would take out, but they seem very happy together. It's her third pregnancy. Last normal menstrual period . . ." He frowned, then said, "March fifth, so she's — thirty-six weeks today. Oh yes, and she plays the balalaika and the penny whistle."

Jenny shook her head. "Doctor Fingal Flahertie O'Reilly, walking department of medical records. Balalaika and penny whistle? I'll bet you know her granny's name too."

"Paternal is Susan, maternal is Joyce." He lit his briar.

She chortled. "I despair. I'd need her chart to remember the half of that."

He bowed his head in acknowledgement. "Jenny, I've been here for nineteen years. When you've been in one practice for as long you'll remember your customers too. And before you say anything, we'll have Barry's answer in three and a half weeks." And God knows, he thought, it's getting to be a toss-up who I'd rather have stay. "Tell me about

Norma."

"I wish she'd sent for one of us," Jenny said. "She'd have been much better seen at home and then packed off by ambulance to the Royal Maternity Hospital. She had an antepartum bleed, but it stopped so she came to the surgery."

"It wasn't painful?"

She shook her head.

"Sounds like a placenta praevia to me," he said. "She should be in hospital."

"She is. I kept her here until the ambulance came. She'll be in RMH now."

"Good," O'Reilly said. "I'm sure she and her baby will be all right. It's not good when the placenta comes before the baby, but it's not as bad today as it was. Prof MacAfee, here in Ulster, did the early work on treating the condition conservatively. He got the maternal mortality down to half a percent and the fetal mortality down to ten percent. Have you any idea what those figures were in my day?"

"Not the foggiest, but I'll bet they were much higher."

"Much higher. Maternal seven percent, fetal more than fifty percent. Seven women out of every hundred with the condition died. And half the babies."

"That's appalling."

"I know. I was a trainee obstetrician for a year. I saw it all. And that's only thirty-odd years ago. People forget what a bloody risky business childbirth was and how the work of a few dedicated physicians like Davidson, MacAfee, Stallworthy, Lewis, Whitfield, have made it seem routine today. Sometimes," he frowned, "sometimes I get a bit tired of some of the evangelical 'natural childbirth' brigade. I'm all for as little interference as possible," he puffed out a cloud of smoke, "but I saw what that was like back then and I know what my colleagues did to improve things out of all proportion and I'd never want to turn the clock back." He shuddered.

"I'm very glad I'm living today," said Jenny, glancing down, then back up at him. "I love medicine, but one day I do want to get married, start a family. It's good to know that's not so dangerous for me as it would have been in your younger days, Fingal."

"At least we did have blood transfusions, reasonably effective anaesthetics, fairly safe Caesarean sections. Can you imagine what it was like prior to that? And we were on the brink of the antibiotic era then too."

"Penicillin, tetracyline, streptomycin, chloramphenicol. I don't know what we'd do without them."

"I do," said Fingal quietly. "We had to watch a lot of people die." He brightened. "But we did have the sulphonamides, the antibacterial drugs that preceded the true antibiotics. The first was called red prontosil.

I'll tell you a story about it one day, but you said you'd to be on your way. I'd not want you to keep Terry waiting."

She rose. "Nor would I. He's a lovely lad." She paused at the door. " 'Night, Fingal. I hope you're not going to be too busy."

O'Reilly blew out a blue cloud and sipped his whiskey. He heard Jenny greeting Kitty, and in a moment she had stuck her head into the lounge. "I'm home."

"I've missed you," he said, standing. "Drink?"

She crossed the room, pulled off her headscarf, and shook her hair free. "Not just now, thanks."

He waited until she was seated and took his own chair.

"I came in through the kitchen. Kinky was able to tear herself away from a conversation with Archie long enough to tell me she's made us lobster thermidor tonight. I thought a bottle of wine would be called for?" She cocked her head and pursed her lips.

Oysters weren't the only denizens of the deep that reputedly got a fellah's juices flowing, and Kitty knew that very well. "Bloody good idea," he said, and by God, Jenny was out tonight. O'Reilly inhaled and cleared his throat.

"I thought so," she said demurely, "so I popped a couple of bottles of Pouilly-Fuissé in the fridge." She raised a wicked eyebrow.

481

"Wonderful," he said, and knew his voice was husky. "Why don't we eat up here? It's horrid out" — The wind rattled the panes and moaned — "but the fire's lovely and cosy and we can put on a lump of turf. I'd not mind a bit of music to dine to, say Mendelssohn's Violin Concerto?" He stood, bent, and kissed her very firmly. "That," he said, "is because I love you very much, Mrs. O'Reilly." He felt her tongue tip on his, stepped back, and took a deep breath.

She crossed her legs demurely with a mere whisper of nylon. "It's our four-months-and-two-days wedding anniversary." Her smile was feral. "I'm sure we can find some way of celebrating after a lobster dinner." Up went her right eyebrow.

O'Reilly choked on his whiskey, then laughed until he cried. "Kitty, my love," he said, "as usual I'm sure you're right." But after dinner. Calm down, boy. He took a very deep breath, swallowed, and said, "It's always important to have something to celebrate. We made it a rule that we couldn't have a ta-ta-ta-ra in the students' mess at Sir Patrick Dun's unless there was a reason. Last one I remember was Monday, June 18, 1935."

"And the reason was?"

"The birthday of the late — as far as we knew — Anastasia Nikolaevna Romanova."

"Who?"

"The last tsar's daughter. Don't you re-

member, they made a film about her with Yul
Brynner and Ingrid Bergman years ago?
When I was a student, people were still talking about whether or not she'd survived the
Russian Revolution. So we celebrated her
birthday, June 18, 1901, it was. Our 1935 do
was a grand celebration, fit for a grand
duchess, I can tell you." He laughed.

"Eejit," she said. "I love to see you laugh,
you old bear." She used a hand to rearrange
her hair, twisting it into a knot at the back of
her neck. "Do you know, I think I might have
a small G and T after all."

"Right." He rose and busied himself making her drink, singing sotto voce,

from city or country, a girl is a jewel
And well made for grippin' the most of the
    while . . .

"And how was your day, my dear?" he asked
to give himself a further chance to calm
down.

"Pretty much the usual, but I saw Cromie.
I'd spoken to him about Helen. He's had a
word with Walter Braidwood in Newtownards
and sight unseen Walter's recommended
Helen for a ward orderly job next summer.
The management committee will decide later
this month."

"Wonderful," he said, and gave her her
drink. *"Sláinte."*

She took it, letting her hand brush lightly on his. "Cheers." She sipped. "What have you been up to?"

He grinned. " 'The daily round the common task —' "

" '—Will furnish all we ought to ask.' I used to sing that hymn when I was a little girl."

"Don't you start finishing my quotes. It was one thing with Barry, now Jenny's at it." He smiled at her. "Jenny's fitting in nicely, but she said something today that I'd simply not considered."

"Oh?"

"She'll want to start a family one day." He frowned, scratched his head, and set his pipe in an ashtray.

"That's hardly unusual, Fingal," Kitty said.

"Yes, but how can she do that and work full time? I've got very used to having a lot of time to spend with you, love." Alone with you, love, he thought, and smiled.

Kitty pursed her lips and cocked her head to one side. "I've no idea how we'd manage, but we don't know Barry's plans yet. And if he's not coming back and you want to keep Jenny on, as I know you will do, then, as a certain Fingal Flahertie O'Reilly of my acquaintance is wont to remark, 'We'll cross the bridge when we come to it.' "

He smiled. "Practical as ever, Kitty O'Reilly née O'Hallorhan. And that bridge might come sooner than later. She's out with Terry

484

Baird again tonight."

"Now, Fingal . . ." She raised an eyebrow. "I don't think you meant it exactly like that."

He frowned, and then the double entendre struck him. "Eejit. I didn't — I mean, I wasn't suggesting —"

Kitty raised the other eyebrow, then, slipping off her shoes, tucked her feet beneath her in one graceful movement and settled back into the chair.

"I meant I've a notion things are serious between those two and he might pop the question. Tonight."

"Better," she said. "She certainly came down the stairs at a gallop. Seemed in a hurry to get somewhere."

"I held her up a bit. I was going to tell her some interesting medical stuff about antibiotics, but I didn't want her to be late so I said I'd tell her some other time."

"Good for you," Kitty said. "A girl does not get dressed up in her best black dress and pearls to hear about antibiotics." She chuckled and took another sip of her drink.

O'Reilly thought of the story he hadn't told Jenny; a story of how things might have been a lot different back in '36 if a certain antibiotic hadn't made Fingal merely late. He'd missed the date altogether. Still — he looked Kitty up and down, perched comfortably in her armchair — it had all turned out for the best.

"Excuse me, sir," Kinky said.

O'Reilly spun and saw her standing in the doorway. He hadn't heard her coming. "Yes, Kinky?"

"Would you mind very much having the lobster cold with just mayonnaise, lemon slices, a potato salad, hard-boiled eggs, and a shmall-little tossed salad?"

"Would I mind? You're offering that feast to a man who could eat the tyres off a truck."

"I'm asking, sir, because, and I know it is not altogether right to ask, but something has come up and preparing the lobsters that way would be much quicker. I'd have been doing the garnishings anyway."

"It's certainly all right by me," Kitty said.

"You see, sir — and Kitty, Archie's mother's visiting from Greenisland across the lough. She's eighty-seven and Archie would like for me to meet her, so, and she'll be leaving first thing in the morning, and —"

Oh ho, O'Reilly thought. Meeting Mama. Interesting. "You do the lobsters, stick 'em on two trays, leave them, give us a shout, and take yourself off with Archie." O'Reilly smiled and looked longingly at Kitty. "And, Kinky? Have a lovely time and don't feel that you need to rush home."

39
. . . Painful Vigils Keep

"Wake up, Big Fellah. Come on wit' you now. Wake up."

Fingal was dimly aware that someone was shaking his shoulder. "Go 'way, Charlie." He tried to roll over, pull the bedclothes round him, but hands were restraining him.

"Wake up, sir, or you'll fall off the feckin' chair." It was a man's voice, but not Charlie's.

Where the hell was he? O'Reilly forced his eyes open, shook his head, screwed his eyes shut and opened them. His surroundings, dimly lit by a guttering, smelly paraffin lamp and the glow of a turf fire, came into sharper focus. "Sorry," he said, sitting upright in the chair. "Must have nodded off. How's Dermot?"

"He's asleep, sir," Minty Finucane said.

Fingal blinked and said, "What time is it?"

"It's six fifteen in the mornin', sir, and you said you'd need to examine him before he'd get his next dose at half past six."

"Right. Let's have a look at him." Fingal

pulled off a threadbare blanket — someone must have covered him up — got to his feet, and looked at the mattress in front of the fire. No sign of Dermot. "Where —"

"Orla took him into our bed, sir. He was still shivering. You nodded off at about t'ree. I've been sittin' up so I could wake you at the right time." He yawned.

Fingal looked at the man's unshaven face, dark circles under his bloodshot eyes, and rubbed his own chin. He felt the rasp of stubble. "Thank you."

Minty, carrying the paraffin lamp, crossed the room, pulled aside the blanket that did duty as a curtain, and said, "Dere dey are."

Fingal turned back a faded rug that once upon a time had been a bright tartan. They lay like two spoons; Orla, her long grey hair spread like a fan, wore only her shift and was on her side with her back to the whitewash-peeling brick wall, arms wrapped round a naked Dermot, who was fast asleep, muttering to himself. His breathing was slower, sixteen rather than the eighteen breaths per minute it had been when Fingal had last examined the boy before giving him his third dose of ten grams of Prontosil at two thirty. There'd been no change for the better since he'd had his first dose, and Fingal had had to discipline himself from examining Dermot every ten minutes hoping for a sign. It was a good thing Fingal had slept. This waiting for improvement was driving him daft.

He touched the lad's forehead. It was clammy, but was it less hot? Fingal couldn't be sure and was not going to be taken in by wishful thinking. "I'll just be a minute." Fingal went to where he'd hung his jacket on his chair, removed the thermometer from the breast pocket, and snapped his wrist several times to shake the mercury level down below the normal mark.

Kneeling, he slipped it into Dermot's armpit, then took his pulse by feeling his carotid artery at the angle of his jaw. Still up, but at ninety-six was down from its earlier one hundred beats a minute. As Fingal waited for the thermometer to register, he said, "Can you hold the light, so I can see his leg?"

He managed to slip two fingers into the crease of the boy's groin without disturbing him. Their tips moved from the inside of the thigh to its outside near the iliac crest, the hinch bone, and did not encounter what Fingal had been dreading. There was no sign of hard, rubbery, enlarged lymph glands.

One of the glands' functions was to act as hubs to collect the lymph and direct it into larger ducts that eventually returned the fluid into the general circulation. If the fluid carried attackers like living bacteria, the lymph glands mobilised the immune system and became barricades, last-ditch redoubts that tried to keep the invaders out.

When that happened, the glands became swollen and hard. But Dermot's weren't. They were not fighting the *Streptococci* — at least not yet. Fingal took a deep breath. The microorganisms must still be confined to the wound and the lymphatic channels of the leg. Either Dermot's own defences were holding their own or, and he hardly dared tempt Providence by wishing it so, the Prontosil was beginning to have an effect.

Fingal moved to Dermot's foot and took off a soiled dressing. The yellow circle cast by the flame was sufficient for Fingal to make out clearly that the ulcer did not seem to be any bigger. Fingal sniffed. The smell was no worse. He looked at the boy's calf and Fingal's left fist clenched. A tiny smile flickered on his lips.

He'd used an indelible pencil at the times of giving the first, second, and third doses to mark the furthest upward extent along Dermot's leg of the red lines of lymphangitis. Three blue lines crossed the ascending red ones at ninety degrees, each about one inch apart. Since six thirty last evening the progress had been inexorable. It had taken all of Fingal's willpower not to call a halt at two thirty, admit defeat, arrange for hospital admission and, he took a deep breath, amputation. He'd calculated that as the rate of progress was about one inch every four hours he could take a chance. If the thing did go

490

higher between then and six thirty, the boy would still only lose his foot, not the whole lower leg and now, glory be, there'd been no more advance. Maybe? Maybe? Added to the noninvolvement of the lymph nodes it was promising. "Hold the light steady," Fingal said. He removed the thermometer and, holding it up to the light, squinted at the silver mercury column. 99.8. It was hardly plummetting from its earlier 100.2, and body temperature tended to be lower in the morning, but it wasn't getting any higher. He pulled the rug over the sleeping mother and son, taking care to leave the ulcer uncovered. He'd re-dress it in a minute. "Let them sleep," he said, stood, and inclined his head to Mister Finucane to indicate that they should move back to the fire.

The warmth was pleasant on the back of Fingal's legs. The scent of burning turf made an heroic attempt, but failed to counter the overpowering tenement smell.

"Well, sir?"

Fingal managed a smile that he hoped might be reassuring. "Dermot's not out of the woods yet — but he's holding his own."

"Will he lose the foot?" Fingal heard the way Minty's voice trembled. "I'd rather dat dan have him —" He looked down then back at Fingal. "— die. He won't die, will he, sir? He's all we've feckin' got." The man's voice cracked.

Orla had mentioned that just before Fingal had rushed off to track down a supply of Prontosil. He'd thought it odd that a Catholic family should still only have one child after thirteen years since the birth of their first, but he'd been so concerned for Dermot that he'd refrained from asking why. And now certainly wasn't the time.

Amputate or go on hoping? Your decision, Fingal O'Reilly, and ask yourself, look in your heart. If you decide to carry on with this treatment, is it for Dermot's sake — or is it to prove you are right, gain kudos from your colleagues? He clasped his hands behind his neck, pushed his head back, wrestled with the question, then looked at Minty and said, "I think we should wait a while longer. Give the Prontosil more of a chance. Give Dermot more of a chance," and hoped to God it was the right choice.

Minty pursed his lips. "I heard a doctor say dat once before. When Dermot was born. Orla nearly feckin' died. She bled after the delivery. The doctor came to me in the waiting room, said he'd packed her womb and that should stop the bleedin' and we should wait a bit longer. The feck it stopped anything." He hawked and made as if to spit before he clearly recognised where he was. "They took out her womb, and dat was all right. I'd rather have her alive with a bit missing than feckin' dead." He looked Fingal right in the eye. "And dat's w'at I t'ink about Dermot, sir."

"I understand," Fingal said, feeling the worries of the world. "We are doing everything we can."

"It was God w'at spared Orla back den as much as her operation." Minty crossed himself.

"And," said Fingal, "we must pray He'll heal Dermot and his foot." The good Lord and an aniline red dye. "Now, I'll make up the next dose and dress the wound. I think," he said, "it's going to be a long day."

Orla was soon up and dressed and Fingal found himself sharing the water she drew from the courtyard pump for her husband and heated over the fire. The two men used a sliver of soap, and cut-throat razor to shave, but Fingal had declined the offer of a share of the family's mixture of soot and salt that universally substituted for toothpaste in the Liberties.

While Dermot slept on, Orla had fed them a watery gruel and cups of tea.

Fingal's belly growled. He'd had nothing to eat since lunch yesterday, except cups of tea, but he didn't want to leave the patient.

"I'll just nip over and ask Skylark Brennan to tell dem at Clery's I'll not be in today," Orla said, and left.

Even if it was a Saturday the big department store needed cleaning.

"It's a feckin' good t'ing she has regular work," Minty said. "I'm lucky myself, I've a friend, a foreman on the docks, and he's decent about gettin' me a job unloading cargo now and again. Ordinarily I'd be out of dis place by now, linin' up wit' the rest of my mates to see if there was any oul' chance today, but —" He inclined his head in the direction of the sleeping area and said no more.

Someone was knocking on the door.

"Who the hell would that be this time of the mornin'?" Minty strode to the door. "It's yourself, Doctor Corrigan. Good morning to you."

"And to yerself," Doctor Corrigan said, "but there's bugger all good about it. It's bucketing down." He pulled off a bowler hat, almost taking his toupee with it, and shook water from the brim.

Fingal rose. "Good morning, Doctor Corrigan."

Phelim patted his hairpiece into place. "I was out on Swift's Alley seeing a namesake of yers, a Fingal Flahertie O'Reilly Kilmartin."

"How is he? I delivered him last April. And how are Roisín and Brendan, and their other son, Declan?" They were all part of his community now.

"The babe is teething, but he'll be grand. His ma was asking for ye, and his da. Bren-

494

dan's still working with another of your ex-patients, a Paddy Keogh, and he'd come round on his motorbike and sidecar to take Brendan off to a hare coursing meet in the Wicklow Mountains. Paddy says hello."

How the hell, Fingal wondered, did a one-armed man drive a motorbike? Still, he learned soon enough that there wasn't much Paddy Keogh couldn't do once he made up his mind to it.

"Do ye know, Doctor O'Reilly, I think half of my practice is yers already?"

"Thank you." Fingal hesitated then said, "But you didn't come round here just for that."

"No. I did not. Yer friend Bob Beresford is a very persistent young man. He tracked me down at home at ten o'clock last night. Asked me on yer behalf if I'd look after emergencies today. Told me why. Told me about the red prontosil." He cleared his throat and looked Fingal in the eye. "Would ye think it unpro-fessional if I asked to see yer patient?"

Technically it would be, unless Fingal asked for a second opinion. He hesitated. What if Doctor Corrigan disapproved, told Fingal to get the patient to hospital at once? What was in Dermot's best interests? Phelim's advice, that was what. "Mister Finucane, you'd not mind if I asked my senior colleague to con-sult?"

Minty, who Fingal had noticed had been

following every word, nodded. "Sometimes," he said, "two feckin' heads are better than one."

"Thank you."

"And," said Minty, "I know how youse medical gentlemen like to have your palavers in private, so I'll nip across the hall to the Brennans. They'll make Orla and me a cup of tea. Will you come for us when you're done?"

"I will," Fingal said.

He waited until Minty had pulled the blanket-curtain aside, kissed his son's forehead, and left.

Fingal rapidly told Phelim the history, his physical findings, stressing that the lymphangitis seemed not to be progressing, and waited until the little doctor had finished his examination. He straightened up. "Aye," Phelim said, "aye."

Fingal waited. Behind his back he held his left hand in his right, squeezing the fingers in its grasp.

Phelim nodded and said levelly, "It's a very grave chance ye're taking, Fingal O'Reilly. The boy might die."

Fingal tightened his grip. "I know, but if the drug can save the boy's foot? Let him live a full life?"

"Say that again."

Fingal frowned. "If the drug can save —"

"That's what I thought ye said." Phelim

496

smiled. "If I thought for one minute ye were risking this boy's life for yer personal glory I'd insist we get him to hospital right now. We're G.P.s, not research scientists, for God's sake. It's not our job to bugger about with untested drugs." He touched Fingal's arm. "But ye didn't say, 'If *I* can save,' you said, 'If the *drug* can save.' Fingal O'Reilly, I admire that. I'm proud of ye. It is only wee Dermot ye're thinking of."

Fingal's hands relaxed. "Thank you." And Phelim had helped Fingal answer the question he'd asked himself when Minty had asked if Dermot could die.

"So," said Phelim, "ye carry on. I trust ye'll do what's right for the lad, whatever that is, as the case progresses."

"I will. Thank you." He crossed his arms and stroked his chin with his right hand.

Phelim clapped Fingal on the shoulder. "So, ye go and get the Finucanes. Explain to them that I concur. I'll run on and I'll look after the emergencies until Monday. Neither one of us can tell how long ye'll be needed here."

40
Upon the Walls
of Thine House

"I don't believe it. I simply don't bloody well believe it," O'Reilly roared as he stood glowering, arms akimbo, in the doorway. What the hell were Kitty and Kinky doing standing on short stepladders in his waiting room? "Holy thundering Mother of —" Control your tongue, O'Reilly, he thought. You're with ladies, not sailors from the lower deck of HMS *Warspite*. But by Beëlzebub's blistering braces, there's a limit.

It was a Saturday morning and no patients were in the room. Nor was there any furniture, and the floor was covered in old newspapers. He looked down at the newspaper closest to him. It was last Thursday's, November 11. *Ian Smith Declares UDI*, the headline screamed. O'Reilly at the time had thought it odd that the man should have chosen Remembrance Day to declare Southern Rhodesia's independence from Britain. Now there'd been another unilateral decision taken — to redecorate a room in his own house without telling him. *Without telling him.* Sacrilege. Blasphemy. Was he master in his own home no more? Bloody hell. Calm down, he told himself.

Normally he would take pleasure from seeing Kinky and Kitty so obviously happy collaborating on a project, Kinky not one bit perturbed that Kitty was changing things at Number One. That would be the final indication that any residual feelings of Kinky being threatened by Kitty had vanished. At that moment, however, he felt as if two of the women in his house had ganged up on him. Made an unholy alliance. He made a growling noise in his throat as he watched, then said, "And Jasus, Kinky Kincaid, I never, never in a month of bloody Sundays thought you'd collaborate in this travesty."

"Come on, Fingal," Kitty said with a grin. She pushed on the wide-bladed metal spatula she was using to scrape the rose-covered wallpaper off the wall. His rose-covered wallpaper. "Don't growl at Kinky. She's only doing it because I asked you what you thought, didn't I, Kinky?"

"You did, and I'm sorry, sir, but I agreed and . . ."

"All right," O'Reilly said. "I hear you."

"And it's not as if you and I haven't discussed it," Kitty said. A long curl of paper rolled up ahead of her scraper then tore free and floated down.

He stared down at the strip, lying lifeless on the ground. "Discussed it? When?"

Kitty started working on another strip. "Back in August, not long after our honeymoon, I said I thought the roses were gaudy, but told you there was no accounting for taste and I'd let the hare sit — for a while. Then I brought it up a second time."

He frowned and tried to remember. "When?"

"The day Colin Brown cut his foot. I recall you telling me a bit of penicillin would soon put him right."

O'Reilly's frown deepened. "I remember Colin's foot." Aye, he thought, and I recall how it had made me think of a lad called Dermot Finucane too, and that, here and now, made O'Reilly realise that maybe there were more important things in life than a change of ancient wallpaper. And there might be a glimmer of hope. Maybe Kitty had bought new roses to replace these old ones?

The next strip whispered as it drifted to the newspaper-covered floor. The paper had been hung on a wall that had previously been painted a bright green.

"But I don't have any recollection of saying you could redecorate. Not then, anyhow."

Kitty stopped scraping and shook her head. Her hair was done up under a headscarf, and despite his irritation O'Reilly couldn't help but notice that even wearing khaki dungarees she managed to look attractive.

"Now, don't get into a tizzy, dear. You were there when Helen Hewitt helped me — us — choose the new paper. The week before Bertie Bishop's coronary I brought home a sample book. We both liked the light turquoise one with the pinstripe."

"Both liked." Did she mean Kitty and Helen or Kitty and O'Reilly? He knew he'd not remarked on it.

"And when I said, 'Those roses have to go,' you didn't object."

Aha. Kitty was invoking "implied consent," the doctrine that said if a doctor suggested treatment and the patient did not refuse it was all right to assume that they agreed and go ahead.

She turned back and assaulted the wall again. "By the way, I forgot to mention to you when I got home last night — you were so keen to tell me about the prospects for the Irish Rugby International side for next season —"

He smiled when he realised that she was putting up a smokescreen, giving him time to settle down.

"— but Cromie's Mister Braidwood has called to say the management committee have approved his request and that there will be a job for Helen as a ward orderly at New-townards Hospital in the summer. You'll need to speak to her about it."

"Wonderful," O'Reilly said, and his smile broadened. "And I do remember you actually saying, 'Those God-awful roses have to go,' but I don't seem to recall agreeing with you."

She smiled at him as a mother might whose ten-year-old has come second in the egg-and-spoon race. "Well, you didn't exactly, but I knew you'd approve." She blew him a kiss.

Game, set, and match to Kitty O'Hallorhan O'Reilly. Either he could give in graciously to the inevitable or start a row. And how could he possibly fight with Kitty or glue the already removed strips back on the wall? Sometimes discretion was the better part of valour. And perhaps — an idea was beginning to crystallise — there might be a way to salvage something after all. The fact that the wall had been previously painted would be a great help. He grinned, took off his jacket, and set it on a chair in the hall. "Did I ever tell you about the night Linfield, the Blues, were playing at Windsor Park against Glentoran and leading two to nil when the floodlights failed? Absolute bedlam. Then a wee man, Jimmy Dalzell from Finaghy, gets ahold of the microphone. 'On the count of th'ee I want everyone of youse til start clapping, so I do,' he roars. Crowd thought yer man had lost his marleys." O'Reilly's accent was now broad Belfast. "They must have decided to humour wee Jimmy. 'One, two, th'ee.' And away they went clapping like billyoh, and begod didn't the floodlights come straight on?" O'Reilly reverted to his normal speech. "Because," he paused for effect, "many hands make light work."

"Many hands make — ? Fingal, that's terrible." Kitty said, but she was chuckling.

Kinky was doubled over. "The humour of the wee north," she said, "it would make a cat laugh, so."

"And I do mean it," O'Reilly said, rolling up his sleeves. "Have you ladies another stripper and I'll give you a hand?" He fell to work with brio, all the while accompanying himself by singing,

'Tis the last rose of summer left blooming
    all alone
All her lovely companions, are faded and
    gone . . .

"Ah," Kinky, said, " 'Tis powerful voice you are in today, sir, and seeing yourself is in good form I would like to ask you a shmall-little favour, so."

"Fire away."

"It would please me greatly if you and — Kitty —" Kinky smiled at her friend and O'Reilly thought back a few months to when Kinky had struggled over the proper form of address for her employer's new wife. "When we have the old stuff off, if you would both join me in my kitchen for tea and hot but-

503

tered barmbrack, for I do think it will be about elevenses time and I've a matter I'd like to discuss, so, before we start hanging the new paper."

And O'Reilly wondered if the fact that Archie Auchinleck had stayed at least an hour longer than usual in Kinky's quarters yesterday evening could have anything to do with the "matter." He could wait to find out, and bent to the task in hand.

"Hanging the new paper, Kinky? I think," said O'Reilly, putting a hand into the small of his back, "that if you two ladies feel half as stiff as I do we may need to come up with a different tactic for doing that." He'd had plenty of time to refine his salvage plan and now, before Kinky started her "discussion," was the time to set the wheels in motion.

"At least the stripping job's done," Kinky said, climbing down from her stepladder into a sea of strips of tattered paper roses. "And in a minute you can rest your back, sir."

Kitty brushed away stray wisps of hair that had escaped from under her headscarf with the back of her hand. "That tea and barmbrack you promised sounds wonderful, Kinky. I could certainly use a breather."

"Come along then." Kinky led them to her kitchen, which as usual was redolent of something wonderful cooking. "I did think that I'd make a nice Dublin coddle for dinner," she said, "and although some recipes use water I prefer to make my own stock, so."

O'Reilly relished the thought of the bacon, sausage, potato, and onion dish that would be coming later and said, "I can hardly wait, but let's get the kettle on now."

"Doctor O'Reilly, Kitty, will you both please take a chair?"

They did, and watched as Kinky fussed round boiling the kettle, preparing the teapot. She sliced the freshly made circular barmbrack horizontally and popped it under the grill.

O'Reilly said, "I suspect you two were going to hang the new paper today so the waiting room will be ready for Monday."

"That's right, dear," Kitty said.

"I think not," O'Reilly said. "I have plans to take you to Belfast, Kitty. There's a Renoir exhibition on at the Ulster Museum Art Gallery I know you'd love."

"But —"

"And it would hardly be fair to expect Kinky to do the job all by herself."

Kinky had removed the dark barmbrack from under the grill. She spread butter on the lower slice, replaced the upper half, and cut the loaf into pie-shaped wedges. "It would not be all by myself," Kinky said, "Archie" — O'Reilly noticed how her voice softened — "would be pleased to help me, if that's what you'd like."

"Bless you, Kinky," O'Reilly said, accepting a cup of tea and a plate with two slices of the warm loaf, "but I've a much better idea. When we've finished our elevenses and you've told us what you want to, I'll nip out to Dun Bwee. Donal Donnelly's always on the lookout for odd jobs, you know, especially now with little Tori on the scene. And he's a damn fine paper-hanger . . ." Fine decorator of Halloween windows too, O'Reilly thought, "so if you have the rolls of the paper you want ready, Kitty, and the tools . . ."

"I have."

"All we have to do is let Donal loose. If he's left in peace the job'll be done by the time we get home for dinner." He bit into his first slice of 'brack, savouring its yeasty flavour and the sweetness of the dried fruit. Of course Donal could be easily persuaded to make some minor modifications, but he would need the privacy to do so.

Kitty sipped her tea. "Wellll," she said, "I'd certainly like to see the Renoirs, and I'm sure Kinky could find better things to do."

"I can."

"Consider it arranged, then," O'Reilly said, "and even if Donal's not available today I'm sure he could do the job tomorrow." He finished his first slice in one enormous bite, then said, "Now, Kinky, there was something you wanted to talk to us about?"

506

41
EXULTING ON
TRIUMPHANT WINGS

"Neither one of us knows how long you'll be needed here." Phelim Corrigan had spoken the truth. The whole day had gone by and all Fingal had been able to do was keep giving Dermot lots of water, examine him from time to time, and administer his four-hourly doses. The boy had slept.

"Are you sure you'd not like another cup of tea, sir?" Orla said. "It wasn't much of a supper for a big lad like you." It was seven thirty in the evening, the daylight was long gone, and the paraffin lamp was guttering and smoking. Dermot still drowsed and Minty paced the floor muttering, "How much longer, for God's sake?"

"It was grand, Orla," Fingal lied. Breakfast had been a bowl of thin gruel and a cup of tea. At two forty-five he'd managed to choke down a boiled pig's cheek with a boiled onion for lunch after he'd examined Dermot. Fingal had not seen any improvement then, yet there had been no further deterioration, no more extension of the red lines either. All he'd managed to say to Minty and Orla had been, "He's holding his own," and had given Dermot his sixth dose.

"I'd feckin' well hope so," Minty'd said.

After lunch the man had snatched his duncher from a peg, said, "Jasus, I hate bein' cooped up in here, worried sick. I can't take it no feckin' more. I'm goin' out," and slammed the door as he left.

Orla had shaken her head. "Don't blame him, sir. He blames himself. He t'inks if he hadn't rolled home stocious the night before you and Doctor Corrigan came . . ." She sighed and folded her shawl round her. "He t'inks if he'd let the stone bruise go sooner all dis wouldn't have happened." Her eyes had glistened. "He loves Dermot just as much as I do, but poor oul' Minty has terrible trouble hiding his feelings. He can work himself up intil a ferocious rage and dis time he's mad at himself. Better he's out." She smiled. "He'll be back by suppertime."

Fingal hadn't known what to say to comfort her. He'd begun wondering how Columbus, DaGama, Cabot, and their likes had felt when the familiar land disappeared astern. Would they find new lands or would they sail off the edge of the world? How had they felt? Bloody terrified, just like me, he thought. He supposed those early explorers had people they could trust, friends who had faith in them and were happy to let them exercise their own judgement. He blessed Phelim Corrigan for his understanding. His faith.

Fingal had already made up his mind that he'd wait until midnight and then get Dermot admitted. Give in to failure. Fingal hated the thought, but by then thirty-six hours would have passed since treatment had begun. He remembered that Sister Oonagh O'Grady had said it was then that improvements usually started in the patients Doctor Davidson was treating with Prontosil at the Rotunda.

Fingal looked around and wished he could get out of here for a while like Minty. Somehow the room seemed to be shrinking. "Where'll your husband go?" he asked.

She shrugged. "The boozer likely. Look for a bit of comfort from his friends. Try to find peace in a pint."

"I hope he'll be sober when —"

"I'll feckin' kill him if he's not," she said, and looked sideways at a serrated bread knife on the counter.

Fingal was not convinced that her words were an exaggeration.

Minty had come home stone-cold sober an hour later. "Sorry about dat," he said. "I had to get some feckin' fresh air. Smoke a fag or two. I walked around on the Quays. How is he, Doctor?"

"He's no worse."

Minty'd pulled his chair over to where Dermot lay and had sat holding his son's hand until Fingal came to give the six thirty dose.

Fingal repeated the examination. No change. "Much the same, I'm afraid." He looked at the red fluid in the beaker. "All I can tell you is that this stuff has worked in France, Germany, and England."

"I hope it's got nothing against us feckin' Irish," Minty said, sighed, and smoothed his son's brow.

Fingal said nothing and together they sat in a silence punctuated by Dermot's steady breathing, the spluttering of damp turf burning.

Someone was knocking on the door.

"Who's dere?" Minty asked. "Mebbe Doctor Corrigan's come back?"

Fingal answered the door then smiled. "Come in, Bob." Fingal turned to the Finucanes. "You remember Doctor Beresford who came here last night?"

Bob came to just inside the doorway.

They greeted him and he returned the pleasantry.

"I'd forgotten I'd asked him to come round tonight and bring my bike," Fingal said.

"It's in my car," Bob said. "How's your patient?"

Fingal sighed. "Holding his own, but no obvious improvement yet."

"Anything I can do?" Bob seemed anxious

to get out of the room, hesitated, then said, "I nipped over to Lansdowne Road Rugby Grounds after my lunch, was able to explain to Charlie why you probably wouldn't show up . . ."

"The Bective Rangers rematch. Damn it, I'd completely forgotten."

"Aye," said Bob. "Charlie said he understood, said he'd explain to your captain."

"Thanks, Bob."

Bob shrugged. "Least I could do for you considering the investment you're making here. Sure there's nothing more I can help with?"

"I'm sure."

"Then I'll be trotting on. Come and get your bike."

"I'll only be a minute," Fingal said, following Bob.

"I hope you don't mind me rushing off," Bob said, opening the car's door and hauling the bike out.

"Not at all. There really is nothing you can do." Fingal took hold of the handlebars.

"I'll be off then." Bob lit a Gold Flake and lowered his voice. "I did get fleas last night, you know. Rather not tonight. Good luck, Fingal. You'll let me know how it all turns out?"

"Of course." As Bob drove away, Fingal waved, turned, left the bike in the hall, and let himself back into the room.

"Come and get your supper, Doctor," Orla said.

Fingal joined the Finucanes at the table. He'd already known what one part of the meal would be. The smell of boiling cabbage had filled the air for the past hour.

Orla bowed her head, closed her eyes, and waited until Minty intoned, "We thank you Lord for this our daily bread."

Fingal joined in the amen.

She said, "I hope you like buttermilk. Dere's a jug on the table, sir." She served him a heap of champ, boiled cabbage, and one rasher of bacon.

He waited. Minty had got champ and cabbage but no bacon — so he, Fingal, had been given their last rasher. She had spread bacon dripping on a slice of white bread for herself.

Fingal poured some buttermilk and growled. It was always the way of it in the tenements. The men got the best of everything. The women held back.

"Please start before it gets cold, sir."

There was no bloody way he was going to demolish all that grub while she had nothing but bread and dripping. "Give me your plate, Orla," he said.

"But . . ."

"Your plate, please." He held out his hand.

She glanced at her husband and did as she'd been asked.

"There." He handed it back with half his

512

own meal on it. He came close to yelling at her when she said, "You have half the rasher, Minty."

Perhaps it was because of Fingal's presence that her husband refused.

The meal was taken in silence and tea was poured. "Are you sure you'd not like another cup, sir," she said when he'd finished.

"No thanks," he said, "but do you mind if I smoke my pipe?"

"You go right ahead, sir," Minty said, "and I'll have a fag —"

"Mammy. I want my mammy. Maaaaaa— mmy."

Orla leapt to her feet, Minty stared at Fingal, who rose and crossed the room.

Dermot was sitting up. He was in tears. His lip trembled. "Mammy."

"It's all right, *muírnin,*" she said, taking her son in her arms. "Mammy's here. It's all right. Dere now. It's all right."

Fingal leant across Orla. The boy's forehead was cool. Fingal got out his thermometer. "Hold this under your oxter, Dermot, like a good lad," he said, lifting the naked boy's arm then folding it down on the glass tube. He held Dermot's wrist. The pulse was strong, regular, and — Fingal had to wait for fifteen seconds that seemed like an eternity, then multiply the number of beats he'd counted by four — eighty-eight per minute. Almost normal. He bent. "Bring over the light, Mister Finucane." Parents' Christian names were infrequently used in front of children. "Shine it on Dermot's leg." Fingal realised he was trembling. He hardly dared look. Yes, yes, sweet Jesus, yes. All that remained on Dermot's calf were the three blue lines. The red, inflamed lymphatic channels had vanished as if they had been simply rubbed away with an eraser. He removed the thermometer and read 98.8, only 0.4 degrees above normal. He had to restrain himself and say, not shout, "It's worked. Dermot's getting better." Fingal would need time alone before he could fully digest the implications of the hugeness of what the red prontosil had achieved. For now all that mattered was that the infection was coming under control and Dermot's foot and life were saved.

"Mammy. I'm hungry."

"Would it be all right, Doctor?" she said, her voice cracking, eyes glistening.

For a moment the adage "Feed a cold and starve a fever" flashed through Fingal's mind, but then he remembered that only applied to enteric fevers where solid food might perforate an inflamed bowel. "Here." Fingal rummaged in his pocket, produced a handful of jelly babies, and gave them to Orla. "For later, Mammy, after you've given him a glass of buttermilk and a piece."

She wrapped him in a blanket and carried the boy to the kitchen table, sat him on a chair, poured tea, and spread margarine on a slice of bread.

Fingal inhaled deeply, feeling the responsibility for what was going to happen if he'd been wrong lift from his shoulders.

"And my wee boy's all better, Doctor?" Minty asked. "All mended?"

"Not quite," Fingal said, "but almost. He'll need to stay in bed, but he can get into the one by the fire and you and Mammy can get a bit of sleep tonight. I'll show her how to change his dressings and I'll make up enough doses so you can go on giving him the Prontosil every four hours, so you'll have to be up at ten thirty, two thirty, and six thirty. I'll come back tomorrow morning to see how he's doing."

Minty stuck out his hand. "We don't know how to thank you, sir."

Fingal shook the hand. "Mister Finucane," he said, "just seeing Dermot on the mend is thanks enough." And it was.

"It is a feckin' miracle," Minty said.

Fingal looked over to where Orla, smiling now though her cheeks were still wet, was asking Dermot, "Would you like another slice, dear?"

Perhaps it was indeed a miracle, but could the boy suddenly get worse? Fingal had no idea. He said, "I'll be going soon, but I'll be sleeping at Aungier Place just in case you need me. All you'll have to do is run over

515

and ring the night bell. And you come, even if you're only a bit worried."

"Och, he'll be grand, feckin' grand altogether," Minty said. "Never you fear."

Fingal wished he could share the man's belief, but he would sleep at Aungier — just in case, and he might see Phelim there, be able to give him the great news. Fingal hugged that thought.

Minty opened a cupboard, took out a bottle and two glasses. He poured a clear liquid and handed a glass to Fingal. "I'd like to drink your health, Doctor Big Fellah," he said. "It's a drop of the pure I keep for very special occasions."

That damn Big Fellah again. Fingal grinned. He liked it. No doubt he was accepted here in the Liberties. And, Fingal thought, the cure of Dermot's foot was special in more ways than one. If this Prontosil's as good as I think it's going to be, doctors won't be so bloody helpless anymore. Even dispensary G.P.s like me will be able to cure a lot of their patients. Really cure them and not simply stand round helplessly waiting for nature to take its course. Acceptance by the locals and at last the ability to cure made the prospect of staying in the job very attractive.

"Here's til you, sir." Minty raised his glass. "Dere's very few doctors who'd t'ink of staying all night and all feckin' day. You're the kind of man who puts his patients before himself. *Sláinte* and thank you."

"*Sláinte mHaith.*" O'Reilly drank the fiery *poitín* and felt a satisfied . . . he sought for the word. It wasn't quite smugness, but it was damn close and he must guard against that. The kind of doctor who put — Oh shite. He choked on his drink. Kitty. He'd been expected at her place for dinner last night. After Fingal had failed to get Bob to call Kitty then, explain to her why Fingal was unable to see her, he'd put her out of his mind. He'd even missed a chance tonight to ask Bob for the same favour. Idiot.

Would she understand why he had simply vanished for more than twenty-four hours and hadn't let her know why? Would she understand, and would she forgive him? He glanced at his watch. Eight fifteen. It was only a couple of miles from here to her flat, five or ten minutes on his bike.

"Right," he said, finishing his drink. "Let's have a last look at you, Dermot, and then folks, I'll be off."

42
I Have Heard
of Your Paintings

Kinky perched primly on the oak chair, looking neither to right nor left. "I hope you are enjoying my barmbrack, so. Now, there is this matter I'd like to discuss."

"Fire away, Kinky," O'Reilly said, taking another swallow of tea and starting on his second slice of 'brack.

"You will recall, sir, a conversation we had last month, the day you came in here to help me pluck the ducks?"

O'Reilly stopped chewing. "About whether I could manage if you left?" He glanced at Kitty. This wouldn't come as a surprise to her. He had told her all about Kinky's belief that one day soon Archie Auchinleck was going to propose and of her concerns about how O'Reilly would cope. "Has Archie — ?"

Kinky coloured to the roots of her silver chignon. "Last night over tea here he did ask me to be the second Mrs. Auchinleck, him being a widower man, so." She smiled and her dimples appeared.

Fingal was on his feet. "And? And?"

"I said I'd be honoured, and he said —"

O'Reilly let out such a loud whoop that it was answered by a "Woof" from the direction of Arthur's kennel in the back garden. "D'you hear that, Kitty, and I don't mean the dog? By God, this getting wed is becoming contagious. Kinky, Kinky, I wish you every happiness. When's the big day?"

"I'm very happy for you, Kinky," Kitty said. She looked long at O'Reilly then back to Kinky. "Marriage is a condition I'd certainly recommend without any reservations."

Thank you for that, girl, O'Reilly thought, but said, "What time is it?"

"To answer your first question, sir, no, we haven't set a date yet. And it's eleven thirty," Kinky said. "Why, sir?"

"There's a bottle of Pol Roger in the fridge, and damn it all it is twelve thirty in Paris so the sun is over the yardarm so to speak, and this is something marvellous." He headed for the fridge.

"I wonder, sir, if I could ask a favour?" Kinky said.

"Of course." He opened the fridge door.

"Would it be possible to save the bubbles until near your suppertime?"

O'Reilly frowned. "I suppose." He closed the door.

"You see, sir," she said, "Mister Auchinleck does be an old-fashioned gentleman and he's asked me to ask you, sir, if he could pay his compliments this evening at six thirty?" She inhaled. "My da, God rest him, is long gone, so Mister Auchinleck would like you to stand in Da's place so he can ask your permission for my hand."

"So he can ask — Kinky, you and Archie don't need my permission." O'Reilly felt a lump in his throat.

"I think that's sweet and very gallant, Kinky," Kitty said. "And of course you'll see him, dear."

"If that's what Arch — Mister Auchinleck wants, of course."

"Thank you," Kinky said, "and like the gentleman he is, Mister Auchinleck will be bringing my ring this evening, to put on my finger after his interview with yourself, and I do think that would be a time for my family, and that's what you are, sir, and Kitty." Kinky's eyes glistened. "My northern family, for Fidelma and Tiernan and Sinead and theirs are far away in County Cork. I'd like you to drink a toast to us then, so."

O'Reilly grinned. "By God, we will. We'll drink a toast to you and Archie. And perhaps more than one. I'll stop at the off-licence when I go to get Donal so he can finish the papering and I'll get a couple more bottles. Kinky, Kinky —" He stood in front of her. "Stand up."

She did, and he folded her in the most

enormous bear hug. "Good luck to you and Archie," he said, "and as my ma's housemaid from Rasharkin, Bridgit, who was full of country wisdom, might have said, 'The blanket's always the warmer for being doubled,' " he held her at arm's length, " 'and may the Lord keep you and Archie in his hand and never close his fist too tight on you.' " He let her go.

"Thank you," she said softly. "Thank you very much."

"We're absolutely delighted," Kitty said. "Number One's not going to be the same without you, Kinky. I imagine you'll be going to live with Archie once you're wed."

"I will," she sat, "but I have been giving some thought to what we discussed last month, sir."

O'Reilly snaffled a third piece of 'brack on his way back to his seat. "Go on."

"Archie is a milkman, so. He does rise up very early in the morning to do his rounds. There's no reason he can't arrange to swing by his house and pick me up and drop me off here at about six thirty. I can get the breakfast ready so you both won't need to fuss about it before you both go to work. I'll do the lunch, and even make a start on the dinner if Kitty's too busy to do it. The phone will get answered every morning. I can do the housework and the shopping like always, so." She frowned. "If I could work three full days here and two mornings, sure Archie's wee place needs the half of no upkeep, I'd like weekends off, all you'd need, sir, might be a bit of extra help on the three weekday afternoons I'll not be here to answer the phone — like Helen Hewitt did when I was sick. And I'd not feel I'd be letting you down, so if we could come to that arrangement."

O'Reilly glanced at Kitty. "It certainly would make life a lot easier. What do you think, Kitty?"

"I think it would be wonderful, but I think it would be too much to expect Kinky to run two households."

O'Reilly saw Kinky start to bristle, hunch her shoulders. "Too much . . ." she said, her voice starting to rise.

"Kinky," he said, "I agree with Kitty, and there's no point you huffing. How would you feel if we got somebody to do the heavy housework here?"

"Well . . . I . . . I suppose . . ." Her shoulders relaxed and she smiled.

"Consider it done," O'Reilly said.

"Thank you, and perhaps your assistant, sir, would be more comfortable down here . . ." She glanced slowly round. ". . . in my old home after I'm gone?"

"I don't mind having them upstairs," Kitty said, "but we'd certainly have more privacy, Fingal."

"We would, and they'd have more privacy

522

too. It'll all take a bit of getting used to, but the main thing is Kinky's happiness, and if she can have that and go on working here, well . . . ? Today is a great day. Grand day altogether." He finished his third slice of 'brack. "Now," he said, "we've things to do. Kitty, out of those overalls and into something fit for a Renoir exhibition. Kinky, I've no doubt you'll want peace to get the lunch ready," he headed for the back door, "and I'll get off right now to see if Donal can work this afternoon." And, he thought with a grin, as he closed the door behind him, I've got time to nip into the off-licence and the painter's and decorator's supply shop in Bangor and organise a little surprise.

Arthur appeared from his kennel, a look of anticipation on his face.

"Come on, lummox," O'Reilly said, "let's go and see Bluebird or Buttercup or Brandywine or whatever the hell that buck eejit calls his dog now."

"I hadn't realised that Claude Monet was such a shaggy-looking bloke," O'Reilly said as he neared the back door of Number One.

Kitty had been in her artistic element at the exhibition and had talked about nothing else on the way home. "Renoir painted that portrait of his friend in 1875," she said, "when Monet was thirty-five."

"Died of lung cancer not long after his

eighty-sixth birthday, I believe," O'Reilly said. "Did he? I didn't know that." She waited while O'Reilly opened the door. "The curator of the exhibition worked wonders with the exhibits," she said. "That portrait of Monet and *Dance in the City, Dance in the Country* and *Nude in the Sun* all usually hang in either the Musée d'Orsay or L'Orangerie in Paris. I can never quite remember which Impressionist is where. Thank you for taking me to see them, Fingal." She chuckled. "It beat hanging wallpaper all afternoon."

"Mmmm," said O'Reilly, wondering how Donal was getting on. "Maybe next year I'll take you to see those museums and the Louvre. I'd love a trip to Paris. There's a wonderful hotel, the Regina du Passy, near Chausée de la Muette. I stayed there in 1959. Went to watch the Irish Rugby team beat France nine to five." He looked over to catch Kitty sending him a look of despair. "No, I am not a Philistine, my love. I also, I'll have you know, visited L'Hôtel Biron to see the Musée Rodin."

Kitty chuckled. "It might be heresy, but I've always thought his *Thinker* looks like a man who could really use a laxative."

O'Reilly was still laughing when he opened the back door and waited until Kitty had gone in before following.

"Kinky, you look lovely," Kitty said.

She did. Under her pinafore, Kinky was

524

wearing the embossed silk bridesmaid's outfit she'd worn at his wedding. O'Reilly put the champagne into the fridge.

"Well," said Kinky, "it does not be every day that a body is going to get engaged to be married, so." She indicated with a lift of her head. "Mister Auchinleck arrived a little early. I have taken him up the stairs to the lounge, sir."

"I'll go straight up, but when I send him down to you, Kinky, Kitty, you bring up the bubbles and five glasses. We'll give Donal a wee tot when he's finished." O'Reilly left.

"And I'll keep you company, Kinky, until then," Kitty said. "Teach me about Dublin coddle while we're waiting. I know it's one of Fingal's favourites."

He closed the kitchen door and opened the one to the surgery. All he could see with his head barely inside was Donal's dungaree-clad back as he used a broad brush to hang what was probably the final strip of the pinstriped paper. "How are you getting on?" O'Reilly kept his voice barely above a whisper.

"Rightly," said Donal, half turning. He winked. "First I done that wee special touch you asked for, sir. Made it a lot easier seeing the wall had been painted and didn't need priming. You can't see it unless you come right into the room, so you can't. It took a wee while. I thought I might have til come back the morrow for til finish the papering,

525

but hanging the paper's been a doddle. Just this here last piece, you know, then Bob's your uncle."

"Great. I won't look now. It'll be a surprise," said O'Reilly. "We'll be with you soon." He closed the door and climbed the stairs.

Archie Auchinleck stood in O'Reilly's upstairs lounge. Archie was rigidly at attention and for a moment O'Reilly thought the man might salute. Not surprising. He'd been a colour sergeant with the First Battalion, Royal Ulster Rifles, which had become an airlanding brigade after Dunkirk. Archie and hundreds of his comrades had been taken by Horsa gliders to France on D-Day and across the Rhine in Operation Varsity in 1945.

"Doctor O'Reilly," he said, "thank you for taking the time to see me."

"It's my pleasure, Mister Auchinleck," O'Reilly said, and offered his hand. He stood level with Archie, who was a good deal thinner than O'Reilly. Let's see what a few months of Kinky's cooking did to that, thought O'Reilly with an inward smile. The man's greying hair was neatly trimmed in a short back and sides and combed flat. He wore what must be his best blue serge three-piece suit, starched white shirt, regimental tie with its crown and harp emblem, and highly polished black shoes.

Archie hesitated then took the hand and

shook it with a strong grip. "Doctor O'Reilly," he said stiffly, "you might think a man of fifty-six like me coming to you like this a bit odd, but all my life I've done things the proper way, so I have. By the book. No muckin' about, no hanky-panky. The first time I was wed back in 1938, a man was expected to ask."

O'Reilly nodded and waited.

Archie took a very deep breath. "Everybody knows me and Maureen's been keeping company since April." His next inhalation was even deeper and his voice hesitant when he said, "Her and me's in love and it's time."

To save Archie further embarrassment, O'Reilly said, "I understand." He knew from past experience what a great effort it took for Ulstermen to confess their love to their girl, never mind another adult. It took a kind of courage to propose marriage and to ask for a daughter's hand. God knew, O'Reilly should have in 1936. "You think you need my permission?"

Archie frowned. Stiffened. He sounded as aggrieved as a vegetarian might if offered a ham sandwich. "It's the usual custom, sir, in these parts, and God rest him, Maureen's da's long gone. Who else would I ask?" His voice softened. "I'll take good care of her, so I will. I promise. Honest to God."

Not so long ago a father would have been expected to enquire into a future son-in-law's prospects and whether he could support his wife in the manner to which she was accustomed. At least the days of having to provide the bride with a dowry were long gone too. He said, "Archie, if you feel you need my go-ahead, and I'm touched you'd ask, you have it from the bottom of my heart and my blessing and Mrs. O'Reilly's too."

"Thank you, sir. Thank you." The man's smile, which revealed a gold tooth, was radiant. "Thank you very, very much."

O'Reilly offered his hand, which was shaken. "Now," he said, "you trot down to the kitchen, Kinky's waiting, and send Mrs. O'Reilly up here, and when you're ready, bring Kinky back and we'll seal the bargain with a jar or two."

"Right, sir." Archie bent and picked up a bunch of red roses that O'Reilly had not noticed lying in an armchair.

"Good man-ma-da," said O'Reilly to Archie's back.

In what seemed like no time Kitty appeared carrying a tray bearing a bottle of Moët Chandon and five tulip glasses. She set it on the sideboard.

"Fingal," she said, "if you'd seen the look on Kinky's face when Archie appeared with the bouquet of red roses and the ring, you'd have wept. I've never seen her so happy." She stretched up and kissed him. "You're very good at making women happy, pet."

He took her in a hug, kissed her, and said, "Thank you." He looked down. "It's taken me a fair bit of time to learn how, but I think I am getting the hang of it."

"You are," she said, "quite definitely." She glanced at the bottle. "And what's champagne for but to celebrate happiness?"

O'Reilly took the hint. Shortly after the cork went *pop,* he had poured four glasses and Kinky and Archie arrived.

"Let's see?" Kitty said, reaching for Kinky's left hand. "Beautiful. That's one of the loveliest princess-cut diamonds I've ever seen."

"And Kitty should know," O'Reilly said. "She's taken courses in gemology." He handed out the glasses of bubbles.

Kinky smiled. "Thank you, sir, and thank you, Kitty. I'm a very lucky woman, so." She beamed up at Archie and took his hand.

The tall Ulsterman smiled down and said, "The luck's all mine, so it is, Maureen."

"Now," said O'Reilly, raising his glass. "To Archie and Kinky. May they always love and find comfort in each other."

"To Archie and Kinky," echoed Kitty. "I hope you'll let Doctor O'Reilly and me give you a party soon to celebrate with family and friends?"

"Good idea," O'Reilly said. "Some time in the next few weeks before Christmas."

"Thank you, Doctor," Archie said. "Me and Maureen'd like that very much, so we would."

As he drank deeply, O'Reilly's gaze caught Kitty's. May they all love and find comfort in each other. True, he thought. How very true. "All right, but now I'd like you two to excuse Kitty and me for five minutes, then we'll be back up because we want to hear all your plans. But first I want to take a glass down to Donal, pay him, and let him get home. Come on, Kitty." He poured another glass.

They went down the stairs. "That was very tactful, Fingal," Kitty said, "giving them a few moments together. For all your bluster, you really are a pussycat, you know."

"For goodness' sake, woman, don't tell anybody. I've my reputation to think of." He pushed open the waiting room door. "It's us, Donal," he said, standing in the doorway and effectively blocking Kitty's view of the room, now smoothly papered in the subdued pastel shade.

"Just finishing tidying up, sir," Donal said with an eyelid-drooping wink. "Wheeker. Thanks." He accepted the glass. "Champagne? What's the big event?"

"I'll tell you in a minute," O'Reilly said, barely able to hide his smile, "but come on in, Kitty." He stepped aside. "How do you like it?"

Kitty came in looking straight ahead and obviously admiring Donal's work. "Lovely. Thank you, Donal. You've done a marvellous job. Now, Fingal, don't you think it's much more restful than those God-aw . . ." She turned through 180 degrees. "I'll kill you, Fingal Flahertie O'Reilly, you gobshite," but she nearly spilled her drink she was laughing so violently. "I'll kill you. Oh dear." Tears ran down her cheeks. "Oh dear me. Wonderful."

"Do you approve, Mrs. O'Reilly?" Donal asked in his most innocent voice, the one he used on unsuspecting punters just before he scalped them. "Doctor O'Reilly said you especially liked murals and he lent me one of your art books for to copy, so he did."

And there on the rear wall was an unpapered strip of previously green-painted wall upon which in acrylic paint not yet dry were the stems, leaves, and heads of three bright red floribunda roses. Donal had shown remarkable talent, even to having put glistening dewdrops on three of the leaves.

"Oh, Donal, Donal," said Kitty, as her guffaws subsided into a series of throaty chuckles, "I never liked the wallpaper, but I've never had any quarrel with roses." She took a deep breath and once her chuckles had subsided said, "And you've made them look so natural. I think Donal should sign it, don't you, Fingal?"

O'Reilly inclined his head. "I do, in soul I do."

43
PART AT LAST WITHOUT A KISS

Despite the late-October rawness, Fingal was sweating when he rang the bell and waited on the steps of the converted Leeson Street terrace house where Kitty had her flat. He'd pedalled furiously from Bull Alley, rehearsing his speech of apology all the way. "Kitty. I'm so sorry about last night. It was an accident —"

She opened the door. The Kitty he saw standing in the doorway was a far cry from the smartly dressed, well-coiffed young woman he'd become used to seeing. She was wearing a tartan dressing gown, felt slippers, no makeup, and her hair in paper curlers. "Fingal?" her voice was expressionless. He'd been prepared for a relieved, "Are you all right? Thank God you're here," or an exasperated, "Where the blazes have you been. I've been worried sick." She certainly had every right to be angry, but it would be all right when she understood why she'd been stood up.

He pursed his lips. "Can I come in? I'd like to explain."

She nodded, said, "Put your bike in the hall," and stood aside.

He grabbed his doctor's bag from the basket — it would be silly to leave it in a public hallway — and followed her into the flat.

"Sit down," she said once she'd closed the door. The living room was cosy and the gas fire burbled and popped. "Virginia's out. You know she and Cromie came to the parting of the ways. There's too big a distance between Dublin and Belfast."

Fingal had felt sorry for his friend when Kitty had mentioned last month that Cromie and Virginia Treanor had parted, but understood that, like Fingal himself, his friend was on the threshold of a career, too junior to settle down and working even worse hours than Fingal.

"Virginia decided to cut her losses. She has a new man now. He's not a doctor. He doesn't work on weekend nights. Lucky Virginia." Fingal detected a wistful tone. Kitty's laugh was clipped. "It's Halloween tonight, and she's gone to —"

"Halloween? I'd lost track," he said. "I've been working." He didn't take a chair. "Look, I'm so sorry about last night."

She stood, arms folded across her chest. "I'm listening. Go on."

"Kitty, you won't believe what I'm going to tell you."

She tapped her foot. "I'm sorry, Fingal, I just hope it's a good explanation. I was worried sick. That time last year when you couldn't get back from the north because your brother's car broke down — at least then you got a message to me through one of your friends. I understood then. Circumstances . . ."

"And I should have sent a message this time too. I'm sorry." Boy, should he have? You bet he should. Yesterday evening, when he'd asked Bob to explain things to Phelim Corrigan, Fingal could have asked his friend to nip round and tell Kitty as well. But Fingal had been totally preoccupied with Dermot Finucane, and by the time Fingal had thought of it, Bob had gone. "I'm sorry. I know I should have tried to let you know, but I was with a very sick boy —"

"And the patient always comes first," she interrupted. "I know." She shook her head. "Fingal, I'm trying to be understanding, but back in August you made that pretty clear. I have tried to understand. Three weeks ago when you spent ages chatting to that tugger —"

"Lorcan O'Lunney? But —"

"That's the one. I didn't mind, truly I didn't. But I did wonder aloud if you ever stopped thinking about your patients. That some doctors should be like priests, take vows of chastity. You told me you loved me, that you'd make a bigger effort —"

"I do and I have been."

"And I said, 'All right, let's see how it goes,'" Kitty continued on, as if he hadn't spoken. "I don't think spending half a Friday getting myself ready for you, for you, Fingal, cooking a meal I thought you'd really enjoy . . ." Her voice caught in her throat. "Then watching it shrivel up and have to be chucked out. It made me wonder about chucking other things out too."

And he knew what she meant. He hung his head. "I am sorry, Kitty, and —"

"Damn it, it's not the inconvenience, it's not the waste, it's —"

"Please, Kitty —"

"No. Let me finish." Her voice cracked.

He shook his head. All his prepared words fled. Surely once she understood the marvellous enormity of what had happened in the last twenty-eight hours she'd forgive him? "Kitty, please. Please listen."

She sighed. "No, Fingal, you listen. Last June you put me aside because of your final exams. I cried. I told you you'd killed my laughter. I hurt." She pursed her lips. "Perhaps I was selfish, but I didn't want to play second fiddle to your career. I met another doctor. Somehow he always had time for me, and I'm not the possessive type. You know that. I'm a nurse. I understand about doctors being on call. But last night was your night off."

"I know, and I was on my way here, but —"

"Don't you see, Fingal? There'll always be a 'but.' " Her eyes glistened. "My trainee surgeon from Galway proposed last year and I did think I was in love. If I hadn't thought so I'd have turned him down flat. I wasn't wanting to get married simply because it's what women are meant to do. I was, I still am, hoping one day to find a man who'll be a full half of my life. I want a family. I'd like to settle down."

"So would I." Don't say "but." Propose now, man, or you're going to lose her.

"Last year I didn't think that you were that man, Fingal. I didn't think I could compete with your mistress, medicine. When you called here to apologise I sent you away, but everything I'd ever felt for you came flooding back."

"Kitty, I love you —"

"Damn it all, Fingal, I know you do. I turned the Galway man down, and the night you passed your finals and you took me to meet your parents, my mind said, 'Watch yourself, girl,' but my heart?" She shook her head. "I was in love with you. I still am."

"I love you, Kitty." Fingal took a huge breath. "If you'd only let me explain how we were able to save a fourteen-year-old's leg and his life." He knew his voice must sound excited.

Her tears started. She didn't sob, but the water ran slowly down her cheeks. "Don't you see, Fingal, you and Phelim Corrigan are two of a kind? He's single. He puts his patients first." She dashed her hands across her eyes. "I'm sorry. I shouldn't be weeping, but, Fingal, don't you see? There'll always be a child with diptheria, a life to save." She looked right into his soul. "You're going to be a saint of a doctor — but the saints were single men."

"Kitty," he said, stepping forward to embrace her, soothe her, tell her it was going to be all right. That he'd change. But the damn doctor's bag got in the way. Before he could set it down, she had stepped back.

"No, Fingal," she said. "I had a visitor this afternoon. Do you remember I mentioned my friend Agnes Brady?"

He shook his head. Why wouldn't she listen to him? "Vaguely," he said.

"The Connolly Column of the International Brigade will be leaving in December to train in Perpignan in southern France."

"But you said you weren't interested in going to Spain to support the Republican side." He shook. Fingal felt as if he'd walked into quicksand and no matter which way he turned, his feet were stuck and he was sinking.

"I'm not, and neither's Agnes anymore."

"Thank God for that." The earth became firmer. "Now, please, Kitty, please let me tell you about why I didn't come until now, and it's miraculous." He knew he sounded excited, but he had good reason.

"No, Fingal. No. You don't understand. I'm trying to tell you I want us to take a break and you're not hearing me. You're too excited — and not about us. About something at your work."

His jaw fell. "A break?"

"Yes. This afternoon Agnes told me she'd been given permission to leave the International Brigade before they sailed because she's been contacted by a nondenominational group who have established an orphanage for the poor wee mites who have lost their parents in the fighting. You know how much I've worried about the children? I thought the orphanage sounded like a good idea. Agnes asked might I volunteer to work there with her." Kitty shook her head. "By this afternoon I'd heard nothing from you, decided you couldn't really care if you could forget about me so completely —"

"It's not like that, it's just that I —"

"No, Fingal. No explanations. I was so angry with you I said yes, I'd need to give notice at Baggot Street Hospital but, then,

538

when can we leave?"

"But the night we saw *Bride of Frankenstein* you said, 'I'd hate to leave Dublin . . .' "

"I will, but I have to go."

His shoulders slumped. "So you are going to Spain?" Dear God, he'd been, in a desultory fashion, following the fighting. Franco's troops had nearly reached Madrid. She could get hurt. Killed.

"No," she said. "Not Spain proper. To one of the Canary Islands. Tenerife. In a small village called San Blas on the south coast. There's no fighting there. The orphanage is near Mount Teide."

Tenerife? He remembered calling at its port, Santa Cruz de Santiago de Tenerife, during his time in the merchant marine. Lord Nelson, whose statue stood on his pillar in O'Connell Street, had lost his right arm there leading a failed assault on the port in 1797. And he, Fingal O'Reilly, was going to lose something more precious to him than his own right arm. "Please, Kitty. Please don't go."

"I'm sorry, Fingal," she said. "I see now that it was my anger at you that tipped my decision, but my mind's made up. You care for your patients. I'm going to children who need love."

"But I'm trying to explain."

She shook her head. "Too late. I've promised. I'm going. That's final. The ship leaves from Southampton next month. I'll be back

539

next year on leave. If you wish, I'll let you know when. I might be willing to give us one more chance then, but for now I need to step back. Clear my mind."

"If that's what you want." Fingal was lost and didn't know where to turn. At least there was a glimmering of hope. "I'll wait," he said. He'd no other choice. "I'll write."

She went to a small desk, picked up a sheet of paper, and handed it to him. "It's a forwarding address for the society," she said. "Fingal O'Reilly, I'll always love you, but . . ."

Her few words hung as limply as the piece of paper in his hand, and there was no need for more.

Fingal, with his coat collar turned up, cycled slowly through a chilling drizzle along the familiar streets, barely noticing that he was passing Saint Stephen's Green on his way to Aungier Place. He knew he'd let Kitty down, hurt her, knew it was his fault. He struggled to understand her anger. Damn it all, he was a doctor, trained to accept people when they were upset, as all patients inevitably were. He was meant to be able to make allowances for folks who had reason to be angry, but — he swerved to pass a parked car — when it came to Kitty O'Hallorhan? Fingal couldn't just dissect her feelings as Bob Beresford might dispassionately look at one of his bugs under the microscope. Fingal loved her pure and simple and did not want to lose her. But he also knew her well, and he knew himself.

He stood on the pedals, sprinted the last few hundred yards, and dismounted in the courtyard. Shoving his bike in the rack, he blew out the calcium carbide headlamp, grabbed his bag, and headed for the dispensary. There was a light on in the upstairs kitchen. Phelim must be there. Pity. Fingal would have much preferred to have been on his own for a while.

He let himself in, left his sodden coat in the hall, and climbed the stairs. Aye, he nodded, he knew Kitty was a strong-minded woman, and when she'd made her mind up? Damnation. He hit his fist twice against the wall.

And he knew himself. He could be stiff-necked, and he thought of how he'd defied his own father, God rest him, to train as a doctor. Nor did Fingal believe that pleading with Kitty, if he could bring himself to do so, would have any effect. She said she'd promised. And Kitty O'Hallorhan was not a woman to go back on a promise. She'd be home on leave next year. He could keep in touch, and hope. He could see no other choice.

"Jasus, Fingal, ye look like a rat that's gone ten rounds with a cat and been dumped in the Liffey," Phelim said, turning from the gas stove when Fingal entered the kitchen, "so would ye like a cup of tea?" His colleague's hairpiece too, looked like a rat that had suffered a grave misfortune, but for once it failed to amuse Fingal.

"Aye. Please." Fingal set his bag on a shelf. He wondered should he tell Phelim about Kitty?

Phelim, with his back to Fingal, poured, added the milk and sugar the way Fingal liked, turned, and gave him the chipped enamel mug. "I'm assuming ye had to send the child to hospital," Phelim said, "for yer face is as long as a wet Sunday. Sit down and tell me all about it."

Fingal accepted the tea, sat at the table, and waited for Phelim to do the same, but before he did the little doctor went to a cupboard, rummaged in a tin box, and filled a plate with fig rolls and coconut creme biscuits from Jacob's biscuit factory. "Here," said Phelim, sitting and offering the plate, "have ye a biccy." He helped himself. "I'm very partial to fig rolls."

Fingal shook his head.

Phelim leant forward, cocking his head. His remark was softly spoken. "It's not like ye, Fingal, to refuse grub. I hope to God I'm wrong, but — but did the little lad die?"

"No," Fingal said, "quite the contrary. I'm just tired, a bit preoccupied."

"So what did happen?"

Fingal smiled. "A miracle. The stuff worked. Damn it, it worked, Phelim."

"Get on with ye. Ye're fooling me. In all my years I've never seen anything that cures infections." But Phelim Corrigan was grinning.

"Red prontosil does work. Honestly, at least it did for Dermot. We were finishing our supper tonight and suddenly he calls for his mammy. Says he's hungry. His temperature and pulse were nearly normal, he wasn't sweating, and the lymphangitis had vanished. Completely vanished."

"Jasus Murphy and all the saints. Honestly?" Phelim shook his head. "I'm not doubting ye, Fingal. I'm just flabbergasted."

"I was too," Fingal said, "and delighted for the lad — and for the future."

"The future?"

"Phelim, we're soon going to be able to cure infections. Think what that means."

Phelim pushed his chair back. "And ye still haven't thought what it means for ye, have ye?"

Fingal shook his head.

"Ye'll be famous."

"I'll what?"

"If ye want to be, ye can be the most famous doctor in Ireland. All ye'll need to do is write a letter to the *Lancet*."

What had Fingal said when he was trying to persuade Bob to get the Prontosil in the first place? "There might be a prize in it for one of the professor's top students." It hadn't dawned on Fingal that there might be a prize in it for him too. "I'm not sure I want that," he said.

"And why the hell not?"

"I'd have to explain where I got my hands on the Prontosil. It said right on the bottle, 'Not for use in humans,' and Bob Beresford told me, 'Professor Bigger will kill me if he finds out.' " Fingal also remembered how Bob had said he would have helped Fingal even without the carrot of possible fame. He'd have helped because they were friends. "I'd not like to queer his pitch with his prof." Fingal and Bob were friends, and friendship was a two-way street.

Phelim munched his fig roll. "Do you not think Prof Bigger would forgive Bob?"

"He might." Fingal shook his head. "But you know, Phelim, that would be a gamble and I've already taken one that's paid off against the odds. What's important is that Dermot's better and his foot's saved. I'm not interested in fame."

"So it's just the outcome that matters, is that it?" Phelim reached for another roll. He narrowed his eyes. "I'll never forget what ye said, boy, 'If the medicine cures the patient,' not a thought of, 'If the great Doctor O'Reilly cures the lad.' I am proud of ye."

Fingal blushed and said, "I — I just wanted to see the boy better and, yes, I do want the world to know and I do want us in the profession to be able to do something huge for patients, but Bob's told me that the real, proper research is just beginning to suggest Prontosil, or its active part, sulphanilamide, does work. Can you imagine what harm I'd do bellowing one case from the rooftops if it was only a lucky chance? A fluke? I said we'd soon be able to treat infections. I'd just like a bit more proof, maybe from the study Doctor Davidson's doing at the Rotunda. I don't want to go off half-cocked."

Phelim's fig roll never got to his mouth. He stood and offered his hand.

Fingal frowned and took it.

"Doctor O'Reilly. Ye are a remarkable man."

"No such thing." Fingal blushed.

Phelim took his seat and bit into his second roll. "There's one thing I don't understand."

"What?"

"Ye've come damn close to finding the Holy Grail, yer patient's going to get better, and still ye came in looking like ye'd lost a guinea and found tuppence. What's wrong?"

Fingal pursed his lips. There was no reason not at least to tell Phelim. "My girl and I . . ."

Phelim choked on his roll and Fingal leapt to his feet, used the flat of his hand to smack the man on the back. Phelim coughed, spluttered, said, "Thank you," and dried his eyes with a hanky. "Fingal," he said, "I know what ye're going to say — Ye were meant to see her last night, but ye stayed with your patient."

"How did you know?"

Phelim's smile was wistful. "I'm still single, aren't I?"

And Fingal realised that Kitty's suspicion about Phelim's bachelorhood was right, and it might be prophetic for Fingal's future too.

"I wish," said Phelim, "I could say I could free up more time for ye to make it up to her."

"I don't think that would matter," Fingal said. "She's a nurse and she's leaving next month to help with orphans of the Spanish Civil War." He took a deep breath. "But it was a generous thought."

"No, it wasn't." Phelim put down the uneaten half of his fig roll. "I was going to tell ye and Charlie on Monday anyway."

"Tell us what?"

"Ye know I've been having these meetings with the dispensary supervisory committee?"

"Yes."

"So, Fingal, they're going to redraw the boundaries of the Aungier Street Dispensary. On Monday I was going to have to tell ye and Charlie that I'll have to let at least one of ye go —"

At least one of them? Charlie was pretty set on leaving anyway, but what if they both had to go? Fingal knew, knew completely, that his future was here in Aungier Place working with a man who must be the best senior colleague any young doctor could ask for. He gritted his teeth, and said levelly, "I'm sure between us Charlie and I can work it out." Charlie'd understand. Probably be relieved to have an excuse. Fingal smiled, but the smile vanished when Phelim said, "It may not be just one. The new boundaries may not even support two doctors. I'm sorry."

"Jesus," Fingal said. Kitty gone, probably the job he had finally decided was the right one for him gone, and — trivial in comparison, but still important to him, by missing playing rugby this afternoon he'd probably jeopardised his chances for selection, and a place on the Irish team. All taken from him in the space of twenty-four hours.

Who'd said bad things come in threes? Damned if he knew or actually gave a tinker's curse about the source, but everything Fingal cared about had been overthrown like the shattering of the ramparts of a sand castle by the waves of Killiney Bay.

44
CHOOSE THOU WHATEVER SUITS

Barry Laverty didn't seem to be able to stop laughing, but managed to say, "Donal painted those roses? He's quite the artist."

Immediately after letting the young man in through the front door, O'Reilly had taken Barry to view the redecorated waiting room. "What my Dublin patients would have called 'spec-feckin'-tacular,' " O'Reilly said. "Not quite up to the standard of the old wallpaper, but, 'Not so deep as a well nor so wide as a church door . . . but . . .' "

"Mercutio, *Romeo and Juliet,* 'but mind you, 'tis enough.' "

"Indeed it is," O'Reilly said with a smile. "You haven't changed much, Barry, have you? But you'd be amazed by some of the things round here that have since you left. I'll tell you about them soon, but, and I'm sure it will come as no surprise to you, I still like my jar. Come on upstairs and we'll have a quick one." He led and Barry followed. The young man had phoned yesterday to say he'd like to see O'Reilly at five o'clock today. Hall Campbell, the fisherman from Ardglass who last week had his patent ductus arteriosus repaired successfully, may have wondered if O'Reilly's first name was Sherlock, but it had taken no great powers of deduction to guess why Barry'd asked to come. What he was going to say was another matter.

While Barry settled in one armchair with his glass of John Jameson, O'Reilly filled his briar and lit up before sitting himself. *"Sláinte,"* he said, raised his glass, and drank.

"Cheers," Barry said. He pointed to the curtained bow windows. "It doesn't seem like nearly eighteen months since I first sat with you in this room, sipping a sherry, admiring the view. Do you know, Fingal, I got so used to it I can picture it now even with the curtains closed? You can see past the moss-grown lopsided steeple, down over the rooftops of the cottages on Main Street, over the foreshore, across Belfast Lough, and out to the Antrim Hills." He sipped. "You said, and I'll never forget, 'You couldn't beat it with both sticks of a Lambeg drum.' You were right."

"Aye," said O'Reilly, belching smoke. "And it's not just the scenery or the slow pace of life. It's a place and people that will get under your skin if you let them."

"I have done," said Barry quietly.

O'Reilly wondered if it was the place, its

inhabitants, or a certain schoolmistress. He waited.

"I promised you a decision before the end of November, Fingal." Barry stood, walked to the window, and came back. "I didn't want to talk about such an important thing over the phone last evening. It has to be face-to-face."

"I agree." That was the sort of approach folks used if they were delivering what they thought their listeners would perceive as bad news. Did that mean in spite of loving the place Barry wasn't coming back?

"I won't muck about . . ." And he grinned. "If you'll have me, Fingal, I'd like to be your partner starting in January."

"Bloody marvellous." O'Reilly rose, extended his hand. "Welcome back, Barry. We've missed you."

Barry too, rose and shook hands.

"When can you start?" O'Reilly said.

"I need to give a month's notice in Ballymena. Would Monday the third of January be all right?"

"Make it Monday the tenth. I'm sure you could use a break and Jenny won't mind staying on for as long as that. She may need a bit of time to find another spot." How was he going to break the news to Jenny? She was going to be very disappointed and O'Reilly hated to disappoint people. He sat and motioned Barry to do the same. "What made you decide?"

Barry sat, frowned, and shook his head. "It's hard to explain."

"Barry, I'm just delighted you're coming back, the reasons don't really matter." But they did. Fingal wanted to know if whatever had swung Barry's heart in this direction was anything like the decision-making a younger Fingal O'Reilly had had to wrestle with in 1936 and '37.

"I think," Barry said, "I missed the feeling of belonging. I missed seeing how things turned out with the patients. I liked walking down the street here and being greeted with smiles and a 'How's about you, Doc?' Knowing I fitted in. There's no Mucky Duck in Ballymena. I missed feeling we were making useful changes here in the village that had nothing to do with medicine. Like helping Donal and Julie get their house."

History repeats itself, O'Reilly thought. Pretty much the same reasons why I chose to come back here in '46 after the war.

"And like stopping Bertie Bishop from buying the Duck and turning it into a chrome-and-plastic tourist trap with piped Mantovani and Percy Faith? Bertie, by the way," said O'Reilly, "had a coronary three weeks ago. That's one of the changes I was going to tell you about. He'll be getting home on Monday."

"I'm sorry to hear that, Fingal," Barry said,

"and I don't mean I'm sorry he's getting home. He's not the most amiable of men, but you'd not wish a coronary on your worst enemy."

O'Reilly laughed. "You're right, Barry, but there have been occasions I'd have wished the plagues of Egypt on the bloody man. Let's hope he makes as good a recovery as can be expected." He raised his glass. "To you, Bertie. Get well soon."

"To Bertie." Barry drank.

A white blur shot acros the room, roared "Meroooowww," launched herself into Barry's lap, and began purring and indulging herself in what Kinky called dough-punching, kneading Barry's lap with her forepaws. He glanced down and fondled Lady Macbeth's head. "I missed your lunatic menagerie, Fingal."

"You can give old Arthur his walk anytime," O'Reilly said.

"Of course, the great lummox." Barry sipped. "And it's not just the things here to come back to that helped me decide," he said. "I've learned something about myself too. I love obstetrics, but I've discovered that I didn't like doing well-woman clinics. I know Pap smears are critical for the early detection of cancer of the cervix. I know they're important to the individual woman, but in the hospital they come in and out so fast their faces are a blur. They're barely people.

Simply a procedure to be performed as efficiently as possible, then move on to the next." He shrugged. "And much as I enjoy the difficult technical aspects of gynaecology, I like to get to know the customers and" — his grin was wry — "I also much prefer working with them when they're conscious." He looked up and smiled. "I think I'm a more natural G.P."

"That's honest of you," O'Reilly said. "And you're going to be a fine G.P. I've watched you grow. I've been at it for more than twenty years — in Dublin, and here before the war. I don't think you could ask for a better job." He glanced at his whiskey. "My glass seems to have a hole in the bottom. Top up?"

Barry shook his head. "No thanks. I'm having dinner with Sue in Holywood."

O'Reilly rose and poured for himself. "Nice girl, your Sue," he said, back turned to Barry. Was she part of his reason for coming back? O'Reilly would love to hear but would not ask Barry directly.

"Very," said Barry. "I never thought I'd say it, Fingal, but leaving was the best thing Patricia Spence could have done for me." Barry sat forward, glass held between both hands.

O'Reilly took his own seat. "Because?"

"Because I'd never have found Sue." There was a softness in Barry's voice. "I think, and let's keep it between you and me, Fingal —"

Father O'Reilly, confessor of this village and

553

townland, O'Reilly thought, and smiled. Here we go again.

"One day soon, next year when I can afford it, I'm going to ask her to become Mrs. Laverty." Barry blushed.

"Thundering Jasus, lad, that's marvellous." O'Reilly rose, grabbed Barry's glass. "Good for you. Good for you, and by God, if I'm willing to drink to Bertie Bishop, you and I sure as all bedamned are going to raise a glass to you and Sue. If you're as happy as Kitty and me, you can't ask for better."

"All right, Fingal," said Barry, laughing, . "But just a wee one."

Fingal rose and poured. "I think," he said, "Kitty and I have started an epidemic. Archie Auchinleck proposed to Kinky two weeks ago and she said yes. That's another change you didn't know about."

"Good Lord," said Barry. "That's absolutely wonderful. As our old friend Donal might say, 'More power to her wheel.' " He accepted his topped-up drink.

"It was the most touching thing, you know. She came to me to see if Kitty and I'd be able to manage if she moved out. Said if we couldn't she'd turn Archie down."

"Typical of the woman to put other people first," Barry said. "It's going to be a very different Number One without her." He frowned. "I'll certainly miss her cooking. It was one of the things I had in mind as worth returning for. The junior doctor's mess at the Waveney wasn't exactly Cordon Bleu."

"She'll still be cooking and working part time, Barry," O'Reilly said, "and I thought you might like to move into her quarters after she leaves. It would be more comfortable than your old attic bedroom."

"That would be great."

"I'm pleased you're coming back, Barry," O'Reilly said. "And don't worry about the details. I'll have my solicitor draw up a contract. At least it's not like in my younger days when a doctor often had to buy into a practice."

"A good thing too," Barry said. "I'm poor as a church mouse. I couldn't afford —"

Jenny stuck her head round the door. "Just popped in to say, cheerio, Fing— Oh, hello, Barry. How are you?" She grinned at him. "Still liking obstetrics?"

Barry looked at O'Reilly, clearly not wanting to be the one to break the news to Jenny.

"Jenny," O'Reilly said, "I think you've known all along this could happen. And your work here has been superb —"

Her smile fled. "I see." She swallowed.

"I'm sorry," O'Reilly said, feeling like a chaplain telling the condemned prisoner that the warden had rejected the plea for clemency, "but Barry does want to come back."

Jenny sucked in her cheeks, nodded. "Lucky you, Barry," and to O'Reilly's surprise she smiled again. "You know," she said, "I am disappointed. Very."

O'Reilly flinched.

"I did want the job a great deal, but no hard feelings. It was yours to come back to, Barry. Fingal, you made that very clear from the start. I shall miss the people here and the work very much, because I am breaking down the 'I don't want a lady doctor' opinions. And I'll miss you, Fingal O'Reilly, you old toasted marshmallow."

"Toasted what?"

"Crusty as bejasus on the outside, but —"

"Say no more," O'Reilly said. "You'll ruin my local reputation." And inside her words warmed him.

"You deserve the job, Barry," she said. "You've earned it."

"That's generous, Jenny," Barry said. "Thank you."

"You know, I was beginning to wonder if I should perhaps be looking for something in Belfast."

O'Reilly guessed why. Terry Baird was becoming an important part of Jenny Bradley's life. "If you like," he said, "I could have a word with a friend of mine, Doctor Jack Sinton."

"I know Doctor Sinton. On the Stranmillis Road, right?" she said. "I've done weekend locums for him. Keen wildfowler. Shoots on the Long Island on Strangford with his twin

556

brother Victor and two Bangor men, Jamsey Bowman and Jimmy Taylor. All of them doctors. The man loves his Mozart." Her smile widened. "He'd be a delightful senior to work with. I'd be really grateful — and I'll start looking for jobs myself too. There's a rumour that the Lord helps those who help themselves."

"Originally used as the moral in one of Aesop's fables, 'Hercules and the Waggoner,' " O'Reilly said.

"People often think it was Benjamin Franklin. But a chap called Algernon Sydney way back in Charles II's time wrote it down first," Barry said. "Poor chap was later executed for treason."

O'Reilly guffawed so loudly that Lady Macbeth leapt off Barry's lap. He looked from Barry to Jenny. A middle-aged G.P. could not have wished for two better young assistants. It was a shame to have to lose Jenny. He frowned. The practice couldn't support three full-time doctors, could it? He shook his head. For once, O'Reilly couldn't begin to see a way round a difficulty.

45
WIND OF CHANGE IS BLOWING

"Please do be careful with that chest of drawers. It's George III mahogany."

Fingal smiled at his mother's words and glanced across at Lars. The brothers were at Lansdowne Road to lend moral support during the move, and Lars would be taking Ma and Bridgit to Portaferry as soon as the removal men were finished loading the furniture. He shared a tiny smile with his brother and guessed they were thinking the same thing. Ma was particularly fond of that piece and, as always in major family matters, she was in charge and making sure everything was being done exactly, exactly, to her satisfaction.

"Don't you worry yer head, missus. Me and Lacky here's been shiftin' furniture since yer man Mister Chippendale, who likely designed dis t'ing, was learnin' to use a feckin' chisel. Ain't dat right, Lacky?" The speaker was a brawny man wearing moleskin trousers tied at the knee with leather thongs, a striped collarless shirt, and a leather waistcoat. Popeye the sailor, corncob pipe and all, was tattooed on the man's right forearm.

"True on you, Ignatius," Lacky said, mopping his bald head. Even in the late November drizzle, carrying the furniture down the long flight of stone front steps to the waiting removal vans would be sweaty work. "We'll treat it like one of our own chisslers, missus, and beggin' your pardon —" He knuckled his forehead then replaced his peakless, leather dustman's hat. "— the work'd go a lot easier if you and dese two gentlemen would give us a bit of peace to get on wit' it, like." They trundled a dolly bearing the carpet-swaddled piece along a hall now bare of furniture and paintings. The lighter paint beneath where the pictures had hung for years made Fingal think of a rare disease, vitiligo, where the skin lost its pigment in patches.

"Come along, boys. Upstairs is all done, and the dining room, study, kitchen, and servants' quarters. Movers can be clumsy, but I've made sure of everything I wanted to look after. They'll be clearing the lounge last. Let's go in there for a minute or two. It'll soon be time to leave."

Fingal, following Ma and his brother, glanced into a now-empty room, Father's study when he'd been well, his ground-floor bedroom in the days before his death. Fingal thought of times in there; of scoldings as a child, the rows about Fingal's refusal to read nuclear physics, the reconciliation when Father had accepted Fingal's choice to study medicine. He could picture Ma fighting back tears after Professor Connan O'Reilly had taken his last breath in July. Fingal swallowed, thinking how those memories had all been borne out of here along with the rolltop desk, the bookshelves, the library of books. He wondered what those who were left were meant to do with Father's diplomas? They were pieces of paper that had marked the successes of a young man's striving to achieve his goals and now were of no more value than the secondhand price of their frames.

He looked up the bare wooden staircase, its upper flight masked in shade. The house had been Fingal's home since his fourteenth year and by this evening all that had passed here would be starting to fade like the hues of a sunset on a cloudy night until only the shadows would remain. It must be hard for Ma.

Bridgit, already wearing her outdoors coat and a blue felt cloche hat, sat on a hard-backed chair in the lounge, thin-lipped, knees together, handbag firmly clasped in both hands on her lap. Fingal knew that her and Ma's suitcases were loaded into Lars's car. Cook had left on November first to work for the Carsons. Fingal stopped at Bridgit's chair and put a hand on her shoulder.

"It's very hard to leave this place, Master Fingal." Somehow the "Doctor" title had slipped. "I mind your mother and me nursing you when you had the measles. You were fourteen." She sniffed. "And you were forever skinning your knees on the gravel drive. Memories," she said, "a brave chunk of our lives."

"I know," he said, and squeezed, "but you'll enjoy Portaferry."

Ma went to her usual armchair and motioned for her sons to be seated. In here, as in the rest of the house, the pictures had all been crated yesterday. The landscape Ma had painted in Donegal near Ramelton was gone, the curtains taken from their rods. Outside the drizzle had turned to a steady rain that tapped insistently on the glass for admission, was refused and, sulking, ran down the panes.

"So," Ma said, glancing round, "it was a good old house, but it's looking sad now. I'll always remember it fondly. I wonder if it will remember us? I'm sure the nice couple who have bought it will take good care of it."

"And I know you and Bridgit will be comfortable where I've rented for you in Portaferry," Lars said.

"And you're sure you'll be all right on your own in Dublin, Fingal?" she said.

He shook his head and smiled. "Ma, I turned twenty-eight last month."

"I'm aware of that, dear, but there's not a mother who doesn't worry about her children and will always do so. I shall miss you, Fingal." The stoic look slipped for an instant and she turned her head to stare out at the rain.

"I'll miss you too, Ma."

"And you'll have that nice Miss O'Hallorhan to look after you. And Bob Beresford and Charlie too."

It was Fingal's turn to stare out the window, hoping his face didn't betray him. He'd decided there was no need to let Ma know about Kitty's imminent departure, about Charlie Greer's decision to specialize in Belfast, and other disruptions that might yet be on the horizon in Fingal's life. Some bridges crossed, some yet to come. He looked round the partially stripped room. Everything in flux. Everything changing. "When I have a free weekend I'll get the train to Belfast if Lars will collect me there."

"Of course I will, Finn," Lars said. "Just give me a call and I'll —"

" 'Scuse me, missus," Lacky said, "but me and Ignatius is ready to get goin' in here now and we'd like til get finished by teatime."

"Very well." Ma rose and removed a change purse from her handbag. "Here." She gave each man a half crown with an Irish harp on one side, a racehorse on the other. "I've already settled the account with your employer. This is to thank you both for all your hard work and for taking care of my things."

"T'ank you, missus," Lacky said, and grinned. His two top front teeth were missing. "T'anks very much. We'll sink a pint of plain til you tonight, your ladyship, won't we, Ignatius?"

Ignatius nodded. "Fair play. If you was a man I'd call you a right toff and a proper gent, lady."

Ma inclined her head. Fingal could see her trying not to smile at the backhanded compliment. "Come along, boys, Bridgit — and, dear, there's no need to cry." And Ma, shoulders back, head erect, strode from the room.

Fingal stood in the rain as Lars helped Bridgit into the backseat and Ma into the passenger's. Not once on the short walk to the car had she looked back. "You take care of yourself, Fingal," she said. She reached out through the open window and patted his hand. "And, oh dear, I had quite forgotten. I did speak to Mister Jackson last week."

Jackson? Fingal frowned and flinched as a trickle of rain found its way under his coat collar.

"I'm afraid he has no work at his factory in Chapelizod for your friend. I am sorry."

Work for John-Joe. Of course. Fingal had not only forgotten Mister Jackson, he'd not had much time to spare a thought for John-Joe Finnegan either. "Thank you for trying."

563

Lars started the engine.

"Safe trip. I'll be in touch." Fingal turned to go as Lars pulled into Lansdowne Road. The last Fingal saw of them was Ma staring fixedly ahead, but Bridgit was turned in her seat and was staring up at the big old house. Her face was crumpled and sad.

Fingal collected his bike and headed for his flat. Pity about John-Joe. Fingal was feeling guilty that he'd forgotten the man and then something niggled. The Carsons. They lived a short ride away and Robin Carson was a director of several companies. Why not give it a try for John-Joe? Fingal felt he owed the man one last effort. Mount Street Upper where the Carsons lived was on the other side of the Grand Canal. All he'd have to do was cross Mount Street Bridge.

Bridges. Huh. That's all Fingal seemed to have been dealing with for the last four weeks, since Halloween when Kitty had broken it off. She'd be leaving in two weeks for Tenerife, damn it, and he missed her sorely. That bridge was well and truly burned.

He stopped, one foot on the ground, and waited for the traffic to thin on Haddington Road. The next bridge to be anticipated was professional. Charlie'd not been upset when Phelim had announced on the Monday after Dermot's cure that either Charlie or Fingal would have to be let go.

Charlie'd simply said, "Then I'll be the one.

I've enjoyed my time here, but I'm going to see if there's a surgical trainee spot at the Royal Victoria Hospital in Belfast. I have a hankering to specialise in bones."

"Fair play to ye," Phelim said, "and I wish ye luck."

Fingal pedalled ahead. All very well for Charlie, but would Fingal have a place in the new year? It still was not clear.

The sound of his tyres on the road changed and Fingal glanced over to see rings of raindrops on the still waters of the Grand Canal. He wanted the job. Phelim hadn't said anything about the dispensary committee all month and Fingal had let the hare sit in the belief that no news was good news, but the uncertainty was unsettling. He hunched his shoulders and pedalled faster.

"Fingal, my friend, how are you?" Robin Carson rose with a smile from where he sat in an armchair in front of a black enamelled Coalbrooke Dale hob fireplace. Another man was sitting in a wingbacked chair with his back to Fingal. "She's visiting her mother in Roscommon, but Jane will be sorry to have missed you. There's no stopping her since she got over her surgery."

"Robin." Fingal shook the offered hand. "Sorry to pop in unannounced like this —"

"Always a pleasure. May I offer you something to drink?"

"Small Jameson, please."

Robin headed for a sideboard. "Make yourself at home. You know Doctor Davidson, of course."

"How are you, Doctor O'Reilly?" Doctor Andrew Davidson, who held a nearly empty cut-glass tumbler, smiled, but did not rise.

"Very well, thank you, sir." Fingal wondered what the senior obstetrician from the Rotunda Hospital was doing here. It was four months since Jane's operation and clearly she was still doing well. "Thank you, Robin." Fingal accepted his drink.

"Jane asked Andrew to see Milly, the cook's assistant. Some woman's difficulty, I believe," Robin said. He indicated a third regency-striped armchair. "Please. Have a seat."

Fingal did, grateful for the warmth of the fire after his ride through the rain. His trouser legs steamed. It was very decent of Robin to pay Milly's medical fees, and while Fingal would have liked to enquire how Cook was managing, he thought it polite to make conversation with his senior first. "If you don't mind me asking, and I don't think I'm being indiscreet, sir, how's your Prontosil study coming on?" and before Doctor Davidson could answer Fingal went on to explain to Robin, "The doctors at the Rotunda are testing a new medicine that might cure infection."

"That would be something," Robin said.

"It is, and there's no 'might' about it." The obstetrician's grin was huge. "We'll be publishing the study early next year, but we have confirmed the work of our English colleagues. It works."

I know, Fingal thought, and there's going to be a revolution worldwide when sulphanilamide becomes available. He'd be able to make a real difference in a small way here too — if he still had a job.

Doctor Davidson's smile faded. "I'd appreciate it, O'Reilly, and you, Robin, if you'd keep it to yourself until it's public knowledge. We don't want to be sensationalist about this."

Fingal's first thought was that perhaps he had been hasty asking the question, but he knew Robin would say nothing. His second thought was one of relief that apparently no one had mentioned his attempt to get some Prontosil from the postpartum ward last month. "I understand, sir," he said, and managed to keep his face straight, but inside he exulted. And he'd been right to tell Phelim that even if the stuff seemed to have worked for Dermot, it was too early to broadcast the news. "But it is amazing. Have you any idea when it might be available to G.P.s like me?"

"Probably very soon, because the active principle was synthesised in 1903. It was widely used in the dyeing industry, its patent has expired, so anyone can manufacture it."

"That's wonderful," Fingal said, forgetting for the moment what had brought him here.

"And you're still happy working with Phelim Corrigan?" Doctor Davidson asked. "I hear there are cutbacks in the dispensaries." He turned to Robin. "Even with the money coming in from the Irish Hospitals' Sweepstakes since 1930 there's still not enough to fund the system."

"Phelim has had to let Doctor Greer, my classmate, go. He's staying until he finds a job in Belfast," Fingal said. "But yes, I'm enjoying the work tremendously. I just hope there'll be no more cuts." He took a drink.

"Don't forget, young man, if you do ever have second thoughts, or find you are out of a job and fancy giving obstetrics and gynaecology a go, my offer stands. You'll remember I mentioned special moneys?"

"After Jane's surgery."

"Right. I can create a position any time I like from an endowment fund set up specifically to attract truly promising young people."

"Thank you, sir. I will remember that." And the mention of jobs jogged Fingal's memory. He turned to Robin. "I think, though, it's time we stopped talking about medicine —"

"Quite right, young man. Doctors can be frightful bores." Doctor Davidson rose.

Fingal stood.

"Milly will be fine if she takes the medicine, Robin, and keeps to her bed for a week. I'll

568

look in again in a day or so. My secretary will send my account." He finished his drink. "I'll be running along. And good luck in your work, O'Reilly."

"I'll see you out, Andrew." Robin Carson led the way to the door.

Fingal sat and stretched out his booted feet in front of the fire, took another drink, and smiled wryly at Doctor Davidson's "My secretary will send my account." Naturally it would be in multiples of guineas, that archaic coin worth one pound and one shilling — and one guinea was probably as much as a cooper made in a day. "Bloody miserable out there," Robin said, coming back rubbing his hands and blowing out his cheeks. He went to the sideboard and topped up his drink. "Another?"

Fingal shook his head.

"So, how's the rugby going? Any word?" Robin parked himself in his chair. "Cheers."

"Not yet, but I'm hoping," Fingal said. "Charlie's not heard either, so no letters will have gone out. He's bound to get a trial if not a place."

"I'm sure you will too."

"I hope so, but it's not why I called, Robin. I want to ask you for a favour, but of course I'll understand if you can't grant it."

"Fire away," Robin said. "If I can help, I will."

Fingal leant forward. "Last July a young

man was hit by a tram. Smashed his ankle. I gave him first aid. He's a cooper by trade and had secured a position with the Guinness Brewery. That fell through and —"

"And you'd like me to see if I can find him work?"

Fingal sat back. "Well, yes. How did you —"

Robin sighed. "If you knew how many requests I get, all us directors of companies get, you'd weep." He set his glass on a coffee table. "Contrary to popular opinion, not all the people who live in the Liberties, the Quays, the Northside are work-shy drunken bowsies. You'd be amazed how many men are wanting to work."

"John-Joe certainly is." He remembered the man's tears of frustration.

"Of the companies where I sit on the boards, most are in finance and insurance. They need clerks who at least have their School Leaving Certificate."

"My friend's a cooper."

"Not much call for coopers, but I have interests in three concerns where skilled tradesmen are needed."

"Do you think —"

Robin shook his head. "We've a policy so there's no favouritism. Each business has appointed a foreman in charge of hiring. Anyone like your friend can apply. If they seem suitable, names are put on a waiting list and jobs are offered to whoever is at the top of the list. It's a bit harsh, but it's fair. The best I can do is give you the names and addresses of the hiring foremen. I'm sorry. The lists are very long, but your friend could ask."

Fingal pursed his lips and inhaled. "I do understand," Fingal said, "and thank you, but I don't think I'll take the addresses. Poor old John-Joe needs something now, not a forlorn hope." He sipped his drink. He wanted to get back to his flat, but it would be impolite to leave now, seem as if he was going in a huff. "We'll say no more." He smiled. "Now, do you think King Edward will abdicate over this American Wallis Simpson woman?"

"I fear so. The Anglican Church won't accept marriage to a double divorcée. Mister Baldwin, the British PM, is opposed, so are the PMs of Canada, Australia, and South Africa —"

"DeValera has publicly announced his indifference."

Robin shrugged. "It's not much concern to the Irish Free State, even if we are technically still a dominon. I can't see that lasting much longer."

And so the conversation went until Fingal had finished his drink and made his excuses.

He cycled slowly back to his flat on Adelaide Road. At least the rain had stopped, and as he pedalled he thought of John-Joe and remembered the promise of the loan of five pounds for Christmas. That at least Fingal could do for the man who was possibly facing a life of unemployment. It was in marked contrast to Fingal's own case. If the money did run out and he had to leave Phelim, there was at least a safety net waiting at the Rotunda.

46
A CHANGE OF HEART

"You'll be glad to be home, Bertie," O'Reilly said from where he sat on a button-backed slipper chair beside the councillor's bed. A quick examination had reassured O'Reilly that Bertie Bishop's pulse was firm and regular, his blood pressure normal. The chintz curtains were closed, blocking the view of Belfast Lough. "I had a letter from Doctor Pantridge. I'll not beat about the bush. You're a very lucky man to be alive."

"I know." Bertie's voice was little above a whisper. He was propped up on pillows, their pink cases clashing with the maroon of his silk pyjamas.

"There, there, dear," Flo said, patting his hand from where she sat on a chair on the opposite side of the bed. The bedside table behind held a large bunch of grapes and a fleet of get-well-soon cards.

"And from now on you're going to have to do as you're bid," O'Reilly said. "Behave yourself and you'll be able to go back to work by February, but it's stay in bed for another week, then we'll start getting you up and about a bit more every day."

"Donal Donnelly's coming round this afternoon to move the telly in here, dear," Flo said. "You can watch your favourites, so you can."

"Thank you, Flo," Bertie said listlessly.

"Bertie loves *The Magic Roundabout,*" Flo said, "don't you, dear?"

Bertie grunted.

O'Reilly smiled. He had a soft spot himself for the stop-action characters, Dougal the dog; Dylan, a guitar-playing hare; Brian the snail; Ermintrude the cow; and Zebedee the jack-in-the-box. The programme was aired on BBC1 at 5:44 just before the six o'clock news. Like the *Winnie the Pooh* books, which were nominally for children, most adults found them and the *Roundabout* immensely appealing.

"Aye," Flo carried on, "and the *Flintstones* and *Thunderbirds* and *Noggin the Nog.* Pity they've stopped showing that one this year."

So Bertie had a penchant for children's programmes. Interesting. "It'll stop you getting bored, Bertie," O'Reilly said.

"Aye, mebbe, but who the hell's going to look after my business, that's what I want til know?"

O'Reilly coughed and ignored the temptation to say, "Your executor if you snuff it, you eejit," and instead remarked, "I've a suggestion. Last year, when you kindly repaired Sonny's roof, you made Donal the foreman. He did a good job."

Bertie frowned, then said, "Right enough, he's a good worker, so he is."

"Maybe make it a permanent position? Take some of the load off your shoulders?" said O'Reilly. Donal and Julie and the wee one would always be able to use a few bob more, and Bertie could afford it.

"Wellll . . ."

"I think thon's a great idea, dear. You need to be taking it easy," Flo said.

"That's true," added O'Reilly.

"I suppose."

"And a pay rise for Donal?" O'Reilly suggested, quite ready to back up his original suggestion by turning it into doctor's orders — for the sake of Bertie's health, of course.

"Pay rise? Do you want me til have a relapse, Doctor?" Bertie said, but O'Reilly could see a weak smile on the councillor's face. The man was starting to cave in. O'Reilly was delighted both for Donal and for Bertie, who must indeed start slowing down if his heart was going to recover. "Fair enough. I'll do it," Bertie said.

"Good man-ma-da."

"Thank you, dear," Flo said to Bertie, and smiled at O'Reilly.

"But will I be able to advise your man?"

Bertie said. "Donal knows the half of sweet bugger all about contracts and accounts, that end of the business."

"I think you might be pleasantly surprised by Donal's business acumen," said O'Reilly wryly. "And do you not have a solicitor and an accountant? And could they not advise Donal until you're better?" O'Reilly asked.

"More money," Bertie said, and rolled his eyes to the heavens.

"Bertie," O'Reilly said, "there are no pockets in a shroud. Do it."

"In soul, Doctor O'Reilly's right, Bertie," Flo said, and fluffed his pillow. "Them other nice doctors in the Royal had a wee word with me, you know. You're not til exert yourself, nor get your knickers in a twist about nothing, so you've not. And I've for til feed you right, and all."

"Not worry about nothing? Easier said nor done," Bertie said, "but I'll try, and I'll eat whatever you set before me, so I will." He turned hopeful eyes on his medical advisor. "Youse doctors is the great ones for prohibitions. 'No smoking.' Well, I've not had a cigar since I was took ill."

"Good for you," O'Reilly said. "It's not easy to give up tobacco. I know." And he did. Years ago his first wife, Deirdre, had asked him to quit his pipe. He'd tried and it had damned near killed him.

"Huh," Bertie said, "and no drinking." He

576

sighed. "I'm not a raging drouth, but I enjoy my jar." He sounded sad and O'Reilly could empathise.

"No reason why you shouldn't have a nightcap. I'd suggest a wee half of Jameson's. Less calories."

"I like my pint," Bertie sighed, and said, "but it'll be a week or six before you'll let me out of the house, won't it?"

"In the new year," O'Reilly said, and came close to offering to take Bertie for his first trip to the Duck, but doctor-patient relations only went so far.

"Fair enough." Bertie took a deep breath. "But I'd prefer Paddy's whiskey if that's all right?"

"A grand drop from County Cork," O'Reilly said. "You go right ahead. Do you know why it's called Paddy?"

Bishop shook his head.

"It was called Cork Distillery Company Old Irish Whiskey when it was founded in 1779, a mouthful you'll agree —"

"It's long enough to gag a maggot," Bertie said, "but if you put an air to it you could sing it," and smiled.

It was the first time in all the years O'Reilly had known the councillor that he'd heard the man try a little levity, and moments ago he'd agreed to part with money. Had Bertie suffered a sea change?

"So why is it called Paddy?" Flo said.

"The company had a salesman, Paddy Fla-
herty, who was so good at his job that in 1912
they changed the name in his honour."

"See what a learnèd man Doctor O'Reilly
is, Bertie?"

"Not really," O'Reilly said. "Kinky told me
about it. She's very proud about anything
from her home county."

"And Kinky and Archie's getting wed. Isn't
it sticking out a mile?" Flo said.

"I think so," O'Reilly said. "We're all very
happy for her." He rose. "Now I'd be happy
to chat about Kinky and Archie, but I've a
few more calls to make, so if you'll excuse
me I'll be —"

"Can you wait a wee minute, Doctor
O'Reilly," Bertie said. "I'd like til say something, so I would. I've had a whole month
with bugger all to do but think things over."

"Go right ahead." Fingal wondered what
was coming.

Bertie looked down. "It's like, uh, it's not
easy for me, but . . ."

"Come on, dear. You can do it," Flo said,
patting Bertie on the shoulder then turning
to O'Reilly and remarking, "Him and me's
talked this over, so we have, and I'm right
proud of my Bertie."

"Aye. Well. I hear my heart stopped." He
looked up at O'Reilly. "And you and Mrs.
O'Reilly give me the kiss of death."

O'Reilly struggled to keep his face straight.

That's what Ulster folks called mouth-to-mouth resuscitation.

"And then your Doctor Bradley knew to send for the firing squad."

"Flying squad, Bertie."

"Aye, that. And they told me in the hospital if it hadn't been for it —" He looked at Flo and a single tear dropped along his cheek. "The next time I see Doctor Bradley if she has a minute I'd like for to tell her, like . . ." He stared at the floor. "I'd like for to tell her I'm sorry."

"See, Bertie," Flo said, "that wasn't too hard, was it?"

He managed a weak smile and shook his head. "I'm going to get a wee thing for her, and —" Bertie heaved himself up on his pillow.

"Go on, dear," Flo said.

"She can be my doctor any time she likes, so she can."

"I'll tell her," O'Reilly said, wondering if perhaps Saul, who changed his name to Paul, might also have had a coronary on the road to Damascus. The medical event had certainly wrought as big a change on a certain misogynist named Bertie Bishop. "I think you'd be doing the right thing, Bertie, but we'll wait until you're up and about in the next week or two."

"Thank you, Doctor."

O'Reilly hesitated. Apart from the folks at

Number One, no one in the village and townland knew that Barry would be coming back and, damn it all, Jenny leaving in January. The word had to get out sometime. "You may not need to see her professionally, Bertie. Doctor Laverty'll be coming back and Doctor Bradley'll be moving on in January."

"Och, that's great about Doctor Laverty, he's a right good head," Flo said, "but there's a brave wheen of people who'll miss our wee lady doctor, so there is. Wait 'til I tell Cissie Sloan and Aggie Arbuthnot."

47

END IS BITTER AS WORMWOOD

"It's his finger, sir." A beshawled woman in a floor-length grey skirt stood in front of Fingal. She had one arm protectively around the shoulders of a boy of ten or eleven in a darned woollen pullover and patched short trousers. With her other hand she supported his right wrist.

As Fingal climbed down from the high stool and took a couple of paces across the surgery floor he noticed the boy's boots. They were laceless and the uppers of one had parted in front from the sole, letting his grubby toes peep out. Fingal squatted and looked the lad in the eye. "What's your name, son?"

The boy dashed the back of his left hand across his snot-stained upper lip, sniffed, and said, "Damien Pádraic Costello. From Dean Swift Square."

"And, Damien Pádraic, what happened to your finger?"

The boy sniffed again and buried his face in his mother's skirts.

Fingal looked up. "Mammy?"

She tossed her head, making her long auburn hair fly. "Dere was a wedding at Francis Street Chapel, Doctor. Nobody we knew, personal like. I hear they was from somewhere over at Meath Place, but sure the whole street always comes out to watch newlyweds leave the church. When the bride and groom come out after the service and Damien and his pals was going after the grushie, some feckin' bollix in hobnailed boots trod on his hand. You should have heard the gulders of him, poor wee lad."

Fingal frowned. "Grushie?"

"It's a custom here in the Liberties. When the happy couple comes out of the church, the groom has a brown paper bag and in it dere's copper coins, pennies and ha'pennies and farthin's, like. He chucks them into the street and all the gurriers yell, 'Grushie, grushie,' and scramble like buggery to grab as many coins as dey can."

"I see." Fingal had heard of the custom but not its name. "And Damien's hand got injured in the scrum?"

"Dat's right."

He transferred his attention to Damien. "I'll bet it's sore."

The boy turned his tearstained face to Fingal. "You'd win your feckin' bet, sir. It's t'umpin' like a drum."

"Can I see?"

Damien slowly extended his hand.

Fingal bent forward. He could see bruising and swelling between the second and third knuckles of the middle finger. It was probable that the bone between, the phalanx, was broken. The finger seemed to be twisted to one side. That might need to be straightened in an adult, but in a child of ten, healing would be rapid, complete, and without deformity as long as the finger was immobilised. "We can fix that for you, son, and it won't hurt."

"Promise?"

"Promise. Cross my heart." Fingal did.

"Dat's all right, den. Here."

Fingal, who never ceased to be humbled by the trust shown by his patients, rummaged in his jacket pocket and produced a bull's-eye. "Open big."

Damien did, and Fingal popped the hard sweetie in.

"Dere now, Damien, didn't I tell you Doctor Big Fellah always has sweeties for chisslers?"

The lad nodded his head.

Fingal smiled and stood. "I'm pretty sure the bone's bust, Mammy," he said, "but all I need to do is strap it to the index finger. It'll be mended in about three weeks."

"T'ank you, sir," she said.

It was the work of moments to use adhesive tape to strap the wounded digit to the one next to it. He'd learnt that trick back in July when Phelim had strapped two of Joe Mary Callaghan's fingers after a ruggy-up the night before. "There you are, Damien. Good as new." Fingal put a hand in his trouser pocket. "And this'll make up for the grushie you weren't able to get." He slipped a nickel Irish sixpence with its distinctive wolf hound into Damien's left hand.

"Jasus, Mammy. I'm feckin' rich," Damien said, his tears now fled. "T'anks very, very much, sir."

Fingal tousled the boy's untidy mop. "Don't spend it all in the one shop." He turned to the mother. "Bring him back in three weeks and I'll take the strapping off, and sooner if you're worried about him."

"I will, sir." She took Damien by the hand and followed Fingal to the door. "T'ank you, sir. T'ank you very much."

"Go on with you," said Fingal, ushering them out. "It's my job." And it was and he loved it. He crossed the hall. The waiting room was empty. His tummy rumbled. Lunchtime.

Today had started out well and was still shaping up to be a good one, despite the ache for Kitty, which was never far from the surface. The late November sun spilled in through the waiting room windows, making dust motes sparkle. He'd seen interesting cases this morning. His easy acceptance here in the Liberties as Doctor Big Fellah warmed him, and to crown matters he had in his inside jacket pocket a letter that had arrived at the flat first thing this morning. On its envelope it bore the crest of the Irish Rugby Football Union and inside was a letter inviting Fingal Flahertie O'Reilly to play for the probables, the players most likely to be capped for Ireland after the trial match at Lansdowne Road on Saturday, December 12, a little over two weeks away. Charlie had got one too. And there'd be no distractions like last year when he'd had to cry off from the trial. Fingal knew he'd play his heart out. He could almost savour his selection. They were going to Davy Byrnes tonight with Bob to celebrate.

He started for the stairs, but Phelim Corrigan hailed him. "Fingal, could ye spare me a minute?" He inclined his head to the surgery.

Fingal hadn't seen the senior man this morning. He'd been out making home visits. "Of course." Fingal went in and heard Phelim close the door behind him. "And before you say anything, Phelim, I've got it."

The little doctor's brow creased. "What've ye got? I'm in no mood for conundrums this morning." His voice was flat.

Fingal ploughed on. "I've got the letter from the IRFU. I've been selected for a trial. So has Charlie."

Phelim ran the flat of one hand across his

toupee and sighed. He held out his hand, which Fingal shook. Phelim didn't smile.

"Are you not pleased? I remember what you said to me in July. 'An Irish cap or bust, is that a promise?' I'm as close as I can be to getting that cap. I'm playing in the trial — for the probables."

"Jasus," said Phelim, and managed a smile, "if I was a dog with two tails I'd wag them both for ye. I am pleased and I wish ye well, but —"

"But? There's no but about it —"

"Wheest. Let me speak." Phelim took a deep breath. "I hate to do this to ye today when ye've nearly reached yer dream, but —" He reached into his pocket. "— I got a letter too." He looked Fingal straight in the eye. "I'll come to the point. There's been another budget cut." He offered Fingal the envelope.

Fingal shook his head, held up one hand as if to ward off evil, and said quietly, "You're letting me go." After five months of vacillating, doubts about his choice of career, encouragement from the success of the Prontosil, getting comfortable in his ready acceptance in the community, Fingal had thought himself perfectly happy to be a dispensary G.P. and was looking forward to a long career. Now? He shrugged. "I see," he said levelly.

"I'm truly sorry, Fingal."

"No need to apologise, Phelim. You gave

586

Charlie and me fair warning. He's been offered a trainee position in Belfast, by the way, but he says if there's the money for it he'll be happy to stay until after the rugby trials and on into January."

"I'm pleased to hear that. I'm glad he'll stay on."

"It's not your fault if there are more budget cuts."

"Damn British," Phelim said. "All their doing."

Fingal wondered if his colleague, who had never discussed politics except months ago when he had damned all political parties, was a Republican at heart. But if he was, what had that to do with the budget of the dispensary system? "I'm sorry? I don't understand."

"Two years ago the British government banned the sale of Irish Sweepstakes tickets in the United Kingdom. They didn't like all that sterling coming here to the Irish Free State. The money from the Sweeps is what keeps our hospitals and G.P.s going. There's a thriving black market for tickets in Britain now." He winked. "Ye'll never stop people indulging a vice if they want to. Look at Prohibition in the States. But even so, the amount of money coming in is down considerably. British contributions, which used to account for sixty percent of ticket sales, have fallen to forty percent. The organisers are putting a lot more effort into selling to Irish

587

expatriates in the United States, but it will take a while before we see any effects. Not enough money in the system for all the demands on it. I'm truly sorry. Ye have the makings of a fine G.P. I shall miss ye, boy."

"Thanks, Phelim." Inside Fingal was hurt, angry, but he understood there was no point making a fuss. "When do you want me to leave?"

"There's money left to keep you and Charlie on into the new year if you want to stay. But I'll understand if you find something sooner." He scratched his head. "Finding a dispensary job for ye won't be easy."

"I know." Fingal pursed his lips. "There's not a hell of a lot to keep me in Dublin now anyway. My mother's gone north, Charlie's getting a job there, one of my other close friends, Cromie, has been there since the summer." He swallowed. "And I've told you Kitty's going to Tenerife." Fingal bit his lower lip.

Phelim clapped him on the shoulder. "I'm truly sorry, lad. It doesn't seem that much is going your way . . . except the rugby."

Fingal looked Phelim Corrigan straight in the eye. "There's that . . . and Doctor Davidson."

"Davidson?"

"You remember I assisted him at Jane Carson's ovarian surgery? I saw him at the Carsons last week. I was hoping Robin Carson could help me find a tradesman's job for a friend of mine. That was a washout too, but Doctor Davidson said he'd have a job for me any time at the Rotunda." And Fingal remembered the day he'd first met Phelim Corrigan, the same day Ma had painted that stormy skyscape. His dying father had tried to persuade Fingal to specialise and his parting words that day reverberated in Fingal's mind. "Think about my opinion, after I'm gone." Perhaps Dad had been right after all.

"Ye take it, son," Phelim said. "Give yerself a year. Ye may find ye like the work even better than G.P."

"I might," Fingal said. "I might." But he doubted it.

"Is there a rush for ye to start?"

"I'll have to ask Doctor Davidson. I'll go and see him as soon as I can."

"Do that, but see if ye can get him to let ye stay here until the end of February."

"Why until then?"

"Because the first two rugby internationals will be played in that month, and by all that's holy I'll make damn sure you, and Charlie if he's still here, will be free of medical duties so ye can play."

"I'll be seeing him tonight for a jar. I'll tell him about all of this," Fingal said. There was a lump in his throat when he continued, "Thank you, Phelim. Thank you very —"

"Blether. Don't embarrass me, man. Think

of it as yer going-away present. I shall miss ye, Doctor Fingal Flahertie O'Reilly — the Big Fellah."

"And I'll miss you, Phelim, and Aungier Street, and the midwives, Jimmy Corcoran the apothecary, and the Liberties. I shall miss them all very much." And the truth of how much hit Fingal like a blow from a sledge-hammer. It was all he could do to hold back the tears.

48
AND WOMEN GUIDE THE PLOT

"We should be next," Brenda Eakin said, "but I think you'd better see Colin Brown first, sir."

O'Reilly eyed Brenda, wondered why she had said "we." The only other people in the waiting room were Julie and Donal Donnelly — who was carrying Margaret Victoria — Mairead Shanks, Mary Dunleavy, and Colin and Connie Brown. And it was obvious why Brenda had said Colin should go next. His face was sooty, his eyebrows gone, and his usual donkey fringe had been singed away. His left hand was wrapped in a towel. "Come on then," O'Reilly said, and turned to go. What the blue blazes had Colin been up to now?

O'Reilly sat in his swivel chair and adjusted his half-moon spectacles. Connie and Colin took the wooden seats, the ones with the front legs shortened. "So," O'Reilly said, "what happened this time?"

"You tell Doctor O'Reilly, Colin," Connie

said, making a tutting noise and shaking her head. "Sometimes, Doctor, I despair of the wee eejit, so I do."

Colin was nursing his left hand and occasionally wincing. "I've already said I'm sorry, Mammy, and I won't do it again. Not never. Honest to God."

Connie shook her head. "You're lucky you didn't do yourself serious hurt."

In her voice, O'Reilly heard a mother's concern wrestling with her anger.

"Go on please, Colin," O'Reilly said.

"I'd come home from school for my lunch and when I'd finished I went out for to try out my new cannon with Art O'Callaghan. Him and me went down to the dunes on our way back to school, so we did. Nobody knew we had it, like, and it's nice and private there."

"Your new . . . cannon?" O'Reilly could remember himself and Lars when not much older than Colin experimenting with sulphur, charcoal, and saltpetre to make gunpowder. What was it about explosions that fascinated little boys and, indeed, grown-up Irishmen? From 1956 until '62, the Irish Republican Army had waged the ineffective "Border Campaign," blowing up Northern Irish police barracks and customs posts. That nonsense was over now, thank goodness.

"It's not really a cannon like them ones on the walls in Londonderry, but the bang the thing makes is dead on, so it is, or was. It's busted now." Colin sighed. "Art's big brother showed us how to make it."

"Did he now? Go on."

"Do you know about carbide, sir?"

"I do. I used to have a bike with a carbide headlight." And that wasn't yesterday, O'Reilly thought, seeing himself pedalling at night through the Liberties. The image of blowing the flame out at Aungier Place after Kitty had told him she was going to Spain was still vivid.

Colin started to unwrap the towel. "You buy it in a metal cylinder so you empty it all out and put it in a jam jar for til keep it, like. You drill a wee hole in the cylinder's side just above its bottom, put a single lump of carbide back into the metal cylinder, pour in water —"

"That'll make a gas called acetylene," O'Reilly said. "Highly flammable."

"Aye, you can hear the fizzles and spits and bubbles of it. Then you push the lid of the tube in tight."

Good Lord. O'Reilly sat back in his chair. "You didn't — ?"

"We did." Colin grimaced. "And it worked dead wheeker the first time. If you hold a match over the wee hole you've drilled there's a bloody great 'boom,' and the lid gets blew out. Goes a brave way, so it does." He finished unwrapping his hand. O'Reilly could see a red burnt area on the back between the knuckles and wrist. Sometimes, because of nerve damage, the pain of a burn wasn't experienced immediately.

"The second time we tried it, I held the match. 'Boom' goes the cannon, even louder, but because the lid stayed in, the whole bloody lot exploded."

Which would account for Colin's appearance.

"Art took off like a liltie," Colin took a breath, "and I went home to my mammy because . . . well," he thrust the wounded hand under O'Reilly's nose, "I'd burnt my hand."

"You're lucky you didn't blind yourself, or blow your hand off," Connie said.

"Your mammy's right," O'Reilly said, hiding a smile as he remembered the ferocious telling-off he and Lars had been given by Ma when one of their infernal machines had blown a hole in a neighbour's hen-house, sending the terrified chickens running all over hell's high acre clucking and squawking, feathers flying. "Now, let's have a look at that hand."

O'Reilly peered at it and said, "Lucky for you it's a superficial burn. Only the skin's red and damaged, it's dry, and there are no blisters. It'll be easy enough to treat. You'll be better in a week."

"It's starting to sting like buggery," Colin said.

"Colin. Language."

"Sorry, Mammy."

"Come over to the sink, Colin." O'Reilly rose and pushed a small instrument trolley ahead of him, Colin and Connie following.

"Hold your hand up over the sink," O'Reilly said, and Colin did as he was asked. "This'll be cold but it won't hurt." He poured a 1 percent solution of Cetavlon over the burn.

Colin sucked in his breath. "That's freezing, so it is."

O'Reilly lifted a tube of penicillin ointment — he daily blessed the antibiotics — and gently smeared the white unguent over the burn. "Now for a dressing."

In a very short time the wound was dressed with Jelonet, a paraffin-impregnated gauze netting that wouldn't stick to the damaged area. Cotton wool on top of the Jelonet was held in place with a bandage.

"There," said O'Reilly, returning to his desk to write. "Now you look like a proper wounded soldier. Mammy, give him two kids' aspirins every six hours for the pain and bring him back in a couple of days and I'll change the dressing." He wagged an admonitory finger at Colin. "And you stay away from explosives. Do you hear me?"

Colin hung his head. "Yes, sir. Thank you, sir." Then he looked up and grinned. "But it did make a couple of wheeker 'booms.' "

"Here," said O'Reilly, handing a piece of paper to Connie. "It's a note for Miss Nolan."

"Cracker," Colin said, grinning more widely. "Am I getting time off from school? You said I'd not be better for a week."

"Certainly not," said O'Reilly. "The note's just to explain why you're late this afternoon."

"Bollix," said a disgruntled Colin.

"Here," said O'Reilly, giving the boy an enormous gobstopper. "That's for being brave." He rose. "Off you go so I can finish the surgery." And finally get a late lunch, he thought. As he strode for the door, he heard Connie say, "Say thank you to Doctor O'Reilly, Colin."

The boy's response was muffled by a mouthful of sweetie.

The mystery of why Brenda Eakin had said "we" was resolved as soon as O'Reilly went into the waiting room. "Who's next?"

All four women stood. Donal, still holding Tori, remained seated. "Is wee Colin all right?" Brenda said.

"He will be."

"That's grand. None of us is sick, sir —"

"And I just come for til keep Julie company and til show her my handiwork." Donal pointed to the roses. "I think they're dead on and the ladies like them too, isn't that right?"

There was a chorus of agreement and Mairead Shanks spoke up. "No harm til you,

596

sir, but the whole place is a lot easier on the eyes than the way it used to be."

"Thank you," O'Reilly said. "I'm sure Mrs. O'Reilly will be gratified by your vote of confidence. But if no one is sick, why —"

The women all turned to Brenda Eakin. "Doctor O'Reilly, us four wondered if we could have a wee word, like?"

"Of course." His gut growled. The sooner he'd heard what the women had to say, the sooner he could get to his lunch. "Now let's go along to the surgery." He led the way.

"I'm afraid I'm a bit short of seats, but if you'll have the swivel chair, Brenda, and Julie — how's Margaret Victoria coming on, by the way?"

"She's already standing if she can hold on to something, and she waves bye-bye."

He heard the pride in her voice and she was right to be so. Only a very few kiddies of seven months would have mastered those two skills. "Terrific," he said. "Now, if you and Mairead would take the other two chairs I'll nip through to the dining room and get one more."

Jenny was on her own at the table. Kitty was at work on this the first Wednesday in December. "Kinky's keeping your kedgeree warm," Jenny said.

"Just need a chair," he said, lifting one. "Won't be long." The spicy aroma wafting from Jenny's plate of half-eaten dinner made him salivate.

Back in the surgery he set down the dining room chair so that when Mary Dunleavy, the publican's daughter, had taken her place he'd be facing a semicircle of seated young women. "Now, what's all this about?"

Clearly Brenda was the spokeswoman. She wriggled in her chair, clasped one hand in the other, looked down at the carpet and finally back to O'Reilly.

"Go on, Brenda," Julie said. "We've come with you to give you a bit of moral support, you know."

Brenda took a deep breath and the words came out in a rush. "You told Flo Bishop that Doctor Laverty'll be coming back in the new year. She told Cissie Sloan and then Cissie told . . ."

O'Reilly was having a mental picture of the Biblical Genesis: "And Adam begat Seth. Seth begat Enos. Enos begat Kainân . . ." "And you four found out," he said, hoping to cut the litany short.

"That's right," Julie said, "and when I think what that nice young doctor has done for all of us in Ballybucklebo, we're powerful pleased to have him back in the village, so we are."

" 'At's right," said Mary, who was normally a reticent girl. "We think he belongs here."

"I'm pleased too, and you're right, Mary, he does," said O'Reilly, his mind more on Kinky's kedgeree and hoping that this welcoming delegation had come to the point.

"But," said Brenda, blowing out her breath against pursed lips, "and I know I'm as guilty as the rest, but we didn't like the notion of a lady doctor."

" 'At's right," Mary said, and the other two nodded in agreement. "Not at first."

O'Reilly thought he was beginning to understand.

"But some of us younger women," continued Brenda, "and cross my heart, no harm til you or Doctor Laverty, sir, there's women's things like them smear tests."

The Papanicolaou cervical smear for the early detection of cervical cancer had only recently been introduced to Northern Ireland.

"And," Julie joined in, "Flo said Doctor Bradley'll be leaving us soon."

"And she was quare nor smart about my endometriosis," Brenda said.

"And you ladies would like me to keep her on?" O'Reilly said, and it was no lie when he continued, "And so would I."

He saw all four women smile and Mary nudge Brenda and say, "See? I told you he's no oul' targe and he'd understand, didn't I."

He let the remark pass. "Trouble is," he said, "there's really not work for three doctors in this practice. I'd really love to keep her, but . . ."

A silence hung — and hung.

"I'll tell her what you said. Doctor Bradley will be flattered, I know."

"We thank you for that, don't we?" Brenda said. "And for your time, sir. We understand, but it's a pity. When it comes to doctoring, Doctor Bradley's dead on, so she is. There's a brave wheen of the younger lasses of the village and townland who'll be disappointed, so there is."

O'Reilly took no offence at the implication that he and Barry were now a disappointment. It wasn't really a popularity contest.

The other women murmured in assent and all four rose.

"We'll not hold you any longer, sir. It's your lunchtime," Julie said, "and I need to be getting back to Donal and Tori."

"It was good of you til see us, sir," said Mairead Shanks, the last to leave. "We'll all be very happy to see Doctor Laverty too." She closed the door.

O'Reilly fished out his pipe and lit up. That had been very gratifying and it bothered him to have to disappoint some of the women of the village, but a promise to Barry was a promise. Come on, man, he said to himself, the warm kedgeree nearly forgotten, think. There must be something you can do to keep Jenny, but what? He rose and went next door.

Jenny looked up from her empty plate. "Finished?"

He nodded and took his pipe out of his

mouth. "The last lot were four ladies who want you to stay. I'd like that myself." He took his usual place. "I am really sorry."

"Please, Fingal. Don't worry. I'm doing fine. Doctor Sinton has offered me a part-time job. I've told him I'd like to think about it because if you can manage without me this afternoon there's something else I'd like to pursue in Belfast."

"Away you go," said O'Reilly, "and good luck with it, whatever it is."

"Thanks." She rose just as Kinky appeared.

"There you are, Doctor dear," she said, setting a steaming plate in front of him. "Eat up however little much is in it."

49
. . . A Broken Thing Mend

"Another pint, Fingal?" Diarmud called over the long bar to where Fingal, Charlie, and Bob Beresford sat at one of the tables in Davy Byrnes. The place was half empty. Subdued voices rose and fell.

"Two, and Bob?"

Bob nodded.

"A small Jameson, and, Diarmud?"

Diarmud, who was drawing a pint from the high barrel, said, "W'at?"

"Will you have one yourself?"

"Is the Pope feckin' cat'lic? I'll put one in the stable for after nine turty, t'anks, Fingal." Nine thirty was closing time and he'd not pour his drink until then.

"So I'll have the pleasure of the company of the pair of you in Dublin until the end of February?" Bob lit a Gold Flake. "Doesn't seem like five months since we were in here, just out of medical school, all dewey-eyed about our futures. Hardly discussed anything else that night. Lot's happened since then."

"You can say that again," Charlie said.

"Doesn't seem like five months since we —" Bob began solemnly.

"Stop it, Bob." Fingal chuckled. "And you are right. It doesn't."

"Funny how it's turned out," Charlie said. "When I start more training I'll be working in the same hospital as Cromie." He took a pull on his pint. "I saw him when I was up north applying for the position. He's being taught by a Mister Calvert. Seems to be very happy."

"Absent friends," Bob said, and sipped his Jameson.

Fingal and Charlie drank.

Over at the bar, a man in a bespoke overcoat and a bowler hat said in a hectoring voice, "I'll have another claret, my good man, and get a move on. I haven't got all feckin' night."

Fingal and his friends looked over to see how Diarmud would reply. He had his back to the customer and the look of a man who has found something unpleasant on the sole of his shoe. He winked at Fingal, who had expected Diarmud, no respecter of self-appointed superior persons, to use a simple Dublin dismissive like "gerruptheyard — sir," a politer version of "feck off." Instead Fingal lip-read the barman's, "Bite the back of me bollix, you miserable gobshite," before he turned and said, all sweetness, "Certainly, sir."

It was a moment or two before the three stopped laughing and Charlie said, "Getting back to job prospects, after I leave here in March I'll be doing a locum for a G.P. in Bangor up north until August, that's the start of the hospital junior doctor hiring year in Belfast, then I'm to work at the Royal Victoria under Mister Samuel Irwin. I think it helped in my interview that I'm a rugby player. He's been capped nine times for Ireland and was president of the IRFU for '35 to '36."

"And you two'll find out about your sporting future soon, won't you?" Bob said, blowing a smoke ring.

"Trial's next Saturday," Fingal said, "and it's important, but so are our medical futures. You seem to be all set, Bob."

"I think so. The people at the Rotunda told Professor Bigger about Prontosil working for puerperal sepsis. So now we're pretty sure that drugs can kill bacteria. And it seems that not only aniline dyes can affect germs." Bob leaned forward in his chair. "Did you know healers have been treating infected wounds effectively with blue-mouldy bread in Europe since the Middle Ages?"

Fingal shook his head.

"Mouldy bread?" Charlie let out a bark of laughter. "Away and feel your head, Bob."

"Don't laugh. In 1871, Joseph Lister tried an extract from a fungus called *Penicillium* as part of his regime for aseptic surgery. It was too weak, but then in 1928 Alexander Fleming showed that *Penicillium rubens* could kill bacteria in the lab. Damn frustrating because it doesn't work in people. Although one of Fleming's students, a Doctor Paine from Sheffield, actually cured a few eye infections with it in 1930. My boss now has me looking at the effects in the lab of a whole bloody host of different moulds on bugs. So far no luck, but you never know." He grinned. "It's fun finding out new things, and I love working in the library stacks looking at old documents." He looked down. "Sometimes I think I'd have been happy as a historian, but Auntie's legacy . . ."

Fingal was well aware that Bob had originally studied medicine only because of an aunt's bequest that specified his course of study.

"And even so, and saving your presence, Fingal, my work beats toiling with the great unwashed. And who knows, perhaps all of this research will lead to something really useful one day."

Fingal chuckled and took the last swallow from his glass. "I for one like working with the great unwashed," he said, "but it doesn't look like I'll be doing it much longer. I've to move on, and through no choice of my own."

"I know, and I'm sorry about that," Bob said.

"Gentlemen, your gargle." Diarmud set the glasses on the table and accepted payment from Fingal. "T'anks. And pay no attention to 'Rags' Rafferty." He nodded toward the demanding customer. "He's a bookie from Blackrock in for a jar and he's still pissed off because I took him for fifteen quid on a daily double last summer. Youse were in here dat day. Youse all rubbed my rabbit's foot."

"I do remember," Fingal said.

"Anyroad, Rags likes to t'ink he's Lord Muck from Clabber Hill, but I pay no attention to the gurrier." Diarmud took Fingal's coins and left.

"Jasus," said Charlie, looking round, "Diarmud's true value for money. I'll miss him and Davy Byrnes." He took a swallow. "Still, we have until the end of February and you'll be staying on in Dublin, won't you, Fingal?"

"I expect so. Doctor Davidson's a man of his word. I'll just need to sort out the details with him." Fingal puffed on his pipe. "I'll probably enjoy obstetrics," he said. "I mean, bringing new babbies into the world. How can you argue with that? But," he sighed, "I've had a great time as a G.P."

Bob stubbed out his cigarette. "What'll you do once Charlie moves north? Keep on the flat on Adelaide Street?"

"I hadn't thought much about it."

"If you want to save a few bob, you could always let it go. Move in with me," Bob said.

"Couple of bachelors together."

"I should have thought you enjoyed having the place to yourself," Fingal said, eyeing his friend. Bob had been without a girlfriend since the glamorous Bette Swanson had moved on.

"I'm still licking my wounds from Bette's departure. You know she left me for some entrepreneurial type with pots of money. I suppose a lowly medical researcher isn't up to dear old Bette's standards. She was fun, though." For a moment Bob sounded wistful, but brightened and then said, "Truly, Fingal, I would enjoy your company."

"Thanks, Bob. I'll let you know once I'm certain I've got the Rotunda job."

"Can one of youse doctors come quick?" Diarmud had returned. His voice was urgent. "A wee mott's gone arse over teakettle on the cobbles outside and hurt herself."

Fingal set his pipe down. "I'll see to it," he said. "Probably only bruised feelings, but just in case it's not —"

"I'm right behind you, Fingal. No point you coming, Bob. You're hopeless with patients."

"Hey, steady on," Bob said, and laughed. "All right, go off and play the white knights."

Outside, a small crowd had gathered. Fingal simply said, "Coming through," then knelt. "Hello," he said, and raising his voice, "I'm a doctor." Those closest to the victim

607

drew back. She was a petite blonde with the most piercing blue eyes. Her oval face was pale and she was biting her lower lip. Surrounded by a half-dozen scattered books, she sat on the kerb with her feet in the gutter. She was nursing her right wrist with her left hand. Her arm was bent at the elbow, the palm of her hand facing her chest. "What happened?" he asked.

She looked up at him and spoke through clenched teeth. "I was in a hurry, trying to get from Trinity to the flower seller on the corner of Saint Stephen's Green before she packed up."

He squatted beside her. No hint of a Liberties accent. Probably comes from a good family and, judging from the books, she's an undergraduate.

"I feel like such a fool. I tripped over a cobblestone, put out my right hand to save myself . . ." She grimaced and cradled her hurt. "Oooh, that's sore. I heard a snap and there was a horrid pain. When I sat up, my wrist looked stupid." She ground her teeth again. "I think I've broken it."

It was the classic history of how a Colles fracture of the wrist was caused, often in older women. He hadn't been out of medical school for so long that he also didn't remember that the fracture was named for a Regius Professor of Surgery here at Trinity in the nineteenth century. "Sounds like it," Fingal said, "Miss . . . ?"

"Elaine Butler," she said.

"Doctor Fingal O'Reilly." He gently laid his fingers on her left wrist. Her skin was chilled and her pulse was rapid, but he didn't bother counting exactly how fast. She clearly was not in shock.

"Anything I can do?" Charlie asked.

Fingal looked up. "I'm pretty sure she's got a Colles. Nip in and see what Diarmud has that we could use to splint it and bring a couple of tea towels for bandages."

"Right." Charlie left.

"That was Doctor Greer," Fingal said. "I'll not disturb your arm now, Miss Butler. I'll get a good look at it when we put a splint on, but my guess is that you'll have to go to hospital, have a short anaesthetic, and have it set properly and put in a plaster cast."

She frowned. "So why splint it now?"

He shrugged. "The ends of broken bones rubbing together can be pretty damn sore, Miss Butler. The splint will immobilise it so we can get you to hospital more comfortably."

"I see. Thank you, and please call me Elaine."

"Right."

Charlie reappeared and handed Fingal two pieces of wood that looked like slats from the back of a chair, and three tea towels. "Here you are, Fingal."

Fingal accepted them and said, "Charlie, this is Miss Butler. Now, give me a hand with the splint." He looked into those blue eyes. "I'm sorry, this will hurt for a moment, but we'll be as quick as we can."

"Please go ahead."

Charlie needed no instructing. He held his hands so that one was under her right hand, the other supporting the forearm. When Elaine took her left hand away, the fork-shaped deformity of the injured wrist typical of the Colles fracture was immediately apparent. Fingal took no pleasure from the rightness of his diagnosis as he put one slat along the forearm's front, with the end of the wood level with the outstretched fingertips. The second slat went on the back of the forearm and in moments they were bandaged in place with two tea towels held in place by strips torn from the third. "Done," Fingal said. As he had worked, he had hardened his heart to her subdued whimpering. He'd been impressed. Many grown men roared and howled when a Colles fracture was being splinted.

"Thank . . ." she took a deep breath, "you very much, Doctors." Although sweat beaded her forehead, she said, "That's more comfortable already."

"Now," said Fingal, "Charlie, why don't you nip back in, send for the ambulance, and ask Diarmud for another tea towel to use for a sling."

"Just a minute," a familiar voice said.

Fingal looked up to see Bob Beresford standing beside them, Elaine Butler's books under one arm, his Trinity tie held in an outstretched hand to Fingal. "Use this for a sling and I'll be happy to run Elaine to Sir Patrick Dun's."

"Hello, Bob," Elaine said, and managed a tiny smile.

So, these two knew each other already. He used Bob's tie by knotting the ends around her neck to form a loop that supported the splinted forearm.

"Small world," Bob said. "The last time I saw you, you were only fourteen at your big brother's twenty-first birthday."

"I've grown up," she said. "I'm in my second year of a BA."

"You certainly have," Bob said. "And a student too. So you tripped on one of Duke Street's cobbles, did you? You always were better on a horse than you were on the ground."

"Bob." She grimaced, shook her head, but managed a smile. "I swear to goodness you haven't changed a bit since you used to help me up onto my pony."

"I hope not changing's a good thing," Bob said, running an appraising eye over the young woman.

And why not, thought Fingal. They already knew each other and it wasn't as if Bob was directly involved in her care. There was no doctor/ patient bond and if Bob was taking a fancy to young Elaine more power to his wheel. He'd always had an eye for the ladies.

"The car's on Grafton Street," Bob said. "Here, let me help you up."

The girl got to her feet and then sagged against Bob. "Gosh, my knees feel like jelly."

Bob handed the books to Charlie, bent, and gently scooped Elaine up, avoiding contact with her arm. "Bring the books, Charlie. I'll carry you, Elaine. You don't look like you're in shock, but adrenaline leaving your system can do strange things."

"Don't tell me you're a doctor too?"

"'Tis strange but true. Come along, Doctor Greer. Carry Miss Butler's books, will you?"

"Thank you so much, Doctors," she said, and allowed her head to rest on Bob's chest.

"Good luck," Fingal said as he watched the little party move away, and wondered if he had just witnessed a simple Colles fracture or the rejuvenation of Robert Saint John Beresford's love life. On that front, there'd be no such luck for Fingal. He shrugged and went back into the pub to find Diarmud taking away his and Charlie's pints and replacing them with new ones.

"The last ones had gone as flat as feckin' flounder fishes," Diarmud said. "Fresh ones on us, and t'anks, Fingal."

"You're welcome. But I'm afraid you've lost your tea towels, Diarmud. I'd to send the young lady to hospital."

Diarmud laughed. "Sure hasn't Byrnes got more tea towels than there's grains of shingle on the beach at Dingle? Nobody's goin' to miss the feckin' t'ings." He headed back to the bar.

Charlie appeared. "We put her in the back of the motorcar and Bob's gone off. Those two have known each other since Elaine Butler was in pinafores."

"I suspect Bob has made a new conquest," Fingal said. He nodded at the table. "Diarmud's poured us fresh pints."

"Thank you, Diarmud," Charlie called, then sat and took a pull on his. "Mother's milk." He wiped the foam from his upper lip. "Funny," he said, "minutes ago Bob was reminiscing about us being in here pondering our futures. Wonder where we'll all be this time next year? I've a suggestion to make about that."

"Go on." He picked up and relit his discarded pipe.

"I don't want to lose touch with my friends once I go to Belfast. I know we'll *say* we'll get together, but life gets busy. We'll both be in new jobs, Bob may have a new girl in his life, Cromie's turning into a bookworm because he's finding the surgery fascinating.

It'll be the first Friday in December at the end of this week. Why don't the four of us, you and Bob, me and Cromie, the old four musketeers from Trinity days, solemnly agree to convene here in Davy Byrnes on the first Friday of December every year, catch up, renew our old friendship, find out how everybody's doing?"

Fingal thought for a moment and the more he thought, the more he liked the idea. "Begod, Charlie, you've said a mouthful. It's a brilliant idea."

"In that case," said Charlie, "let's drink to it, and," he raised his voice, "when these are finished, Diarmud, we'll have the same again."

50
WORDS ARE ALSO ACTIONS

"It was a brilliant idea, Fingal, to have the Culloden Hotel cater and provide the glassware and china," Kitty said, loading a tray with plates of canapés warm from the oven. On this occasion the with-drinks nibbles had not been prepared by the redoubtable Mrs. Maureen "Kinky" Kincaid, who, after a strong but futile protest, was very definitely off duty tonight.

"Most of the invitees have arrived and are upstairs in the lounge," Fingal said, helping himself to a cocktail sausage from a plate waiting its turn to be put on the tray. It was Kinky and Archie's night, their promised engagement party on Saturday, December the fourth. "I think we managed to invite everyone who should be here. And Kinky's family was wise to decide not to come up from County Cork. There was a whiff of snow in the village this afternoon and the roads could very well be treacherous."

"They'll come up for the wedding in April,"

Kitty said.

"Tonight is Kinky and Archie's night. Now, I think we're still waiting for Flo and," he sighed, "Bertie Bishop." The front doorbell rang.

"I'll go," Fingal said, putting the tray on the shelf — and snaffling another sausage.

He let Helen Hewitt in. "Sorry I'm late," she said. "The trains were running slow. There's a lot more snow up by Sydenham."

"Glad you could come," O'Reilly said. "How are you getting on at Queen's?"

"Och, it's great, sir. And thanks again for fixing me up with a job next summer."

"All Kitty's doing. How are the exams going?"

"Remember back in October when I told you about the boys making the row in Doctor Emaleaus's lecture about static electricity and Van der Graaf?"

O'Reilly chuckled. "I do." He hung her duffle on the coatstand.

"And you told me to study it in case Doctor Emaleaus took a bit of revenge for not letting him finish that lecture. Guess what question was on the physics paper?" Her grin was wicked. "Your man Van der Graaf's generator. I've passed physics and botany. Only chemistry and zoölogy to do next June and then after my summer job I'll be in second year and only have five more years to go. It's wonderful." She sighed with every indication of bliss at the prospect. For a moment, O'Reilly envied the energy of the young. For him, the prospect sounded daunting.

"I'm delighted," O'Reilly said. "Now trot on up and have fun. I've some Babycham in an ice bucket for you."

"Just the jibby-job," she said.

As Helen climbed the stairs, Fingal went back to the kitchen. "Helen Hewitt," he said picking up the loaded tray. "Back in a jiffy."

He delivered the canapés but was interrupted on his way back to the kitchen by Jenny letting herself in.

"Jenny."

"Just made it, Fingal," she said. "It was snowing to beat Bannagher at the Holywood Arches. I'll be surprised if Terry gets here."

"But you did," O'Reilly said. "How was the patient?" Jenny had agreed to call on her way home with Hall Campbell, the fisherman whose patent ductus arteriosus had been successfully closed surgically and who had been discharged yesterday.

"Still a bit sore, but he's doing fine." She looked O'Reilly in the eye. "And that job in Belfast I've been investigating? Very interesting. When you get a moment, Fingal, can we have a word?"

He grimaced. "It's Kinky's party. Tomorrow?"

She looked crestfallen.

617

"Okay. Hang on. I'll take the tray in to Kitty and be right back. Why don't you go into the dining room."

In the kitchen, he found Kitty pulling a tray of vol-au-vents and stuffed mushroom caps out of the oven. "Jenny needs to talk to me for a minute. Can you cope?"

"Course. I'm hardly being Julia Child here. The Culloden's done everything beautifully. Take your time."

"Thanks, love."

Jenny was staring out the window as snow-flakes drifted lazily in the twilight. He went in and didn't bother to close the door. "So," he said, "what have you to tell me?"

"I've had two meetings with Doctor Graham Harley, the gynaecologist. The second one was this afternoon." She was wringing her fingers so forcibly they were blanching.

"And?"

"I'll give you some background. A Canadian doctor, David Boyes, introduced a province-wide cervical cancer screening in British Columbia starting in 1960. He's been getting Papanicolaou cervical smears taken from every eligible woman, having the slides read, and then following up if necessary. It's working. Cervical cancer rates are falling there. Doctor Harley knows Doctor Boyes and wants to start a similar screening programme in Ulster — in Belfast and Northern County Down — but aiming to cover the whole province eventually."

"Anything that stops women getting cervical cancer would be a blessing. It's a horrid disease," O'Reilly said.

"Graham's got a budget from the Cancer Authority and the Northern Ireland Hospitals Authority to train doctors and pay their wages once they're trained and working."

"Sounds wonderful," O'Reilly said.

"He'll start me in January, train me for four months, and his idea is that I and people like me can run well-woman clinics, do Pap tests, give contraceptive advice, baby immunisations."

"Innovative," O'Reilly said.

"Isn't it just? The thought of doing something that prevents disease rather than treating it."

The same pleasure and excitement that he had heard in Helen's voice was in Jenny's. "And I imagine it would be part-time work," he said, "that might suit a married woman?"

She smiled and looked down. "Yes, that's what I thought too, although Terry hasn't said anything yet. Anyway, Doctor Sinton has known about this so he'll not be upset when I turn his offer down."

"I'm glad for you, Jenny," O'Reilly said. "If it's what you want, I hope it all goes wonderfully. I shall miss you."

"But don't you see —"

The doorbell rang.

"Hang on," he said. "I'll answer it."

It took some moments to let Bertie and Flo Bishop in and hang up their coats, hats, and scarves.

"Bloody brass monkey weather out there, so it is," Bertie said, blowing on his hands.

"It's nice and cosy up in the lounge," Fingal said.

Bertie and Flo began to head for the stairs, but Bertie must have seen Jenny in the dining room. "Run you away on, Flo," he said. "If it's all right with you, Doctor O'Reilly, I'd like a wee word with Doctor Bradley. I've not had a chance since you come til see me a couple of weeks back."

"In private?"

"No. I'd like for you til be there so you can see I'm a man of my word, so you can."

O'Reilly was pretty sure he knew what was coming. "Go right on in." He followed Bertie into the dining room, but then stood back and listened.

"Doctor Bradley," Bertie said. "I'd like very much for til say something til you."

"Good evening, councillor," Jenny said. "Please go right ahead."

Bertie shifted from foot to foot, looked down, looked up, inhaled, and said in a rush, "Them nice doctors in the Royal says you saved my life, so you did."

"Not me," she said. "Doctor and Mrs. O'Reilly kept you alive until the flying squad arrived. Doctor Geddes saved your life with his defibrillator."

Modest, O'Reilly thought. Good for you, Jenny.

"Aye," said Bertie. "Aye. That may be so." He narrowed his eyes and continued in a serious voice, "But who knew til send for that there firing squad? You tell me that now, young lady. You just tell me."

O'Reilly shook his head. Leopards and spots. Even when it was meant to be an apology Bertie had to score points.

"If you won't," said Bertie, "I'll tell you, Doctor." He nodded to himself. "If it wasn't for you I'd be six feet under and Flo a widow woman." He pursed his lips and his voice trembled and cracked. "I owe you my life, so I do. I can never thank you enough — and I'll never say nothing bad about lady doctors again, so I won't. Not never. I'm dead sorry that I did, so I am and —" He inhaled.

O'Reilly could see the effort it was costing the man.

"I apologise, completely and teetotally, so there." He took another deep breath.

"That is generous of you, Mister Bishop," Jenny said, "very generous, and I accept your apology." She smiled. "Teetotally too."

"Thank you very much," Bertie said, "and —" He fished in the pocket of his jacket and produced a small parcel. "Here. It's just a wee thank-you, so it is."

O'Reilly remembered Bertie saying he'd have something for Jenny. "I'm proud of you, Bertie," O'Reilly said, and clapped him on the shoulder.

"Aye. Well. Doctor Bradley, are you not going to open it? Flo helped me pick it out at Sharman D. Neill's."

The same high-class Belfast jewellers where O'Reilly had bought Kitty's engagement ring.

"Of course," she said, and began carefully to unwrap the packet. She pulled back. "It's beautiful," she said, showing O'Reilly an exquisitely crafted brooch of shining green and black Connemara marble set in silver with matching pendant and earrings. "Thank you, Mister Bishop. Thank you very much, for your apology and your gift. I'll think of you every time I wear them."

"And good health to do so wherever you are, Doctor," Bertie said. "Doctor O'Reilly says you'll be leaving us soon. I'll be sorry til see you go."

"I'm not so sure about going —"

"Fingal," Kitty said from where she stood in the doorway, "I'm sorry to interrupt. Hello, Jenny, and councillor, but I do need some help now getting those last trays upstairs. And we are neglecting our other guests."

"Coming," O'Reilly said. "You help the councillor upstairs, please, Jenny, and Kitty and I'll be along in a minute." And what the hell did Jenny's "I'm not so sure about go-ing" mean? Couldn't be. There wasn't room for three doctors. Anyway, the answer was going to have to wait. Time to join the ta-ta-ta-ra, and as he climbed the stairs he mar-velled. In all his years in practice, Fingal O'Reilly had never seen a man as utterly transformed as Bertie Bishop. But how long would this turn for the better last?

51
THERE'S A GOOD TIME COMING

"Still at the tugging, Lorcan?" Fingal asked as his bicycle drew level with his old patient and his cart as he trudged along Golden Lane. This was the street where Jam Jars Keegan and Joe Mary Callaghan had injured each other in a ruggy-up the day Phelim hired Fingal and Charlie.

"Oh, aye," said Lorcan, the words coming out with a puff. He looked over to Fingal. "It's you, Doctor Big Fellah. I heard you was leavin' us soon. I'm sorry to see you go." Fingal looked along this well-known lane and thought of all the other familiar streets and alleys where he usually ran into folks he knew. News travelled fast in the Liberties. He slowed his pedalling.

"Thanks, Lorcan. I've not seen you for a brave while, not since —" Not since the night he and Kitty had walked along High Street after seeing *Modern Times.* The night she had started talking seriously about Spain.

"I remember. You was wit' a wee mot, a

nurse. Pretty t'ing." Lorcan regarded Fingal. "Is dat why you're leaving us then. Goin' off to get married and move to a new part of town. Where the toffs live, like?"

"No, Lorcan, no. Nurse O'Hallorhan has moved to Tenerife — to Spain — to look after children orphaned in the Spanish Civil War."

"Has she now?" Lorcan stopped to pull off his duncher and wipe a hand over his brow. "Well, that's a t'ing, isn't it? Fancy her up and doin' a feckin' thing like dat. Women." He spat. "Dey're about as predictable as the Irish summer." Lorcan chuckled. The thought seemed to give him energy and he picked up the cart, this time quickening his pace along the cobbles, with Fingal falling in beside him. Perhaps Lorcan was right and Kitty's decision was just the unpredictable actions of the female of the species. But more likely it was Kitty who was right, and he had been too scared to make things more serious between them. But her ship had left for Tenerife and it was long past the time to change anything now. "How's the back?" he asked.

The cartload of scrap metal clattered and jangled as the wheels jounced over a pothole.

"The back? Grand altogether. I've not needed more of the liniment or ground-up pills you give me mont's ago. Dey worked a treat."

Or time passed and the backache got better

625

by itself, Fingal thought. Still, it was good for Lorcan.

"And dat's a feckin' good t'ing. I've a regular job wit' Harry Sive —"

"Who has a shop on Meath Street?"

"The very fellah. He came over from Rooshia after they had dat dere Bollixshevik Revolution, you know, and he opened his shop when he was only sixteen. He's a feckin' good skin. Dis is one of his forty-six carts and he doesn't charge us to use dem."

Fingal saw that Lorcan's old plank-sided cart had been replaced with one made of wickerwork. WASTE SALVAGE and the letter S, for Sive, were painted on the side.

"It's a feckin' sight lighter to pull. Harry doesn't pay wages, but by Jasus he gives a fair price for the stuff we bring in, and he'll see you right wit' a few bob if you've not been able to collect much from the toffs."

"Where were you today?" Fingal knew that Sive's tuggers scrounged used materials from the better-off districts of Dublin.

"I was doin' Rathgar."

"That's a fair stretch." It was two and a half miles from there to Meath Street.

Lorcan shrugged. "Sure I'm fit for it."

"And I'm glad to hear it." Fingal started to speed up. "It's been good to see you, Lorcan. I'm delighted you're feeling better. You take care."

"Fair play to you, Big Fellah. And good luck

to you wherever you're goin' next." Lorcan waved as Fingal cycled away.

He rode along narrow streets lined with many-storied terraces of decaying Georgian houses. Alleys and lanes teemed with skinny, ragged, underfed children; more tuggers; street balladeers; cyclists; men smoking on street corners. When Phelim had told Fingal last week that he would have to let him go, he'd resolved to pop in to see John-Joe when he was in the neighbourhood and lend him the promised five pounds so he could buy his family some treats for Christmas. Fingal wished he could have some job prospects to offer as well. With only three weeks until the twenty-fifth, that would have been a real Christmas present.

A barrel organ player cranked his odd instrument that was known locally as a hurdy-gurdy. Its notes had to compete with the yells of children, the rumble of cartwheels on cobbles, the clop of horseshoes, the tinkling of bicycle bells. Several times Fingal was greeted, "How are you, Big Fellah," and waved his reply. Overhead washing hung to dry. A cat ran by, carrying a dead rat almost as big as the tabby. Fingal's nose was filled with the odours of the Liberties — dirt, offal from the butchers' slaughterhouses, the Liffey — he was inured to them now. And most prominent of all, borne on a westerly breeze, came the rich smell of barley being roasted at the Guinness Brewery a mile away at Saint James's Gate. The people, the sights, the sounds, the smells. Dear God, he still didn't fully understand why, but he loved this place.

Fingal crossed Bridge Street and stopped on the corner of Bull Alley, where an urchin wearing an oversized, stiff-peaked, floppy cap tilted at an impossible angle stood touting his wares. "Get your *Independent,* get your *Daily Mail,* get your *Irish Examiner.*" He was in a thick pullover, short pants, and, Fingal was delighted to see, a stout pair of boots. "Back at work, Dermot?" Fingal said.

Dermot Finucane turned and grinned. "Ach, Jasus, it's yourself, sir. And it's the feckin' trut' I'm back at me work, Doctor. How are you?"

"I'm fine, Dermot, and are your da and mammy keeping well?"

"Grand altogether. Hang on." He lifted an *Irish Independent* from a pile and turned to a well-dressed man in a camel-hair coat and Homburg hat with a neat dent in its gutter crown. "Here y'are, sir, dis mornin's *Indo.* T'anks very much." He pocketed a coin and turned back to Fingal. "It's a good job. I buy the papers at eightpence a dozen and sell dem for a penny each. Dat's fourpence profit, and five Woodbine only cost tuppence." He produced a packet. "You like a fag, sir?"

Fingal shook his head. "No thanks." He knew he'd be wasting his breath telling Dermot he shouldn't be smoking.

The youngster lit up and puffed out smoke like a hardened smoker — which he was. "Aah, grand," he said. "And t'anks again for making me foot better. Me ma said it was a miracle cure and dat you're a feckin' angel of mercy."

Fingal laughed and shook his head. "It's my job," he said, heart swelling at the thought that now that Prontosil was a proven remedy, doctors would at last be able to cure the people here of the many infections that brought them down. But "my job"? Not for much longer. He was losing the job here he was growing to love. And it couldn't be helped. He fished in his pocket. "If I remember, you like clove rock?"

Dermot nodded.

Fingal, despite his earlier thoughts about wasting his breath, decided it was worth a try. "Do you know what the big chimney said to the little chimney?"

Dermot shook his head. "Nah."

"You're far too wee to be smoking."

Dermot laughed loudly. "Ah, you're a gas man, Doctor. 'Too wee to be smokin.' "

"And so are you, Dermot Finucane. I'll swap you a bag of rock for your gaspers."

Dermot frowned, took a deep drag, shook his head. "No t'anks," he said, and Fingal felt sad for the lost childhoods of the hundreds of tenement kids like Dermot Finucane.

"Here. Take it anyway."

"T'anks very much."

"I've to be getting on," Fingal said. "Give my best to your folks."

"I'll do dat, Doctor Big Fellah."

And as Fingal rode away he heard Dermot's on the verge of adulthood voice cracking, "*Indo,* get your *Indo.* Five t'ousand Germans land in Cadiz. Read all about it. A few more flamin' feisty forces to fight ferociously for fearless feckin' Franco." Fingal chuckled. Twelve, and already the alliterative Dermot was displaying his native flair for the language. Dubliners. Fingal's feet were lighter on the pedals.

In less than five minutes he was propping his bike up outside number ten High Street. He went into the lobby barely conscious of the all-pervasive tenement smell as he knocked on John-Joe Finnegan's door. The man himself answered.

"Och, Doctor O'Reilly. Come in. Come in. W'at's the *craic?* How the feck are you?"

"I'm well, John-Joe, and yourself?" Fingal walked into the dingy room. Nothing had changed since he'd last been here in October. "How's the hind leg?"

"Sit down. Sit down." John-Joe pulled a chair in front of the turf fire and waited until O'Reilly was seated before sitting himself. "My ankle? The feckin' t'ing's still stiff and swollen, but I'm gettin' about all right. Can I make you a cup of tea, sir? I was just goin' to have one meself."

"Please. I'd like that."

John-Joe rose and went to work. A kettle was already boiling on a gallows over the fire. It wouldn't take long.

Fingal vividly remembered the last time he'd been here and he'd made the tea for a weeping John-Joe. Clearly as he was at home mid-week he still hadn't got a job. Fingal knew he'd nothing to blame himself for, but he was disappointed that despite his best efforts he'd been unable to help. He decided that he'd simply not raise the subject. It would probably embarrass the man.

"Here we are." John-Joe set a teapot with a couple of chipped mugs on the hearth tiles. "We'll let it stew for a minute."

"Fair enough."

"Now, Doc, I know you're a busy man, and it's a pleasure til see you, but what brings you here?"

O'Reilly hesitated, but a promise was a promise. He produced his wallet. "I believe," he said, "we have an agreement about Christmas?" He opened the wallet.

"We do, sir," and to Fingal's surprise John-Joe seemed not the least bit put out, in fact he was smiling.

Fingal frowned. This wasn't the fiercely proud man who eight weeks ago had refused charity and had been reduced to tears at the thought of accepting even a loan.

Fingal withdrew a blue-on-white five-pound note on which was inscribed, "The Governor and Company of the Bank of Ireland, Belfast, Donegall Place, promise to pay the bearer on demand the sum of Five Pounds Sterling." The currencies circulated easily on both sides of the border. "Here. Get your kids and your wife —"

John-Joe took the note. "I will, sir, and t'ank you." He smiled widely. "I believe the interest was to be a pint in the pub of my choice?"

"Well — yes, but only after you've got a job." Fingal was confused.

"If you would meet me, sir, in The Blue Lion on Parnell Street."

"That's where Sean O'Casey wrote *The Plough and the Stars.*"

"I didn't know dat, but it's a bit feckin' fancier than places round here like Swift's on Francis Street or Kennedy and Lalor's on York. The Lion's more suitable for a gent like yourself. Anyroad, if you'll meet me there on the first Saturday in February at six o'clock."

Fingal did a quick calculation. The first Irish rugby international against England at their home ground at Twickenham wasn't until the 13th of February — if he was good enough to be selected in the trial this Saturday. "I can do that, but I don't understand. Have you fallen into a fortune?"

"Like Paddy McGinty?" John-Joe laughed,

and sang,

Mister Patrick McGinty an Irishman of note
Fell into a fortune and bought himself a
    goat . . .

"Do you know, sir, that Irish song was written by a couple of feckin' Englishmen who'd
come to Dublin to work in the music halls?
The nerve of the fellahs pretendin' to be
Irish."

"I did not," O'Reilly said, laughing, "and
you haven't answered my question. Where
are you going to get the money?"

John-Joe stopped grinning. "You'll not
believe this, sir. There's a fellah called Casey
Dempsey —"

"His wife's Dympna and they have a lad
called Jack?" The boy whose rickets Fingal
had treated.

"Dat's right. Casey's the one who looked
after my allotment at Dolphin's Barn when I
was in the hospital. Anyroad, Casey knows a
man from Swift's Alley, Brendan Kilmartin."

"I delivered his wife last year," Fingal said,
well remembering Roisín and her baby boy,
Fingal Flahertie O'Reilly Kilmartin.

"Brendan got Casey work on a building site
two weeks ago. The pay's feckin' brilliant."

Fingal felt the hairs on his forearms stand
on end. This was eerie.

"His foreman's a lad wit' only one arm —"

633

"Sergeant Paddy Keogh," Fingal said. "He was a patient of mine once."

"Well, Brendan fixed it for me to see Mister Keogh last week. He said a cooper should know how to use a feckin' saw and hammer and adzes and bradawls, but he was a little hesitant. I was honest with him about my ankle, how I'd lost the job with Guinness, and how you'd helped me that day and come to see me in hospital. He said you'd treated him at Patrick Dun's, he owed you a favour, and dat any old patient of yours was all right in Mister Keogh's book, and then he offered me work startin' January the second, praise be."

Fingal leapt to his feet and clapped the man on the shoulder. "Bloody marvellous, John-Joe. Bloody wonderful."

"Aye, sir, it is. In a way, I feel like you helped me get this job. So t'ank you." Fingal could hear the relief in John-Joe's voice. "I'll have your money and if you don't mind I'll pay interest of not one but two feckin' pints for you by February. It's the least I can do."

"Mind?" said O'Reilly. "Mind? I'll be happy to drink your health. Indeed," he said, "there's a pub on the corner of Back Lane." He rose. "With all due respect, tea be damned. Come on, John-Joe Finnegan. I'll buy you a pint right now."

He may be losing his job here by March, but he'd still be working in Dublin. He wouldn't abandon his friends here in the Liberties. The fabric of his life here was woven too tightly for that. John-Joe's story proved it. In some ways, he had helped his friend get this job. And, damn it all, didn't the Liberties' women who didn't go to the Coombe Lying-in Hospital all end up in the Rotunda where he'd be working? 'Course they did.

52
KEEP RIGHT ON TO THE END OF THE ROAD

"Nice little crowd," said O'Reilly to Kitty as he started to unload the tray of canapés onto the upstairs lounge sideboard. The drone of conversation and laughter rose and fell above the strains of a softly played recording of Glenn Gould's *Das Wohltemperierte Klavier* by J. S. Bach.

"And a great spread," O'Reilly said, piling a plate and handing it to Kitty, who had picked up her previously poured G&T. There were plenty of sandwiches, cheeses on sticks, chicken liver paté on toast, and stuffed olives to choose from as well as the newly arrived hot hors d'oeuvres.

"Thank you," she said. "Don't forget about yourself."

He didn't, and soon his own plate was piled high. He lifted his Jameson. "I think it has the makings of a very good hooley. We should circulate."

The lounge was warm, cheery. Slack banked the fire and crackled as it burnt slowly enough for the room to stay comfortable without becoming intolerably hot. Kinky wore her best blue outfit, the one she'd worn at O'Reilly and Kitty's wedding. She sat in an armchair, chignon immaculate, a smile perpetually on her lips as she chatted with Cissie Sloan and Aggie Arbuthnot, a small glass of sherry in one hand.

O'Reilly watched Aggie finish a sausage roll and delicately brush the pastry flakes from her fingers. "That was dead nummy, so it was," he heard her say to her friend, "but not a patch on one of yours, so it's not, Kinky."

Kinky's smile grew even wider.

"Excuse me, sir," Donal Donnelly said, wriggling past O'Reilly, "but you said, and you were dead pacific —"

Donal suddenly turned to Julie, who was mouthing the word "specific" to her husband.

"Right, that's what I said. Dead specific, that we was to help ourselves if we wanted another drink. Can I have one of them Baby-chams for Julie, please?" He pointed to where his wife, her long blond hair shining, continued to watch them.

"Pacific or specific, of course you can. Help yourself." O'Reilly had no difficulty remembering exactly what he'd said fifteen minutes ago. He'd rattled a spoon on a glass and when enough folks were paying attention had announced, "Now, listen. I've got everyone their first jar, but after that I want you all to pour your own. I learnt from my father that if all guests do, no one can ever accuse their host of sending them home stocious. Any lack of sobriety on your part would have been regarded in the navy back in the '40s and today will still be considered a 'self-inflicted injury.' "

"And will you court-martial us, Doctor, if we get one?" Archie's son, the recently promoted Sergeant Rory Auchinleck had enquired, to a general wave of laughter. Today he was in mufti. His battalion was stationed at Palace Barracks near Holywood.

"As the naval equivalent, retired, of a lieutenant-colonel in the army I do outrank you, Sergeant, so what I will do —" O'Reilly let a long pause hang, sufficient for Rory reflexively to come to attention. "— is remark that your dad and Kinky, his fiancée, must be very proud of your extra stripe, and so am I, lad. And even if you're not in uniform tonight — so stand at ease — I'll ask everyone to raise their glass in your honour and drink to the health of our new sergeant."

The room had rung with the toast and a round of applause.

O'Reilly had glanced at Kinky to see both she and Archie beaming. Good. It was their night and O'Reilly knew how Archie doted on his only son.

Now Rory was standing beside his father. O'Reilly overheard Archie say, "I don't agree.

I think England'll win the soccer World Cup next year."

"It'll be Germany," Rory said. "I watched their team play when I was stationed at Wuppertal. Bet you they win."

O'Reilly remembered how, long after he'd first tried red prontosil, he'd discovered that Wuppertal-Elberfelt was where a German doctor had done the very first clinical trials on the drug that had been so much bound up with Dermot Finucane and young Fingal's life in the '30s. Funny that the place should crop up in conversation tonight.

Donal Donnelly must have overheard Rory. "Who's betting what?" he asked, and Julie, fresh drink in hand, sang out, "I thought, Donal Donnelly, you were giving up the betting."

His reply was drowned by a gale of laughter from a group that included Sonny and Maggie Houston née MacCorkle, whose yellow felt hat had a scarlet poinsettia in its band. Kitty had joined them as they surrounded, of all people, Bertie and Flo Bishop. Bertie was repeating the punch line of a joke O'Reilly recognised as one of Dublin comedian Dave Allen's. "If you don't get his arse out of the Grand Canal you'll be at that all day." More laughter. Bertie? Telling jokes? Good Lord.

O'Reilly's glass was empty and he moved to the sideboard. As he passed the front of the fireplace he jerked back, hardly believing his eyes. Arthur Guinness, who was allowed indoors in inclement weather, lay on his side in front of the fire, and curled against his tummy Lady Macbeth slept soundly, her body swaying back and forth as Arthur breathed. The dog raised his large brown eyes to O'Reilly as if to say, "Och, sir, she's only little. I'll let her off with it — this once."

"And the lion shall lie down with the lamb," O'Reilly heard, and turned to see Barry Laverty standing at his shoulder and watching the animals in front of the fire.

"No, Barry, it's a wolf cosying up to a lamb and 'the calf and the young lion and the fatling together.' Isaiah eleven verse six, King James Version." O'Reilly glanced at the still-rotund Councillor Bishop.

"I stand corrected," Barry said, raising his empty glass.

O'Reilly clapped Barry on the shoulder. "I'm getting another jar. Coming?"

"I," he said, "am your man. I'll not have far to drive. I'm staying at Sue's tonight." He leant over and whispered in O'Reilly's ear, "I think I'll have enough saved to pop the question soon."

"Fair play, Barry. I'm delighted," O'Reilly said, and glanced over to where Sue, who was looking stunning in a lime green mini-dress that complemented her copper plait, was deep in conversation with Kitty. "My offer stands about letting you have Kinky's quarters after she gets wed and moves in with Archie. Plenty of room for Sue too."

"That would be grand, Fingal. Thanks."

"We'll say no more tonight. It's Kinky and Archie's do." He handed Barry a Jameson, lifted his own, popped two sausage rolls on his plate, and said, "Let's go and say hello to them."

O'Reilly stopped in front of Kinky and Archie. "Enjoying yourself, Mrs. Maureen Kincaid, soon-to-be Mrs. Auchinleck?" he said.

Archie dropped a hand on her shoulder and smiled. "The whole thing's dead on, so it is. Thank you and Mrs. O'Reilly, sir, very, very much."

Before O'Reilly could reply, Kinky said, "I'm so pleased you and Miss Nolan could make it tonight, Doctor Laverty. And Doctor O'Reilly, dear, you and Mrs. O'Reilly have done this old Cork woman proud and Archie and I are so content in our own way, aren't we, dear?" She hesitated. "And I want to say, nobody could have asked for a better employer these near on twenty years, so, and only for how much I care for this old goat," she looked adoringly at Archie, "I'd be glad to stay here full time for another twenty."

"I know, and I appreciate that very much," said O'Reilly, "but this is your evening so you two keep on enjoying yourselves. The night's a pup yet."

"Arragh," said Kinky, "but we'll not overdo it. A shmall-little fire that warms is better than a big fire that burns, so."

"Jasus," said O'Reilly with a grin, "you have the wisdom of the ages, Kinky Kincaid. Just enjoy yourself."

He became aware of something happening near to the door, glanced over, and saw Jenny embracing Terry Baird, who looked to be very cold. O'Reilly made his way across the room. "You made it, Terry. Well done."

"I let myself in," he said. Terry's lips were blue, his teeth were chattering. "I'll tell you, Doctor O'Reilly," he said, "I can feel for Captain Scott and his men coming back from the South Pole. My car heater broke down. I'm foundered." He blew on his fingertips.

"You poor dear," Jenny said.

O'Reilly glanced round. The little party was in full swing. Nobody would miss him for a few minutes. He put his plate and glass on the sideboard, grabbed a bottle of Jameson, took Terry by the elbow, and said, "Come on, young fellah. Downstairs. Doctors can't cure the common cold, but they can cure this kind of cold."

Jenny followed.

Once in Kinky's kitchen, O'Reilly said, "Jenny, stick a chair for Terry in front of the range."

As Jenny did, O'Reilly filled a kettle and shoved it on a burner. "Now," he said, "I'll soon have your medicine." He took a tumbler, put in two teaspoonfulls of sugar, a large dose of whiskey, three cloves, and a squeeze of lemon juice. Even down here he could hear voices and footsteps. Things must be heating up upstairs.

He turned. Jenny was helping Terry take off his overcoat and scarf.

The kettle started to whistle, a cheerful sound. O'Reilly grabbed it, poured a measure of boiling water into the glass, and stirred the mixture briskly, making the black cloves spin and dance. The aroma of spiced whiskey was heady. "Here," he said to Terry, handing him the glass. "Get that into you. I'm told it'll revive a corpse three days dead."

"Thank you," Terry said, accepting the glass and sipping, "I think you're right, sir. Life is returning." He laughed.

"Thanks, Fingal," Jenny said.

"Think nothing of it." He picked up the whiskey bottle and said, "Keep Terry company, Jenny, then bring him on up. I'd better get back."

"Fingal," she said, "before you go, I've a question."

"Fire away," he said. "I'm all ears."

"Were you not curious when we were in the dining room with Bertie Bishop and I said, 'I'm not sure about going'?"

"I bloody well was, but it slipped my mind." He smiled. "Parties do that to you. So what

643

did you mean?"

She stood, shoulders braced, hands in front of her, fingers laced. "You told me there'd been a group of younger women approach you to see if I could stay."

"That's right."

"And they talked about things like Pap smears."

"They did."

"What would you say if I told you Graham Harley's programme would rent your surgery three half days a week and pay me to do well-woman clinics there? We'll be the centre for all of the north of County Down outside Belfast."

"Here?" O'Reilly said. "You mean, here, at Number One Main?" He knew his voice had risen. "Mother of God." He hugged her. "When?" He let her go. "When can you start?"

She laughed. "There are other details to work out because I might be able to take call occasionally, run a surgery on Saturdays for, saving your presence, women who would be more comfortable with a woman doctor."

"Details," said O'Reilly, "can wait. I've a party to run so I'm off upstairs. But this is great news, Jenny. We've a wheen of talking to do tomorrow to get this organised."

"Thank you, Fingal," he heard as he strode out of the kitchen.

Oh Lord, he thought, as he climbed the

stairs. Kinky'll come in and work part time. I'll have Barry and Jenny as partners, I'll have more time for Kitty. Our women patients who want to see a woman doctor will be happy. We'll be helping to prevent a cancer. He danced a little jig from tread to tread. "By the name of all that's holy I couldn't ask for better." And, he thought, sometimes difficulties to which he could see no solution happily solved themselves. It had happened way back in 1936 when a job had opened up for an unemployed cooper, and had happened again today when Jenny announced the answer to keeping on a talented young doctor when there didn't seem to be enough work for three in the practice. See, he told himself, and grinned, sometimes you flatter yourself that you are the solver of all problems medical and otherwise for your patients. Not so. The universe unwinds in its own good time and often without a shove from Doctor Fingal Flahertie O'Reilly.

He went back into the lounge. Good. Nobody seemed to have missed him. His plate of grub was waiting on the sideboard where he'd left it. So was his whiskey. He stood watching a grinning Kinky accepting her friends' good wishes. Fair play to you, Kinky Kinkaid. Fair play.

Kitty was waving from across the room where she was chatting with Sonny Houston. O'Reilly grabbed his plate and glass and began to make his way in their direction. He passed a group that had formed round Cissie Sloan. Aggie Arbuthnot, Flo Bishop, and Maggie Houston were hanging on Cissie's every word.

Her voice carried. "Did youse see *Coronation Street* last night on the telly? Ena Sharples — no, I tell a lie — it was Minnie Caldwell was in the snug at the Rover's Return, nicer-looking pub than our oul Duck, so it is, no harm til anybody. When in comes Ken, or was it Frank Barlow? Anyroad, your man says, he says, says he . . . you'd not believe it what he says . . ."

And a chuckling Fingal Flahertie O'Reilly laughed and laughed. The foundations of his own cosmos, like the ever-loquacious Cissie Sloan, were firmly in place here in Bally-bucklebo, the best village in the six Ulster counties of the wee north. He laughed until the tears ran and he reckoned himself the luckiest man in the whole of those six counties, indeed in all the thirty-two counties of Ireland, on the greatest island on God's green earth.

AFTERWORD

BY MRS. KINCAID

Well, now the excitement of our engagement party is all over and I've a couple of weeks' breather before I start thinking about Christmas meals, it's time again to sit in my kitchen and pen some more recipes. It's what himself wants, so, and I'm happy to oblige. And by the way, he says that when that Taylor fellah told the last story, he left out a couple of things and would I please tell you here so you'll know? The Dublin story about Doctor O'Reilly when he was much younger and his dispensary job fell through, that story finished before he'd been able to meet with Doctor Andrew Davidson or have his trial match to see if he could play rugby football for his country, stupid rough game if you ask me, bye, but to each his own.

He did well on both counts. He started as a clinical clerk, that's a junior doctor in training, at the Rotunda Hospital in March 1937. And both Doctor O'Reilly and that nice Mister Greer, the brain surgeon — he was simple Doctor Greer back then — got to play for Ireland together in the '37 season. They lost to England but beat Scotland and Wales. Himself would never tell you, but Mister Greer told me. Doctor O'Reilly scored a try against Wales. I've seen himself's three caps with their silver tassels and green shamrocks.

And he says — and God bless him, I remember how her death tore the heart out of him, but he says it's all right to talk about it now — if you want to know about how he met Deirdre, his first wife, how he came here to Ballybucklebo, and what he did in the war, please be patient. That fellah Taylor's long-winded enough, but he's a slow storyteller and he'll not have that one ready until a year after this one comes out.

And that's enough of that. Now for the recipes.

RECIPES

Pea and Mint Soup
1/2 stick / 1 oz. / 28 g butter
Small bunch spring onions, chopped
675 g / 1 lb. 8 oz. fresh or frozen peas, shelled
A large handful of mint leaves, chopped
3/4 L / 1 pint / 6 oz. chicken or vegetable
    stock
Salt and pepper to taste
237 mL / 8 oz. / 1 cup cream or crème
    fraiche

Melt the butter in a large cooking pot and add the spring onions. Sauté gently for a few minutes, until soft. Then add the peas, mint leaves, stock, and seasoning. Boil for 3 or 4 minutes, until the peas are cooked. Remove from the heat and allow to cool. Blend well and chill. Mix in the cream before serving and decorate with mint leaves.

This soup has a coarse texture but if you would prefer it to be smooth you could blend it for longer or push it through a sieve.

And of course on days when the wind is howling like a stepmother's breath you can serve it hot.

Kedgeree

700 g / 1 1/2 lb. undyed smoked haddock (or use half salmon and half haddock)
2 bay leaves
40 g / 1 1/2 oz. butter
1 yellow onion, finely chopped
1 heaped tablespoon of medium curry powder
225 g / 8 oz. long-grain basmati rice
3 tablespoons cream
2 tablespoons spring onion, chopped
3 tablespoons chopped parsley
Juice of half a lemon
Freshly ground black pepper
3 hard-boiled eggs, quartered

This quantity will serve about 6 to 8 people

and is very good with either my wheaten or Guinness bread. Doctor O'Reilly likes it for breakfast nearly as much as he likes my kippers, but it is also a very appetising lunch dish.

First bring the fish and the bay leaves to the boil in about a pint of water and simmer gently for about 10 minutes. Throw away the bay leaves but don't discard the cooking liquor, as you will use this to cook the rice. Now flake the fish into bite-sized chunks and make sure that no bones remain.

Melt the butter in a largish pan and fry the yellow onion gently, but don't let it colour, then add the curry powder, the reserved cooking liquor, and the rice, and cook for about 8 to 10 minutes.

When the rice is cooked, add the cream, spring onion, parsley, lemon juice, black pepper, and finally the flaked fish. Stir gently and place the hard-boiled eggs on top. You can keep this warm in a very low oven, covered with a lid, for about 20 minutes. I like to put it in a silver chafing dish and leave it on the sideboard so that they can help themselves at breakfast time.

Himself is very fond of it and he told me that this was one of those dishes that came from India in Victorian times and had originated as a means of using up leftovers for breakfast before there were refrigerators.

Scotch Eggs

225 g / 8 oz. sausage meat
1 teaspoon fresh thyme leaves, chopped
1 tablespoon parsley, chopped
1 spring onion, chopped
Salt and freshly ground black pepper
4 hard-boiled eggs with shells removed
Seasoned flour (with salt and pepper added
  to taste)
1 beaten egg
125 g / 4 oz. bread crumbs
Oil for frying

Mix the sausage meat with the thyme, parsley, spring onions, plenty of black pepper, and a little salt, and make into 4 flattened ovals on a floured surface.

Coat each hard-boiled egg with the seasoned flour and wrap the sausage meat mixture round each egg, making sure to seal each egg completely. Coat with the beaten egg and then with the crumbs. Now heat the oil in a deep frying pan or wok to 180–190° C (350–375° F). If you do not have a thermometer you can test the temperature by dropping a small cube of bread into the oil, and if it sizzles and turns golden brown then the oil is hot enough. Please be very careful with the hot oil and never turn your back on it.

Now carefully lower each egg into the hot oil and cook for 8 to 10 minutes until the sausage meat is a nice brown colour and thoroughly cooked. Remove with a slotted spoon and drain on kitchen paper. Serve cool with a salad. They keep well in the fridge for a couple of days. And sure doesn't himself like to take these in the game bag when he goes on a shoot?

Queen of Puddings
(Bread and Butter Pudding)
8 to 10 slices of buttered bread
Grated rind of a lemon
100 g / 4 oz. raisins
3 eggs
275 mL / 1/2 pint milk
135 mL / 1/4 pint cream
100 g / 4 oz. sugar

Heat the oven to 180° C/350° F.

Arrange the buttered bread in layers in a greased ovenproof baking dish, sprinkling each layer with grated lemon rind and the raisins. Then you whisk the three egg yolks and one of the egg whites in a bowl with the milk, cream, and half of the sugar, and pour this over the layers of bread.

Bake for 30 minutes or until set, and remove from the oven.

Now beat the 2 remaining egg whites until stiff and whisk in the rest of the sugar. Cover the top of the pudding with this meringue mixture and return to the oven for a further 10–15 minutes or until the top is golden.

Serve warm with cream or crème fraiche.

Variations

You could use barmbrack (see recipe in *An Irish Country Doctor*) and omit the raisins.

Or spread the buttered bread with marmalade and omit the lemon rind and raisins.

For a savoury pudding you can omit the meringue topping, raisins, and lemon rind and add about 170 g / 6 oz. of grated cheese between the layers and on top.

Apparently Queen of Puddings dates back to the seventeenth century.

Cheese Straws

250 g / 9 oz. "ready to bake" puff pastry
Mustard, preferably Dijon
200 g / 7 oz. sharp cheddar or Parmesan cheese
1 egg, beaten

Roll out the pastry to make a rectangle of about 20 cm (8 in.) and spread half with mustard. Sprinkle the grated cheese over the mustard half and bring the other half over the cheese. Now seal with the rolling pin and roll out again to about 15 cm (6 in.).

Cut into strips and twist at each end. Now leave in the refrigerator for about half an hour. Brush with egg and bake for about 10 minutes at 190° C / 375° F / gas mark 5.

AUTHOR'S NOTE

I've never done it personally, but I've known many women who have given birth, and sitting here knowing that at last book eight in the Irish Country series is written, I suspect I am feeling a lot like a new mother. Tired, proud of my offspring, relieved not to be carrying it all day every day for nine months — and yet a little lost and sad now it's all over.

And just as each child of any large family is a unique individual, so is *Fingal O'Reilly, Irish Doctor* different in its own way from all its siblings in the Irish Country series.

Please let me explain and start by offering new readers *cead mile fáilte,* a hundred thousand welcomes, and a short note of introduction. This work, by telling two parallel stories separated by twenty-nine years, continues to explore the character of Doctor Fingal Flahertie O'Reilly and ask what formed him in his medical youth in 1930s Dublin and turned him into the man he has become in 1960s Northern Ireland. I hope you enjoy the journey with him, and no prior knowledge of him and the other characters in this work is required, so please feel free to climb aboard.

Many regular readers (and welcome back to you, good to see you again) post notes on my Facebook page or write to me through my Web site. Thank you not only for telling me how you've enjoyed (or disliked) my work but also for asking such questions as "Will Doctor Barry Laverty marry Sue Nolan? Will Barry come back to work in Ballybucklebo in the '60s? Why did Fingal and Kitty split up in the '30s? What career did he choose immediately after he qualified and why did he choose it?" It was from such questions that the framework of this book developed.

Why not, I asked myself, answer those and other questions by telling two stories, one which followed on from *A Dublin Student Doctor* in Dublin in 1936 and the other set in Ballybucklebo in 1965, picking up where *An Irish Country Wedding* left off? It seemed to be a reasonable skeleton to work round.

The setting of the Dublin story in the tenements of the Liberties owes much to *Dublin Tenement Life: An Oral History* by Kevin C. Kearns, to whom I will be eternally grateful. The timing of the story, 1936, allows young Fingal's character to be shaped by two vital forces: the patients he works with as a G.P. in the dispensary system of the slums, and the primitive but increasingly science-driven medicine of that time, about to be revolutionised by the development of antibiotics.

I hope you will be interested in a short historical note about that subject. In Germany in 1932, a Doctor Gerhard Domagk had been studying aniline dyes produced by his colleague Josef Klarer. Domagk experimented with mice infected with *Streptococcus*. Those treated with red prontosil survived. Those left untreated died. Further trials seemed promising in humans. The work was done in Wuppertal-Elberfeld, where, as an aside, as a reserve soldier I attended a military summer camp in 1960 and from where we were taken to inspect the Möhne Dam, one target of the famous Dam Busters raid in 1943. In 1935, Domagk's six-year-old daughter Hildegarde drove an embroidery needle into her palm. A few days later she was dying from septicaemia (blood poisoning), and it was doubtful if even amputation of the infected limb would save her life. Domagk gave her massive doses of Prontosil. Two days later she walked out of the hospital. He did not mention her when he published his findings in 1935, so Fingal would not have known about her. Domagk's initial report was largely pooh-poohed by the medical establishment at the time. He subsequently was awarded the Nobel Prize.

In 1936, a sulphonamide medication, the

active agent of Prontosil, cured President Roosevelt's son FDR Jr. of a potentially lethal streptococcal throat infection, and following extensive press exposure of this cure in November 1936 the sulpha drugs gained rapid and widespread acceptance. The antibiotic era had begun.

How his own experience with Prontosil changed Fingal O'Reilly is part of the Dublin story.

Nor was Fingal's life in Dublin insulated from events in his wider world. The involvement of Irish men and women on both the Nationalist and Republican sides in the now-being forgotten Spanish Civil War affected him and Kitty O'Hallorhan deeply. My interest in this war was initially sparked by a wonderful work, *Winter in Madrid* by C. J. Sansom, and my introduction to the Irish Blueshirts came in the pages of the haunting *The Secret Scripture* by Sebastian Barry.

Interwoven with the Dublin story is the tale of the doings in Ballybucklebo in 1965. This juxtaposition illustrates how radically the practice of medicine had changed in the twenty-nine intervening years and how O'Reilly had matured and was continuing to do so.

By 1965, although his ways were becoming more set, those closest to him, like Kitty O'Reilly née O'Hallorhan, Kinky Kincaid, Doctor Barry Laverty, and Doctor Jenny

Bradley, influenced the still-growing man that he was. And so did the practice of medicine, which once more was on the threshold of two massive innovations: electrical cardiac defibrillation leading to the portable defibrillator, and laparoscopy, which was the beginnings of minimal-access surgery and in vitro fertilisation. Both are things we take as routine today.

Purely by chance I was houseman to the remarkable Doctor Frank Pantridge in 1965 when he introduced cardiac defibrillation to the Royal Victoria Hospital and, with Doctor John Geddes and Mister Alfred Mawhinney, was developing a portable defibrillator. I have taken a one-month liberty with the first use of the cardiac flying squad, which used the world's first portable device in 1966. I trust you will forgive me.

And I have, for reasons of personal conceit, once more played a little with dates when the story involves another, for the time, revolutionary technique. When, in 1965, Jenny Bradley suggests that one of O'Reilly's patients be sent to Dundonald Hospital, laparoscopy was still a few years away from coming to Northern Ireland. In 1969, I had just qualified as an OB/GYN specialist and my then chief at Dundonald, Mister Matt Neely FRCOG, a most prescient man, arranged for me to be sent to Oldham in England. There I was taught the then revolutionary technique of laparoscopy by a Mister Patrick Steptoe, whose work with Professor Robert Edwards led to the birth of Louise Brown, the world's first test-tube baby in 1978. In 2010 Professor Edwards won the Nobel Prize and was knighted a year later. The laparoscope is also the foundation stone of all of today's minimal access surgery.

In a much lesser way, that month in England gave me a lifelong interest in laparoscopy and the treatment of human infertility. My last textbook on the subject, *Diagnostic and Operative Gynaecological Laparoscopy,* first edition, written in conjunction with Professor Victor Gomel of Vancouver, Canada, was published in 1995 and is now considered more medical history than medical textbook.

And on a further historical note, although doctors like Fingal O'Reilly, Phelim Corrigan, Charlie Greer, and Bob Beresford in 1936 and Fingal's young colleagues in 1965 are all figments of my imagination, all other figures are real. Those senior doctors alluded to in the Ballybucklebo story were all known personally to me. For example, Doctor Adgey, now Professor Adgey, was a classmate; Mister Jimmy Withers was the first Ulster specialist orthopaedic surgeon; and Mister Cecil Calvert set up the first neurosurgery unit. Sir Samuel Irwin, president of the IRFU when Fingal was trying to achieve the honour of playing for his country, had a son, Sinclair, who followed in his father's footsteps both in the game of rugby football and as a surgeon. I was his houseman in 1965.

Doctor Jack Sinton was a G.P. in Belfast, and he did go wildfowling with my father, Doctor Jimmy Taylor, and me as I grew old enough.

Doctor Graham Harley, who became Professor Harley, was instrumental in my training as a gynaecologist, and I was privileged to work in my final position in the department of obstetrics and gynaecology in Vancouver, British Columbia, as a colleague of Doctor David Boyes.

It is my hope that this book will amuse, inform, and please you — and finally put to rest many, but not all, of my readers' questions. I'm afraid I must ask those who want to know about Doctor Fingal Flahertie O'Reilly's first wife, Deirdre Mawhinney, and his wartime naval service on HMS *Warspite* to be patient — but tomorrow I promise I'll be starting to write number nine in the Irish Country series as fast as I can.

PATRICK TAYLOR
Salt Spring Island
British Columbia
Canada
September 2012

GLOSSARY

To each of the seven previous Irish Country books I have appended a glossary. Judging by the letters I receive, they are appreciated. The English spoken in Ireland not only differs from standard English, but the language of regions is equally diverse. So is the Irish Gaeilge, but that is another story. Aspects of the Ulster and Dublin dialects are as far apart as those from Brooklyn, New York, and Bowling Green, Kentucky. Despite these differences many of the expressions in Ireland are shared, so in this glossary by preceding the definition with "Dublin" or "Ulster" I have tried to identify those more likely to be heard in the city on the Liffey and those prone to crop up near where the Lagan flows. Without those modifers the expressions are fairly universal.

I spent October '07 to May '10 in Ireland and frequently visited Dubh Linn, the Black Pool, or as it is properly known in Gaelic,

Baile Atha Cliath, the town of the ford of the hurdles.

In my early years in the north of Ireland I had never heard expressions like "gameball," evincing great approval. My northern versions would be "wheeker" or "sticking out a mile." "Mind your house," exhorting a sports team to be on the lookout for a tackle from behind, would be translated by us roaring, "Behind, ye." A scruffy individual in Dublin would be "in rag order." Up north they would have looked "as if they'd been pulled through a hedge backwards," or "like something the cat dragged in."

But, not all is different. North and south we'd both "go for our messages" when running errands, wonder what that "yoke" (thingummybob) was for, and might end up "shitting bricks" (very worried) because our pal had got himself "steamboats" or "elephants" (utterly inebriated).

I have in previous works explained the ubiquitous use of "feck" and its variants in Dublin. Believe me, it is now so hackneyed by overuse it has ceased to be offensive and I could not render the speech of Dubliners without it.

Usually I try to avoid phoenetics in writing dialogue, but in Roscommon, where I lived from 2008 to 2010, "ye" for "you" is universal and in Dublin the "th" sound does not exist and, for example, "them" becomes "dem," nor does the letter "g" have any place in "ing." I hope the apostrophes are not feckin' irritating.

Here are the words, expressions, and explanations. Please enjoy them.

Aldergrove: Belfast International Airport.

An Gorta Mór: Irish pronounced "an gortash more," literally "the Great Hunger." The potato famine of 1845–52.

anyroad: Anyway.

arse: Backside (impolite).

astray in the head: Insane.

at myself, not: Ulster. Unwell.

away off and chase yourself/feel your head: Ulster. Don't be stupid.

babby: Baby.

banjaxed: Exhausted or broken.

banshee: From the Irish *Bean sidhe,* literally "woman of the mounds," whose keening foretells a death.

barging: Trying to force one's way past. Also (Ulster) a serious telling-off.

barmbrack: Speckled bread. See Kinky's recipe in *An Irish Country Doctor.*

barrister/solicitor: Attorney. Barristers represented clients in court, solicitors did not, but handled legal matters not requiring judicial intervention.

bashtoon: Bastard.

beagle's gowl: Ulster. The gowl (not howl) of a beagle dog can be heard over a very long distance. Not to come within a beagle's gowl of something means missing by a very long way.

beat Banagher/Bannagher: Ulster. Far exceed realistic expectations or to one's great surprise.

bee on a hot brick: Running round distractedly.

beeling: Suppurating. Producing pus.

bejizzis/by Jasus: By Jesus. In Ireland, despite the commandment proscribing taking the name of the Lord in vain, mild blasphemy frequently involves doing just that. Also commonly heard are Jasus, Jasus Murphy, or Jesus Mary and Joseph.

bespoke: Tailored rather than ready-to-wear.

bide: Wait patiently.

bite the back of me bollix: Dublin. Slightly more polite version of "feck off."

black pudding: Traditional Irish blood sausage.

blether: To talk excessively about trivia or an expression of dismay.

blow out: End a love affair, or a big night out.

bog trotter: Pejorative. Country person (bumpkin implied).

bollix/bollox: Testicles (impolite). May be used as an expression of vehement disagreement or to describe a person of whom you disapprove.

bollixed/bolloxed: Ruined.

boozer: Public house or person who drinks.

bowsey/ie: Dublin. Drunkard.

boxty: Potato pancake.

braces: Men's suspenders.

'brake: Abbreviation of "shooting brake." English term for a vehicle that used to be called a woody in North America.

brass monkey weather: In Nelson's navy, cannonballs were kept ready for use by being stored in small pyramids held in place at the base by a brass triangle called a monkey. In very cold weather the brass would contract and the cannon balls roll off, hence, "It would freeze the balls off a brass monkey."

brave: Ulster. Large or good.

brave wheen: Ulster. Large number of.

brung: Brought.

buck eejit: Imbecile. See eejit.

bull's-eyes: Hard, boiled, black-and-white candies.

bye: Boy.

capped/cap: A cap was awarded to athletes selected for important teams. Equivalent to a letter at a U.S. university.

carbuncle: Boil (abscess) with multiple cores.

champ: A dish of boiled potatoes, butter, chives, and milk.

chemist: Pharmacist.

chiseller/chissler: Dublin. Child.

chuckin' it down: Pouring with rain. See rain.

clatter (a brave): A quantity (large).

clove rock: Boiled, clove-flavoured hard candy.

confinement: Delivery of a preganant woman, or incarceration.

Continent: Europe.

corncrake: Bird also known as a landrail (*Crex crex*).

cracker: Ulster. Excellent, often used admiringly of a young woman.

craic: Pronounced "crack." Practically untranslatable, it can mean great conversation and fun (the *craic* was ninety) or "What has happened since I saw you last?" (What's the *craic*?). Often seen outside pubs in Ireland: *"Craic agus ceol,"* meaning "fun and music."

crayture: Creature.

crick: Painful strain.

cross: Angry.

cruibín: Irish, pronounced "crewbeen." Pickled boiled pig's trotter, usually eaten cold with vinegar.

culchie: See Jack.

currency: In Dublin in 1936 the coins, although bearing different emblems from their British counterparts, were pegged to sterling and had the same names. In 1965, prior to decimalization, sterling was the currency of the United Kingdom, of which Northern Ireland was a part. The unit was the pound (quid), which contained twenty shillings (bob), each made of twelve pennies (pence), thus there were 240 pennies in a pound. Coins and notes of combined or lesser or greater denominations were in circulation often referred to by slang or archaic terms: Farthing (four to the penny), halfpenny (two to the penny), threepenny piece (thruppeny bit), sixpenny piece (tanner), two shillings piece (florin), two shillings and sixpence piece (half a crown), ten-shilling note (ten-bob note), guinea coin worth one pound and one shilling. Five-pound note (fiver). Most will be encountered in these pages. In 1965 one pound bought nearly three U.S. dollars.

dander: Ulster. Leisurely stroll or temper. Literally horse dandruff.

dead (on): Ulster. Very (hit the mark).

deadner: Dublin. A blow to the upper arm muscles, often affectionate, but can be painful.

delivery room: Case room.

desperate: Ulster. Immense or terrible.

digs: Lodgings.

divil: Devil.

divil the bit: None.

doddle: Short walk or easy task.

doh-ray-mi: Dough, as in money.

domiciliary: Visit at home by a specialist. G.P.s made home visits (house calls).

do rightly: Be adequate if not perfect for the task.

dosser: Dublin. Homeless man who slept in

tenement halls.

dote/doting: Something (animal) adorable/ being crazy about or simply being crazy (in one's dotage).

dripping: Congealed animal fat often spread on bread.

drop of the pure: A drink — usually *poitín* (see page 679).

drouth (raging): Thirst or drunkard (degenerate drunkard).

drumlin: Ulster. From the Irish *dromín* (little ridge). Small rounded hills caused by the last ice age. There are so many in County Down that the place has been described as looking like a basket of green eggs.

dudeen: Short-stemmed clay pipe.

Duffy's Circus: A travelling circus that was begun by the Duffy family more than three hundred years ago and is still running. I used to be taken to it in the '50s.

duncher: Ulster. Cloth cap, usually tweed.

dungarees: One-piece coveralls. Originally from the Hindi describing a coarse Indian calico used in their manufacture.

Dun Laoghaire: Port near Dublin. Pronounced "Dun Leery," literally, Leary's Fort.

Dutch: Used to modify certain activities or objects. "Dutch treat," each party paying half the costs. "Dutch courage," bravado brought on by liberal quantities of alcohol. "Dutch cap," contraceptive diaphragm.

eat the tyres off a truck: Dublin. One of a number of expressions like eat the arse off a farmer through a tennis racquet, or eat a baby's arse through the bars of a cot, all signifying ravenous hunger.

eejit: Idiot.

estate agent: Realtor.

fag: Cigarette, derived from "faggot," a very thin sausage.

fair play to you: Dublin. To be fair or well done or good luck.

fair stretch of the legs: A long way.

feck, and variations: Dublin corruption of "fuck." For a full discussion of its usage see the Author's Note in *A Dublin Student Doctor.* It is not so much sprinkled into Dublin conversations as shovelled in wholesale, and its scatological shock value is now so debased that it is no more offensive than "like" larded into teenagers' chat. Now available at reputable bookstores is the *Feckin' Book of Irish* — a series of ten books by Murphy and O'Dea.

Feile na Marbh: Irish. Pronounced "fayle na marev." Festival of the dead celebrated on November 1.

ferocious: Extremely bad or very upsetting.

festering: Infected and draining pus.

fey: Posessing second sight.

fierce: Severe.

fire away: Go right ahead.

fist of: Attempt.

florin: Silver two-shilling piece about the size of a silver half-dollar. Worth about forty cents today. In 2010, 120 florins, about twenty-five dollars, would be required to purchase the same amount of goods as a single florin would have in 1930. This must be interpreted in light of today's wild currency fluctuations.

flounder: Flat edible fish.

fly your kite (go): Have a good time. (Go away and stop annoying me.)

fornenst: Ulster. Near to.

foundered: Frozen.

gander: Look-see, or male goose.

gansey: From the Irish *geansaí.* A jumper (sweater). Used in the Anglicised form by Irish and non-Irish speakers.

Garda Síochána: Pronounced "Garda Sheekawna," State Guards. National police force of the Republic of Ireland. Used to be RUC in the north. The Royal Ulster Constabulary is now PSNI, Police Service of Northern Ireland.

gargle: Dublin. Alcoholic drink. "The gargle's dimmed me brain," is an alternate line to "The drink has dimmed my brain" from the song "Dublin City in the Rare Old Times" by Pete St. John.

gas (man): Very amusing/comedian.

gasper: Cigarette (archaic, no longer used).

gee-gees: Horses.

gerruptheyard: Dublin. Literally "get up the

yard." Polite rendition of "feck off."

gobshite: Dublin. Literally, dried nasal mucus, used pejoratively about a person.

gobstopper: Literally "mouth [gob] filler." A very large spherical candy made of multicoloured layers. Jawbreaker in North America.

going spare: Totally losing one's temper.

gombeen man: Irish moneylender.

good man-ma-da: Ulster. Literally "good man my father," but is actually used as an affectionate term of encouragement or approval.

good skin/head: Dublin/Ulster. Decent person.

go up one side and down the other: Deliver a ferocious verbal chastisement.

go 'way (out of that): Dublin. I don't believe you, or I know you are trying to fool me.

grand man for the pan: One who really enjoys fried food.

grushie: Dublin. After a wedding it was the custom for the groom to throw out copper coins — the grushie.

gulder: To scream (v.), a scream (n.).

gurn: Moan and groan irritably.

gurrier: Dublin. Street urchin, but often used pejoratively about anyone.

gymkhana: Competitive event where horses demonstrate their paces show jumping.

half-un (hot): Measure of whiskey. (With cloves, lemon juice, sugar, and boiling water added. Very good for the common cold.

673

Trust me — I'm a doctor.)

hang about: Belfast. Wait a minute.

hare coursing: Hunting hares with grey-hounds, a traditional field sport which preceded greyhound racing. It has been illegal in the UK since 2005, but is still legal in Ireland.

head case: Idiot.

Heath-Robinson: A British cartoonist who preceded the American Rube Goldberg but was his British equivalent. They both invented enormously complicated machines for doing simple tasks.

hinch bone: Iliac crest. The bone that encircles the lower abdomen and forms part of the pelvis.

hirple: Limp.

HMS: His 1936/Her 1965 Majesty's Ship.

holdall: Canvas general-purpose bag, often used to carry sporting gear.

hold the lights: Dublin. Expression of extreme surprise.

house floors: The first floor in a multi-storey house in America would be called the ground floor in Ireland, thus the U.S. second floor is the Irish first floor and so on.

houseman: Medical or surgical intern. In the '30s and '60s used regardless of the sex of the young doctor.

how's about ye?/ 'bout ye? Ulster. How are you?

I'm your man: I agree to and will follow your plan.

in soul: Emphatic agreemeent.

Irish Free State: In 1922, after the Irish war of independence twenty-six counties were granted Dominion status within the British Empire and were semi-autonomous. This entity was the Irish Free State, later to become the independent Republic of Ireland.

Jack/culchie: Dublin. The inhabitants of Ireland are divided between those who live in Dublin, "Jacks" or "Jackeens," sophisticated city dwellers; and those who live outside the city, "culchies," rural rubes. Both terms now are usually applied in jest and "Jack" has been superseded by "Dub."

jam piece: Ulster. See piece. Slice of bread and jam or jam sandwich.

jar: Alcoholic drink.

John Bull top hat: A top hat with a very low crown as depicted in cartoons of the British mascot, as the exaggerated top hat is worn by Uncle Sam. Popular headgear for ladies hunting and Winston Churchill before World War I.

just the jibby-job: Terrific.

knackered: Very tired. An allusion to a horse so worn out by work that it is destined for the knacker's yard where horses are destroyed.

knickers: Females' underpants.

knockabout: Dublin. Homeless man who

slept in tenement halls.

ladder: Of stockings. Runner.

Lambeg drum: Ulster. Massive bass drum carried on shoulder straps by Orangemen, and beaten with two sticks (sometimes until the drummer's wrists bleed).

let on: Acknowledge or pretend.

let the hare sit: Leave the matter alone.

liltie/y: Irish whirling dervish.

lime tree: Deciduous tree known as linden or basswood in North America.

linnet: A small passerine bird of the finch family. Much prized for its song of fast trills and twitters and popular as a caged pet.

Lord/Lady Muck from Clabber Hill: Someone with a grossly inflated opinion of their own importance with a tendency to putting on airs and graces.

lorry: Truck.

lose the bap: Ulster. Bap (literally a small round loaf) means "head." To lose it is to become violently angry.

lost his marleys: Ulster. Literally "lost his marbles." Gone mad.

lough: Pronounced "lockh" as if clearing one's throat. A sea inlet or large inland lake.

lug (thick as a bull's): Dublin. Ear. (Very "thick," stupid.)

lummox: Big, stupid creature.

marmalise: Dublin. Cause great physical damage and pain.

measurements: All measurements in '30s

Ireland were imperial. Of those mentioned here, one stone = fourteen pounds, 20 fluid ounces = one pint, one ounce = 437.5 grains. It can be seen that 1/150th of a grain was a very tiny dose and required extreme accuracy in measuring.

midder: Colloquial medical term for midwifery, the art and science of dealing with pregnancy and childbirth, now superseded medically by the term "obstetrics."

mind: Remember.

more power to your wheel: Words of encouragement akin to "The very best of luck."

mot/mott: Dublin. Girlfriend. Wife. Girl. Made famous in an eighteenth-century street song composed by blind Zozimus, "The Twangman's [toffee maker's] Mott."

mufti: From the Arabic. Originally an Islamic scholar, adopted by the British Army to mean civilian dress.

muírnin: Irish. Darling.

nappies: Diapers.

National Trust: British charitable organisation that preserves sites of historical interest or of outstanding natural beauty.

never know the minute: Totally unpredictable.

niff: Offensive smell.

niggle/niggly: To irritate/irritating.

night's a pup: The party's just getting started.

no goat's toe: Ulster. Have a very high (usually misplaced) opinion of oneself.

no side taken: Ulster. No offence taken.

not a patch on: Nowhere nearly as good as.

not backward in coming forward: Definitely not shy or afraid to offer an opinion.

nursing home: Small private hospital or seniors' home.

och: Emotive multipurpose exclamation that can express anything from frustration, "Och, blether," to admiration, "Och, isn't the babby a wee dote?"

off-licence: Liquor store.

old goat: Usually a term of affection for an older man.

operating theatre: Operating room, OR.

OTC: Officers Training Corps, for reserve soldiers who were university undergraduates. Equivalent to the American ROTC.

oul hand: Ulster. Old friend.

oul ones/wans: Old ones, usually grandparents or a spouse. "Says my oul wan to your oul wan" is a line from the traditional song "The Waxies' Dargle."

oxter: Ulster. Armpit.

Pac-a-mac: Foldable cheap plastic raincoat usually carried in a small bag.

Paddy hat: Soft narrow-brimmed tweed hat.

palaver: Discussion.

paralytic: Drunk. Paul Dickson in *Dickson's Word Treasury* (John Wiley and Sons, New York, 1982) cites 2,660 euphemisms for "drunk." Many have come from the Emerald Isle.

pavement: Sidewalk.

Peeler: Policeman. Named for the founder of the first organised police force in Great Britain, Sir Robert Peel, 1788–1846. These officers were known as "Bobbies" in England and "Peelers" in Ireland.

people's bank: Dublin. Pawnbroker.

petrified: Terrified, or drunk.

piece: Ulster. Slice of bread or sandwich, usually qualified by its condiment. See jam piece.

pinkeen: From the Irish *pincín,* technically a stickleback, but applied to any small fish usually of the carp family. In Newfoundland the term "sparny tickles" is used.

pint of plain: Dublin. Guinness. This expression was made famous in a poem, "The Working Man's Friend" by Flann O'Brien (Brian O'Nolan).

plaice: Edible flatfish. *Pleuronectes platessa* of the flounder family.

plough the same furrow twice: Repeat a task needlessly.

poitín: Pronounced "potcheen." Moonshine. Illegally distilled spirits, usually from barley. Could be as strong as 180 proof (about 100 percent alcohol by volume).

porter: A dark beer. It was brewed by Guinness until 1974 when it was replaced by its stronger relation, stout, which rather than being brewed from dark malts uses roasted malted barley called "patent malt."

potato crisp: Potato chip. In Ireland, French fries are chips. The first flavoured crisp (cheese and onion) was developed by the Irish company Tayto in 1954.

power or powerful: Very strong or a lot.

punter: Bettor.

put one in the stable: Take the money in a pub for a drink to be taken later.

put out: Annoyed.

quare: Queer. Used to mean very, strange, or exceptional.

queer his pitch: Ulster. Make trouble for someone.

quid: Ulster. One pound, or a measure of chewing tobacco.

Raidió Éireann: Irish State radio network.

rain: Rain is a fact of life in Ireland. It's why the country is the Emerald Isle. As the Inuit people of the Arctic have many words for snow, in Ulster the spectrum runs from sound day, fair weather, to a grand soft day, mizzling, also described as that's the rain that wets you, to downpours of varying severity to include coming down in sheets/stair-rods/torrents, or pelting, bucketing, plooting (corruption of French *il pleut*), and the universal raining cats and dogs. If you visit, take an umbrella.

rashers: Bacon slices from the back of the pig. They have a streaky tail and a lean eye.

red-biddy: Cheap red wine.

ricked: Hurt.

right: Very.

rightly: Perfectly well.

ruggy-up: Dublin. Fight.

Saint John Ambulance Brigade: A charitable organisation dedicated to teaching and providing first aid. In Ireland it is not closely associated with the Venerable Order of Saint John.

Saint Vincent de Paul: An international Catholic organisation dedicated to fighting poverty and operational in Ireland since the mid-1800s. Their work in the tenements cannot be lauded sufficiently.

sarky: Sarcastic.

scrip': Shortened form of "script." Prescription.

scuttered: Drunk.

scutting: Dublin. Stealing a ride on a vehicle.

see you?: Emphatic way of drawing attention to the person being addressed, usually before something derogatory is said.

shite/shit: "Shite" is the noun ("He's a right shite") "shit" the verb ("I near shit a brick").

shooting stick: A walking stick which at its lower end had a conical spiked centre and a circular flange to prevent it sinking into the ground. The handles were two large wings which were folded up when it was used as a walking stick and folded out to become a seat when the user wanted to rest.

shout (my, his): Turn to pay for a round of drinks.

shufti: Word from Arabic meaning look-see. Brought back by UK servicemen during World War II.

sister (nursing): In Ulster hospitals, nuns at one time filled important nursing roles. They no longer do so except in some Catholic institutions. Their honorific, "Sister," has been retained to signify a senior nursing rank. Ward sister, charge nurse. Sister tutor, senior nursing teacher. (Now also obsolete because nursing is a university course.) In North America the old rank was charge nurse or head nurse, now nursing team leader unless it has been changed again since I retired.

skin (good): Dublin. Decent person.

skate: Flatfish of the family *Rajidae.*

skivvie: Housemaid of the lowest rank.

slagging: Hurling of verbal abuse which can either be good-natured friendly banter or verbal chastisement.

Sláinte: Irish. Pronounced "Slawntuh." Cheers. Here's mud in your eye. Prosit.

snaffle: A kind of bridle bit, or to steal.

sound (man): Terrific (trustworthy, reliable, admirable man).

sticking out (a mile): Ulster. Wonderful (the acme of perfection).

sticking plaster: Medicated adhesive tape.

stocious: Drunk.

stone: See measurements.

stoon: Shooting pain.

stop the lights: Dublin. Expression of utter amazement.

surgery: Where a G.P. saw ambulatory patients. Equivalent to North American "office." Specialists worked in "rooms."

sweets/sweeties: Candies.

take yourself off (by the hand): Ulster. Run on, often kindly meant. (Don't be so stupid, or go away, always unkindly meant).

targe: Ulster. Very bad-tempered person.

taste (wee): Ulster. Amount, and not necessarily of food (small amount). "That axle needs a wee taste of oil."

ta-ta-ta-ra: Dublin. Party.

tea: An infusion made by pouring boiling water over *Camellia sinensis,* or the main evening meal. "I had a great steak for my tea."

teetotally: Nothing to do with abstinence from alcohol. A Belfast emphatic version of "totally."

terrace: Row housing, but not just for the working class. Some of the most expensive accommodations in Dublin are terraces in Merrion Square, akin to the terraces in New York's Park Avenue.

the day: Ulster. Today.

there now: Ulster. At this moment.

thole: Put up with. A reader, Miss D. Williams, wrote to me to say it was etymologically from the Old English *tholian,* to suffer. She remarked that her first encounter with the word was in a fourteenth-century prayer.

thon/thonder: That/there.

thruppence: Three pennies. Worth about five cents.

til: To.

'til: Until.

toilet: Washroom.

townland: Mediaeval administrative district encompassing a village and the surrounding farms.

traipsing: Struggling to make a journey.

true on you: Dublin. You are absolutely right.

uncle: Dublin. Pawnbroker.

value for money: Has certain worthwhile attributes.

walking out: Going steady.

warm ear: Slap on the ear.

wean: Pronounced "wane." Child.

wee: Small, but in Ulster can be used to modify almost anything without reference to size. A barmaid, an old friend, greeted me by saying, "Come in, Pat. Have a wee seat and I'll get you a wee menu, and would you like a wee drink while you're waiting?"

wee buns: Ulster. Very easy.

wee man (the): The devil.

wee north: The six counties in the northeast part of Ireland, properly called Northern Ireland, which remained part of the United

Kingdom after partition in 1922.

well filled: Dublin. Fit and well.

well mended: Healed properly.

wheeker: Ulster. Top notch. Terrific.

wheen: Ulster. An indeterminate number.

wheest: Hold your tongue.

whigmaleery: Thingummybob, what-do-you-ma-call-it.

whippet: Small dog, like a miniature greyhound.

ye: You, singular or plural.

yiz: You, singular or plural.

yoke: Thing. Often used if the speaker is unsure of the exact nature of the object in question.

you-boy-yuh: Ulster. Expression of encouragement.

you know: Verbal punctuation often used when the person being addressed could not possibly be in possession of the information.

youngwans: Dublin. Young ones, usually unmarried.

your man: Someone either whose name is not known, "Your man over there? Who is he?" or someone known to all, "Your man, van Morrison."

youse: You, plural.

ABOUT THE AUTHOR

Patrick Taylor, M.D., was born and raised in Bangor, County Down, in Northern Ireland. Dr. Taylor is a distinguished medical researcher, offshore sailor, model-boat builder, and father of two grown children. He is the author of the beloved Irish Country novels, beginning with *An Irish Country Doctor*, as well as *Pray For Us Sinners* and its sequel, *Now and in the Hour of Our Death*, a duology centered around The Troubles. He now lives on Salt Spring Island, British Columbia.